Praise for M...
and her novels of "cu...

"[Monica Burns's] excellent love scenes and bold romance will have readers clamoring for more."   —*Romantic Times*

"A cinematic, compelling, and highly recommended treat!"
                                        —Sylvia Day, national bestselling author

"The love scenes are emotion filled and wonderfully erotic . . . Enough to make your toes curl."   —*Two Lips Reviews*

"Elegant prose, believable dialogue, and a suspenseful plot that will hold you spellbound."   —Emma Wildes

"Historical romance with unending passion." —*The Romance Studio*

"Wow. Just wow."   —*Fallen Angel Reviews*

"A satisfying read complete with intrigue, mystery, and the kind of potent sensuality that fogs up the mirrors."   —*A Romance Review*

"Monica Burns is a new author I must add to my 'required reading' category . . . Everything I look for in a top-notch romance novel."
                                        —*Romance Reader at Heart*

"Blazing passion."   —*Romance Junkies*

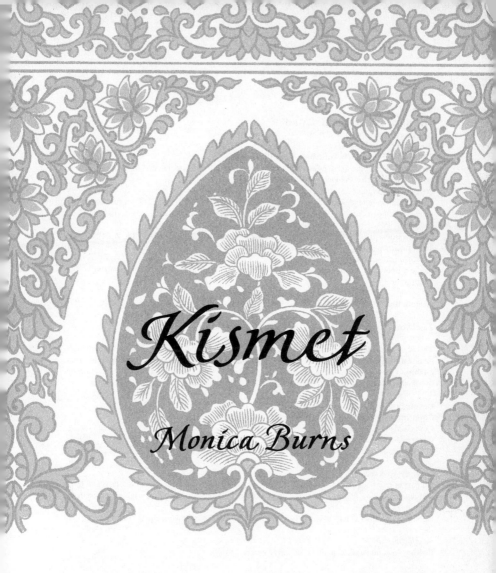

Kismet

Monica Burns

BERKLEY SENSATION, NEW YORK

THE BERKLEY PUBLISHING GROUP
Published by the Penguin Group
Penguin Group (USA) Inc.
375 Hudson Street, New York, New York 10014, USA
Penguin Group (Canada), 90 Eglinton Avenue East, Suite 700, Toronto, Ontario M4P 2Y3, Canada
(a division of Pearson Penguin Canada Inc.)
Penguin Books Ltd., 80 Strand, London WC2R 0RL, England
Penguin Group Ireland, 25 St. Stephen's Green, Dublin 2, Ireland (a division of Penguin Books Ltd.)
Penguin Group (Australia), 250 Camberwell Road, Camberwell, Victoria 3124, Australia
(a division of Pearson Australia Group Pty. Ltd.)
Penguin Books India Pvt. Ltd., 11 Community Centre, Panchsheel Park, New Delhi—110 017, India
Penguin Group (NZ), 67 Apollo Drive, Rosedale, North Shore 0632, New Zealand
(a division of Pearson New Zealand Ltd.)
Penguin Books (South Africa) (Pty.) Ltd., 24 Sturdee Avenue, Rosebank, Johannesburg 2196,
South Africa

Penguin Books Ltd., Registered Offices: 80 Strand, London WC2R 0RL, England

This book is an original publication of The Berkley Publishing Group.

Copyright © 2010 by Kathi B. Searce.
Cover illustration by Jim Griffin.
Cover design by George Long.
Cover hand lettering by Ron Zinn.
Interior text design by Laura K. Corless.

PRINTING HISTORY
Berkley Sensation trade paperback edition / January 2010

Library of Congress Cataloging-in-Publication Data

Burns, Monica.
  Kismet / Monica Burns.—Berkley Sensation trade paperback ed.
    p. cm.
  ISBN 978-0-425-23215-6
  1. Courtesans—Fiction. 2. Nobility—Fiction. 3. Middle East—Fiction. I. Title.
  PS3602.U76645K57   2010
  813'.6—dc22   2009039463

PRINTED IN THE UNITED STATES OF AMERICA

10 9 8 7 6 5 4 3 2 1

For my sister Marsha, because you believed.

Acknowledgments

Many thanks to Katie D for her insightful critique of the book and its characters. Your input was invaluable.

A warm thanks to Marie-Claude Bourque who kindly confirmed my translations of French. *Merci, mon amie.*

Thank you to D'Ann Dunham, Jerrie Alexander, Lucinda Betts, and Candace Rice who generously offered up their equine knowledge and graciously answered my repeated questions about what a horse can and can't do.

Author's Note

Bedouin is a term often used to describe the nomadic tribes that have inhabited North Africa and the Sahara Desert for more than three thousand years. Different tribes are often grouped together under the Bedouin term.

These collective groups of people are often referred to as Berbers, but the ethnic group call themselves Amazigh, which means "free man." Within the Berber/Amazigh group are tribes such as Tuareg, Zenaga, Chaouis, Fulani, Riffians, Kabyles, and a number of other tribal groups.

France's interest and influence in Morocco was seen as early as the beginning of the Victorian era. This created a blend of language and culture. Even today, there is a mix of French and Arabic spoken throughout various regions of the country.

Marrakech, Morocco, 1893

Organized chaos. Allegra could think of no other way to describe the train station. The rhythmic sound of the Berber dialect mixing with the French language created a colorful cacophony of sound that engulfed her the moment she stepped onto the crowded platform. A whoosh of steam from the engine blasted its way out into the air, adding to the din.

It wasn't any louder than London's Paddington Station, but it was much more colorful and interesting. Spices and exotic fruits scented the air in a tantalizing fashion, while people pushed their way in and out of the one-story station house. A man, dressed in the flowing white robes of the Bedouins she'd read so much about, made his way along the platform followed by a woman dressed in a bright blue garment with a veil across her face. A porter dodged the couple and headed straight for Allegra. The small, wiry man came to a halt in front of her and bowed deeply.

"Mademoiselle Synnford, I am Ali. I come from Major Hastings and his *bien-aimée*."

"Wonderful," she said as she turned to see her maid directing the removal of their luggage from the railroad car. "Millie?"

"Yes, Miss Allegra." The older woman turned her head toward her.

"This is Ali. He's here to take our luggage to the carriage Isabelle's fiancé arranged for us."

Millie nodded before she gestured for the porter to see to one of the trunks sitting on the platform. Allegra bit back a smile as her maid started to bark orders like a general commanding a strategic assault.

Efficient and thorough, Millie managed everything in a way that always ensured a positive outcome. Over the years, numerous attempts had been made to lure Millie away from her and into the employ of others. Her friend would have none of it.

The shrill, high-pitched scream of a horse broke through her thoughts and she turned toward the sound. Hooves crashing against wood followed the animal's loud shrieks. Over the past fifteen years, she'd learned a great deal about horses. She'd even acquired a sizable stable of thoroughbreds, which she ran at Newmarket in all the major events. Since her first riding lesson at the age of seventeen, she'd learned to recognize the difference between animals in distress and those that were merely high-strung.

This particular horse wasn't suffering, although it was clearly agitated. Curiosity got the better of her and she carefully made her way along the crowded platform toward the disruption.

She'd passed almost five coaches when she saw a railcar designed to transport cattle and other animals. A wide plank ran from the straw-strewn floor of the car down to the platform so animals could be led off the train. Another shrill whinny erupted, followed by a violent thrashing of hooves on the sides of the car. Excited shouts filled the air, and in the next instant, a white Arabian stallion bolted down the wooden ramp and onto the platform with a young boy valiantly clinging to its halter rope. The already crowded platform exploded with panicked shouts as the horse released a shrill cry and reared up on its haunches before falling back onto all four legs.

Despite the panic around her, Allegra could only stare at the magnificent animal. It was the most beautiful horse she'd ever seen. Not even her champion thoroughbred, Seabreeze, could compare to this stallion. She was still caught up in the beauty of the horse when someone charged past her, knocking her off balance. Several more people rushed by, bumping her aside as they raced toward safety. Her balance precarious, she had almost righted herself when a man shoved her out of his path—she staggered to one side then tumbled to the ground.

Eyes rolling wildly in its head, the stallion reared up and brought its front hooves crashing back down in a vicious blow near where she lay. The boy still struggled with the animal, but he was no match for the stallion's strength. The realization sent fear streaking through her as a pair of hooves pounded the wood floor of the platform, which reverberated beneath her with the force of the blow. The horse seemed close to gaining its freedom, and she froze as the animal reared up over her head.

In that breathless instant of terror, a dark shadow abruptly blotted out the image of the uncontrollable horse. The man took charge of the animal and brought it under control. His voice low and hypnotic, he soothed the animal in the language of the Bedouins. As the horse slowly grew quiet, she pushed herself up into a sitting position. Dazed, she pushed a loose strand of hair away from her face with a trembling hand.

The strand of lace that had ripped away from the cuff of her sleeve brushed across her cheek causing her to study it ruefully.

She was extremely fortunate it was the only damage to her person. Gratitude swelled in her for the man who'd come to her rescue.

She was just about to stand up when strong hands gripped her waist and lifted her to her feet. The light scent of bergamot tinged with an exotic spice teased her nose as she stared up at the man towering over her. It was impossible to stifle her gasp as the rest of her senses absorbed the full impact of his close proximity.

When she'd arrived in Morocco yesterday, she'd seen men who epitomized the romantic image her travel guide had painted of a Bedouin sheikh. But this man defied all those impressions. Dressed entirely in black, his kaffiyeh was draped across his face so all she could see were his dark brown eyes.

A rush of heat warmed her skin at the intensity of the look in his hooded gaze. She was accustomed to being in the presence of powerful men, but never one such as this. This man possessed a raw, savage mystique about him that sent her heart skidding along at breakneck speed.

He was at least six feet tall, with wide shoulders and equally strong hands. Hands that only just now were releasing her. Even with her limited knowledge of the nomadic tribes of the Sahara and surrounding regions, she knew his height was unusual for a Bedouin. Instinct told her it was an advantage he used on a regular basis, just as he was doing now.

Transfixed, she couldn't remember the last time a man had intimidated her. But this one did. The invisible, unrestrained aura of his maleness enveloped her. Here was a man of power. A man who bowed to no one. A man who conquered everything in his path.

Including her.

A shiver raced down her spine as she took a quick step back from him. His gaze narrowed and she realized her trepidation showed. With one hand pressed to the base of her throat, she swallowed hard.

"Thank you," she choked out from her suddenly dry mouth.

"You are unhurt then."

His voice was just like him, dark and mysterious. His French was impeccable and mimicked that of the bluest of aristocrats, yet she doubted there was a drop of Gallic blood flowing through his veins. Still, it was easy to understand why the horse had been so easily soothed. The man had the seductive voice of a dark angel, the sound of which could easily make the most pious of women consider the possibility of sin. Realizing she'd not responded to him, she brushed her hand across her temple in another attempt to straighten her appearance.

"I'm a bit shaken, but none the worse for wear."

She dropped her gaze and swatted at the dirt still layering her skirt. Those deep brown eyes of his made her feel as if he could see straight through her. It was a disconcerting sensation, and she didn't like it. It made her feel out of control, something she never allowed herself when she was with a man. Fire blazed through her as strong fingers captured her lower jaw. He tilted her face to one side.

"You should ask the hotel manager to give you ice for that cheek, *ma belle*."

It appalled her that she liked hearing him call her pretty. She knew it was ludicrous to take pleasure in such a small compliment. Even worse, her body was responding to him in a way it had never done with any other man. The elemental force of personality that flowed from him set off alarms in her head. Swallowing hard, she put distance between them. The moment she did, he arched an eyebrow at her and his eyes became unreadable mahogany.

"Thank you for your concern, monsieur. I shall ask for your suggested remedy when I arrive at my friend's home."

"Then we say, adieu, mademoiselle."

He gave her an abrupt nod then turned and moved back to

the stallion he'd saved her from. Flabbergasted by his sudden departure, she felt her mouth fall open as he walked away without another word. Unaccustomed to men simply walking away from her as if she were of no consequence, she watched in disbelief as he took the horse's halter rope from an older Bedouin. It was an unpleasant experience to have a man ignore her. Annoyed, she grimaced at her emotional reaction.

The older man said something to the dark stranger then nodded in her direction. Horrified that her rescuer might turn around to find her watching him, she spun around on her heel and hurried back to where she'd left Millie. She reached the train car and frowned when her maid and the porter were nowhere in sight. She turned around to face the direction she'd just come from and across the distance saw her mysterious Bedouin watching her.

The unexpected frisson sliding over her skin appalled her. This wasn't a man to be toyed with. That she found him intriguing and mesmerizing made him even more dangerous. He was the type of man who would demand total submission, and not since that first night in Madame Eugenie's had she ever allowed a man to control her. That night had taught her a hard lesson and she'd turned it to her advantage. She knew when to leave well enough alone, and this Bedouin sheikh was a man to avoid at all costs.

She drew in a deep breath and directed a polite nod in his direction before dragging her gaze away from him. Despite her desire to run, she forced herself to walk at a sedate pace until she reached the interior of the railway station. The moment she escaped his watchful eyes, she hurried through the building toward the doors leading out to the roadway.

The chaos from the railway platform had moved out into the city street. A man with a monkey on his shoulder walked by her, while a vendor across from the railroad station hawked his wares at the people passing his small shop.

"Miss Allegra," Millie called out with a note of relief in her voice. "Thank heavens. I thought we'd lost you."

With a smile, she turned to face her maid. "I'm sorry, Millie. I was distracted by the most incredible horse I've ever seen."

"Another horse." The older woman snorted with disgust as she pulled out a handkerchief and dabbed at the side of Allegra's skirt. "Look at your gown. Did you ride the beast as well?"

Although she'd been intrigued by far more than the horse, Millie's question made her realize she'd missed the opportunity to make an offer for the white stallion. Irritated that she'd allowed the mysterious stranger to be such a distraction, she pursed her mouth with rueful frustration. If the man hadn't addled her brain so much she might have been the new owner of that splendid animal. Shaking her head, she touched her companion's shoulder.

"No, I didn't ride him, although I should have made an offer. I'm certain he'd make a wonderful sire."

"I admit you have an eye for horses, Miss Allegra, but bless me if I understand why you'd need another one."

"I suppose you're right, Millie." She smiled as she followed the maid toward a waiting landau. "I don't really need another horse, but he was magnificent."

Once they settled themselves inside, their coachman guided the vehicle into the busy street and set off for Isabelle's. Seated beside the driver, Ali occasionally pointed out an item of interest to them. Well into the middle of the day, the sun lashed its heat downward. The parasol she carried deflected a large amount of sunlight, but the temperature was still stifling. She would be grateful to reach Isabelle's, where she could quench her parched throat with a cool drink.

Seated across from her, Millie eyed the scenery warily. The maid had never been comfortable journeying outside of England, but Allegra had given up suggesting the woman remain at home when she traveled. Her friend refused to be left behind. She returned her attention to the exotic setting they were driving through. It was beautiful and mysterious with its Moorish arched windows, small alleyways, and the minarets rising up toward the crisp blue sky. The seductive sounds, the pungent scent of spices, and the vivid colors created the impression of a rich opulence that stirred an emotion deep inside her that she was unable to define.

"It's beautiful isn't it?" Allegra didn't expect Millie to actually answer her. The customary response was generally a grunt, but the maid surprised her.

"A bit too heathenish to my liking, but it is interesting."

Laughing, Allegra shook her head. "I'll make a traveler of you yet, Millie."

"I highly doubt that." The older woman sniffed her dissension at the idea.

With a fleeting smile, Allegra turned her head to study the lovely intricacies of the large building they were passing. The architecture was beautiful and mysterious. Almost as darkly inscrutable as her Bedouin sheikh. She released a small sigh of disgust. What was it about the man that intrigued her so much?

He'd been far too arrogant for her liking and dismissive as well. Was that what bothered her? She had to admit that she didn't like the fact she'd not made the slightest impression on him. Even happily married men didn't walk away from her like the stranger had. Perhaps her age was beginning to show. She frowned. *Ridiculous.* She was barely past thirty.

No, she was nettled because she'd been unable to capture his attention completely. Her ego smarted from his blatant dismissal of her. It had not happened before. That was the only reason she couldn't forget him. She suppressed a sigh at the thought. Was it? She wasn't so sure.

Not even the Prince of Wales had intrigued her quite this much.

But then Bertie had been a known quantity, just like her other lovers. The dark-robed sheikh represented the unknown to her. Many of her lovers had often been more like spoilt schoolboys with power. Always amorous, yet prone to the occasional tantrum.

She allowed herself a small smile as she recalled one of the Prince of Wales's ill-tempered moments. It had been easy to feel affection for him, just as it had been easy to feel affection for all the other men she'd allowed into her bed. Affection, but never love.

There were many men who'd thought themselves in love with her, but she knew better. Although she was attractive enough with her green eyes and dark red hair, it wasn't her beauty that drew men to her. The image of her as a courtesan unparalleled was what intoxicated them. It was the illusion that had evolved out of Arthur's death that drew men to her.

She understood how the persona had developed, but the creation of it had been far from pleasant. The one positive in the entire nightmare of Arthur's death had been her ability to choose the men she welcomed into her bed. It had cultivated an independence she would never have known at Madame Eugenie's. It was a liberty she protected by avoiding the emotional attachment of love. The emotion was even more of an illusion than the misguided notion that she was an incomparable lover.

Quite possibly Arthur might have protested her ideas about love, but he wasn't here to chide her or challenge her on the issue. All the same, she was certain he would be proud of her. It would have pleased him to see her so self-sufficient. Arthur's patronage and tutelage had brought her a long way from that frightened girl he'd first met at Madame Eugenie's. Even Millie had changed since her days cooking in the brothel's kitchen. The woman was more than her maid and occasional cook. Millie was a friend and companion who watched over her.

Devoted and incredibly stubborn, Millie was one of the few

people she could count on to stand by her in even the worst of circumstances. Her friend Isabelle was made of the same cloth as her maid, but then the three of them had all emerged from the bowels of the East End at almost the same time.

Her gloved fingers tightened on the wood handle of her parasol as she banished the memory. This was a time of celebration. Isabelle had found her heart's desire in the form of Major Brant Hastings. The couple were to marry in two days' time and she couldn't be happier for her friend. She only wished she could be happy about the second invitation she'd received just before leaving London.

With an adept move, she used her free hand to open the drawstring reticule in her lap and retrieve Cordelia's letter. The missive already showed distinct signs of wear, evidence of the numerous times she'd read and reread her niece's words. This time wasn't any different than the hundreds of other instances she'd studied the letter. The content was always the same. She heaved a sigh.

Married.

Her sweet, lovely Cordelia was to be a countess.

She'd always imagined that a country squire or perhaps a wealthy merchant would steal her niece's heart. It had never occurred to her that the girl might actually marry a member of the Marlborough Set. But not even in her wildest dreams would she have envisioned her niece becoming engaged to the nephew of her first patron.

Arthur would have found the entire matter uproariously funny. That his nephew, the current Earl of Bledsoe, was to marry the niece of his one-time mistress would have appealed to his sense of humor. But as much as it would have amused her paramour, she was equally certain his wife, the Dowager Countess of Bledsoe, would *not* find it humorous if she discovered the truth.

The chill coursing its way down her back forced her to adjust her parasol so the sun's heat could warm her shoulders. If the dowager were to find out she and Cordelia were related—no. She wouldn't let that happen. She just wouldn't go to the wedding. She sighed. It wasn't quite that simple, and she knew it.

The carriage turned off the street and rolled through the black wrought iron gates outside a small mansion. As the vehicle came to a halt, Allegra returned the letter to her reticule and focused her attention on the government residence. The Petit Palais was appropriately named. Isabelle's new home was a beautiful little palace. Rounded arched windows culminating in a sharp point were complimented by sculptured stonework that gave the impression of stiff lace across the façade of the mansion. The stone itself had a delicate pink tinge that only enhanced the image of something magical and fragile.

Accepting the coachman's assistance, she stepped out of the carriage as she continued to admire the Petit Palais. Although elaborate in its Moorish design, there was a welcoming quality to the house that made her suddenly realize how fortunate her friend was. Isabelle hadn't just found love, she'd found a home.

It was something she'd never had. There was her house in London, of course, but it was simply a place to live. A home was much more than a place to rest one's head. It represented something more intangible. It was a symbol of comfort, acceptance, and happiness. And it was that intangible she was determined to give Cordelia, no matter what the price.

"Allegra! Oh, how wonderful. You're here at last," Isabelle Denten exclaimed as she hurried out of the enchanting house with her arms outstretched. "I'm so happy to see you."

Her friend's excitement contagious, Allegra hastened forward to embrace the dark-haired beauty. Stepping back to look at her friend, Allegra smiled as she shook her head in admiration.

"Belle, you look positively radiant!"

"It's Brant's doing. I never thought it possible to be so happy."

Isabelle laughed as she turned toward Allegra's maid. "Hello, Millie. Are you keeping my friend here in line?"

"I do my best, Miss Isabelle. I do my best."

The woman's world-weary sigh pulled another laugh from Isabelle as she issued a quick order to the butler who'd joined them outside and stood discreetly a few feet away. "Teabury, please have Ali see to the luggage and ensure Millie is settled in the room adjoining Miss Synnford's."

Satisfied everything was running smoothly, Isabelle wrapped her arm around Allegra's waist and drew her inside. "I can't tell you how much it means to me that you've come to be my witness at the wedding."

"How could I possibly refuse," Allegra said with a warm smile. Arms entwined, they moved through a cool foyer into a cheerful, brightly lit salon. "Although I confess I was relieved to escape London."

"Escape? Whatever from?"

"Cordelia is engaged." Allegra sank down onto a green chintz-covered sofa.

"But that's wonderful."

"She's to marry the Earl of Bledsoe."

"Oh dear Lord." Isabelle, an expression of horror on her face, collapsed onto the seat beside her.

"Quite." Allegra closed her eyes for a brief moment. "I received her letter just before I left London. Apparently, she met Arthur's nephew while on her holiday in Italy."

"My dear Allegra, I am so sorry. What are you going to do?" Isabelle reached over and squeezed her hand in a gesture of comfort.

"I don't really know." She shook her head at her friend's question. "I only know I cannot do anything that might jeopardize Cordelia's happiness."

"What if you told her the truth?" Isabelle asked.

"The thought of doing so terrifies me."

"Cordelia loves you, Allegra. She'll understand."

Isabelle turned her head at the sound of china rattling. A smile on her face, she instructed the maid to set the tray on the coffee table in front of the couch. With a sense of detachment, Allegra watched her friend pour a tall glass of lemonade. *Would* Cordelia understand? She wasn't so sure.

It was true, her niece loved her, but she could easily lose that love if she tried to explain the lies of the past fifteen years. Falsehoods that had been difficult and expensive to maintain. And all of it paid for by some of the most prominent members of the Marlborough Set. Men who'd showered her with money and jewels in exchange for her company and the right to share her bed.

"I'm not convinced Cordelia will be as understanding as you think." Allegra shook her head as she accepted the glass Isabelle offered and took a sip of the cool drink. "She'll be hurt and angry. And she'll feel betrayed. I understand far too well what that means."

"Betrayed in what way, dearest? Do you really think not telling her the truth is betrayal? You protected her." Isabelle stared at her with an expression of fierce affection and protectiveness. "Your mother betrayed you and Elizabeth. You have nothing to be ashamed of. Cordelia is a sensible girl. Her anger will be for what you and her mother went through—not because you kept the truth from her."

"That may be true, but it's too large a gamble for my peace of mind. I have no desire to involve Cordelia in a scandal. The last one was vile enough."

"Ah yes, Lady Bledsoe has a strong predilection for vicious behavior, doesn't she," Isabelle said with a resigned sigh. "But if young Lord Bledsoe is of Arthur's character he'll stand by Cordelia regardless of what his aunt says."

"Perhaps." Allegra closed her eyes for a brief second. "It would have been so much easier if Cordelia had fallen in love with someone other than Lord Bledsoe."

Somehow, she'd convinced herself that Cordelia would never need to know the truth. It had been a foolish assumption to make on her part. She sighed. She couldn't help who she was or where she'd come from, and her current lifestyle was infinitely preferable to working in a brothel. It had also given her niece the kind of life Allegra had never had.

Nor could she deny cherishing the independence she'd gained due to the generosity of the rich and powerful men she'd chosen as her lovers. And she *had* chosen them. Her selective decisions as to whom she allowed into her bedchamber had only enhanced her elusive image. It made men all the more eager to seek her favors.

Cordelia had no knowledge of what her aunt did to ensure that she received only the best money could buy. Nor did she have any idea as to her less than illustrious parentage. Telling the truth meant she might easily lose Cordelia's love. But what other option did she have? The moment someone discovered their relation, a scandal would be inevitable. Of that, she had no doubt. Keeping the truth from her niece would only make matters worse in the end. She knew firsthand how devastating scandal was. Cordelia was unprepared for the malicious gossip, the vicious innuendos, and outright lies.

All of which would be exacerbated if Lady Bledsoe had any say in the matter. The scandal would be far more savage and poisonous than the last time. A shiver raced down her spine. The storm she'd weathered at the time of Arthur's death had been horrible, but she'd survived. This was a different type of tempest altogether, but it would be no less terrible, and quite likely worse.

Allegra took another swallow of her lemonade and met Isabelle's sympathetic look with a sense of sardonic self-pity. "I suppose I could disappear into the desert for several months. Cordelia would have no choice but to marry without me being present."

"What a splendid idea," Isabelle exclaimed with sarcasm. "Simply ignore the problem and hope it goes away. Look what happened the *last* time you refused to face something."

"I suppose you mean Charles."

"Precisely." Her friend sent her an abrupt nod of confirmation.

Isabelle was right. She'd disregarded all the signs that the Viscount Shaftsbury was becoming enamored with her. Her hope had been that he was merely infatuated. She'd been wrong. It had taken his offer of marriage to open her eyes. He was the first man who'd ever made her such a proposal, and for the briefest of moments, she'd actually considered accepting. The fleeting thought had been discarded at almost the same moment it occurred to her.

Still, rejecting him had not been an easy thing to do. There had been a part of her that liked the stability and companionship a marriage to Charles might bring her. But she didn't love him, and even if she had, her independence would have been too high a price to pay for such a permanent arrangement. Up until Charles, she and her lovers had always parted on good terms. Many of them were still close friends. But ending her affair with Charles had been a disaster. The gossip had been particularly vicious, and even on occasion the public, and especially cruel, denouncements from Charles had cut deep. Even more painful had been the destruction of a friendship she'd valued dearly. She met her friend's censorious gaze and sighed.

"You're right. I have no other option except to tell her the truth. Although how I'll do that, I've no idea."

"Between us, we'll develop a plan of action." Isabelle patted her arm. "For the moment, I think you need some rest. You look fatigued, and your journey here would have been difficult enough without this matter about Cordelia weighing on you."

"Surely I don't look *that* exhausted." She sent her friend an amused look.

"Of course not, but tonight we dine at the Sultan's palace. Mulay Hassan is hosting a celebratory reception for Brant and me. It's a tremendous honor."

"Oh, Belle, I don't know if I'm up to a lavish affair."

"But you must come. The only women attending are wives of officers and attachés. They're most likely to ignore me unless forced to acknowledge me. I'm afraid Brant has rather scandalized the Imperialists by marrying me." Isabelle sniffed her disdain delicately. "I'll be bored to distraction unless you're there."

Unable to help herself, Allegra laughed at her friend's determined expression. Belle had always been adept at persuading people to do as she wanted, but there was a hint of loneliness in her plea. It reminded Allegra that her friend's social circle was most likely limited given her social position. Even once she was married, Belle would have a difficult time being accepted into many circles.

"Very well, since it means that much to you, I'll go."

"Wonderful," Belle exclaimed as she impulsively leaned forward to hug Allegra. "Who knows, perhaps you'll meet a handsome sheikh tonight who'll fall madly in love with you and whisk you off to his desert tent."

"Good heavens, perish the thought." Allegra shook her head sharply as her heart skipped a beat at the memory of a darkly robed Bedouin. "You know I'm far too strong-willed to submit to the edicts of a demanding sheikh."

"Perhaps, but even you might find such a man exciting." Springing to her feet, Belle gestured for Allegra to follow her. "Come, let me show you to your room."

As she trailed after her friend, Allegra recalled the Bedouin she'd met earlier. He represented a danger she knew better than to long for, but there had been something about the man that tugged her thoughts to him. Would he be at the Sultan's palace tonight?

Dismayed by the thought she frowned. What on earth would possess her to consider such a notion? She had no desire to be conquered, and the man would do precisely that. He would take what he wanted, and in the end he'd bend her to his will.

The prospect appalled and excited her in the same breath. Swallowing her fear, she fervently offered up a plea that she wouldn't see her dark sheikh tonight or any other night. But even as she climbed the steps with Isabelle, a small voice in the back of her head begged for just the opposite.

2

Standing in the shadow of a decorative palm tree, Shaheen studied the room and its occupants with guarded interest. Bejeweled mosaics covered the walls of the Sultan's drawing room and most of the furniture had gold inlays. Although he knew the wealth inside the palace was the accumulation of several hundred years, it was hard to ignore the fact that just one ruby from the wall's artwork would be enough to feed one of the poorer Bedouin tribes for months.

Rich and opulent, the palace interior was a sharp contrast to the simple tent Shaheen lived in almost year-round. Although his adopted people were quite prosperous, even they had years when the herd was not as good as others and the riches here would ease hardship.

Still, the Sultan, for all his wealth, was a man of simple tastes and he was generous to his people if he saw a need. If Mulay Hassan had any faults when it came to excesses, it was his fondness for the social customs of the British Empire. It explained the abundance of bright red military uniforms and colorful evening gowns filling the room this evening.

It would please the Sultan if he knew this particular affair emulated London society perfectly. His jaw tightened at the remembrances threatening to flood his head. He seldom thought of England anymore, but when he did, the old wounds opened up as easily as if they were fresh cut. He shoved the bad memories aside, burying them as deep as he could. It had been more than fifteen years since he'd left London, and there was little reason to return. The Amazigh were his people now, and his home was here.

He scanned the room for Hakim. The boy had been insistent they attend the reception honoring Major Hastings and his bride-to-be. Shaheen had consented partly because he knew his young charge would enjoy himself. Social events such as these were perfect training for the heir to the largest tribe in Morocco. When Hakim eventually succeeded his father, Khalid, as Sheikh of all the Umayyad Amazigh, the boy would need social skills that only events like this could give him.

After several seconds, he saw Hakim deep in conversation with Major Hastings and the French ambassador. Hastings had been the other reason for attending the dinner party. He'd come tonight out of his respect for the British officer. The man had become a valuable ally in Shaheen's efforts to negotiate treaties between the different Bedouin tribes in the Sultan's name.

Thanks to Hastings, the French and Spanish governments had been amenable to the unification of the Bedouins under the Sultan's rule. More importantly, Hastings's interventions enabled Shaheen to work behind the scenes without jeopardizing the treaties. He'd been a part of the Amazigh nation for so long that most

Bedouins, including himself, had forgotten he was actually British. But political repercussions could destroy all his hard work if someone were to raise questions about his nationality.

Arms folded across his chest, he continued his surveillance of the room. It was unlikely Hakim was in danger here in the palace, but vigilance was a habit Shaheen had developed living among the Amazigh. Even Hakim's ability to defend himself didn't alleviate Shaheen of his duty. A soft chuckle off to his left made him turn his head. He immediately bowed low as the Sultan stopped at his side.

"Good evening, Excellency."

"You watch over Sheikh Mahmoud's son like a worrisome mother hen."

"It's important to guard the Amazigh's future, sire, particularly when he will be a staunch ally of yours, just like his father."

"True. And you are among my strongest supporters as well, Shaheen." The Sultan clasped him on the shoulder. "Without your clearheaded reasoning, many of the treaties we've made in the last two years would not have been possible."

"I am honored you think so." Shaheen bowed his head in a gesture of gratitude and respect. "The well-being of the Amazigh tribes is all I desire."

"Were there more like you and Sheikh Mahmoud, my friend. Then I would feel more confident that this fragile peace we have would not be trifled with by those who wish more wealth and power."

The veiled reference to Sheikh Nassar made Shaheen grimace. Nassar was one of the main reasons for the tribes to band together. The man's lust for power was surpassed only by his unscrupulous nature. It didn't matter what it was. If Nassar wanted something, he took it, either by force or subterfuge. A leader of one of the larger tribes in the Amazigh nation, Nassar coveted the title Hakim would inherit. It was a title the man didn't deserve, and Shaheen would give his life to ensure Nassar never possessed it. Beside him, the Sultan released a soft noise of pleasure.

"Ah, I see Major Hastings's bride-to-be has brought with her the newest arrival to Marrakech."

Shaheen looked in the direction the Sultan nodded. The sight of a familiar face pulled the air out of his lungs in a quiet rush. He'd experienced the same sensation today at the railway station. He hadn't liked it then, and he liked it even less now.

His gaze narrowed as he watched her being introduced to Hakim. In the candlelight, gold flecks shimmered in her dark auburn hair. He could only see her profile, but it was all too easy to recall a pair of green eyes slightly tilted up at the corners giving her an exotic look. Then there had been her small, yet plump, mouth. It was the kind that begged a kiss. His jaw grew painfully stiff at the thought.

As much as he hated to admit it, he'd been preoccupied with the thought of tasting those lips for most of the afternoon and into the evening. He saw her smile at something Hakim said, and a pang of irritation nipped at him. She exhibited none of the vulnerability and discomposure he'd seen in her this afternoon. Tonight she was a confident, graceful siren, and men were gravitating toward her like sailors hearing Circe's call.

Despite his determination to remain unmoved by her, the gown she wore did nothing to aid him in his resolve. Luxuriant blue green silk wrapped its way seductively around her lush figure while accentuating the beautiful line of her neck and soft shoulders. Like this afternoon, he once again noted the fullness of her breasts. She'd be soft and full if she were naked beneath him. He swallowed hard at the vivid image forming in his head and resented the way his cock stirred beneath his *gambaz*. Out of the corner of his eye, he saw the Sultan watching him with interest.

"She's quite lovely," he murmured with a slight nod.

"Lovely?" Mulay Hassan sent him a look of disgust. "That, my friend, is Allegra Synnford. It is said that one night with her and a man will die a thousand pleasurable deaths."

"A courtesan?" Tension held him rigid as he studied her closely.

"Ah, not just any courtesan, my friend. This is a woman of such skill in the art of pleasure that *she* chooses her lovers. I am told that men vie for her favor as children beg for candy."

"Then it is fortunate I'm not a child," Shaheen said as a thread of bitterness wound its way through him. He'd been a child once— tempted by the favors of a woman like Allegra Synnford.

"You disappoint me, Shaheen." Mulay Hassan frowned. "I would have expected you to find a woman such as this, intriguing."

"One can be intrigued by a rose, but one must always remember it is laced with thorns." Shaheen's gaze narrowed as he studied Allegra Synnford from behind the fronds of the palm tree that partially concealed him and the Sultan. Where courtesans were concerned, thorns could be deadly.

"Come, let me introduce you. Perhaps you will find Miss Synnford fascinating enough to weather whatever thorns she possesses."

"Thank you, sire, but I think it best I remain focused on my responsibilities where young Hakim is concerned."

"As you wish. I admire your ability to withstand the charms of Miss Synnford and your commitment to Hakim, my friend." The Sultan laughed. "But I, on the other hand, am fascinated by the woman and have no desire to avoid her charms."

With a light clap on Shaheen's shoulder, Mulay Hassan headed in Allegra Synnford's direction. Anger slid through him as he watched the stout ruler join Hakim and the other men circled around the woman. *A courtesan.* What a fool he was. He'd spent the better part of his day preoccupied with thoughts about her only to discover she was the type of woman he avoided with resolute determination.

Her complete lack of guile and flustered behavior this afternoon had made him think she might be a widow or a spinster visiting a family member. When she'd disappeared into the train station, he'd debated going after her. He wasn't certain which had irritated him more, his fascination with the woman or his indecisiveness as to whether to go after her. The need to know more about her had overridden his desire to stay away from her.

When his men had lost her trail, he'd tried to put any thought of her out of his head, but even as he'd entered the palace this evening, he'd found himself wondering if she might be present. He clenched his teeth. It had been a long time since any woman had piqued his curiosity as this one had, and the fact that she made her living by accepting favors from men only heightened his annoyance. He should have listened to his gut and ignored his fascination with the woman.

The sound of her laughter echoed in his ears as he saw Hakim offer her a glass of champagne off the salver a footman held. He frowned at his charge's expression. *Damm gahannam*, Hakim was already besotted with her. The woman would have the boy for breakfast then discard his rotting carcass when she was through.

She laughed again, her heading tipping backward as she did so. He didn't understand how, but she made the slight movement appear erotic and seductive. His fingers dug their way through the soft wool of his *gambaz* to pinch deeply into his upper arms.

One would think that after all these years he'd know better than to be intrigued by a woman of Allegra Synnford's ilk. With perhaps the exception of this woman's mastery of seduction, he doubted there would be any difference between her and Frances.

The sudden onslaught of emotions made his body grow taut as

he remembered his one-time mistress. Calculating, greedy, and without a heart, Frances had been interested in one person and one person only. Herself. It hadn't bothered her in the least to take two lovers at the same time. Nor had she cared that both of them had thought themselves in love with her.

He returned his attention to Hakim, and he clenched his jaw at the expression of adoration on the boy's face. Christ, had he looked like that when he'd been in love with Frances? No, not love. He'd been in lust with the woman, never in love. If he'd realized that all those years ago, would it have mattered?

His skin grew cold as he remembered how the feathery snow had brushed across his face that wintry, dark night. If he'd been late reaching Frances that evening, perhaps things might have been different. He grimaced at the wishful thought. The past was written, and it was useless to consider what might have been.

He focused his attention on Allegra once more to see her smile at one of the men in her circle. With a low growl of annoyance, he watched her continue to weave her spell on the men around her. Even from here he could understand why her audience was so captivated.

She had an elusive, mysterious quality that served as a silent temptation to every man around her. With a simple tilt of her head or a soft smile, she invited every man to lure her into a liaison. He might know what she was, but he couldn't help but feel the urge to answer her unspoken challenge.

Every laugh, every turn of her head pulled at him, enticed him to join her. His lack of self-control infuriated him. He took pride in his ability to avoid temptation, but this woman fascinated him more than he cared to admit. Muttering a violent oath, he strode quickly out to the open terrace that led down into the Sultan's gardens. He could just as easily monitor threats to Hakim's safety from the patio.

The night air was cool and he drew in a deep breath of it. *Merde*, he'd gone without a woman for too long. When this hellish event was over he'd take Hakim back to the house the family maintained in Marrakech, then he'd find a brothel where he could wear out his cock. Maybe he'd even take the boy with him, just to convince him that whores were all alike. The scent of citrus floated up from the gardens and filled his nostrils. It reminded him of Allegra Synnford. He pinched the bridge of his nose with his fingers and blew out a hard breath. Behind him the sound of applause made him turn his head and he saw a small contingent of dancers begin to perform for the Sultan's guests.

Instinct made him search the small gathering for Hakim's familiar figure. Mere seconds later, he saw the young man enjoying the performance in front of him. His gaze continued to sweep the room in search of Allegra. To his surprise, he saw she'd freed herself of her circle of admirers and was moving away from the other guests. Slowly, she put distance between the gathering and herself, and it took him a moment to realize she was headed toward the terrace.

He wasn't sure why, but he retreated into the shadows as she stepped out onto the balustrade-enclosed patio. When she reached the marble railing, she gripped the smooth stone and stood there quietly. Eyes closed, she tilted her face up toward the moonlight. Several long moments passed before a soft sigh escaped her and she turned her head to look back into the palace.

The vulnerability he'd witnessed in her earlier today had returned. She seemed reluctant, yet resigned to going back into the drawing room. A surprising behavior for a woman who made her living the way she did. But then the worried expression on her face was startling, too. It stirred in him a sudden desire to offer her comfort from her troubles. The idea created a restlessness in him, and he shifted his position slightly. The moment he moved, his *gambaz* brushed against the branch of a small pomegranate tree that hung over the railing. She jerked her head toward the rustling sound with a low cry.

"Who's there?"

"Someone else who sought a moment's solitude," he said, not leaving the shadows.

The moonlight illuminated her surprised expression, and she took a step toward him, peering into the shadows in an effort to see him. "I know you. Your voice. You were at the train station today."

"Most fortunate for you it seems," he said with a touch of irony.

She winced at his words. "I know it was foolish of me to be so close, but I was spellbound by your horse. He's magnificent."

"I agree."

"I don't suppose . . ." She nibbled at her lip in hesitation. "Would you consider selling him? I would give you a fair price."

"Abyad isn't for sale."

"Oh."

The soft word reflected a disappointment that was unexpected. She turned away from him, and moonlight drifted across the side of her neck like pale, translucent silk. It surprised him that she would give up so easily. It wasn't the reaction he'd expected. Frances would have immediately switched tactics and tried to seduce him into getting what she wanted. But this woman wasn't even making an attempt to persuade him to change his mind about Abyad.

Was it possible for a courtesan not to use her wiles to get what she wanted? The thought intrigued him. Fascinated, he moved closer without leaving the shadows. His fingers itched to trace the moonbeam's path and he almost gave in to the temptation.

"Perhaps other arrangements could be made," she mused as she stared out at shadows of the garden.

"What sort of arrangements, *ma belle*?" he bit out through clenched teeth. It infuriated him that he'd actually contemplated the possibility that she was different than Frances. She might be the most sought after courtesan in Europe, but she was no less manipulative than the next whore. No doubt she thought she could earn the horse by lying on her back.

"I could purchase a mare from one of the traders in Marrakech and then breed her with your horse. I would pay you a fair price."

She turned back toward him with a hopeful expression on her face. For a moment, he couldn't believe his ears. The woman wasn't propositioning him; she wanted to conduct an ordinary business transaction. In the next instant, he realized he hadn't just expected her to propose a liaison, he'd been hoping she would.

Frustrated by the traitorous thought, he silently berated himself. The only reason he wanted her to offer herself to him was so he could prove she was no different than Frances. But she hadn't done that. No, she was more interested in discussing the possibility of breeding Abyad. And to make matters worse, he didn't enjoy coming in second to his horse. Any horse. He stepped completely out of the shadows and he watched her green eyes widen. In the moonlight, her gaze was darker and more mysterious than he'd expected.

Although her features were rather ordinary, she had a mystique about her that made her exquisite. With the tip of his forefinger, he lightly traced the line of her jaw. Beneath his touch, she quivered before she abruptly tipped her head away from him. But not even the dim shadows of the terrace could hide the way her breasts rose and fell at the same rate as her rapid breathing.

That he affected her shouldn't have given him any pleasure, but it did. The best course of action would be to tell her to stay away from Hakim and leave her on the patio. He chose to ignore his own advice. Instead, acting solely on impulse, he reached out to touch her again. The smoothness of her shoulder was like a rich, lustrous satin beneath his fingertips. She immediately put distance between them at his touch. Her reaction made him smile.

"Tell me why I should say yes, *chérie?*"

"Because it will be a profitable venture for you," she said in breathless voice. There was a guarded expression on her face as she met his gaze.

"Hmm, perhaps." He took a step closer, but she stood her ground.

"I'm certain we could reach an agreement on a sum you'd find acceptable."

Excitement lit up her face and she leaned toward him ever so slightly. His gaze took in the myriad of emotions dancing in her eyes as she waited for his answer with a touch of impatience. She clearly understood the significance of Abyad's pedigree, otherwise she wouldn't be so insistent on settling for the opportunity of off-spring. The fact impressed him.

He didn't want to be impressed. He didn't want anything to do with her. The lie stabbed at him with vicious glee. With a jerk, he turned back toward the moonlit garden. *Damm gahannam*, he was insane. Why draw out this ridiculous barter session? It accomplished nothing when he knew full well he had no intention of accepting anything less than a night in her bed. He didn't like admitting it, but he wanted her.

"I must refuse, mademoiselle. I believe you will consider my price too high."

"I think you should let *me* decide whether or not I have the funds to meet your price."

The fresh scent of honey and lemon made his nostrils flare as he breathed in the essence of her. She'd moved closer, her expression filled with the hope that he would agree to her request. It was the fact that she didn't even attempt to use her charms in any way that made her even more persuasive.

Her manner indicated nothing more than an earnest desire to convince him their transaction would benefit them both. The smell of her was soft and enticing as she leaned into him, creating an overwhelming desire to give her what she wanted. Sweet and warm, her breath brushed his cheek as her hand touched his arm. Electricity pulsed from her fingers through his *gambaz* and into his body. He immediately stiffened at the shock of her touch, while alarm bells clanged wildly in the back of his head. His attraction to the woman was far more dangerous than he'd realized. The sooner he ended this farce, the better.

"All the same, if what I've heard is true, you will not agree to the transaction, *ma belle*," he murmured, and she abruptly took two steps away from him. He turned his head and saw her face was devoid of emotion. That she was still even on the patio told him how badly she wanted Abyad to sire a foal. A tiny sliver of guilt nicked at his conscience, but he shoved it aside. She was a courtesan. She gave herself to men for other things, what made this transaction any different?

"What do you want?" She held herself rigidly, her voice icy and distant.

The answer was immediate. He wanted to see her naked on top of him, riding him with abandon. The erotic image tugged the air out of his lungs as he pictured his sun-darkened hands sliding across the lusty curve of a peach-colored hip and thigh. His fingers dug into his arms as he fought to destroy the sudden blast of desire barreling through him.

"One night, *chérie*." He clenched his jaw as he realized it might take more than one night to ease his lust for her.

Her gaze slid over him with a scathing look he knew was

designed to humiliate him. It didn't work, but he begrudgingly admitted to himself that if looks could maim, he would be bleeding heavily. A small voice in the back of his head told him it would be no less than he deserved.

She turned her head away from him, a frown marring her features as if she were in deep contemplation. There it was again, that air of vulnerability he found puzzling. Intriguing. Perhaps he'd been judging her unfairly. He crushed the thought. Silence stretched between them for a long moment before she pulled in a deep breath as if reaching a decision. The change in her was instantaneous. The vulnerable woman vanished, replaced by a creature so sensual and enticing, she was breathtaking.

"One night?" Her voice was a low, beguiling whisper that wrapped its way around him with gentle yet relentless persuasion. "No more than that?"

The witch thought to turn the tables on him. She was doing a damn good job of it, too. Tension flowed through him as he resisted the urge to pull her into his arms. Experience had taught him to avoid this type of temptation, and yet each passing moment in her presence made it difficult to do so. He hadn't experienced lust this strong in years.

"One night," he bit out, not about to admit that he should have asked for more.

"And what is it you want for this one night, monsieur?" Her voice was soft and seductive, but he could still hear a hint of anger behind her words. He forced himself to smile if only to keep her from realizing her attempt to tie him into knots was succeeding. But he refused to give her the upper hand.

"I'm not one for games, Allegra. We both know what I want."

She stepped forward and brushed her fingertips across his mouth. Her touch was light, almost nonexistent, and yet his entire body grew taut with need. The seductive smile curving her lips signaled her confidence in her ability to tempt him. Slowly, she leaned closer and the heat of her breath warmed his ear.

"You want me," she whispered.

Instantly his cock was hard as iron. With the grace of one of the Sultan's dancers, she put several feet between them before facing him again. The moonlight draped its softness over her entire body and he was certain the move was a calculated one. Somehow she knew the pale light would only heighten the sensuality of her figure. Silently, he watched her fingers brush across the side of her neck in a slow stroke. It was the same type of caress his own hand itched to perform.

Lips parted in a small, knowing smile, she closed her eyes and allowed her hand to fondle her skin in a light caress. Mesmerized, he watched her continue the stroke downward to the base of her throat and beyond until two fingers slid into the valley between her full breasts. With a leisurely stroke, she caressed the darkened slit in an up and down movement that had his body howling for release. He dragged in air between his clenched teeth in a soft hiss, and she opened her eyes at the sound.

Across the small space between them, she met his gaze with a sultry smile and his heartbeat thundered in his ears. Eyes gleaming with confidence, the tip of her tongue slid out to lick her upper lip in a quick stroke, leaving it glistening in the moonlight. It wasn't just an invitation; it was a goddamned command performance. White-hot need lashed through him and he swallowed hard. For the first time, he understood completely why her name was uttered with such fascination by other men.

Her skill at seduction was extraordinary. But she wasn't dealing with a weak-willed Englishman she could manipulate to her own ends. He wasn't one of her infatuated admirers she could control.

The dramatic presentation she'd just shown him illustrated that she fully expected him to fall in line like every other man she'd ever been with. But for the first time, Allegra Synnford had met her match. With a nonchalance he didn't feel, he clasped his hands behind his back and arched an eyebrow at her.

"An exceptional performance, *chérie*. I confess it's quite possible I'll be receiving the better end of the bargain."

In a split second, her expression went flat and lifeless, but the way she held herself rigid revealed her anger. "For anything even *resembling* that performance, monsieur, you would need to *give* me your horse, not his seed, and I confess I no longer have interest in either."

She whirled around and stalked toward the doorway leading back into the drawing room. Despite his surprise, his quick reflexes allowed him to reach her in two strides. His arm snaked around her waist and he dragged her backward into the shadows with him.

"Let me go," she snapped with hushed fury.

"And if I gave you the horse, *chérie*?" He couldn't believe he'd just offered her Abyad for a single night in her bed. He had to be mad to offer her such a proposal even if his entire body ached for a physical release. That she could stir his desire so easily infuriated him. Well, he was damned if he'd let the tempting witch get the best of him.

"I believe I made myself perfectly clear that I have no intention of conducting *any* business with you, monsieur." She struggled against his hold and he deftly twisted her around to face him, while holding her tight against his chest.

"Surely, you're not afraid, Allegra."

"Of you? Not at all," she responded with a vehement shake of her head and glared up at him.

"You should be, *ma belle*."

"And why is that, monsieur?" The sneer in her voice almost covered her trepidation, but not quite.

"Because I'm not like your other lovers," he murmured. As her gaze locked with his, he smiled. "I'm the one man you won't be able to control."

3

His words and the dark emotion glittering in his intense brown gaze sent fire streaking through every inch of her body. From the first moment she'd heard the seductive familiarity of his voice echoing out of the shadows she'd known exactly who he was. At the railway station, he'd been dark and dangerous, but tonight— tonight he epitomized everything male she knew to avoid.

Pinned against his chest, it was impossible not to breathe in the warm spicy scent of him. The effect he'd had on her senses earlier today was nothing compared to what she was experiencing now. Wickedly handsome in a barbaric fashion, the sheer power of his presence sent her blood flowing hot and fast through her veins.

Black, wavy hair brushed against his shoulders at a length that was almost heathenish, but she found herself wanting to lace her fingers through the silky-looking curls. The headdress he'd worn earlier in the day had hidden his strong, narrow nose and the way it emphasized the fullness of his mouth. His high forehead ended in a widow's peak, and a thin scar crested across the browned skin of his cheek in a vivid white line. The mark gave him a rakish air that she found far too tantalizing for her own good.

He was right.

She should be afraid of him.

This man wouldn't be satisfied until she was in his bed. And it didn't help matters that she was sorely tempted to give in to his demand without her usual forethought. That was something she never did. She swallowed hard. She could always cry for help, but she was too stubborn to let any man get the better of her. No, she would find some other way out of the situation.

"I'm afraid, monsieur, that it's you who doesn't understand the rules of this game. *I* pick my lovers, and I *never* enter into a liaison on such short acquaintance."

"And *I* never take no for an answer," he murmured.

She struggled to suppress a tremor. God, but the man had a wicked voice. She immediately clenched her teeth. It irritated her that she couldn't control her reaction to him. Over the years, there had been many men who had arrogantly declared they intended to become her lover, and they'd all failed. But this man's confidence unnerved her. She believed him when he said he wouldn't take no for an answer.

The worst of it was she knew a liaison with him could have devastating consequences. Just the way her body responded to his told her it would not be a simple dalliance. He would bend her to his will, and not since Arthur had rescued her from Madame Eugenie's had she allowed any man to do that.

"It would seem we are at an impasse," she said, trying desperately to keep her voice steady.

"Are we? Then one of us must yield."

Something about the determined glint in his eye kindled a firestorm of panic inside her. He narrowed his gaze at her, his mouth curved in a seductive smile. As his hand captured her chin, her trepidation vanished in a wave of heat and she barely suppressed her whimper of desire when his thumb stroked her lower lip. Dear God, what was wrong with her? She needed to end this madness now, before she really did surrender to him.

"I shall be happy to have *you* yield to me, monsieur," she said in a breathless rush.

"Doing so is not in my nature. But for a kiss I might be persuaded otherwise." The amusement in his voice made her stiffen.

"A ki— You arrogant beast. I have no intention of—"

The scents of cedar and anise drifted across her senses just before his mouth silenced her. The outrage holding her rigid evaporated in an instant, replaced by a sharply pitched desire.

Up until this moment, pleasure had been a simple, uncomplicated experience for her. But this was something altogether foreign. It was raw. Primitive. Completely out of control.

His tongue laced across her lip until she willingly parted her mouth for him. He tasted hot and savage, just like the desert. She'd always enjoyed kissing, but this was a hedonistic assault. He didn't take—he cajoled.

Every stroke of his tongue was a dance of seduction that heightened each of her senses until what little control she had left spiraled away into oblivion. A rush of heat made the insides of her thighs slick, and she gasped as his mouth skimmed across her jaw and down the side of her neck.

His touch demonstrated just how precarious her position was where he was concerned. For the first time in memory, she wasn't the one doing the seducing, and it made her feel powerless. The realization set off alarm bells in her head and she wrenched herself free of his embrace.

The harsh sound of her breathing echoed loudly in her ears as she stared up at his features, visible in the light spilling out from the palace drawing room. He appeared completely unaffected by the kiss. Not even a hint of desire darkened his expression. Horrified, she pressed her hand to the base of her throat. *She* was always the one who seduced. The one in control. Men succumbed to *her*, not the other way around. She flinched at the small smile slowly curving his mouth.

"It would seem we have resolved the question of who will yield," he murmured. "A step forward in the negotiation of your fee, *chérie*."

Dear God, he was mocking her. It was bad enough she'd succumbed so easily to him, but for him to realize it as well infuriated her. And to autocratically suggest they'd been discussing an arrangement—money—it was an insult. She might be a courtesan, but her benefactors had always treated her with respect. Money was *never* openly discussed.

When she did welcome a man into her bed, he simply contacted her attorney at a later date to make arrangements for a substantial allowance that ran for the length of their association. She'd never demanded a specific amount of money for her time, but her lovers had always been generous. Now this man thought he could barter his way into her bed as if she were one of those poor creatures she'd left behind at Madame Eugenie's.

She shuddered. What this man wanted, she refused to give, and she wouldn't let him treat her like soiled goods. She'd not chosen her lifestyle, and she was damned if she'd apologize for the method of her survival. The man thought she had yielded, but she'd only surrendered to his touch. Now he was about to discover exactly how unyielding she could be when it came to selecting a benefactor. Holding herself ramrod straight, she eyed him with cold anger.

"We were *not* negotiating, monsieur. *You* are the last man here tonight that I would consider taking into my bed."

"We both know that's untrue." There it was again, that amused autocratic note in his voice. It appalled and angered her in the same instant.

"Your arrogance has made you delusional. There are at least half a dozen men inside who I would eagerly welcome into my bed over you."

His gaze narrowed and the mocking amusement in his dark-eyed gaze became a hard, bitter gleam. "If you think to impress that fact on me by using Hakim as an example of your allure, think again."

"I beg your pardon."

"I'm sure you've already learned the boy is worth a king's ransom."

"I don't know—"

"Your protests fall on deaf ears, *ma belle*. The boy might be infatuated with you but I'll not allow you to use him to prove your point."

He had to be referring to the young man who'd not left her side since their introduction. The boy was the reason she'd come out onto the patio in the first place. As charming as the young man was, she'd needed an escape from his effusive compliments. She knew the boy was already infatuated with her, but she would never encourage him. Younger men had a habit of demanding more of her than she was willing to give. Namely her heart. She shook her head and glared at him.

"This is absurd. I—"

"Hakim is uneducated in the rules of your game. Stay away from the boy or you'll answer to me." Cold fury hardened his features, and she ignored the flicker of fear sliding through her.

"I answer to *no* man," she snapped fiercely.

"In *this* matter you will." The menace in his words scraped across her spine like an icy dagger. "The boy's my charge, and I'll not have you toying with him."

"You should learn the rules of *my* particular game as you refer to it, monsieur. I *never* welcome schoolboys into my bed." She struggled to keep her tone even as she sent him a baleful look. "How I earn my living doesn't determine my personal conduct."

His hand whipped out to stop her as she turned to walk away. He didn't speak—he simply studied her intently. It was easy to see he was uncertain of her, but it mattered little. She'd experienced the condemnation and contempt of far too many others for this man's opinion to make any difference to her. The sound of mocking laughter whispered through her head, but she ignored it.

"Surprised, monsieur?" she said coldly as she peeled his fingers off her arm. "Don't be. You're not the first to think me unprincipled simply because of my profession, and I doubt you'll be the last."

With as much dignity as her anger allowed, she walked stiffly toward the doors leading back into the palace. Compared to the shadows of the patio, the light of the drawing room was blinding. As her eyes adjusted to the brightness, she fought to control the myriad of emotions raging inside her. Anger, disappointment, pain, and humiliation all converged to make her long for a home. A place where she could go to nurse the wounds he'd inflicted on her.

She was no stranger to contempt, but it always stung when she encountered it. For some inexplicable reason, the man's scorn—God, she didn't even know his name—had cut deeper than she was accustomed to. The knowledge dismayed her. Why should she care what the man thought?

Her hands clenched in fists, she dragged in a deep breath. She would not let him upset her. Slowly, she forced herself to release the emotions holding her tense and rigid. She was enamored with the romantic imagery of a desert sheikh. It was the only explanation for the way she was feeling. She would be back to her usual self by bedtime.

Lying to herself was never a good idea, but this was one time when she took comfort in doing so. From across the room, her gaze met Isabelle's. Concern furrowed Isabelle's forehead as she moved quickly toward her. When her friend reached her side, Isabelle wrapped one arm through Allegra's.

"Where on earth have you been? The Sultan was asking for you."

"On the patio," she answered quietly. "I needed a moment to myself."

"Well, perhaps that's a good thing considering Charles arrived a short time ago." Isabelle took a quick glance over her shoulder.

"What?" she gasped in dismay.

"He's a friend of one of Brant's officers. They came late. I'm so sorry, Allegra. I had no idea he was in Marrakech."

She winced. What were the odds that Charles would choose to visit Morocco at the same time she had. Remote, she was sure. Had he followed her here for some perverse reason? She raised her hand to massage her temple in a vain effort to stave off the beginnings of a headache. She should never have allowed Isabelle to convince her to come this evening. Her friend's grip on her arm tightened and she saw the Viscount Shaftsbury moving toward them.

The solemn expression on Charles's face surprised her. It had been a long time since she'd seen his face free of bitterness or anger when he looked at her. When he stopped in front of them, he bowed politely.

"May I offer you my sincerest best wishes on the occasion of your marriage to Major Hastings, Isabelle. I hope you'll be very happy."

"Thank you." Isabelle's tone of voice was cool, yet polite, as she bobbed her head in his direction.

Charles turned his head toward her. "How are you, Allegra?"

"Well enough." She greeted him with a sharp nod.

"Might I have a word with you?"

His question made her glance at Isabelle, who squeezed her arm in a silent word of caution. Her circle of friends was a small but loyal one, and the protective gleam in Isabelle's violet eyes warmed her heart. If Isabelle were to have her way, Allegra was certain her friend would drag her away as quickly as possible. Any other time she would have followed her friend's lead, but something in Charles's face told her to grant his request. With a light touch on Isabelle's hand, she offered her friend a small smile.

"I'll be all right, Isabelle. Go back to Brant, and I'll join you in a few moments." When her friend looked ready to protest, she gently urged Isabelle in the direction of her future husband. "I'll be fine."

Although it was obvious she didn't want to go, Isabelle acquiesced, but only after sending the Viscount a sharp glance of warning. As her friend moved away, she turned her gaze back to the man in front of her.

"I'm surprised to see you in Marrakech," she said quietly.

"I'm here on family business." He grimaced as she arched her eyebrows. "It's the truth. I'm looking for my cousin, the Viscount Newcastle. The last I heard he was here in Marrakech."

"Please don't take me for a fool, Charles." She sent him a look of disgust.

"Allegra, I swear I didn't know you were here this evening. If I'd known you'd be here, I wouldn't have come."

"Why? You've not let it stop you before." It was impossible to keep the bitterness out of her voice. She'd been exceedingly fond of Charles and when he'd maligned her publicly, it had been a betrayal of their friendship. To her amazement, she saw him wince.

"You're right, and I'm sorry."

For a moment, she wasn't sure she'd heard him correctly. She shook her head in bemusement as she watched the remorse in his expression. When she didn't say anything, he stretched his neck as if to swallow a large lump in his throat.

"I'm sorry, Allegra. For all of it. I was a bastard."

"What do you expect me to say, Charles?" She eyed him with mistrust. "That an apology makes everything all right?"

"No." He grimaced. "I said some ugly things and hurt you. I wish I could take it all back, but I can't, so the only thing I can do is tell you how sorry I am."

"Very well. You've said it," she said coolly and started to move away from him. He immediately grasped her arm to hold her in place.

"Do you think you might be able to forgive me?"

She glanced down at her arm in a pointed manner before meeting his gaze again. He immediately released his grip. Taken aback by the regret on his face, she looked away from him. Any other time she would have found it fairly easy to forgive him, but tonight her nerves were raw. She couldn't trust her instincts where Charles was concerned. Her mysterious sheikh had rendered her far more vulnerable than she cared to admit. She'd been powerless in his arms, and the confidence she prided herself on was shaken badly.

If she gave in easily to Charles's request, it might make him think there was still hope for him. Worse, what if he were simply playing her for a fool? She'd already played that part once this evening and had no intention of doing it again. With a sigh, she returned her gaze to Charles's remorseful expression.

"It's not that easy, Charles. I need time to think about it."

"I understand," he said softly. "Will you at least let me call on you in a couple of days?"

"I don't know . . . I'm not sure—"

"I know I can't have your love, Allegra, but I'll settle for your friendship. I've missed our debates. Of all the women I've ever been with, you're the only one who could ever best me when it came to a sound argument."

The admission tugged a small smile to her lips. She'd enjoyed their debates as well. "In a couple of days, then."

Charles smiled with delight as he captured her hand and brought it to his lips. It reminded her that it was his smile that had attracted her to him in the first place. He brushed his lips across her knuckles. "Thank you, Allegra, you won't regret it. I promise."

With a nod, she gently eased her hand out of his and moved toward where Isabelle stood with her fiancé. She'd only gone a short distance when a frisson across the nape of her neck made her pause. Glancing over her shoulder, she saw a tall shadow just beyond the reach of the salon's candlelight. A shudder rippled through her. It was impossible to read his expression, but instinct told her that she would see him again. And the next time she wouldn't find it so easy to escape.

✧

From the shadows of the terrace, Shaheen watched Allegra join the group of people surrounding Hastings and his fiancée. It was clear the man she'd been talking to was someone she knew well. They had the look of lovers arranging a tryst, and the idea put him in an ill temper.

He uttered a soft noise of disgust. *Damnation.* Why the hell should it bother him to see the woman with one of her lovers? Because she'd gotten to him. She'd managed to make him doubt his assumptions about her.

Damm gahannam, he'd never meant to indulge in a game of seduction. And it had backfired on him in a way he'd never expected. How the devil was he supposed to know she was a courtesan with principles? Frances had never been so idealistic.

"*Merde*, what the hell were you thinking, you bastard?" he muttered as he paced the length of the patio.

None of this would have happened if he'd simply warned her away from Hakim instead of trying to prove she was just like any other whore. Particularly when she'd quite effectively proven him wrong. He grunted with anger as he wheeled about and walked the length of the stone terrace for the second time. It had been a hell of a lot easier to consider her unprincipled than a woman with scruples.

He now understood the fascination other men had with her. All he'd done was kiss the woman and his body had been on fire. His lust for her had been all-consuming and unlike anything he'd ever felt for Frances, or any other woman for that matter. Even now, his cock ached to slide into her warm, silky cunny. It would be a simple thing to relieve his physical ache with his hand or even by a visit to one of the local brothels, but he doubted there would be any satisfaction in it.

At the moment, there was only one woman he wanted. The image of Allegra kneeling in front of him, her round buttocks cupped in his hands as he slid in and out of her slick, velvety heat made his erection jump. Making it worse was the fact that he could still feel her softness against him, smell her fresh feminine scent in his nostrils. She'd left her mark on him.

The simple thought halted his pacing. *Christ Jesus. Halah's prediction.* More than a year ago, the old woman had foretold of a woman of fire who would leave her mark on him. He'd always scoffed at the woman's fortune-telling where he was concerned, but if the crone heard about Allegra, he'd never hear the end of it. Particularly when Halah's description of the courtesan had been extraordinarily accurate, right down to the color of Allegra's auburn hair.

He released another grunt, this time of disgust. The tribe

Sheikh Mahmoud had placed under his leadership revered Halah for what he grudgingly admitted was her uncanny ability to predict the future. The Amazigh were a superstitious people, and they took omens and signs seriously. He turned back toward the salon. Hakim was once more at the courtesan's side.

From what he could tell, she was doing an excellent job of ignoring the boy. The fact pleased and annoyed him at the same time. He didn't like admitting he was wrong, and she was forcing him to do just that. Damnation, whether he'd been wrong about her or not wasn't the point.

The only thing he cared about was ensuring Hakim didn't spend any more time in the woman's company. They were only staying in town another week, and if he kept Hakim occupied with business matters, the boy would soon forget the courtesan. As for him, he'd find a way to dismiss Allegra from his thoughts. He clenched his teeth. He didn't like the mocking voice in his head that said he'd find it difficult to forget her.

Another glance at Hakim's face said the boy was growing frustrated by Allegra's lack of attentiveness. Any minute now, his young friend was apt to make a fool of himself over the woman. *Best to rescue the boy now and save him from any potential embarrassment.* He reentered the drawing room and waited several seconds to catch Hakim's eye.

When the boy saw him, Shaheen gestured toward the door. A stubborn expression darkened Hakim's face, but he nodded belligerently when Shaheen glared at him. He watched the young man begin to say his good-byes, and he debated whether to breach the small crowd encircling Hastings and his fiancée to do the same.

He decided to let Hakim say good-bye for the two of them. Eager to leave, he looked around the room for any sign of the Sultan. The ruler was conversing with another guest close to the salon's entrance, and he made his way toward the man. Mulay

Hassan saw him coming and broke away from his conversation as Shaheen approached.

"Are you leaving us so soon, my friend?"

"I think it best to escort Hakim home before the young fool embarrasses himself."

"The boy has an excellent eye. Unfortunately for every man here, the lady has no interest in *any* liaisons at this time."

The thought of the Sultan with Allegra set him on edge. In the next instant, satisfaction replaced his irritation as he realized Mulay Hassan, like the other men in the room, had failed to capture her interest. On the heels of both emotions came frustration. *He* was one of those men. *Damm gahannam*, the woman had him tied up in knots. The sooner he was away from her presence, the better.

"Ah, Hakim." The Sultan greeted the Amazigh heir with a smile and his hand settled on the young man's shoulder. "Don't despair, boy. There are other birds of paradise to catch."

"I shall call on her tomorrow to persuade her to change her mind."

There was a defiant glint in the boy's eyes that made Shaheen study him carefully. Under his scrutiny, the boy's features grew even more rebellious. Beside him, the Sultan chuckled.

"Persuasion is an admirable skill to possess, Hakim. But if you wish to possess a woman's body, my young friend, you must first conquer her heart."

Hakim's reply to the Sultan's adage was a fierce scowl. Shaheen immediately sent the boy a stern look before Hakim bowed respectfully and bade their host good night. Mulay Hassan chuckled at the young man's sullen good-bye and watched with amusement as Hakim stalked out of the salon.

"Rejection is good for the boy," the Sultan said with a clap of his hand on Shaheen's shoulder. "It will teach him humility."

With quiet agreement and a final farewell, Shaheen followed the younger man into the atrium and out through the front entrance. Hakim's stride was long and fast, evidence of his frustration. He found the boy's behavior disappointing, but he understood it. Allegra was the first woman the boy had ever displayed any real interest in and rejection wasn't easy.

Silence engulfed the carriage as they returned to the house the family kept in Marrakech. Shaheen had always allowed the boy to work through his anger without interference unless absolutely necessary, but something felt different this time. The icy atmosphere between them made him realize Hakim somehow considered him to blame for his lack of success with Allegra.

He released a quiet sigh and yearned for the peaceful sound of a crackling fire and the stars draped overhead in the black sky. The carriage rolled to a stop and Hakim bolted from the vehicle. With resignation, he watched the young man enter the house. The boy would one day make a great leader, but at the moment, he needed to learn how to control his hot temper. As Shaheen walked through the gated doorway into the coolness of the central courtyard, one of the servants hurried forward and handed him a sealed letter. Tearing the missive open, he stared at the single line of script.

A Lord Shaftsbury has been asking about you.

Respectfully, Ali Dabir

The tribe's legal counsel in Marrakech, Dabir always had his ear to the ground and knew what was happening before anyone else. The man was also one of the few people who knew his real identity. But for all intents and purposes, that man was dead. Robert Camden, Viscount Newcastle had died in the desert almost fifteen years ago. No one had even mourned his passing. And the dead were always best left buried.

His gaze returned to the short message. *Shaftsbury.* Visitors had been rare at Pembroke Hall, but he had vague memories of meeting the man after he'd moved to London to live with James. A relative from his mother's side of the family as he recalled. He closed his eyes at the thought of a mother he'd never known. Her death had always been a painful reminder of what could have been. Not even his brother had felt it quite as keenly as he had. He looked at the note again. Whatever Shaftsbury wanted there was little doubt that his father was involved. Maybe the bastard was finally dead.

The thought caused him to flex his jaw as the muscles in his body tightened with pain. He winced then stiffened his shoulders. Whether his father was dead or alive was of little consequence to him. The earl had disowned him years ago, and he had no desire to inherit the Pembroke title or return to the life he'd once known. Shaftsbury and his father could both go to hell for all he cared.

With the note tucked inside his *gambaz*, he crossed the courtyard and walked down a short hallway before entering the suite he shared with Hakim. The young man was standing on the room's balcony that overlooked Marrakech. As if sensing he was no longer alone, the Amazigh heir apparent turned and eyed him coldly.

"I saw you with the *emîra*, Shaheen."

The boy's bitter accusation sailed across the room with the vehemence of a jealous lover, suddenly aware he had competition. At least this confirmed his suspicions about the cold silence in the carriage. Arching an eyebrow at the youth, he remained silent. It would do no good to try and explain his actions to the boy. Hakim's face grew flushed with angry color when Shaheen didn't answer. His stride a brash swagger, the boy moved toward a low couch and threw himself on top of several of the divan's brightly colored pillows.

"If I were Sheikh, I would have you flayed for touching her."

"If you were Sheikh, you would be a man," he said quietly and turned away to go to his room. Despite his lineage, the boy needed to understand the difference between commanding and acting the part of a petty tyrant.

"I will change her mind. A woman like that can always be bought."

For some odd reason, the callous words infuriated him. Allegra Synnford might accept gifts and money in exchange for her favors, but she'd displayed a set of principles tonight that he found honorable. Other women wouldn't have thought twice about taking Hakim as a lover once they discovered his worth. Something deep inside him said Allegra would never consider doing such a thing.

"She turned you away because you're still a boy," he said as he clenched his jaw with anger and continued toward his room. Any other time Hakim's belligerent behavior would have amused him, but tonight it only exacerbated his irritation.

"You lie."

The heated words brought him to an abrupt halt. Slowly, he turned to face the defiant boy he'd guarded for the past fifteen years. He was angry enough to throttle the insolent pup. The boy knew better than to accuse him of lying. Barely restraining his fury, he sent Hakim a cold look.

"I will forgive your insult to me, to your father, and the trust he places in me." He watched the boy blanch at his icy words. "Forget the woman. She's not worth the heartache she would cause you, even if she were to consider taking a mere *boy* to her bed."

Not waiting for a reply, he strode from the sitting room and slammed the door behind him. In the dark, he paced the floor with a restless energy and released a grunt of anger. It had been a long time since he'd miscalculated a situation so badly. Even his exchange with Hakim could have been handled better. The boy

was in the midst of his first real infatuation. That he understood.
He still remembered the pretty ballerina he'd made a fool of himself over. But comparing Allegra to that vacuous ballerina was like
night and day.

He shrugged out of his *gambaz*. Carelessly, he threw it onto
the bed and shoved a hand through his hair. The confines of the
spacious room closed in on him, and he strode toward the balcony that hung low over the house's inner courtyard. He inhaled
a deep breath of cool night air, and the scent of jasmine teased his
nostrils.

It reminded him of Allegra's skin, soft and sweet. The memory of her in his arms made him grow hard again. *Damm gahannam*. The woman was occupying his thoughts far too much. He'd
warned her to stay away from Hakim, and he was confident she
would. The problem was, *he* didn't want to stay away from her.
The woman was like opium—a small taste brought a craving for
more. It had been years since a woman had made him come close
to losing complete control of his senses. Like his young charge, he
would forget Allegra Synnford. It would be a mistake to bed her,
no matter how tempting she might be. Losing control of his senses
was something he could never let happen again. The price had
been too costly the last time.

4

Trees lined every path inside the Agdal Gardens, and the path encircling the small glade Shaheen stood in was no different. More than a dozen pomegranate trees encircled the marble gazebo, their dark green leaves forming a natural canopy of shade against the afternoon sun. Standing at the foot of the stone structure, Major Hastings and his new wife greeted their wedding guests with smiles and laughter.

Having already passed through the short receiving line, Shaheen was content to stand on the fringes of the small gathering and wait. From where he stood, he had a clear view of Allegra standing off to one side of the happy couple conversing with one of the major's subordinates. It had only been two days since that night on the Sultan's terrace, but forgetting her had been far more difficult than he expected. Erotic images of her filled his nights, while he spent his daylight hours testing his willpower against the persistent desire to find some way to see her again.

His willpower had always won out, if only by a thin margin. Then when he'd seen her precede the bride down the aisle just a short time ago, that slim thread had snapped. It had been impossible to take his eyes off her. She looked like a Titian model. Voluptuous curves and skin with the satiny sheen of an unripe peach made her the ideal subject for one of the master's paintings. Even the deep blue satin gown she wore clung to her curves like the caress of an artist's brush, reluctant to leave the canvas.

When she'd turned to watch the bride move toward the gazebo's makeshift altar, her eyes had met his almost immediately. Intense emotion had darkened her lovely features, then in a flash, it had disappeared. A mask of disdain had swept over her face as if he was no more than a horsefly. He'd expected anger, not scorn.

It was one thing to reluctantly believe her principled, but the idea of her being insulted by his proposal the other night seemed too far-fetched. Inwardly, he scoffed at the idea. She was a courtesan. Trading her favors for money and jewels was how she earned her living. Her current demeanor was nothing more than a ploy to manipulate him into paying a higher price for her services.

The thought irritated him. He refused to let her get the best of him, but coaxing her into his bed wasn't going to be as easy as he'd like. And seduction was precisely what he'd decided on where Allegra was concerned. He'd known as much the other night on the terrace and had simply been putting off the inevitable by staying away from her.

Now, as he watched Allegra smile at the British officer facing her, a twinge of annoyance pricked at him. He recognized the possessive emotion flowing through him and frowned. The last time he'd allowed himself to feel such an emotion had been with Frances. The memory made his jaw harden painfully. He needed to remember that bedding Allegra Synnford was simply an exercise in satisfying his cock, nothing more. Almost instantly, his hands flexed into tight fists. He could lie to himself all he wanted, but he knew full well his fascination with the woman went far deeper than he really wanted to admit.

Every muscle in his body tensed as he saw Allegra's suitor accept her glass and hurry away with the clear intent of providing her with more refreshment. The moment the officer was out of sight, Allegra quickly skirted a large bed of yellow roses and disappeared down one of the paths leading away from the glade.

No doubt she'd arranged a tryst with Wilberforth. It didn't matter, because he was about to change her mind. Without hesitating, he took another path that would enable him to follow her with little effort. He lengthened his stride and followed the tree-lined footpath at a quick pace. As he rounded the corner of the path, he saw Allegra bent over a bed of Turk lilies. The dark pink flowers had brushed their pollen across one of her full breasts, and he immediately wondered if her nipples were the same dusky color as the lilies.

The sand beneath his leather shoes did little more than whisper his approach, and when he cleared his throat, she jerked upright with a soft cry of surprise. The moment she recognized him, her eyes narrowed with anger.

"Monsieur?" Coated with icy contempt, the one-word question was meant to wither every part of him into oblivion. He assessed her mood in silence for a long moment before bowing slightly.

"For all its beauty, Marrakech is not always a safe haven. You should not be out here alone."

He half expected her to emasculate him with a blistering response, but instead consternation furrowed her forehead. The dismay on her face decisively crushed his assumptions as to why she'd entered the gardens unescorted. She'd ventured into the gardens for no other purpose than the one she'd had the other night. *Solitude.* The thought didn't please him. Once again, she'd shattered another preconceived notion of his.

"I shall heed your warning, monsieur, and return to the reception." The cool response revealed none of her disappointment, but he saw the emotion darkening the green of her eyes.

As she turned back the way she'd come, he quickly stepped past her to bend over a belladonna lily. The movement effectively blocked her escape route. Silky smooth against his fingers, the lavender-edged flower reminded him of her soft skin. The moment his fingers traced the bell-shaped bottom of the bloom, the image of another delicately curved bottom flashed into his head. He dismissed it as a romantic fancy brought on by lust.

Doing so didn't assuage the tension stiffening his muscles. Nor did it help matters when the honey-lemon scent of her drifted across his shoulder to mingle with the flower's fragrance. His nostrils flared at the pleasurable smell. As it had that night on the Sultan's terrace, her simple scent surprised him. Given her reputation, he'd expected a musky perfume, something exotic, not something so simple and natural.

"I offended you the other evening," he said, without looking at her.

"Is that an apology?" Although anger still laced its way through her voice, he heard the slight crack in her icy demeanor.

"You are an enigma, *ma belle.* You display scruples where other women in your position would not."

"I'll assume that's an apology," she said in a dry voice.

He straightened and turned to face her. The chilly demeanor she'd displayed initially had softened and he pressed his advantage. "Would you like to visit a spot in the gardens where you can see the Koutoubia Mosque and the Atlas Mountains simply by turning around?"

Curiosity swept across her face before she met his gaze and retreated behind a polite mask of indifference. He bit back a smile. Despite her efforts to hide it, he'd piqued her interest. He stretched out his hand to her in a silent invitation. Doubt clouded her face and a pink tongue slipped past her teeth to lick at a plump upper lip. It was a tiny, unrehearsed action, and yet his blood blazed with a sudden desire to pull her into his arms.

Was this what drew men to her? Her ability to entice them with delicate gestures that were completely natural and without artifice? He clenched his jaw. More likely she was so well skilled in arousing a man that all of her movements had become second nature over time. Did it matter? This wasn't the past, and he had no illusions as to what Allegra was, what he wanted from her, or what he was prepared to give her. He arched his eyebrow at her with more than a hint of arrogance.

"Is it me you fear, *chérie*, or yourself?"

"Neither." She sent him a glare of annoyance. "I'm simply debating whether the view would be worth the time I'm forced to spend in your company."

The tart response left him speechless for a long moment before he laughed deeply. It had been a blunt, honest response and he liked her for it. Perhaps a little too much. "I promise the view will not disappoint you."

Her expression wavered between curiosity and distrust. Curiosity won. "I accept your offer, monsieur, but only because there is no other escort available to me."

"You flatter me," he said with sardonic amusement.

"I didn't mean to." She arched an eyebrow at him before waving him to lead the way. "Shall we—preferably in silence."

When he offered his arm, she scorned it with a haughty look and instead walked stiffly at his side. The small slight told him she wasn't happy with herself for succumbing to her curiosity. A tiny smile tugged at his lips, but he remained silent as they strolled along the narrow walkway.

Despite their lack of conversation, her face revealed far more than she realized. The simplest of blossoms was enough to transform her expression into one of delight, and she stopped frequently to appreciate the garden's beauty firsthand. She took pleasure drawing in the scent of a fragrant bloom or touching the leaves of a mint tree in an effort to inhale its tangy perfume. Seeing the gardens through her eyes was almost like visiting them for the first time himself. Up ahead he saw their destination and pointed in the direction of the knoll.

"As promised. A unique view of the mosque and the mountains." When they reached the viewing point, Allegra faced first the mosque then turned around to view the mountains. She stood there for several minutes studying each vantage point with a contemplation that told him she was memorizing the view. Several moments later, she breathed a sigh of pleasure and he smiled.

"I take it the view is well worth the pain you suffered having me as your escort."

She darted a quick look in his direction before looking back at the mountains rising up into the brilliant blue sky. "It's wonderful. My guidebook only has a brief description of the Agdal Gardens and there was no mention of this particular viewing spot. Thank you."

"There are other sights in Marrakech that are equally entrancing," he said softly.

The way she suddenly grew still reminded him of an animal that sensed danger. Tense and uncertain, her posture betrayed her desire to flee. As if aware of his scrutiny, she slowly turned to face him, and the amusement on her face surprised him.

"Entrancing? You must be in need of spectacles, monsieur. One would be hard put to label my features anything but average."

He frowned as she turned and headed in the direction they'd come. Damn, if the woman hadn't deftly sidestepped his subtle invitation. Not only that, there had been enough mockery in her voice and smile to make him feel like a buffoon. It wasn't a pleasant sensation. He drew in a deep breath and slowly counted to ten. It had been a long time since he'd had to cajole his way into a woman's favor, and he was clearly out of practice. But if she thought to outwit him when it came to achieving his goal, she was mistaken.

❧

Allegra could almost feel the force of the Sheikh's frustration as she walked away from him and back in the direction they'd come. First, the man had thought to buy her company. Now, he sought to gain her favor by offering to show her Marrakech. Treating his invitation as though he'd paid her a compliment had helped her avoid the trap of spending more time in his company.

Not to mention how good it had felt to see the wind knocked out of his sails. She coughed in an effort to hide her laugh as she remembered the flabbergasted look he'd worn beneath what she'd learned was a kaffiyeh, held in place by a braided cord called an *agal*. He deserved to have his deportment knocked askew. The man could only benefit from a lesson in humility.

Despite his arrogance, she couldn't deny she was attracted to him. Particularly when he cut such a striking figure. She'd read a great deal about Bedouin clothing in the past two days, and his appearance today was a reflection of the wedding festivities. He'd discarded his flowing black robes for cream-colored *sherwals* and a colorful brocade vest she'd read was called a *kubran*, which fell open to reveal a simple white shirt beneath it.

The light colors emphasized the rich brown color of his skin and his sharp, angular features. In the sunlight, the scar on his cheek was even more noticeable, its white length a stark contrast to his darkened skin. It added to the air of danger surrounding him, and the overall effect was one of earthy male sensuality that sent her pulse hammering through her veins.

All too cognizant of the sensations flowing through her, she fought to control her physical response to the man. She might find him intriguing, but she had no intention of acting on her fascination. She didn't even know his name. Not that it mattered. She didn't want to know his name or anything else about him. All she wanted was to convince the man she had no intention of pursuing a liaison with him, despite her mixed emotions about him.

The way he expected her to fall eagerly into his arms was ridiculous, not to mention most annoying. She was certain there were many women who'd be delighted by his attentions, but she wasn't one of them. Still, she had to admit he wasn't without his good qualities. He had a sense of humor, he was charming when he so chose, and he was intelligent. And although she could easily do without his arrogance, she had to give him credit for showing her a spectacular vista.

That he'd recognized her desire to experience new things surprised her. And she confessed to being amazed that he'd actually complied with her demand for silence as they'd walked to the knoll from which she was now making a hasty retreat.

On their way to the viewing spot, she'd expected him to solicit her favor. Instead, he'd done as she'd asked and they'd walked through the gardens without talking. It had lulled her into dropping her guard to where she'd almost forgotten what he really wanted from her. Fortunately, she'd come to her senses in time. The other night he'd made it clear that he didn't think highly of her profession. That she'd said no to his offer had been a challenge he couldn't ignore.

His approach was barely audible, but the heat of him slowly

warmed her back as he caught up with her and fell into step beside her. Even if her eyes had been closed, her body would have screamed with awareness at his presence. The realization forced her to swallow the knot of tension swelling her throat shut. Her physical attraction to him was unlike anything she'd encountered before. That fact alone was an important reminder that she needed to keep her wits about her when in his presence.

It only made the situation all the more difficult that this wasn't a man willing to accept no for an answer. He'd warned her of that the other night, and today his behavior reinforced his warning, but what he'd not said was how devastatingly charming he could be when he wanted something. In particular, *her*.

It had been foolish to venture deeper into the gardens with him. She was fortunate it was the middle of the afternoon so she could keep her head. The romantic in her had always found the moonlight seductive, and if given the chance, he would use Marrakech's exotic shadows to tempt her into losing her head. She knew it as sure as she knew the word *temptation* was far too simple a word when it came to describing this man. He had the ability to befuddle her senses no matter the time of day or night. No other man she'd met had been able to do that. It was enough of a warning to ensure she kept her distance from him. A shiver skimmed down her spine.

"I've been wondering how you would like to proceed." The smile in his voice made her realize he'd seen her shiver.

"Proceed? Doesn't this path lead back to the wedding reception?"

She offered him a look of innocent surprise, which elicited a scowl from him. Satisfaction slid through her blood. He really didn't like it when she found a way to twist his words into something other than their original meaning. She turned her head away to hide her smile. When he didn't respond, she took a peek in his direction. The frown on his face had evolved into one of amusement.

"You've a quick mind, *ma belle*."

"It's a requirement for fighting off wolves," she muttered with aggravation. The four-legged variety would be easier to scare off than this man.

"Wilberforth hardly qualifies as a wolf."

"I wasn't referring to the lieutenant," she snapped as she met the flash of amusement in his dark eyes.

"Good, because you'd be bored with the man in less than an hour."

"That's rather presumptuous of you, given how little you know about me."

She threw a harsh glare in his direction. *The arrogant bastard.* How in the hell did he know Wilberforth would bore her? Up ahead she spied the banana trees where the path turned and led to the reception. She could even hear the soft hum of conversation filtering through the foliage surrounding the trees. *Sanctuary.*

That and the prosaic company of Lieutenant Wilberforth. She grimaced at her companion's accurate observation. It didn't matter. The British officer was far less dangerous than current company. The man beside her chuckled softly, and she darted a look up at him. His expression said he knew exactly what she was thinking.

"Actually, I know a great deal about you."

"Pray enlighten me with your wealth of knowledge." The scorn in her voice was second only to the look of contempt she sent him.

"You're a woman of principle, you're independent, you have a good eye for horses, and you enjoy experiencing new things," he said with a note of amusement in his voice.

The confidence in his reply sent a shiver skimming across the back of her neck until her skin tingled. His observations unnerved her. He knew far too much about her already, and with each new tidbit he learned, the greater her vulnerability. The man wouldn't hesitate to use his knowledge of her to his advantage. It made him far too dangerous and the sooner they parted company, the better.

"Is that all?" The acerbic note of mockery in her voice pleased her. It gave her the appearance of being self-assured, which couldn't be further from the truth at the moment.

"For the time being." He smiled. "Ah, yes, I almost forgot. You're remarkably stubborn."

"I most certainly am not."

"No? Need I remind you of your refusal to yield to me the other night?" The laughter in his voice was gently teasing, but it was the layer of emotion flowing beneath his amusement that disturbed her.

The potency of it slid across her skin like rich velvet and ignited every nerve ending until she was taut with anticipation. This was precisely why she'd retreated from the knoll. The man had the devil's tongue for persuasion.

Although instinct told her to run from that silver voice of his, she deliberately maintained her pace. Experience had taught her that the more elusive she was, the harder a man fought to gain her favor. More importantly, she wasn't about to let the man know he could intimidate her.

"I hardly think refusing to submit to your demands could be considered stubbornness on my part." She offered him a smile. "However, if you choose that as the basis for your argument, then your refusal to yield to me displays your obstinate nature as well."

"*Touché, chérie.* As I've already said, you've a quick mind. But it changes nothing about how we should proceed with our relationship."

The narrow trail leading to the reception was only a few feet ahead on the main path, but his words brought her to an abrupt halt. Fingers pressed to the base of her throat, she watched him take two strides past her before he realized she was no longer moving. As he turned to face her, she noted the branch of bananas dangling from the tree next to him.

She allowed her gaze to drift over him in lazy appraisal, deliberately parting her lips in a sultry pout. His expression was one of amusement, but his eyes glittered with a telltale emotion she'd seen many times before. The Sheikh, for all his arrogant ways, was like any other man when it came to lust.

"Since we're both determined to have our own way, I propose a wager, monsieur."

"Of what kind?"

"I wager that in less than five minutes, I shall return to Isabelle's reception unescorted."

"And if I agree to this wager, to the victor what spoils?" Arms folded across his chest, he shook his head in amusement.

"If I fail to persuade you into letting me return to the reception alone, then I shall come to your bed as per your original offer." She offered him her most beguiling smile. "However, if I succeed, you agree not to seek me out during the rest of my stay in Marrakech."

His dark eyes narrowed as he contemplated her words. Determined to convince him to take the bet, she stepped forward until she was a hairsbreadth away from him. The spicy scent of him teased her nose, and she reached out to trace the line of his scar with her forefinger. Beneath her fingertip, she could feel the tension tightening his jaw. She marveled at his self-control. There were few men she knew who possessed the steely discipline necessary to hide the desire she instinctively knew he was feeling. When he swallowed hard, she knew without a doubt she would win.

"Why do I sense deception on your part with this wager," he said in a dry tone of voice.

"I give you my word there is no deceit involved. I am simply gambling on the merits of my persuasive abilities, nothing more."

He studied her for another long moment, his dark gaze searching her face with an intensity that made her skin alternate between hot and cold. With an abrupt nod of his head, he captured her chin with his hand.

"Very well, I agree to the wager," he said with a skeptical laugh. "However, I think you're simply putting off the inevitable."

The amused cynicism in his voice sent her heart skittering out of control. He'd regained his confidence, and it unnerved her. Willing herself to calm her rattled sensibilities, she glided her hand over his and gently freed herself of his grip. Stepping away from him, she released a soft laugh, her self-assurance returning as she caught the flash of desire in his dark gaze.

"Tell me, monsieur, if you were to win this wager, what do you expect for your one night of pleasure? Me or the illusion?"

"I have no need of illusion, *chérie*." Although there was amusement in his voice, his eyes glittered with assessment.

"Then you are a most unusual man."

"More flattery?" His mouth quirked with irony.

She smiled but didn't answer. Instead, she looked away from him to study the large cluster of yellowish green bananas dangling from the tree. Each fruit attached to the plant was long and thick and pointed toward the top of the tree as opposed to growing in a downward fashion. Erotic and suggestive, the plant could not have suited her needs any better. Her head tipping to one side, she glanced at him over her shoulder.

"I've enjoyed bananas at home, but I've never seen them growing before," she mused with deliberate curiosity. "Do they all look like this? With the fruit . . . pointing upward?"

Dark eyes narrowing with the realization that perhaps he'd made a mistake in agreeing to the wager, he nodded but didn't speak. She turned away from him before she let her mouth curl in a smile of satisfaction. The man had no idea how persuasive she could be.

"Do you like bananas, monsieur?" She reached out and slid her fingers over the length of one particularly thick stalk of fruit. With a quick snap, she broke off the banana while she allowed her breath to catch in her throat before she released it as a soft gasp of pleasure.

"Not particularly."

The hoarse sound of his voice pleased her. Clearly, she was on the verge of making the fruit appealing to him. Her movements designed to be sensual and elegant, she turned to face him. Biting back a smile, she tipped her head and eyed him with mischief. For the first time since she'd met this man, she was in control. It felt good.

"What a pity. I find them quite . . . enticing," she said with a smile.

Her gaze didn't leave his face as she snapped the stem of the fruit to break open the peel. With delicate moves, she pulled back the yellow skin of the banana to expose the fleshy white meat of the fruit. His expression was unreadable, but he betrayed his rapt attention in other ways. The way he held himself rigid, and the tic flexing in his face. Then there was the fire darkening his intense brown eyes.

Tipping her head back in a slow, elegant manner, she parted her lips and swirled her tongue around the tip of the fruit. Eyes closed, she sighed with pleasure and slowly drew the banana into her mouth. The sharp hiss of his breath filled her ears and she quickly pulled the fruit from her mouth to eye him with innocent concern.

"Is something wrong?" she asked. He swallowed hard, and simply shook his head. Smiling, she sighed. "I hope you don't mind me indulging myself. I adore bananas. They've such an . . . erotic quality."

Not waiting for his answer, she closed her eyes then tipped her head back again to demonstrate the skill she'd learned years ago. Slowly, she slid the firm flesh of the fruit in and out of her mouth. With each leisurely stroke, she took more of the banana into her mouth until he rewarded her efforts with the choked sound of a man struggling not to cry out.

Certain of his undivided attention, she gently bit down on an ample portion of the fruit and freed it from the peel. In the next instant, she swallowed the piece whole. The dark growl he made vibrated across her skin, and she smiled with triumph. As if she were just awakening from an afternoon of lovemaking, she opened her eyes in a lethargic manner.

Lightly, she touched her fingers to first one corner of her mouth then the other as if to wipe away any lingering residue from her lips. The jubilant taste of victory flooded her mouth. The man had just experienced the illusion of Allegra Synnford, courtesan extraordinaire. Her gaze shifted downward to where his erection created a natural tent inside his *sherwals*, and she returned her gaze to his face.

Aware that she needed to retreat before his ardor subsided, she stepped to one side of him, her shoulder pressed into his. She turned her head and noted the taut white lines of tension at the corner of his mouth. He knew he'd lost their wager and he wasn't happy about it. She needed to tread carefully. Gloating might easily be her downfall.

"Forgive me, monsieur, but I must return to the reception before I'm missed," she said softly. Extending her hand, she brushed it over his erection. His jerked at the touch and dragged in a sharp hiss of air. "Thank you for a most . . . stimulating tour of the gardens."

5

Although it wasn't quite the noon hour, the sweltering heat had already engulfed the city as Allegra climbed out of the carriage and looked around the large plaza. Once a place of public executions, the Djemaa El-Fna now served as the gateway to the *souqs* north of the bustling area. Beside her, Millie grunted softly.

"I can't say as I like the looks of this place, Miss Allegra."

"Isabelle said we'd be perfectly safe, Millie, as long as we don't venture off into one of the alleyways."

"All the same, I wish we'd visited this place *before* she and the major had set off for their honeymoon."

"We'll be fine."

With a smile, Allegra patted the maidservant's arm in a pacifying gesture as she led the way across the plaza and into the heart of the *souqs*. The sights and smells that greeted them were almost overwhelming as she meandered through the open stalls with

Millie not far behind. Colorful cone-shaped piles of spices sat on roughly hewn tables at a spice merchant's stall, the scent of coriander, cumin, ginger, and cinnamon drifting off them.

Across from the spice stall was a vendor selling gazelle horns, a sweet pastry stuffed with almond paste and topped with sugar. The delicious smell enticed her to purchase one for each of them. She followed the pastry, fresh and delicate on the tongue, with a cup of juice, freshly squeezed from oranges grown in a local orchard outside Marrakech.

"Isn't it wonderful, Millie?" She turned her head to see her friend finishing off her croissant-shaped gazelle horn.

"I can't deny it's interesting, miss. And I'd like to get the recipe for this pastry. It's quite good," Millie said as she swallowed the remainder of her gazelle horn.

Laughing, Allegra shook her head with amused despair at her friend's less than adventuresome nature. Her gaze drifted past the older woman toward a stall where a veiled woman was having her hand painted by a wizened old woman.

"Oh look, over there." Without waiting on her friend, she walked toward the booth to watch the artist at work. As Millie joined her, Allegra pointed toward the design on the woman's hand. "It's beautiful, isn't it?"

"It looks rather barbaric, if you don't mind me saying so, miss." Millie sniffed.

"Oh no, it's exquisite. Look at the intricacy of the pattern she's drawing."

Fascinated, she watched the woman put the finishing touches on her artwork. A few moments later, the artist looked up with a smile and gestured for Allegra to sit down. With a shake of her head, Allegra laughed and waved her hand no. Speaking in Arabic, the old woman grinned and pointed to a vacant seat in her stall.

"She is offering to henna the back of your hand, mademoiselle," the young woman said. Her hand still damp with henna, she smiled up at Allegra. Despite the veil hiding the lower half of her face, the woman's beauty was dark and exotic. As the henna artist spoke again in the musical language of the desert, Allegra shook her head.

"That's quite nice of her, but I'm afraid I must refuse."

"You must not insult her, mademoiselle," she exclaimed. "Fatima is the henna artist who paints the odalisques in the Sultan's harem. It is a great honor for her to offer to adorn you."

The mention of odalisques gave her pause as she narrowed her eyes at the young woman, but her open expression revealed nothing but friendly encouragement. Allegra suppressed a sigh. Although she'd regained a great deal of confidence by beating her mysterious Bedouin at his own game, she still found herself questioning even the most innocent reference to her lifestyle.

Caution was something she'd learned early, but her ability to know who to befriend or avoid had always been one of her strengths, and it was time she learned to trust her instincts again. With a smile at the young woman, Allegra slowly sank down on the stool the old henna artist had pointed to. Behind her, Millie gasped loudly.

"Miss Allegra, you can't possibly be thinking of letting this woman paint your skin. It's heathenish, I tell you, heathenish."

"Women of Morocco's feet and hands are painted for decoration and religion." Despite the young woman's halting and accented English, her voice held just a trace of rebuke as she sent Millie a hard look.

"You speak English."

Allegra studied the young woman with interest while Fatima took her hand and examined it closely, just as an artist would a fresh canvas. With a nod of her head the veiled woman smiled with amusement as she replied in French.

"Not very well, but I understand enough. I am far more comfortable with French as it is the second language of most Moroccans. It is also a language most *ferengi* understand."

"*Ferengi?*"

"*Ferengi* means *foreigner* in the Berber tongue," she said with a smile before she uttered a gasp of apology. "Forgive me, I've been terribly rude. My name is Laila Mahmoud."

"I'm Allegra Synnford, and this forbidding creature behind me is Millie."

She tossed a glance up at her maid, who seemed to understand that she'd just been introduced as she nodded abruptly in Laila's direction. A cool sensation suddenly laced its way across her skin. Turning back toward the henna artist, she watched the old woman squeeze out a small line of henna paste onto her skin.

With the skill of a longtime artist, Fatima worked quickly and efficiently, creating a design that slowly took the shape of a bird. With its head close to her wrist, the creature's fancy plumage drifted downward over her two middle fingers. She was certain a great many people in the Set would be appalled by the temporary tattoo, but it appealed to her sense of adventure.

As she continued to watch Fatima work, she marveled at the beauty and craftsmanship of the design. Beside her, the young woman leaned forward to watch the old woman at work. She said something in Berber to the artist, who chuckled before replying in the same musical tongue.

"What did you ask her?" She arched her eyebrows with curiosity as she looked at Laila.

"I wanted to know why she's drawn the sign of fire on the bird's feathers. She says it's to ward off evil and help you find your destiny."

"My destiny?" Allegra laughed. "I shape that myself."

With a shake of her head, Laila sent her a piercing look. "Destiny is not ours alone to shape. But the fire charm Fatima has drawn will protect you."

Behind her Millie sniffed her disapproval as Fatima lifted Allegra's hand to show off the design she'd completed. Delighted with the beautiful pattern, she smiled at the old woman as she nodded her thanks. The woman gestured for her to remain still as she retrieved a small roll of white gauze. Gently she wrapped the newly painted design and said something to Laila. When she'd finished speaking, Laila turned to Allegra.

"Fatima said that you should wear the gauze on your hand for a few hours to allow the henna to set."

"Could you ask her what her fee is?"

"She says she will not take money from Shaheen's destiny." There was a distinct edge of bewilderment in Laila's voice.

"I don't understand." Allegra shifted her puzzled gaze between the henna artist and Laila.

"I'm not sure I do either," Laila said, the frown on her forehead deepening. Speaking quickly in Fatima's musical language, she questioned the woman. When she finished Laila turned back to Allegra. "It seems Fatima is convinced you belong to Shaheen. She says you are his destiny."

"Shaheen?" Thoroughly puzzled, Allegra saw Fatima nod her head vigorously. Beside her, Laila's expression was pensive.

"Sheikh Shaheen of the Amazigh. He's a trusted friend of my father and is highly respected by my people."

"Then she's clearly mistaken me for someone else. I belong to no man," Allegra said with a forced laugh.

The last thing she needed was another Bedouin Sheikh entering her life when she'd just managed to get rid of the last one. She ignored the fact she'd been wishing her mysterious Sheikh would find a way to circumvent their bargain and turned to the henna artist to thank her. As Laila stood up, Allegra offered her unmarked hand to the other woman. "It was a pleasure meeting you, Laila."

"And I you," the younger woman said as she gently grasped Allegra's hand. "But perhaps we do not need to part company so quickly. It appears you have no guide. I would be honored if you would allow me to lead you through the *souqs*."

"That's very kind of you, but I couldn't ask you to do that."

"You did not ask, I offered." Laila's eyes twinkled with mischief. "And, while the *souqs* are relatively safe, I can provide an escort as well."

She pointed to two young men watching them from a discreet distance. The offer was a tempting one, and she turned her head to look at Millie. With a frown, the older woman sniffed her irritation. "If you want me to answer a question, then you'll have to ask it in the Queen's English. I haven't understood a word of that French tongue you've been speaking since we stopped here."

"Laila here has offered to be our guide through the *souqs*, and she has two young men to guard us as well," Allegra said. The wary look her friend threw at the proposed escort emphasized how uncomfortable the maidservant was in the strange surroundings.

"I see." Millie sent the young woman a critical look. "Well, then if she's going to be guiding us, perhaps she'd best be getting on with it."

Laughing at her maid's resigned tone, Allegra turned toward Laila. "Since Millie's managed to overcome her reservations, I put us in your knowledgeable hands."

"Excellent," Laila said with a smile. "Come then, there is much to see."

With Millie in tow behind her, Allegra followed her new friend

out of Fatima's stall and into the frenzied chaos of the narrow
street. Once again, the exotic blend of sights and smells reached
out to seduce her as Laila led them deeper into the winding streets
that housed all manner of treasures and delights. Their male escort
followed them, but always several yards behind. They stopped in
the Souq Sebbaghine where a jade green scarf caught her eye. As
she lifted the sheer fabric up and draped it over her arm to admire
the delicate pattern embroidered on the scarf, Millie sent her an
arched look.

"And exactly *where* will you be able to wear such a thing in
London?" she asked.

"I would imagine anywhere I wanted." Laughing, she pulled
some coins from her purse. About to pay the vendor Laila reached
out to stay her hand.

"No, Allegra. It is customary to negotiate your purchase."

Arching her eyebrow slightly, she smiled at the young woman
before turning back to the shop owner and proceeded to haggle
over the cost of the silk. After a lively exchange, she was throwing the scarf over her head with a substantial amount of change
in her purse. She fumbled with the silk until Laila reached out to
help her.

"It will never stay on your head if you leave it like that." Laila
laughed as she adjusted the headdress. "There, that is certain to
entice any man, even Shaheen himself."

"You say that as if the Sheikh would be difficult to please."
Allegra grinned at the Moroccan woman from behind her veil.

"Difficult? Hmmm," Laila mused out loud. With a laugh she
nodded. "No, I simply think Shaheen is more selective than most
men."

"And what man doesn't consider himself discriminating," she
replied with a smile.

"Perhaps, but Shaheen is different. My father has offered to find him a bride on many occasions, but he has been adamant in his refusal."

"What does his name mean?"

"It is the Bedouin name for *falcon*. He earned the name and his title of Sheikh when he saved my brother's life during a *ghazu*."

Laila's voice faltered and her eyes darkened with a deep pain that made Allegra reach out to touch her arm in concern. As if realizing she'd revealed too much of an inner turmoil, the young woman smiled and shook her head.

"That was a long time ago, and they are far less frequent thanks to Shaheen's efforts."

"These *ghazus*, what are they?"

There was a slight darkening of Laila's eyes, but it quickly disappeared. "It's when a neighboring tribe raids another tribe's camp. In most instances it's to steal sheep or horses." Laila shrugged slightly as she averted her gaze. "It's rare that anyone is ever really hurt."

Something about the young woman's expression said she'd witnessed a *ghazu* that had been much more than a simple theft of livestock. Whatever had happened, it had affected Laila deeply.

"Whatever are they doing over there?" An unidentifiable emotion edged its way through Millie's voice. Turning her head in the direction her maid was looking, she heard Laila utter a noise of dismayed disgust.

"It is a slave auction. Parents often sell their children when they're unable to provide for them. Unfortunately, it's quite common." Sadness filled Laila's quiet words. "Father and Shaheen have done much to educate people against such practices, but old customs die slowly."

Laila's voice faded into the background as Allegra moved through the crowd toward the makeshift stage the slave trader was using to hawk his wares. There were at least a dozen children ranging from age five and up. One little girl was clinging to a boy not much older than her. When the slave trader broke them apart, the small child screamed with fear.

The bile rose in Allegra's throat at the sound. She'd screamed like that for her sister a long time ago. The memory sent a wave of nausea cresting over her. It sickened her to admit it, but she understood the girl's fear. A chill crept across her skin, and she shivered despite the blistering heat.

Like a receding wave, the riotous sounds of the market had all the substance of a bee buzzing in her ear as she stared at the faces of the children on the rickety platform. Some were teary-eyed, their bottom lips quivering as they fought to keep from sobbing. In the case of several older boys, their fear made them stand at attention with a vacant look on their faces. It was an expression she knew well.

The dark memories flooded her head, and her throat slowly tightened until it was impossible to swallow and difficult to breathe. What kind of a parent would sell their own child? Slavery was terrible enough, but when they were your own flesh and blood . . . She bit back a sob.

Rooted in place, she watched in horror as a man moved across the stage and jerked a child forward in a clear display of the child's assets and capabilities. Anger thrummed its way through her blood and she pushed her way forward through the densely crowded stage. She'd pay the man whatever he asked to free every child on the stage.

Someone thwarted her efforts to reach the rickety platform by grabbing her arm and dragging her to a halt. Startled, she glanced downward at the grimy, calloused hand holding her in place then up at its owner. The man leaned toward her, and she gagged at the stench coming from his mouth as he grinned menacingly at her.

"Let me go," she snapped as she tried to tug herself free of his grip.

His fingers dug deeper into her skin as he responded in the Berber tongue. The sharp jerk of his head said she was to go with him.

"Go to hell." She sent him a defiant glare and continued to strain against his hold. Her actions made him dig his fingers into her arm that much harder. Wincing with pain, Allegra looked back toward her friends. The sight of a small group of men preventing Laila and Millie from joining her sent an icy finger down her back. Something was terribly wrong here. Her gaze darted to where Laila's bodyguards were roughly shoving their way through the crowd in an effort to reach the young woman.

Again, the ruffian detaining her tugged on her arm, only this time he managed to drag her with him a few steps. Furious, she clenched her fist and drove it as hard as she could into the man's groin. Instantly he screamed out in pain and dropped to his knees. As he sank to the ground in front of her, several of the men holding Laila and Millie hostage turned their heads in her direction.

One of the men headed toward her, while the man on his knees reached for her arm in an attempt to hold her prisoner. In response, she slammed her fist into the man's jaw. His roar of pain filled her with satisfaction as she jerked free of his hold. Her gratification died quickly when she heard an angry cry from the makeshift auction platform. Turning her head, she saw the auctioneer point at her and gesture wildly at the man slumped to the ground.

Several people in the small crowd turned to glare at her, and she took a quick step back only to find her way blocked. Two large hands gripped her from behind and panic settled a knot of fear in her stomach. She didn't understand what the men wanted from her, but their determination was frightening.

Fear sent her elbow driving into the person behind her. A loud grunt of pain said she'd found her mark. She found the target again then jerked free of her attacker's hold. No longer thinking, she simply reacted. She found an opening in the crowd and pushed her way through it. It was in the opposite direction of Millie and Laila, but an angry mob could easily turn on her friends if anyone realized they were all together.

Shoving her way through the crowd, she struggled not to gag on the rank odor of so many people in one place. Behind her, several voices cried out in protest and someone clutched at her veil in an attempt to stop her. Desperately, she clawed at the fabric until it ripped with a loud cry and she was free to continue her flight.

After several frantic seconds, she escaped the crowded square and darted down one of the *souq*'s populated streets. She should have listened to Millie. They should have visited the *souq* before Isabelle left on her honeymoon. With a glance over her shoulder, she saw one of her attackers emerge from the crowd. Frantic now, she moved as quickly as possible through the busy street until she was certain she'd lost the man.

Breathless, she darted into a small alleyway and pressed her back to the wall. Guilt sped through her. She'd deserted her friends. Suppressing a soft sob she bit her lip. No, she hadn't deserted them. They'd not been the ones in danger. She was the one the men wanted. If their intent had been to take Laila and Millie, she would have seen the two women being dragged away. But she hadn't. No, she was the one the men wanted. But why? Who would want to harm her?

None of this made any sense. Straightening, she pushed herself away from the wall to move on. As she did so, her foot caught on the edge of her skirt. Head bent, she worked the heel of her shoe free from the ripped hem. She'd barely succeeded in her task when a hand roughly covered her mouth, and a strong arm jerked her backward several feet into a small, dark room. For the second time in her life, she went numb with fear.

6

Shaheen jerked open the front door of the house and strode across
the threshold. Battered and bruised, he stopped at the fountain in
the middle of the courtyard and flung water over his face. The cut
on his chin stung from the contact and he released a snarl of pain.
Behind him, Jamal snorted with amused disgust.

"If you continue picking fights with men twice your size, you'll
be mending far more than just your pride," Jamal said.

The fierce glare he sent the middle-aged Bedouin only made his
friend laugh as he walked away. Staring after Jamal, he cupped
his hand in the fountain again and drank the sweet-tasting water.
His friend was right, but he didn't want to admit it any more than
he wanted to admit that Allegra Synnford had gotten the best of
him. She'd turned the tables on him so deftly that he'd not even
known what hit him until it was too late.

When he'd agreed to the wager she'd offered him, he'd understood that she would try to seduce him. But the manner in which

she went about it had stunned him. He never would have believed anything as simple as a piece of fruit could be used to make him harder than iron.

Damm gahannam, he'd never witnessed a more erotic gesture in his entire life. All he'd been able to think about since that afternoon in the Agdal Gardens was the thought of her hot mouth taking him deep into her throat and milking him with loving care. It was an image that kept him up at night until he was forced to put his hand where her lovely lips should be—snug around his cock.

He rubbed his jaw gingerly, his fingertips scuffed by his evening shadow. The thing that bothered him the most was that he liked her for beating him. She'd won their bet fair and square, and while he knew she'd been elated at besting him, she'd not gloated. *A woman of principle and a good sport.* He'd kept waiting for her to do something like Frances would have done, but she hadn't.

With a grunt, he sloshed water over his face again. He needed a bath, and then he'd put his mind to work trying to figure out a way to see Allegra without reneging on their wager. It wouldn't be easy, but then the prize would be worth the effort.

The sun had set a short time earlier, and the shadows had already filled the corners of the inner courtyard as his senses detected something unseen charging the air around him. He tensed at the sensation, ready for the unexpected. What he didn't expect was to see Sheikh Khalid Mahmoud's only daughter emerging from the shadows. As Laila raced toward him, he recognized the almost tangible emotion filling the air—fear. She launched herself into his arms with a sob, her voice muffled against his *gambaz*.

"Shhh . . . it's all right," he said as he smoothed the top of her head with his hand. "What's wrong? Where's your father?"

"We must help her, Shaheen. We must."

"One thing at a time. Where's your father? Khalid said he wouldn't return to Marrakech for at least two more months."

"He's still in Sidi Rahal." An odd look crossed her face as she took a step away from him, wiping at the tears on her face.

"Then how did you get here?" The brief flash of guilt across her lovely face gave him his answer. "Christ Jesus, do you mean to tell me you traveled from Sidi Rahal to Marrakech by *yourself*?"

"Of course not! I brought Kasim and Ali with me." She weathered his roar of fury with an indignant look.

"Kasim and Ali." He spat out the names. "Those two are only good at finding food and water. What the devil were you thinking?"

"I was thinking how tired I am of Father treating me like a child. Hakim is allowed to travel to Marrakech with you," she said in a defensive tone.

"Exactly. He's with *me*. Khalid has spoiled you, and I've no doubt he's half mad with worry. This has to be the most outrageous, thoughtless thing you've ever done, Laila."

"I left a note for Father with Halah. She said it was my destiny to come to Marrakech. That I had an important task to perform."

He snorted in disgust. "That old woman tells everyone that. Coming here by yourself wasn't destiny. It was reckless."

"Father will—"

"Understand? Not this time. You'll be lucky if he lets you out of his sight for the next ten years," he growled. With a disgusted shake of his head, he glared at her. "I'll send a message tonight so your father will sleep easier knowing you're safe."

"It doesn't matter what Father does to me as long as we save her."

"Save who?" He frowned as he looked into her guilt-ridden gaze.

"Allegra."

The single word response made him stiffen. What the hell had happened to Allegra and how did Laila know her?

"Allegra Synnford?" he rasped, an icy chill slithering its way through his blood. Fresh tears slid down the young woman's cheeks and her bottom lip trembled as she stared up at him.

"Yes. We met in the *souq*." Laila hiccupped. "Nassar's men took her."

"What do you mean, they took her?" He grasped her shoulders in a grip that made her wince.

"Five of them. They kidnapped her," she exclaimed before rushing on with a description of the events that had transpired in the *souq*.

As her story tumbled out of her, what he heard sent dread slicing through him with the sharpness of a razor. If Nassar really had taken Allegra, she was in grave danger. The bastard had never liked being challenged, and from what he already knew of Allegra, she would defy the man. At least until Nassar had broken her. The thought of what the man would do to her made him grow cold. Perhaps Laila was mistaken.

"How can you be certain it was Nassar's men who took her?"

"It was them I tell you. They wore the crescent over a scarab on their forearms," she said with heated bitterness. "It was the same mark I saw as a child when Nassar killed my mother."

Her words tightened the knot in his stomach as his fear for Allegra's safety deepened. The powerful memories of that fateful day in the desert made him turn away from the pain in Laila's eyes, to stare down into the small fountain.

Water spilled out of the fount, making a musical sound as it tumbled into the basin. The cheerful noise taunted him as he dipped his hand in the cool liquid and allowed it to flow out of his palm. His eyes focused on the droplets rolling off his hand, but it wasn't water he saw—it was blood.

The carnage that day, more than fifteen years ago, was something he hoped never to see again. It was why the treaties were so important. Men, women, even children, had been cut down with calculated ruthlessness by Nassar and his men, all in the name of vengeance. That terrible day was as much a part of him as it was of Khalid and his children. It was also the day the Viscount Newcastle had died, and Shaheen of the Amazigh had been born.

"Please, Shaheen. You must save her." Laila's hand clutched at his arm.

He nodded with understanding as he looked down at the pleading expression on Laila's lovely face. Ever since she was a little girl, she'd managed to wheedle everything she could out of him and anyone else who loved her. But this was one time when her pleading was unnecessary. He wasn't about to let Allegra, or any woman for that matter, suffer at the hands of a man like Nassar.

Even a whore? the voice in the back of his head mocked him.

With a muffled expletive, he began to pace the courtyard's stone floor. Allegra's trail was growing cold with every minute that passed, and he needed to move fast if he was going to have any idea what direction her kidnappers had headed. How to free her would have to come later. Right now, he needed more information.

"Where are Kasim and Ali?" he bit out as he stopped his prowling to face Laila.

"I sent them to see if they could find out anything about Allegra and where Nassar might have taken her."

"Was her maid with her?"

"Yes, but she refused to wait for you to return." Laila nodded her head. "The woman doesn't speak French, and you know my English is not very good. She said something about a Viscount Shaftsbury."

"*Damm gahannam*," he ground out between his clenched teeth. As if things weren't bad enough. The last thing he needed was Shaftsbury interfering in tribal matters. The man could easily make matters worse. *For whom?* a voice deep inside him questioned. What did it matter if Shaftsbury found out who he really was?

It mattered because he'd built a new life here in Morocco. A life that could easily come to an end if his true identity became known. His ability to negotiate treaties between the tribes was a valuable one, and he'd earned the respect of not only the different Bedouin tribes, but the Spanish and French governments that controlled the Moroccan Sultanate. If any of them discovered who he really was, there would be hell to pay.

No, it was vital that Shaftsbury not discover Robert Camden, Viscount Newcastle and Shaheen of the Amazigh were the same man. It could hurt those he now called family, and he had no wish to revisit the pain and guilt that had brought him to the desert to die, only to find a new life among the Bedouins.

"Who is this Viscount Shaftsbury?" Laila eyed him with the same perceptive gaze as her father's. Brushing the subject aside would only increase her curiosity.

"A distant cousin."

"From England," she murmured with a nod of understanding. "And you don't wish him to find you."

"No, I don't."

"Would it be so terrible if he did? Perhaps someone is ill. At the very least I'm sure your family misses you."

"The Amazigh are my family now. There is nothing for me in England," he growled with a bitter harshness that made her flinch.

He knew she wasn't accustomed to him using such a sharp tone with her, but he had no intention of discussing his past with her. She nodded her head and worry darkened her expressive brown eyes again

"How will you get her back when you find her, Shaheen?" she asked.

"I don't know. Nassar isn't one to give up his playthings easily."

Finding the bastard would be easy compared to securing Allegra's freedom. Nassar would want something in return. He simply had to figure out what the man wanted more than Allegra. The thought made him wince. It wouldn't be easy convincing Nassar to give her up. Particularly when Shaheen was the trusted friend of the man Nassar hated with a passion that had lasted for almost twenty years.

The carpet smelled of sheep and stale sweat. The stench reassured her that she was still alive. That and the jerky rocking motion of the cart she was in. She wanted to retch, but the cloth gag in her mouth prevented her from doing so, and she forced back the bile rising in her throat.

What little air she had was hot—barely breathable. It was the reason she'd been drifting in and out of consciousness. She didn't have any idea how long she'd been wrapped in the rug, but she was certain several hours had passed since her capture. Through the layers of the carpet, she heard the muffled sound of voices speaking in that odd Berber and French mixture that the Bedouins spoke.

The gist of the conversation was lost to her because she found herself incapable of moving past the words *enchères d'esclave*—the slave auction. Dear God, were they taking her somewhere to sell her to the highest bidder? Tears stung her eyes as the darkness of the past clawed at her with a vicious tenacity. The memories aroused a sickening helplessness inside her, and the bindings around her wrists bit into her skin the same way her mother's hand had done the day of her fourteenth birthday.

It had been dark and rainy. The normal stench of the streets had evaporated in the downpour, leaving nothing but the damp, musty smell of slick brick walls and cobblestones. The expression on her mother's face was shadowed except for the occasional flashes of light thrown out by the lightning overhead. Whatever looks her mother had once had were gone, replaced by a world-weary hardness that made her look old and beaten.

Desperate to understand what was happening, she'd pleaded to know where they were going. When the light had flickered over her mother's face, the look of haggard stoicism had terrified her. Whatever her mother had planned, she would see it to fruition. It had been the familiarity of the street that had alerted her to the horror to come. Four years earlier they'd come this way. It was the last time she'd seen her sister. She was going to her death, just like Elizabeth had. She moaned as her tears mixed with the sweat on her face, and succumbing to the deadly heat she fell into oblivion once more.

Loud warbling cries penetrated the confines of the carpet, jarring her awake. The wagon she was in came to a halt, and someone lifted her up like a sack of potatoes. Panic swept through her, and she tried to cry out past the gag in her mouth. The guttural sound lingered in her throat as someone placed her on the ground and rolled her out of the carpet. Rough, calloused hands removed her gag, and fresh, sweet air filled her lungs as she inhaled a deep breath.

She dragged her hand across her eyes to remove the sand and grit layering her eyelids. Blinking what was left of the dirt out of her eyes, she stared up at the early evening sky. The stars were just beginning to glow overhead as the light faded. Fear gnawed at her as she slowly sat up to take in her surroundings.

More than two dozen men and women encircled her, and their voices filled the air with chatter. The fury of the sound made her wince. Out of the chaos, a strong voice spoke sharply. The demand in the man's voice indicated he was asking for something, and he was far from pleased with the answers he received.

The gathering parted quickly to make way for a man dressed

in the fine robes of a wealthy Bedouin Sheikh. The man's voice was sharp and angry as he gestured at the men who'd kidnapped her. Dehydration had weakened her considerably, and she didn't move from the carpet. The Sheikh made a hissing sound of anger and issued a sharp order that sent a man rushing toward her. A moment later, her hands were untied and the man lifted her to her feet. She swayed slightly, but managed to remain on her feet as she gently massaged the tender spots on her wrists where the rope had chaffed the skin.

Stepping forward the Bedouin leader touched first his heart and then his forehead. "*Ssalamū 'lekum*, Miss Synnford."

"You . . . know . . . my name."

She winced at the raw dryness of her throat and licked her lips. God, she was so thirsty. Anger twisted the man's face as he snapped another order. Almost magically, a bag of water was placed at her lips. She drank eagerly from the vessel. She couldn't remember the last time something had tasted so good. Her thirst quenched for the moment, she lowered the water bag and stared at the man in front of her. He bowed slightly.

"Allow me to introduce myself. I am Sheikh Yusuf Nassar. One of your many admirers." He spoke in English, each word enunciated in the clipped, precise tones of someone who was fluent in a language that wasn't their native tongue.

He was a handsome man. Black, lush eyebrows arched over brown eyes. They were a stark contrast to the swarthy complexion of his face. The black beard and moustache he wore were trimmed close and neat to his face. Despite his good looks, there was a slightly cruel twist to his thin mouth. He wouldn't tolerate challenges to his authority.

"I must apologize for my men," he said in his precise English. "The fools were supposed to escort you here, not treat you like a common whore."

Refreshed somewhat by the water, she stiffened at the man's arrogant statement. "Escort? Where I come from they call it kidnapping."

"Ah, but this is Morocco, my dear. We do things differently here."

"I don't care what you do here," she snapped in a hoarse voice as fear gave way to anger. "As a subject of Her Majesty, Queen Victoria, I'm protected under agreements between the French and British governments."

"Ah, but I'm not French," he said as his lips curled upward in a feral smile. "The moment I saw you disembark from the boat in Safi, I knew I had to have you."

"Have me? I'm not a piece of property for you to do with as you please," she grounded out through clenched teeth. "It's uncivilized and barbaric."

She didn't flinch under his cold gaze. Something about his manner said it would be unwise to show anything but strength in the face of his harsh examination. He would use whatever weakness he saw in her to his advantage.

"Are you suggesting that I'm a barbarian?" His eyes were flat like a reptile's, and she dodged answering the question by changing the direction of the conversation.

"You obviously brought me here for a reason, monsieur. I'd like to know why and how long you intend to hold me against my will."

"Why?" He laughed, clearly amused by her reply. "Because I intend to enjoy the pleasures of your body, my dear Allegra."

"I see. Are there so few women in Morocco who welcome your attentions that you must kidnap one to service you?"

His laughter died a quick death, and inside she cursed herself for letting her tongue get the best of her. She knew better, but her brain was sluggish. She needed to remember to control her anger or it would bring the man's wrath down on her head. He narrowed his eyes as he sent her a cold look.

"None as special as you, *ma chérie*. It is said you have the ability to drive a man mad with desire. I intend to experience that."

"Your expectations are high, monsieur."

"So the rumors of your skill are greatly exaggerated," he said smugly as if certain she would take umbrage at his snide statement. He made another comment in Berber to the men, which provoked their laughter. The sound angered her.

"My skill is not in question, monsieur. It is a question of choice."

"Choice?" He snorted with amused disgust. "You have no choice here."

"Ultimate pleasure is a mutual exchange. Without choice there can be no such exchange," she said with quiet determination.

The fury rolling across his face sent an icy finger down her back. He stepped forward until there were mere inches between them. The flat expression in his eyes reminded her of men she'd seen in Madame Eugenie's, men who took their pleasure in ways that appalled even the more jaded members of the brothel. She forced herself not to flinch or look away from his malicious stare. To show fear was to show weakness, and weakness was something she could ill afford in her current circumstances. He narrowed his gaze at her.

"Do you think to refuse me?"

"My skills, monsieur, are reserved for the men I choose to be with. I do not choose to be with a barbarian." Her words elicited a sharp inhalation of what she was certain was pure rage. God, she was a fool for carrying her independence to this extreme. Perhaps she should simply give the man what he wanted. It was a disgusting thought.

"You seem oblivious to your situation, *ma chérie*."

"Then perhaps you will explain it to me." She kept her gaze focused on his angry face.

"You are far from home, without friends, and without hope of rescue," he said coldly as he began to circle her as a predator might its prey before pouncing. "You have no choice."

"There are always choices, and I choose to say no." Her heart pounded with fear at her words. She was mad. All she had to do was sleep with the man. When he tired of her, surely he would return her to Marrakech.

"You will change your mind. And you will do well to remember that I am the one in control here, not you." He glared at her, his mouth thin with anger.

"Control is nothing more than a small man forcing his will on others."

She didn't realize she'd spoken the words out loud until his hand struck out like a cobra to grab a large quantity of her hair. Caught unprepared, she cried out as her scalp protested the harsh treatment. Jerking her head backward, he forced her to look up at him, and the cruelty in his smile made her mouth go dry. He *enjoyed* hurting her. With a rough twist of her head, he forced her to look at the men watching their exchange.

"Look at them, Allegra," he whispered, his lips brushing across the edge of her earlobe. "They're eager to see who will win our little war. I have whipped men for less than your insolence. Perhaps the idea of seeing me discipline you in such a way excites them. They're wondering if I'm really willing to mar that creamy skin of yours with my whip. Then again, they might be hoping I'll offer them a taste of your body."

"You're not the type of man who's willing to share his prize," she said quietly, wincing as he tugged her hair tighter in his fist.

"I confess that the idea of sharing your charms is not a welcome one, but then again, I might enjoy seeing you naked with all of these men tasting your body one after the other. I think it would excite me very much. Would you enjoy it? The taste of one man's seed in your mouth while another man fucks you?"

Sickened by his words, she remained silent. Despite the intense desire to rebel, it was clear her resistance only brought him enjoyment.

"It seems you finally understand the nature of your situation." He laughed softly, the sound chilling her skin. "A pity, I was just beginning to enjoy myself."

He released her with a wordless sound of anger. With a gesture in her direction, he snapped an order to several women standing nearby then turned away from her. In seconds, she was quickly surrounded, and one of the women gave her a hard shove in the direction of a large tent.

Without a second thought, she rebelled against the rough treatment and pushed the woman back, refusing to move. The shrill scream of anger coming from the woman caused Sheikh Nassar to turn around. Striding back toward them, he stopped in front of the woman who was angrily gesturing toward Allegra as she spat out words of anger. The Sheikh frowned as he listened to the woman. Annoyance furrowed his forehead as he turned toward Allegra.

"It appears Rana believes you mean to harm her."

"Then Rana's mistaken," she said quietly.

"She said you pushed her."

"Yes." She directed a steady look at the woman before turning back to the Sheikh with a look of defiance. "I assumed because she pushed me it was a native greeting of some sort, so I pushed her back."

Nassar stared at her in stunned amazement for a long moment. Then, tipping his head back, he laughed out loud. She released the deep breath she was holding as she realized what a gamble her response had been. The Sheikh could have easily taken her words as an insult, and the end result might have been much different. In silence, she watched him turn toward the Bedouin woman. Rana tried to argue with him, but he silenced her with a sharp word. With a sound of fury, the woman whirled around and stalked away. He turned back to Allegra and wagged his finger at her.

"You must not tease Rana too much, she can be quite spiteful."

"I shall remember that, monsieur."

Stepping toward her, Nassar caught her chin in a firm grip and tilted her face upward. "See that you do. I don't want this pretty face marred by Rana's knife."

The words crawled across her skin like a hive of bees and her stomach lurched with fear as he released her from his bruising grip. For the first time in years, she was no longer in control of her destiny, and it terrified her.

7

The women guided Allegra past a flap of woolen material into a
large tent. Rana stood in the center of the dwelling. The woman's hatred was visible in her expression and stance. Allegra had
seen this reaction before at Madame Eugenie's when a new girl
entered the brothel and unknowingly stole a regular customer
from another girl.

She was a threat, and Rana intended to put her in her place. It
was clear whose domain they were in, and the attitude of all the
women changed as Rana barked several commands. They immediately pushed Allegra into the center of the tent and began removing her clothes.

Protesting, she tried to shove their hands aside, but someone held her arms to prevent her from interfering, while another
woman ripped the fabric of her shirtwaist while removing it from
her back. Her fear receded, and in its place grew a furious outrage.

With a deep-throated cry, she found the strength to break free, sending two of the women tumbling to the carpeted flooring.

Rana's response was to step forward and slap Allegra so hard her head whipped sideways. The shocking sting of the blow was so unexpected she simply stood there mute and unresisting as the women ripped the remainder of her clothing off her body.

Completely naked, she was immobilized by the humiliation of her situation. She could barely think as two of the women set about washing her. Their efforts were fast and efficient, but it was the whispers and snickering of the other women in the tent that made the entire experience mortifying. Rana smiled smugly as she watched.

Leaning forward, the woman poked at Allegra's breasts then turned her head and said something to the other women, causing them to laugh. Allegra swallowed hard. Not even at Madame Eugenie's had she ever been treated with such contempt. Clearly relishing her power, Rana sent her a malicious look and reached out to viciously pinch a nipple. Allegra's reaction was a mixture of fury and self-preservation as she slammed her fist into the other woman's jaw. The blow sent Rana sprawling across the rug-covered floor into a mass of colorful pillows. Trembling with rage, Allegra glared down at the woman.

"If you ever touch me like that again, I'll kill you," she said through clenched teeth.

She had no idea if the woman understood French, but she doubted the woman knew any English. The woman released a howl of anger, but she didn't move from where she'd fallen. Satisfied the woman would leave her alone, at least for the time being, she turned to see the other women huddled together watching her with an expression of awe.

"*Vous*"—she pointed toward the woman closest to her—"bring me something to wear, *now*."

The woman moved quickly to one corner of the tent and retrieved several articles of clothing. She dressed quickly in the Bedouin garments. The wide *sherwals* covering her legs were far less confining than her own undergarments, but the wool material of the long top she pulled over her head was itchy. Sliding her feet into the smooth leather slippers the woman had provided, she turned and headed for the flap leading out into the encampment. When she reached the exit all the women erupted into wild, shrill cries.

Allegra came to an abrupt halt and glared over her shoulder. The women fell silent. Satisfied they would remain quiet, she pushed the tent flap aside and stepped out into the evening air. A water bag hung from the tent pole, and she quickly reached for it. The liquid soothed her rough throat, and when she'd had her fill, she drew in a deep breath of desert air that still smelled of heat. As she stared out at the open plains that encircled the camp, the barren landscape left her feeling just as desolate as the scenery stretching out before her.

Far off in the distance she saw the Atlas Mountain range that in Marrakech had been so close and now was so far away. Stifling the fear that threatened to regain control of her, she reminded herself how she'd shaped her destiny ever since arriving at Madame Eugenie's.

Destiny, something the henna artist had mentioned earlier today. She looked at her hand and the beautiful painting on her skin. Somewhere along the way, the gauze wrap had disappeared from her hand, but the tattoo was unblemished. *Shaheen's destiny.* She didn't know what the woman had meant by that, but it was clear the only person who was going to save her now was herself.

Thirsty again, she took another long swallow of water from the bag. Slinging the goatskin over her shoulder, she slowly walked along the outer edges of the encampment. It was a small miracle her captors had not kidnapped Millie and Laila as well. Escaping this desert prison would be difficult enough by herself, but with three of them, it would have been almost impossible. But she *would* find a way to escape, and she would do it without entering the Sheikh's bed.

She'd seen too many men of his temperament before not to understand him. The man believed that simply because he wanted something he was entitled to it. But he wasn't, particularly where she was concerned. Her life had given her the freedom to go where she liked and to do as she wished.

And it had given her the right to say no to a man like Nassar.

She had no desire to go back to what she'd been before Arthur had taken her away from Madame Eugenie's. There was only danger, disrespect, and humiliation in that life. She'd come too far to return to a time where her only value as a human being was for what her body could give a man. Even if it meant her very survival, she wasn't certain she could submit herself to that existence again.

She swallowed hard at the thought. The easiest way to keep that from happening was to find her means of escape. She knew which way was west, which told her the other cardinal directions. In her political studies, she'd learned the strategic importance of many different countries, and Morocco had been one of them.

Although she still had much to learn about the country, she was familiar enough with its geography to know the general direction of Marrakech. But staying the course to reach the city would be far more difficult. Daylight meant she had no place to hide when Nassar came after her. And he *would* come after her. Her best chance of escape would be after dark, and astronomy was not her forte. In truth, riding away from this camp was little more than suicide at best.

But the other option was no less dangerous. If she stayed, she had no choice but to deal with Nassar. It had been a long time since she'd endured a night with someone of the Sheikh's temperament. Her first three years in Madame Eugenie's had introduced her to all manner of beasts disguised as men.

She'd forced herself to charm them into doing what she wanted, manipulating the situation to her advantage. She'd hidden her revulsion and distanced herself from the entire experience. But that had been so long ago. She'd been independent for too many years. It would be difficult to act submissive and docile. And that was precisely what the Sheikh expected of her. He would demand her subservience, and if she refused, her very survival might be at risk.

No, she would have to leave tonight. It was the only option open to her.

Something akin to relief filled her limbs. There was a sense of comfort in making a decision and forming a plan of action. She had something to work toward now. The next step was finding transportation. She'd yet to see any guards around the perimeter of the camp, but she was certain there would be someone guarding the livestock.

She continued to circle the camp until she came upon a young boy feeding and watering several horses tethered to a line. For a long moment, she simply stared at the animals. Salvation had never been so close and yet so distant. The boy must have sensed her, because he turned his head and eyed her warily. She forced a smile to her face and continued past the animals without giving them more than a cursory glance. The last thing she wanted was to have the boy tell someone she'd been near the horses. Deliberately, she forced herself to keep her pace moderate as she walked away.

A fragile hope lit its lamp inside her. It had taken her captors less than a day to bring her here by wagon. That meant a horse and rider would be able to travel much faster. Marrakech might not be all that distant if she could slip away with one of the Arabians she'd seen. Her optimism quickly evaporated as she considered what Nassar would do to her if he caught her trying to flee.

She touched her scalp where the roots were still sore from where the man had pulled her hair. The Sheikh wouldn't hesitate to punish her in some way, and it would be something far worse than pulling her hair. He'd threatened to beat her if she committed a smaller transgression. Any attempt to escape would be a challenge to his authority. A challenge she was certain he would punish harshly. She shivered at the notion. It didn't matter.

The only other choice was one she refused to make.

When she returned to the women's tent she pushed aside the flap and entered quietly. The women were seated around a large tray of food centered in their midst. Ignoring them, Allegra looked around for her own clothes, but they were gone. A shudder rippled through her as she saw her nemesis eyeing her with malevolence. The woman's hatred was almost tangible.

Could she use that to her advantage? Would the woman help her escape or betray her for the simple pleasure of seeing her punished? Something told her it would be the latter. She turned away from the women and sank down onto a small pallet. A moment later, one of the women approached her with a small bowl of food.

"*Mangez,*" she said with an encouraging expression on her face. "*Mangez.*"

Allegra's throat closed in protest at the mention of food, and she shook her head. Again the woman urged her to eat.

"You must eat, mistress."

The woman's French was poor, but her concern seemed sincere as she thrust the bowl at Allegra. When she hesitated, the woman grasped her hand and forced her to hold the round dish. Reluctantly, she accepted it and stared down at the contents. It reminded her of the gruel her mother had often made when she was a child. The memory wasn't a pleasant one.

She looked up at the woman, who encouraged her with an eating gesture. Nodding her gratitude, Allegra observed how the other women were eating with their fingers, and she mimicked their actions. The first taste made her want to gag, but she swallowed hard to force the food down. The woman smiled with satisfaction as she left Allegra and returned to the circle of women.

The second bite of food was easier to swallow, and despite the unpleasant taste, she realized she was hungry enough to eat anything. The water she'd been given helped to wash the sticky meal down. She glanced over at the women, and she saw Rana watching her with smug satisfaction. Something about the woman's expression made her uneasy.

She leaned forward to set her bowl down and the interior of the tent spun madly around her. God, she hadn't been this disoriented since that night at Madame Eugenie's when the brothel owner had given her a mild drug to help calm her for her first customer. An invisible layer of ice swept over her skin and made her tremble with fear.

What a fool she'd been. They'd drugged her so she couldn't try to escape. Her eyelids drooped, and she slowly slid down onto the carpet. Just before her eyes fluttered shut, she saw Rana moving toward her with a malevolent smile curling her lips.

The morning sun had inched its way almost to a midday peak as Shaheen and his men rode north across the plains. As the third water well they sought came into view, there was no sign of Nassar. Frustrated, Shaheen pulled Tarek to a quick halt. The chestnut stallion snorted in protest, his teeth gnashing at the bit, and

Shaheen eased his grip on the leather reins. Following his lead, his men halted their mounts behind him.

With a gentle nudge, he urged Tarek forward a few steps and bent over in the saddle to study the dirt and grass for any sign of a large party having recently made camp near the well. It was a worthless effort. After several moments, he uttered a grunt of disgust and straightened in the saddle. Even the occasional goat-herder they'd encountered in their search had little to offer in the way of information.

As he surveyed the landscape in front of him, his jaw tightened as he recalled his initial reaction to Allegra's disappearance. The primal force of his need to have her back had been startling. With every brawl he'd engaged in since she'd left him beneath that banana tree, he'd been fighting a losing battle to forget the woman. Even before the Agdal Gardens, Allegra had managed to occupy his thoughts more than any woman before her. Not even Frances had preoccupied him so tenaciously.

The memory of how soft she'd felt in his arms was only compounded by his recollection of her lips around a piece of fruit that resembled his cock. His body craved her with a hunger unlike anything he'd ever experienced. But it wasn't just the sensual images of her that nagged at him. It was something else. Something he wasn't even sure he wanted to define. What was it about this woman that aroused emotions he'd thought long dead and buried?

Urging Tarek into a slow trot, he forced himself to resume searching for some sign that Nassar had been in the vicinity of the well. He knew it was a futile task. The man hadn't been here. This pretense of looking for tracks was simply an attempt to shut out the past. But as soon as the past receded, thoughts of Allegra pushed their way back into his head.

With a low growl, he shifted restlessly in the saddle.

"We will find the *anasi, yâ sâhib.*"

The dark timbre of Jamal's voice filled the air, and he turned his head toward the Amazigh. It had been Jamal who'd found him in the desert, delirious and half dead of thirst. At the time, he'd been far from grateful at Jamal's interference. He shook his head at the reassurance and confidence in his friend's words.

"And what if Nassar isn't at the fourth well, Jamal? I was certain the bastard would be somewhere between Sarhlef and Bel Azri."

"I do not think your search strategy unwise, Shaheen. What concerns me is that we have not found Nassar yet. He is too far from his own territory. Only a man up to no good is difficult to find."

"I agree," he said grimly. "If he means to stir up trouble, then the only two men capable of helping him in this region would be Abd al Jabbar or Sheikh Cadi."

"Then perhaps we should find him and put our uncertainty to rest." Jamal arched an eyebrow at him, his expression filled with good-natured provocation.

With a sharp nod, Shaheen called out to the men behind him, and he urged Tarek forward into a canter as he headed in the direction of the well outside of Berrechgoun. The men following him, like Jamal, were not only part of his tribe, but his family. When Khalid had given him responsibility for the men and their families, as well as Hakim, he'd questioned the wisdom of the Amazigh's sovereign.

Khalid had simply smiled and stated it was time Hakim learn European ways, which only Shaheen could teach him and that he would need men to protect the royal heir. He'd not taken Khalid's faith in him lightly. Over the past seven years he'd done his best to teach the boy everything he would need to know when it came time for him to take his father's place as Sheikh of the Amazigh. In helping the boy better himself, he was paying penance for his own past.

For almost fifteen years, his adopted family had believed him courageous, but he knew it was an illusion. It had been a penitent need to relieve himself of his guilt. They said suffering was good for the soul, but they'd lied. The guilt weighing on him today was as heavy as it had been that terrible night in London. He tried to shove the dark memories back into the pit he'd dug for them years ago. When they didn't slide easily back into place, his muscles grew taut with tension. They were always with him, but the past week had presented him with more torment than he'd experienced in years. And Allegra was to blame for it. Her presence had dredged up the past and all the pain that went with it.

They rode steadily for more than an hour, and it was just as the sun reached its peak directly over their heads that Shaheen saw the tents. The sight filled him with a sense of relief as he eased Tarek out of his gallop and settled into a gentle canter. A moment later, Jamal rode up alongside him with a satisfied smile on his tanned features.

"So we have found the fox in his den." The other man pointed at the tents that were growing larger and more distinct with each stride Tarek took.

"It would seem so. I wonder what he'll make of our unexpected visit." The thought of surprising Nassar made him smile. If his appearance made the bastard sweat, all the better.

"Have you considered what you are going to tell Sheikh Nassar about our presence here in Sahrawi territory?"

"I see no need to explain our presence unless he explains his." Shaheen shrugged. "But if he does, then we can simply say we're on our way to Hajra to see about putting Abyad out to stud."

"You are hoping that when Nassar sees the stallion he will want him."

"I'm counting on it," he bit out as he saw a large group of men riding out to meet them.

Shaheen did not slow Tarek's stride. Hesitation with Nassar would only show weakness. And if the man found your weakness, he would do everything to exploit it. As the men drew near, he recognized Nassar leading the way. Like all Sheikhs, he led his men out to confront a potential enemy. To assume otherwise could be deadly. Just like that day in Sheikh Mahmoud's camp. But then one would never expect treachery from a member of one's family. He frowned. He and Nassar had more in common than he cared to admit. Wheeling Tarek to a halt just in front of the lead horse of Nassar's group, he sat ramrod straight in his saddle.

"*Ssalamū 'lekum*, Newcastle." Nassar touched his heart and then his forehead in the usual Berber greeting.

The subtle reference to his English heritage was not unexpected, and Shaheen forced himself to smile as he replied in kind. "*Ssalamū 'lekum*, Nassar."

Immediately, the Sheikh's smug expression changed to a bitter glare at the deliberate omission of his title. It was disrespectful not to use the man's title of Sheikh, but Shaheen saw no reason to show respect when none was accorded to him.

"You look as though you've traveled far." A smile barely curled Nassar's thin mouth as he gestured toward the camp. "Come, let us put old differences aside. You will eat with me."

"Thank you." Shaheen nodded his head.

"It is the Amazigh way." Nassar shrugged. "I cannot argue with the customs of our people."

The man spoke as if he was untroubled by their surprise visit, but their arrival had clearly unsettled him. His rigid posture in the saddle and tight grip on the pommel displayed his tension. Glancing over his shoulder, the Sheikh's eyes fell on Abyad. At the sudden gleam of interest in the man's gaze, Shaheen looked away and focused his gaze on the camp. The stallion had caught the man's attention, but now it was a question of how interested Nassar was in the animal. It was also possible the man didn't even have Allegra. He dismissed the thought. Intuition told him differently. The man had her. Allegra would appeal to Nassar's baser instincts. He knew how easily she could drive a man to distraction, and Nassar was no different than any other man in that regard. Hell, she'd managed to twist him into knots without any real effort at all.

Chaos of a nonthreatening nature erupted as they rode into Nassar's camp. A young boy ran forward with feedbags for the horses, while another carried water for the animals. Dismounting, Shaheen instructed two of his men to stay and tend to the horses. With Nassar leading the way, Shaheen and the rest of his small entourage followed the Amazigh Sheikh through the camp until they reached a large tent with the sides rolled up to let the air flow through. One arm stretched out in a sweeping gesture, Nassar bowed in his direction.

"*Ahlan Wa Sahlan*, Shaheen of Mahmoud's Tribe."

"May God return your hospitality to you," he replied as he entered the tent and sat at one of the pommel rests arranged in a semicircle inside the shelter.

A sheepskin covering softened the hard leather of the arm support as he watched Nassar ceremoniously usher in the rest of his guests. With a clap of his hands, the Sheikh called for the traditional coffee, which was brought almost immediately. His movements an exaggerated flourish, Nassar poured three cups from the pot. Dramatically, he made a display of tasting the first cup to show the beverage wasn't poisoned. When he'd finished, he handed the second cup to Shaheen. Accepting the cup from the Sheikh, he took a sip of the strong, cardamom-spiced coffee before handing it back to Nassar to complete the tasting ritual. The coffee now deemed poison free, they repeated the ritual with the *mensaf.* Freshly made, the rice and meat dish was flavored with pine nuts. As they ate, Nassar arched an eyebrow at him.

"Tell me, how does your friend Khalid fare?" There was just enough mockery in his question to warn Shaheen to be on his guard. Revealing where Khalid was camped or that Hakim had taken Laila and Allegra's maid to the Amazigh sovereign would be foolhardy. But mocking the man's query could not go unremarked upon.

"He is well, as are Hakim and Laila. The boy will make his father proud." He swiped a bite of food out of his bowl with the leavened bread he held, keeping his eyes downcast. "Laila is as beautiful as her mother was."

The silence in the tent hung stiff and still over them as Shaheen continued to eat his meal as if nothing untoward had been said. He lifted his head and met Nassar's unreadable gaze.

"You are a long way from Sheikh Mahmoud's territory, Shaheen." Nassar's eyes narrowed with assessment as he abruptly changed the subject.

"And you're far from home as well. Does Sheikh Cadi know you're in his territory?"

"I do not ask any man's permission as to where I travel." Nassar shrugged with indifference. "But at least I am wise enough to protect myself when I do. You travel with such a small escort, Shaheen. Do you truly believe yourself that invincible?"

"Hardly. Only great men are invincible, and I am not great, but you honor me by suggesting it is so."

He bit back a smile at the sight of Nassar clenching his jaw. Having his insults turned into compliments clearly wasn't an experience the Sheikh enjoyed. Equally unsettling for the man had been the reference to Laila and how she resembled her mother. It had raised the past and the question of vengeance. One day, Nassar would pay for his crimes, but for the moment Shaheen would bide his time until Khalid chose to make the man pay. Eventually, Nassar would die the traitor's death he deserved. Setting his bowl aside, he dusted off his hands as if he were ready to leave. Immediately, the Sheikh leaned forward.

"Is your stallion for sale?"

"My stallion?" he asked as if puzzled. "Oh, you mean Abyad. No, I'm afraid not. He cost me a pretty penny, and I intend to find a broodmare that will please him."

"And this is why you're so far from my brother's territory?" The man studied him carefully.

"We are headed to Hajra. I've heard there is a man there with broodmares that are considered to be the finest in Morocco."

"Ah, you must be talking about Abdulla." Nassar nodded his head. "I bought one of his prized mares just last month."

"Then I count that as a recommendation given your expertise in horseflesh."

The Sheikh beamed with pleasure, his expression suddenly open and pleasant. Shaheen marveled at how compliments fed the man's sense of self-importance.

"What if I had a rare jewel to trade for the stallion? Would you consider an exchange?" Stroking his beard, Nassar studied him with just a hint of anticipation.

"It would have to be an exceptional jewel for me to part with Abyad."

"I can assure you that this jewel is exceptional. She is a queen among women."

"A woman?" Shaheen waved his hand in a dismissing gesture. "I have no need of a woman."

"But this woman is a creature beyond all imagination."

"She sounds like a story I might tell a child."

"Trust me, she is quite real." Nassar gestured to one of his men and quietly issued an order. As the servant left the tent, the Sheikh turned back to him. "The paramour of kings and the odalisque of many, and her abilities are exceptional."

"Exceptional?" He eyed Nassar coldly. If the bastard had touched her, he didn't think he'd be able to keep from killing the man.

"So I've heard." Nassar shrugged. "I've not yet had time to indulge myself and experience her skills in the art of pleasure."

"Then why part with her?" He took a sip of coffee. Nassar hadn't touched her. The relief spreading through his body was sharp and fierce.

"I've searched for an animal like Abyad for years. A horse is worth its weight in gold. A woman? Bah!" The Sheikh shook his head with an expression of disgust. "Useless, fickle creatures."

The muscles inside his stomach coiled tight with anger at the words. God, he was ready to slit the man's throat right now. If the bastard— Without lifting his head he knew she had entered the tent. His body responded to her presence with a primal edge of tension that he remembered from that night at the Sultan's palace. The sensation gnawed at him with the fierce frenzy of a wild animal devouring a meal.

Seated beside him, Jamal revealed his consternation with a sharp hiss. Surprised by the sound, he glanced at his friend. The look of shocked horror on the Bedouin's face compelled him to immediately jerk his head toward Allegra. Raw and merciless, the fury twisting his muscles into tight, sharp threads of tension blurred everything in his sight except for her.

8

"By all that is holy, woman, what have you done to your hair?" Nassar grabbed Allegra by the arm and jerked her toward the center of his tent.

"You will have to ask Rana that question, not me."

With what was left of her pride, she lifted her chin to a proud angle and stared at a point over Nassar's shoulder. She refused to let the man see how devastated she was. He'd only take pleasure in her pain, just like Rana had this morning.

"Rana knows better than to incur my wrath."

"She might know better, but Rana is responsible for shearing me like a piece of livestock," she snapped without looking at her jailor.

Her mind flashed back to how she'd awakened to find her hair strewn all over her pallet in large clumps. The horror of that moment washed over her as she recalled the desperate way her fingers had tried to clutch at hair that no longer existed. Even now she had to fight the urge to reach up and touch her cropped head. Any sign of anguish and Nassar would consider her beaten. No, she refused to give the bastard that satisfaction.

"You are a liar." Nassar's roar of disbelief destroyed what little reserve of common sense she had and she sent the man a scornful look.

"And you are a fool."

Her head snapped sideways beneath his hand, the sound of the blow splitting the air with a vicious crack. Fighting to remain upright, she stumbled back into one of the guards. Rough hands shoved her back into place. Her hand touched her cheek, and she winced at the agony the slight touch triggered. By morning, her cheek would be black and blue.

A sharp exclamation of disgust made her jerk her head toward the sound. Stunned, she saw her Bedouin Sheikh seated on the tent's carpet glaring up at Nassar with angry disdain. Certain she was imagining things, she closed her eyes for a moment then opened them again. He really was here. He wasn't a figment of her imagination. Her shoulders sagged with relief as she stared at his handsome profile. He'd come to rescue her.

"You must think me a fool, Nassar. I have no intention of accepting this pitiful creature even as a gift."

The contempt in his voice eroded some of her relief. *Pitiful creature?* She watched him rise to his feet and cross the short distance between them, his gaze empty of any recognition. As if she were invisible, he walked in a circle around her, a skeptical look on his dark features.

She flinched at his careless disregard. A moment later, his fingertips pressed into the skin under her chin and forced her to turn her head while he examined her face where Nassar had hit her. A low-pitched sound rumbled in his throat. Her gaze jerked up to his face, but he'd already turned away from her.

"Even if she were of interest to me, she's damaged." His words made Nassar wave his hands in protest.

"Do not allow her appearance to deceive you, Sheikh Shaheen. I can assure you the woman will please you."

Again, her mysterious Bedouin looked her up and down then turned his back on her with a wave of his hand. Still struggling to understand what was happening, she trembled at his abrupt dismissal. Surely, he wouldn't leave her here.

"She is too defiant. Even Abyad is not so stubborn."

"Are you saying you cannot tame her?" Nassar stroked his beard and raised his eyebrows at Sheikh Shaheen.

"It's easy to use a whip to control a creature, but taming requires patience and a gentle hand." He turned his head to look her up and down again before shaking his head. "It is something I do well, but I don't think she's worth the price of my stallion."

Price. It was as if he'd thrown her into a lake of icy water. A wild tremor rippled through her and her heart slammed to a halt for a long second as she fought to breathe. *Worth the price.* Dear God, Nassar was offering to trade her for a horse. Her stomach lurched and sent bile rising in her throat. Closing her eyes, she fought against the nausea. After a few seconds, the sickness passed and in its place was a cold rage that forced her hands to knot into tight fists. She watched as Nassar's face took on a crafty expression.

"Very well, I'll give you the woman and a quarter of the gold you paid for the stallion."

Sheikh Shaheen's scoffing laugh sent humiliation sweeping through her. Fierce and terrible, her mind clawed at old wounds until they were bloody and raw just as badly as they had been that first night at Madame Eugenie's. Her mother's harsh voice had mixed with Madame Eugenie's softer, more refined one as the two of them argued over a price. When the final price of ten pounds was agreed to, she'd looked on in horror as her mother walked out the brothel doorway without a backward glance. Allegra drew in a slow breath that reflected her pain.

The sound captured Sheikh Shaheen's attention, and for a fraction of a second, she thought she saw regret flash across his face. She immediately realized she was wrong as his gaze ran over her figure with a critical look before he turned his attention back to Nassar. Knuckles white beneath the pressure of her clenched fists, she could feel her rapid pulse spill hate and anger through her blood. To these men, she was nothing more than human cattle to be bought and traded.

"The woman and 75 percent of the gold I paid for Abyad," Shaheen said carelessly and folded his arms across his chest.

"Forty percent." Nassar shook his head.

"Sixty."

"Done," Nassar said with a jubilant smile and offered his hand to seal the transaction. "You drive a hard bargain, Shaheen."

Rage swallowed her like a turbulent, dark river. Its undercurrent dragged her down into a primal place that blinded her to everything except the desire to kill them both. With an unintelligible cry of fury, she lunged toward Nassar and her fingers wrapped around the jeweled handle of the knife he wore. With a vicious tug, she yanked it free of the scabbard. Nassar's curse and shouts from the others in the tent barely registered with her as she flung her hand upward in an attempt to plunge the blade into Nassar's chest. Strong fingers caught her wrist and held her in place.

"Drop the blade, *ma chérie*." His voice was almost gentle, and was that regret in his voice? No, that wasn't possible for a man who'd just bought her like a piece of livestock.

"I'm a free woman! A subject of Her Majesty Queen Victoria. You cannot sell me like cattle, you bastard."

She tried to free herself from Sheikh Shaheen's firm, yet gentle, grip, but failed. Still holding her prisoner, he removed the knife from her hand and returned it to Nassar. Cruel amusement curled Nassar's mouth.

"Bringing her to heel might require more than the gentle patience you believe is such an effective training tool, Newcastle. But then you English have always been a stubborn people, perhaps you'll succeed after all."

Nassar's words made Allegra jerk her head in the direction of the man who'd just released her. *Newcastle? Dear God.* He wasn't a Bedouin. He was English, and he'd bought her. The shock of what he'd done threw her back into the darkness of her past. It was such a long time ago, and yet the sharp, wrenching pain of it tore at her with the same intensity as it had when the horror of it had been new. He'd stolen her ability to choose. She'd been sold for the second time in her life.

"Jamal, take her to the horses," Sheikh Shaheen said quietly.

She heard his words, but as though from a great distance. She was back at Madame Eugenie's. Any moment now, she'd find herself drinking in the rank odor of sweet wine left standing overnight, cheap perfume, and stale tobacco. Shame and humiliation crawled through her until her stomach roiled from the onslaught. When had the present become the past?

In the course of just one day, she'd been reduced to the child she'd once been—helpless, unwanted, and devoid of any control over her future. Was it possible she'd been wrong all along? Was she incapable of forging her own destiny? *No.* She couldn't believe that. She'd come too far from that pitiful existence in the East End of London to lose faith in her ability to overcome the worst of circumstances.

Still, the mortification was all too familiar. For Nassar to sell her in such a cavalier manner was despicable, but it was no more than she expected of a barbarian. But to have been bought by *him*—the thought sickened her. At least Madame Eugenie hadn't lied about what she was. Trembling from shock, she didn't move, and the Englishman calling himself Shaheen narrowed his gaze in her direction.

"You have one of two choices, *ma belle*, you can go with Jamal or you can stay here. The choice is yours."

He lied. He wasn't offering her a choice. She didn't hide her loathing for him as she tilted her head in a defiant manner. Although his expression revealed nothing, his narrowed gaze leveled a silent challenge to her. The feeling of helplessness returned, and she reluctantly followed Jamal out of the tent. Behind her, Nassar grunted with anger as he tossed a bag of coins to Sheikh Shaheen.

"The *jahannam meshsh* will not have you."

She tossed a quick glance over her shoulder at both of the men and saw Sheikh Shaheen shrug.

"You may be right, but since she belongs to me now, that is my problem."

If Nassar answered him, she didn't hear. Blindly, she stumbled along behind the Bedouin called Jamal. God, how could he have been so casual about trading a horse and some gold for her. She flinched. Why hadn't he simply demanded Nassar release her? Surely, the man wasn't above the law in Morocco. She nibbled at her lip as she bit back tears. Nassar's behavior showed him for what he was. A man of little character. But how could she have been so wrong about this Englishman who'd bought her without flinching?

From the moment they'd met she'd recognized the raw magnetism he possessed. He was the type of man she'd learned to avoid because they always presented the possibility of emotional entanglements. But she never would have thought him so callous, so dishonorable as to do what he'd done. She couldn't remember ever being so wrong about someone before—a shudder ripped through her. God in heaven, she'd taken pleasure in kissing him.

She'd found him desirable. Worse, she'd even thought he'd come to rescue her. Her throat swelled with tears.

No. She refused to cry. But, oh God, how she wanted to. She wanted to cry long and hard like she had this morning. Ahead of her, the man called Jamal came to a halt in front of a group of horses and several men. Unlike her new master, who wore black, these men wore white robes similar to what she wore. She saw one of the men look at her then speak to the man beside him and nod in her direction. Her hand automatically reached up to touch what was left of her hair.

Shame spiraled through her again as her fingers brushed over the short, stubby clumps of hair. It wasn't until Rana and the other women had left the tent this morning that she'd allowed herself to succumb to tears. And she had sobbed until she had no tears left. She wanted to cry like that again. Cry until she fell asleep and this nightmare ended. A light touch on her arm made her jump, and she turned her head to see Jamal's expression of concern.

"To cover your head, mademoiselle." In halting French, he offered her a linen scarf.

The kindness of his actions made tears blur her vision. Crushing the desire to sob, she hastily wiped her eyes dry with the back of her hand as she accepted the offering. Not worried how it might look, she wrapped her head with the material. As she tied off the scarf, her neck tingled with a familiar sensation. Instinct cried out for her to turn and face him, but she refused to give in to the impulse.

He came to a halt beside her, but she kept her gaze averted, determined not to look at him. With a low growl of displeasure, he moved to a chestnut stallion and swung himself up into the saddle. Nudging his horse forward, he extended his hand to her.

"Come *helwa jahannam meshsh.*"

Dear God, he actually expected her to ride with him. She

shuddered at the thought. No, she couldn't bear to be so close to him. Besides, if they gave her a horse to ride, she could possibly escape. Arthur had always said she rode as if born in the saddle. She would make use of that skill if she could. She shook her head fiercely.

"I know how to ride. Let me have my own horse."

"The only horses we have are the ones you see before you. I just traded my best horse for you." With an impatient gesture, he snapped his fingers and stretched out his hand to her again. "Now come, or I'll leave you here for Nassar to deal with you as he chooses."

Anger whipped through her with the power of the afternoon heat. The last thing she wanted was to ride with him. Ignoring his hand, she turned and moved to where Jamal sat astride a quiet black Arabian. Although her options were limited, she preferred to ride with someone whose conduct toward her had at least been sympathetic.

"Monsieur?" she pleaded as she stretched up her hand to the dark-skinned native.

He hesitated, his gaze flickering to the man on the horse behind her. The silence wrapped itself around her with a tense edge, but her eyes didn't leave the face of the Bedouin. A moment later, Shaheen's anger exploded over her head as he said something in Jamal's native tongue. With a nod, the Bedouin stretched out his arm, helping her mount the horse. Relieved, she wrapped her arms around the man's waist and scooted into place on the rear of the animal.

With a loud command, Shaheen wheeled his horse around and rode off, not waiting for anyone to follow him. Immediately, Jamal and the others urged their animals forward. As they rode after his dark-clad figure, the uncertainty of her position terrified her. She was relieved they were taking her away from Nassar. But the uncertainty of what lay ahead was no less terrifying.

Exhausted and unable to think clearly, she clung to Jamal's waist. Mile after mile they rode across the sparse landscape. Unchanging and unforgiving, it stretched out in front of them, relentless in its barren form. They crossed one or two small riverbeds that were mere trickles of water, only stopping long enough to let the horses drink before they pushed onward. It was late afternoon before she realized the sun was behind them. When had they changed course? She was certain they had been heading north when they left Nassar's camp.

Over Jamal's right shoulder, she saw the Atlas Mountains in the distance, their rocky formation rising up into the sky. They were the only thing that stood between Morocco and the ever-encroaching Sahara desert. Her heart skipped a beat. Was he taking her back to Marrakech? She was certain it was in this direction. Hope crested inside her, easing some of her weariness. Straightening, she searched the horizon for signs of the famed city, but there was nothing to suggest a city at all. At that moment, one of the men released a loud, warbling cry and urged his horse into a full gallop. Turning her head she saw a cluster of tents spread out on the horizon, and her heart sank. He wasn't taking her to Marrakech. Jamal prodded his horse to move faster as the entire party raced toward the tents.

The horses covered the distance quickly, and in moments they were met by a welcoming party of armed men who escorted them into the camp. Women and children rushed out to meet them just as they had at Nassar's camp. The sight made her sag wearily against Jamal as they came to a halt. Lithely dismounting from his horse, he gently lifted Allegra to the ground. Her legs wobbly from the exhausting ride, she leaned against him for a moment. Seconds later, strong arms swung her upward to rest against a solid chest. The heat of him sank into her aching body, warming and relaxing her sore muscles. It was a soothing sensation and for an instant, she allowed herself to relax against him. Horrified by her reaction, she stiffened and pushed against the hard wall of his chest.

"Put me down." Her voice was too hoarse to sound even remotely commanding.

"You can barely stand, let alone walk."

"I'd rather crawl than have you touch me." The bitter words didn't even cause him to falter, but she knew he was angry from the hard line of his set jaw.

"Take care with your tongue, *helwa jahannam meshsh*," he growled.

"Why," she rasped. "Will you punish me like Nassar did?"

She glared up at him, her rage feeding the bitterness inside her. As he carried her into a large tent, he dropped her unceremoniously to her feet. Caught off guard, she had to brace her hands against his muscular arms to steady herself. Looking up at him, she flinched at the icy fury carving his features into stone.

"I'll have one of the women draw you a bath," he said grimly.

Without another word, he left her alone. Burying her face in her hands, she fought back the tears. She needed to think—come up with a plan. That helpless feeling coiled around her again, and she stared around the spacious tent. Unlike Nassar's tent, there were no silken cords or tassels hanging from the tent walls. Instead, white sheepskins covered the bedding, while colorful pillows littered the floor around a large silver tray sitting on top of a basket.

Two trunks were set off to one side, their leather lids covered with woven rugs trimmed with brightly colored tassels. The one extravagance in the tent was the carpet lining the floor. It was a beautiful mosaic of color that cushioned her feet even in the leather slippers she wore. But nothing about the tent made it any less of a prison.

The soft rustle of clothing caught her attention, and she turned to see three women entering the tent with a large leather object, which they proceeded to unroll and erect in one corner of the tent. One of the women looked up to smile shyly at Allegra before returning to the task of setting up the portable tub. They finished just as two young boys entered the tent and proceeded to dump water into the vessel. Another woman entered the tent carrying soap, towels, and clothing. In silence, she offered the items to Allegra before ordering everyone out of the tent with a clap of her hands.

Uncertainty flooded through her as she approached the bath the women had prepared. Would someone return to bathe her as they had in Nassar's camp? Her nerves stretched thin and raw, she waited for someone to burst into the tent. Several minutes passed before she realized there would be no invasion of her privacy. Setting the towels and clothes aside, she bent over and swept her hand through the bathwater.

It was lukewarm, but the water would feel wonderful against her hot, sticky skin. For a brief second, she considered foregoing a bath purely as a matter of protest. It was a fleeting thought, and she hurriedly removed her clothes. Citrus brushed across her senses as she sank into the water with a soft splash. Outside the tent, she heard female voices and tensed with fear. When no one entered the tent, a shudder wracked her body and she reached for the soap.

With a harsh stroke, she scraped the square bar of rough soap across her skin. She repeated the motion. Steady and precise, she scrubbed her skin. A tear slid down her cheek as she increased the pace of her bathing. Another tear rolled down her face as she scoured her body as hard and fast as she could.

Rana's taunting features fluttered through her head, and she rubbed the soap over her skin that much harder in an effort to shed the memories of her captivity. The rough edges bruised her arms and legs as the memory of Nassar's vile threats churned her stomach.

Rubbing the soap between her hands in a vigorous motion, she worked up a glob of lather and ran it over her head. The short, spiky points of hair undid her completely. Hunkered down in the tub, she wrapped her arms around her legs, rested her forehead on her knees and sobbed quietly. She wasn't sure how long she cried, but after a time her tears became dry sobs. Inhaling a deep breath, she sat upright and forced herself to finish her bath.

She'd just stepped out of the leather tub, when the flap of the tent flew open and Shaheen strode in. Frozen where she stood, she simply stared at him in mute surprise.

"Christ Jesus," he rasped. "They assured me you would be dressed."

His liquid brown gaze was a hot wind across her skin as he studied her with a look she'd seen on the faces of many different men. She swallowed hard at the heat suddenly pulsing through her body. Not one of her past lovers had ever affected her this way with just a look. As their eyes locked, fire skimmed over her skin. If it were possible for a man to devour her with his gaze, this one could.

She looked away from him. What was wrong with her? The man had traded his horse and accepted gold coin for her. How could she be attracted to him? And yet she was. Her body seemed to have a mind of its own the way her senses hummed in his presence.

Infuriated at responding so easily to him, she bent over to retrieve a towel from the floor. One of the first skills Madame Eugenie had taught her was to rejoice in the beauty of the human body. Since learning the skill she'd never felt uncomfortable standing naked in front of a man—until now. This man made her feel vulnerable, and she didn't like it. Nonetheless, the skills she'd learned in the brothel stood her in good stead as she forced herself to ignore him and dry herself off with a nonchalance she didn't feel. He cleared his throat in an obvious sound of unease as she dried the water off her skin. The sound returned a precious sense of control back to her.

"I'll"—he paused for a fraction of a second—"come back in a few moments."

"There's no need. I believe it's customary for a buyer to inspect his purchase." She didn't try to keep the bitterness out of her words as she slid a pair of aquamarine *sherwals* up over her hips.

"*Damm gahannam*, it wasn't like that," he bit out with a fury that increased the already warm air inside the tent. "I didn't have any other choice."

"Then tell me what it was like," she sneered.

Wearing nothing but the wide-legged pants, she turned to face him. His eyes flashed with an emotion she knew well. Her sense of power and control grew as he closed the distance between them to tower over her. The warmth of him enveloped her body. It was far too pleasant a sensation. She breathed in quickly at the fire blazing in his eyes. It stirred something deep inside her—an emotion she knew better than to feel. She swayed slightly on her feet and his hands seared her arms as he steadied her.

"You misjudge me, *ma belle*." The instant the back of his hand glided along her bare shoulder she trembled. With one seductive caress, he'd stolen back the sense of power and control she'd regained just moments ago. "I didn't buy you, Allegra. I bought your freedom."

"I don't recall you saying anything to that effect when we left Nassar's camp *or* when we arrived here." She shook her head partly in denial and in a halfhearted effort to ignore the hypnotic way her name rolled off his tongue.

"Believe what you want, but it was your freedom I bought, not you." Desperately she fought to keep the flame of her anger burning inside her as the palm of his hand glided over her skin to the base of her throat.

"Then I'm free to go?"

"Do you wish to be free?"

The seductive note in his voice tugged at her senses with a relentless enticement. With a gentle tug, he pulled her against him, while his hand blazed a trail of fire down between her breasts. Flushed with heat, her body ached with a familiar vibration, but there was something more to it. Something new and far more intense. Reluctantly, she met his penetrating gaze. The desire flaring in the dark depths of his eyes was a tantalizing invitation. In that brief moment before he lowered his head toward her, she lost her ability to refuse his unspoken proposition.

The moment his mouth captured hers, a whirlwind of sensation consumed her. He smelled of cedar and citrus mingled with the bite of something else she couldn't identify. A gasp escaped her as he nipped at her lips with his teeth, demanding access to the inner warmth of her mouth. She obliged him willingly, her tongue mating with his in a demand of her own. The soft wool of his *gambaz* rubbed across her nipples. Her breasts swelled as the material intensified the hard and achy sensation of her sensitive skin. Never afraid to ask for what she wanted, she caught his hand and forced him to cup her. A deep groan rumbled in his chest as his thumb roughed over her nipple. Then with a suddenness that startled her, he released her. He muttered something beneath his breath and bent to pick up the pink *gambaz* lying next to her feet.

The garment made a loud crack as he snapped out its folds. His manner abrupt, he thrust it at her in a gesture that commanded her to dress. Snatching it out of his hand, she threw the large calf-length shirt over her head, adjusting it as she shot a quick glance in his direction. He was watching her with a scowl on his face and another emotion she couldn't decipher. Not so much desire as indecision. It made him more approachable.

"Why didn't you just demand that Nassar release me?" she asked with a catch in her voice. The degradation and helplessness of that moment welled up inside her, forcing her to look away. "Why did you . . . *buy* me like that?"

Silence hung between them for a long moment. She peeked at him from out of the corner of her eye. His expression was grim with regret and it sent a jolt through her. As if aware that she was watching him, the emotion vanished from his features and he turned to face her.

"It was necessary. Nassar and I are old enemies." He folded his arms across his chest. "If he'd realized you were the reason for my being in his camp, he would never have released you without a fight."

"Why didn't you explain this when we were leaving?"

"Would you have listened?" Warm mahogany eyes mocked her with more than a hint of amusement. The look sent a frisson skating over her skin.

"No, but you can hardly blame me for thinking the worst."

"My only priority from the moment I left Marrakech was your safety and that of my men."

His words made it sound as if he'd deliberately set out to rescue her. The top of her hand tingled, and she rubbed at her mark on her skin. In that instant, she remembered the moment in the *souq* when the henna artist had painted her hand. She'd said a man called Shaheen was her destiny. A frown furrowed her forehead. Was it possible the old woman had foreseen this man rescuing her?

"How did you find me?" Her abrupt change of subject clearly surprised him, but he simply shrugged.

"Laila's father and I are old friends. When she was unable to reach her father, she came to me for help, explaining that Nassar's men had taken you."

"She's all right?" She took a step toward him. "And Millie? They're safe?"

"They're both safe and well," he said in a gentle tone.

"Thank God," she whispered as she briefly closed her eyes in relief. Her friends were safe. Perhaps she *had* misjudged him.

"Then you didn't just happen to stumble across me at Nassar's camp. You knew I was there."

He folded his arms across his chest and a nonchalant expression crossed his strong features. "I had enough information to track Nassar's movements, but I wasn't really sure until he had you brought to his tent."

He'd come after her. The realization made her heart skip a beat. And for the first time she realized he wouldn't have left Nassar's camp without her. Somehow, the knowledge eased the humiliation of being bought like an animal. The raw pain of how he'd secured her freedom still cut deep, but she owed her life to him. And she'd be lying if she said she wasn't grateful. That he'd found her at all amazed her.

"Then I am in your debt," she said with quiet sincerity.

"I'm glad to see we can finally agree on something." The irony in his voice sent tension slipping through her body.

The emotion in his gaze was unreadable. She was quite skilled at reading men, but this man revealed nothing to her. If she couldn't anticipate his thoughts, he was in the position of power, not her. It was how he managed to throw her off balance so often, and she desperately needed to feel as though she were in control of what happened to her. She was certain that wouldn't happen until she returned to Marrakech and then home to England.

"Then we leave for Marrakech tomorrow?"

"No." The simple refusal was straight to the point and unyielding.

"I don't understand. You said I was free to go."

"No." Still frowning, he shook his head. "I said I bought your freedom."

"But you can't just keep me here," she gasped. Appalled, she stared up into his unreadable features.

"And who will stop me, *ma chérie?*" he said tersely.

"How long do you intend to hold me prisoner?" she asked as she glared at him with dislike.

"That remains to be seen." He shrugged, and the insouciant gesture infuriated her.

"If you think to induce me to share your bed, then you're as deluded as Nassar," she snapped. "I told you once before that *I* decide who my lovers are."

"I remember," he said in a curt tone. "I also remember seeing you with Lord Shaftsbury at the Sultan's palace."

The accusation in his words puzzled her. What did Charles have to do with his decision not to return her to Marrakech? Confused, she shook her head.

"What does my relationship with Lord Shaftsbury have to do with anything?"

"Do you deny you were Shaftsbury's mistress?"

"I fail to see how that's any of your concern." She glared at him. What did it matter that she and Charles had been— Newcastle. Charles had come to Morocco to find a Viscount Newcastle. She narrowed her gaze at him. "Charles is looking for *you.*"

"*Très bon, ma belle.* And I don't wish to be found." The grim look on his dark features emphasized the harshness of his tone.

She flinched. It didn't matter to her why he wanted to remain hidden in this desolate, half-desert terrain. If he wished to stay lost here, she didn't care. She simply wanted to return to Marrakech and then home to England. Cordelia would be worried about her when she didn't reply to her letter. Her niece would need support to weather the scandal Lady Bledsoe was certain to instigate.

It was madness on his part to think he could get away with holding her here. People would notice. Millie wouldn't let her disappearance be overlooked. And when Isabelle returned from her honeymoon, her friend would insist that her husband launch a search. The man clearly hadn't thought things through.

"You can't possibly believe that Millie will simply let me disappear." She shook her head in disbelief. "She'll have Charles contact the authorities."

"Your friend is in Sheikh Mahmoud's camp. I thought it best she go with Laila as a safety precaution. Laila's father will protect them both. The servants at the Hastings household are under the impression that you and your maid left for England this morning."

"You bastard," she whispered as a bitter taste filled her mouth.

"Perhaps, but a thorough one."

"All of this simply to avoid Charles discovering your whereabouts?" she said with a growing sense of fear as she studied his implacable features. "Did it never occur to you that I didn't know who you were?"

"I assumed as much, but I believe in planning for every possible contingency, including the most volatile one—Nassar." He paused for a split second. "If he'd not mentioned my name, you would be in Marrakech right now."

"If I gave you my word that I wouldn't tell Charles anything, would you let me go then?"

It wasn't difficult to make her voice a soft plea of desperation when it was exactly how she felt. He studied her for a long moment, his dark brown gaze searing her skin with a fiery intensity that was alarming. Then with a sharp shake of his head, he turned away from her.

"No. There's far too much at stake."

"You cannot keep me here against my will," she exclaimed with vehemence and skirted his side to confront him face-to-face.

"And who will stop me?" His arrogance took her breath away

as he met her angry gaze with supreme confidence. He was right. Who would stop him? His harsh expression softened somewhat as he sighed. "In truth, *ma belle*, you are free to go, but I'll not help you return to Marrakech, nor will anyone else in this camp."

"Then I'll find my own way." Furious, she glared at him with outrage.

"I don't think you're that foolish." A somber expression on his face, he shook his head. "Even if you managed to head in the right direction, you would be prey for predators of both the four-legged and two-legged kind."

The quiet simplicity of his words was far more devastating than any threat he could have made. She turned away from him. For a few brief moments, she'd thought she might have regained control of her life, but it had been an illusion. A warm hand touched her shoulder, and with suppressed violence she jerked away from him.

"*Don't. Touch. Me.*" She enunciated each word with an icy calm she didn't feel as she sent him a vicious look. "You're correct about predators, my lord, but I don't have to leave this camp to find any of the two-legged kind. You emulate Sheikh Nassar's predatory manner so easily."

The sharp breath he drew in told her the insult had struck home. Chiseled stone could not have been harder than his features as he took a step toward her. Although the movement alarmed her, she didn't flinch. Instead she straightened her shoulders and met his harsh glare with equal intensity. Eyes narrowing, a muscle twitched in his cheek from the tension sharpening the line of his jaw.

"Have care with your words, *ma belle*."

"Or what?" she sneered with a sharp laugh.

"Or you might discover that Nassar isn't half as dangerous as I am." Ice was warmer than the glacial look in his eyes. But she held her ground as he leaned into her. "He simply toys with his prey. I, on the other hand, devour mine."

His words weren't a threat. They were a cold, brutal promise. His gaze raked over her with scathing disdain before he spun away from her and stalked out of the tent. It was the raw, menacing power in his gait that made her swallow hard. Had she merely been pulled from a small fire, only to be tossed into an inferno?

9

Christ Jesus, he wanted to throttle the woman. She'd actually had the audacity to compare him to that bastard Nassar. He strode through the camp, a grunt the only form of greeting he offered up to those he passed. Worse yet, he didn't like the way her accusation was so close to the target. He *was* keeping her against her will. And he knew his rationalization for doing so was only part of the reason. The treaties were important, but it was pointless to deny his attraction to her. An attraction he'd admitted when he'd made his decision to rescue her from Nassar's camp. When he'd seen her covered with nothing but the moisture of her bath, a raging lust had swept through him with the force of a Sahara wind.

It had taken control of his senses, blinding him to everything. And the sultry creature had immediately recognized the effect she had on him. She'd used her voluptuous body to her advantage. With a graceful wave of her hennaed hand, she'd exuded supreme confidence in her nakedness. Not even Frances had been so self-assured with her body. But Allegra hadn't been the least bit disconcerted by his presence. Naked curves glistening with water, she'd dried herself off with a sangfroid that hadn't just astonished him. It had aroused him.

The sight of her had sent desire twisting through him. Urgent and hot, his need had made his cock swell tight and hard until he ached to thrust into her soft core over and over again. He'd been driven to kiss her simply to prove to himself that he could control his carnal need. He'd been a fool to think that. God Almighty when she'd grabbed his hand and forced him to touch her, his body had betrayed him with a vengeance. Cupped in his hand, she'd been firm and full, her nipples hard with desire. The feel of her had made him think he'd come right then and there. Not even Frances had demonstrated such a raw, potent sexuality, let alone used it with such skill. It explained why men said Allegra's name with such hunger.

Having reached the edge of camp, he braced his hands against his waist and stared out at the Atlas Mountains. Their rocky façade was awash in the varying hues of red and orange the setting sun painted so vividly on the craggy cliffs and furrows. The sight of them soothed his soul. Despite the sometimes harsh Amazigh lifestyle, he'd found peace here on the plains of Morocco. But that contentment was being rocked by one woman.

A courtesan no less. The type of woman he'd sworn never to become involved with again. He grunted as he remembered that moment in the Agdal Gardens when she'd challenged him to that ridiculous wager. He'd known she would try to seduce him, but he'd been unprepared for her virtuoso performance. She'd more than earned her right to leave the gardens without him with that incredible display of sensual pleasure.

The image of her slowly sliding a banana past her lips still had the power to suck the air from his lungs. The unspoken images her performance conjured up had been enough to make him hard as an iron pole in seconds. And when she'd swallowed the damn thing, she'd created a burning need in him to have her hot mouth drawing down on his cock in the same fashion. Even his nights refused to give him rest from the memory. Over the past week, he'd found himself awake more than once in the middle of the night, forced to use his hand as a poor substitute for Allegra's skilled mouth and tongue.

No, he needed to get her out of his system, and he wasn't quite sure how to do it, except to send her back to Marrakech. Send her back to Shaftsbury. The thought made him grimace. He wasn't ready to give her up to his cousin just yet.

The mere thought of doing so stirred a primitive emotion inside him that he didn't like. It signaled a departure from his usual clear-headed thoughts. For almost fifteen years, Morocco had absorbed all his passion, but in less than two weeks, Allegra had distracted him in a way nothing else had ever done.

A strong hand gripped his shoulder for a brief moment, and he turned his head to see Jamal standing beside him. His gaze focused on the mountains, the Bedouin squinted as he stared at the landscape.

"Are you certain it is wise to keep the *anasi* here against her will, Shaheen?"

"It's unfortunate, but necessary." He shrugged, but didn't look at his friend.

"This Viscount who is trying to find you. He's your cousin?"

With a grimace, he nodded. "A distant one, but part of the family. I met him once or twice while living in London."

"Is it possible he has a message from your father?" There was a bit of censure in his friend's voice, and his jaw clenched.

"Whatever the message is, I have no wish to hear it."

Silence stretched between them for a moment before Jamal bent and gathered a handful of dry dirt in his hand. Straightening, he examined it carefully. As if coming to a decision, the Amazigh extended his arm to show the earth filling his palm. "This dust contains the ashes of those who came before us. Things that die eventually become dust and the land reclaims them."

He watched as Jamal allowed the dirt to slowly drift through his fingers back to the ground. With a small sound of irony, he shook his head at the Bedouin's actions. "I'm guessing all of this musing is leading somewhere."

"Unlike the bones of our ancestors, memories never return to dust. They're a part of us until the day we die." Jamal looked toward the mountains. "The past is always there, waiting for that one moment when we least expect it to rise up and torment us."

Holding himself rigid, he glared at his friend. "I've never been willing to discuss my past before. What makes you think I'll do so now?"

"I do not think you are willing." Jamal shrugged. "But I consider you to be the son I never had, and I cannot remain silent. The *anasi* is a reminder of your past. Keeping her here will not rid you of the demons locked inside you."

"Allegra is here to ensure the treaties aren't jeopardized. We both know my impartiality would be questioned if the English or French discover I'm not Amazigh. The only reason Nassar hasn't used the information against me is that he fears the Sultan."

"As a member of Khalid's council it was natural for you to negotiate the treaties. You were Amazigh then just as you are now." Jamal's face grew pensive. "Do you remember the day I found you, Shaheen?"

"Yes," he said with just a hint of amusement. "As I recall, my gratitude was less than apparent."

"True." A smile crossed the Bedouin's face. "For a man near

death, you were quite adamant in your demands that I not help you live."

"Clearly you didn't listen to me."

"Ah, but I did," Jamal said quietly. "I listened to the feverish ravings of a young man tortured by something he believed was his fault."

Muscles growing taut, he met his friend's steady gaze. "Whatever you think you heard, they were the mutterings of a man dying of thirst, nothing more, nothing less."

"Perhaps, but with each passing year, I find myself wondering when you will return to your homeland to free yourself of the memories that haunt you."

"This is my home now. The Amazigh are my family. There's nothing for me in England."

"Perhaps, but I think your past has suddenly become much more difficult to avoid. The *anasi* has stirred up memories of an old love."

"The past is dead," he ground out. "Allegra's presence here has simply complicated matters with regard to my identity, nothing more."

Jamal heaved a sigh. "You are even more stubborn than Khalid. It is as if you truly were of his bloodline."

He grunted softly at the Bedouin's words. Sheikh Mahmoud was definitely stubborn, but for Jamal to suggest he was of Khalid's bloodline was the highest form of flattery the Bedouin could pay him. It was Jamal's way of saying there was no doubt that he was an Amazigh. Dusk had almost completely replaced the warm light of the sun, and his friend's face was darker in the dim light. Out of the corner of his eye, he saw the other man turn to face the encampment. In a fatherly fashion, Jamal's solid hand came to rest on his shoulder once more.

"Remember, Shaheen. No matter what you might think, a father always has need of his son."

With that the Bedouin walked away, leaving Shaheen to ponder his friend's words as he stared out at the darkening landscape. Overhead, the purples and blues of twilight danced their way across the sky. The moon was almost full, and it was already lighting up the harsh landscape with a pale glow. He would have to stand guard near the horses tonight. Allegra might understand the treacherous nature of fleeing the camp, but she was stubborn enough to try to escape.

Behind him, he heard the sound of laughter. Turning his head, he saw a spray of embers shoot upward from a nearby fire. His home in England had never felt this comfortable. His head dipped downward so he could study the sandy dirt. Jamal was wrong. The Earl of Pembroke had never had need of him. Not even the morning after James's death had his father needed him. Rather, the earl had bitterly told him it should have been him who died that night—not James.

Throwing his head back, he stared up at the early evening sky. Pain threaded its way through him as he recalled walking into Pembroke Hall that terrible morning. It had been hard enough making preparations for James's return to their childhood home. Filled with torment and guilt, telling his father about his brother's death had been the hardest thing he'd ever done. In the end, his father had emphatically said he never wanted to set eyes on him again.

The guilt of James's death doubled in that moment. For a second time he'd been responsible for the death of someone his father loved. It became a burden he tried to discard inside bottles of liquor as he stumbled his way out of England and across the continent. His activities had consisted of nothing but drinking, whoring, and fighting for almost a year. The fights had been numerous and bloody with instances of mental jubilation when he was certain he was at death's door. But death eluded him every time.

It wasn't until he reached Morocco that he was certain he'd achieved his goal. He'd sought out the worst tavern in Casablanca in search of a fight. In a card game, he'd deliberately accused one of the players of cheating. The end result was a beating unlike any other with his body carried out into the desert plains and left as carrion for the vultures. Jamal had found him instead.

The Bedouin had refused to leave him to die in the desert. There had been little to live for then or for weeks after that. It had been Nassar's rage that had brought him back to life and given him a new purpose. The attack on Khalid and his family had been an act of barbarism unlike anything he'd ever witnessed. Instinct had driven him forward that early morning as he'd killed the man intent on plunging a sword into Hakim, who was just a toddler at the time. A few yards away, he'd seen Khalid's wife covering her daughter's body with her own as Nassar struck her down with one vicious blow of his sword.

From that day forward, Shaheen had been one of Khalid's trusted warriors, assigned the task of guarding Hakim. Where he'd failed James, he vowed not to fail Hakim. He'd become the uncle Hakim and Laila would never know in Nassar. After the attack, Khalid had been determined to avenge the murder of his wife. And if it hadn't been for Jamal's levelheaded arguments, the Sheikh would have gone after Nassar that same day. Jamal had convinced Khalid to consider the welfare of his children over the desire to avenge his wife's death.

"Shaheen, Shaheen!" The excited cry interrupted his musings on the past.

Turning around, he grinned as Malik sprinted toward him. The boy's father was one of his regular outriders. Although barely six years old, the boy exhibited the same natural horsemanship his father had. The lad wasn't even afraid of Ahmar Jinn. That troubled him, because the stallion was still too dangerous for anyone but the most experienced to ride. Swinging the child up onto his shoulders, he walked back toward the encampment.

"Well, little man. Did you watch over the camp while your father and I were gone?"

"Yes, but Father told me you gave Abyad to that traitor Nassar." There was a note of disgust in the boy's voice. It reflected the loathing the entire tribe shared for the man.

"True, but I had no choice."

"I think you made a poor trade, Shaheen."

"A poor trade?" He laughed.

"You gave up Abyad for an *anasi*."

"The woman's name is Allegra, and I gave up Abyad to save her."

"Why?"

The innocent query made him swallow hard. Answering that question was as difficult as negotiating a complex treaty. It was easy to keep telling himself that he'd saved Allegra because Laila had asked him to do so. He knew better. He knew he would have gone after her no matter who'd asked him.

"She's Laila's friend, and Nassar was holding her prisoner."

"Father says you like her."

"He does, does he," he muttered with a frown.

"Yes, he said you called her a *helwa jahannam meshsh*." Puzzlement flooded Malik's voice. "Why would you do that? I thought hellcats were mean and nasty, not sweet."

The boy's words caused him to come to an immediate halt just short of Malik's family tent. Swinging the child down to the ground, he shook his head. "I think it's time your mother put you to bed."

"Oh all right, but I still think you made a poor trade," Malik said with a sad shake of his head as Shaheen gently pushed him toward his family's campfire.

"Go," he said. "And let me to worry about whether I made a good trade or not."

With a look of skepticism arching his small eyebrows, Malik rolled his eyes before he scurried off, leaving Shaheen to stare after him with more than just a touch of irritation. He should have known his rescue of Allegra would incite gossip. His bachelor status had been the topic of discussion for some time now, and several of his friends had been hinting it was time to do something about the situation. He wasn't ready to contemplate the idea of marriage, and certainly not with a courtesan.

Snorting in disgust, he headed toward Jamal's tent for a bedroll. He'd need to sleep near the horses to ensure Allegra didn't leave the camp. Between the hard ground and standing watch, he wouldn't get much sleep tonight. In truth, he could think of far more pleasurable ways to spend the evening. Unbidden came the image of Allegra fresh from her bath. *Damnation.* He needed to find some other outlet for this craving he experienced where the woman was concerned. If he didn't, life would become even more complicated than it already was.

⚜

The night air was chilly as Allegra stepped out of Shaheen's tent. It hadn't taken long at all for her to start thinking of him in that manner. Not one person she'd come into contact with this evening had referred to him as Lord Newcastle. They'd only called him Shaheen. Begrudgingly, she'd admitted that the name suited him. The sound of it was strong and solid. Just like the man himself.

She grimaced as the skin beneath her tattoo tingled. It didn't matter that he'd rescued her from Nassar. He was still holding her prisoner. But tonight she'd be free of him, just like she was free of Nassar. Hovering in the shadows, she wasn't sure whether to be grateful for the fullness of the moon or not. The celestial body illuminated everything, and it would be easy for anyone to see her moving through the camp if she failed to stay in the shadows. The hair on her skin rose slightly at the memory of Shaheen's warning. She shivered. Maybe this wasn't a good idea. Shaking off her fear, she slipped through the darkness and worked her way toward the horses. Perhaps the brightness of the moon was a good sign. There would be enough light to help her avoid riding in the wrong direction. With luck, she'd be in Marrakech by morning. There was every possibility that she could be in the city by dawn's light.

The quiet sound of horses moving against each other caught her ear. It was the sound of freedom, and she sucked in a sharp breath of triumph. Slipping around the corner of a tent, she saw the hobbled Arabians dozing quietly where they stood. As quietly as she could, she quickly retrieved a tassel laden bridle from a nearby pole and approached a golden brown mare. The horse snorted softly as she rubbed the animal's neck.

"You wouldn't get far with Naaja. Her name might mean *escape*, but she's not known for her speed."

She jumped at the sound of Shaheen's voice, barely stifling her cry of surprise. Whirling around, she saw him step out of the shadows into the moonlight. She'd come so close to freedom, only to have him steal it from her at the last moment.

"Then perhaps you might tell me which of these horses is the fastest, so I can reach Marrakech by morning," she said through clenched teeth.

"That would be Tarek, although I doubt you have the strength to handle him." He nodded toward the large chestnut horse he'd ridden that afternoon. "But then we both know you aren't going anywhere."

The quiet confidence in his voice made her want to scratch his eyes out. All she wanted was to return to Marrakech and then to England. She excelled at keeping confidences. It was a necessity for someone in her position. She had no intention of telling Charles that the man he sought was living in the desert as a Bedouin. But convincing this man of that fact was another matter altogether. Furious, she flung the bridle at him.

Not bothering to wait for his reaction, she stalked back toward the tent she'd been using. *His tent.* For a brief moment, she wondered where he'd been forced to sleep. She squashed the thought. Where the man slept wasn't any concern of hers. If he insisted on keeping her prisoner, he could damn well give up his tent in return. She stumbled over a tent stake and nearly fell. A strong hand pulled her upright, and the heat of his touch washed over her skin with the strength of a hot sun. Jerking free of his grasp, she increased her pace. It was bad enough the man was holding her against her will, but for her body to react to him in such a fashion was maddening. She stormed into the darkness of the tent and stumbled again, this time over a pillow on the tent's carpet floor.

"Damn it to hell," she exclaimed as she recovered her balance.

"Your temper matches the fiery color of your hair."

The deep note of his voice reached out to stroke her senses, and she spun around to face him. A small amount of moonlight streamed through in the places where the tent walls didn't quite meet, making it easy to see his tall, dark form directly in front of her. The mention of her hair sent her hand shooting upward to touch her head. Tension locked her jaw as her fingers brushed over the short, jaggedly cut locks.

"Don't you mean what's *left* of my hair?" she asked with a bitterness that matched the bile rising in her throat. She knew he wasn't responsible for what Rana had done, but he deserved every ounce of her resentment and hostility.

"It will grow back, *ma chérie*." He stepped forward to caress the top of her head. She slapped his hand away.

"Being my jailer doesn't give you the right to touch me. Now get out."

He was silent for a long moment, his face unreadable in the darkness. But the stubborn set of his jaw was easy to see as he leaned toward her. The warmth of him soaked its way into her skin, and her heart skipped a beat as she breathed in his crisp cedar scent.

"You forget this is *my* tent, *helwa jahannam meshsh*." The words were spoken softly, but the sharp edge of command was unmistakable.

Frustration crashed through her. She wanted to scream and rage at him for refusing to let her leave. Never had she met a man like this one. One moment solicitous, the next arrogant and commanding. What did she have to do to convince him to let her go? The internal question made her inhale a sharp breath. What a half-wit she was. When had she forgotten that she could control a situation simply with a stroke of enticement? She knew how to pleasure a man, entice him into giving her whatever she wanted.

Appalled at the direction of her thoughts, she bit back a gasp. Never before had she used her skills to manipulate one of her lovers. How could she even contemplate seducing this man? The simplicity of the answer stunned her.

She wanted him.

Even despite his refusal to release her, she still desired him. Since that night at the Sultan's palace, she'd wanted more of his caresses. Seducing him would achieve her freedom, while satiating the desire she felt for him. The question was whether Shaheen would resist her. He'd resisted temptation before, but not without difficulty.

She knew when a man desired her, and he was no different than any other. He wanted her. It was simply a matter of making him blind to anything but the sensations of pleasure. And given that day in Agdal Gardens, seducing him might not be difficult at all. She turned her back on him and removed her *gambaz*. Behind her, she heard him suck in a harsh breath.

"*Damm gahannam.*" The way he choked out his exclamation made her smile to herself. She hid her amusement and looked over her shoulder at him.

"What's wrong?"

"What the devil are you doing?"

"If you won't return me to Marrakech, I'm going to bed." She tossed the *gambaz* to one side then turned her attention to the drawstring of her *sherwals*. "I sleep better without any clothes."

She heard him inhale another sharp breath as she prepared to slide the *sherwals* off her hips. Large, warm hands prevented her from removing the pants as he grabbed her from behind and pulled her close. Soft wool caressed her bare back as a hard muscular body pressed into the length of hers. She didn't fight him as he prevented her from removing the garment.

"You seem to enjoy playing with fire, *ma chérie*," he rasped.

"It is you who plays with fire." She relaxed against him, feeling him accept her weight without hesitation. "You forget who you hold prisoner."

His soft laugh blew heat across her shoulder. "A man would be a fool to forget such a thing."

"I trust you're not a fool then." She smiled as his mouth nibbled at her ear. The back of his hand glided down the side of her neck and across her shoulder. It was a light touch, and it sent a tremor through her.

"Hardly," he murmured. "But I do know when I'm being manipulated."

Caught off guard by his comment, she stiffened in his arms.

With a quick movement, she jerked away from him and whirled around to face him. Reluctantly, she admitted that the only reason she could do so was because he'd allowed it. The shadows hid most of his expression from her, but she could see the firm, resolute line of his mouth.

"Then leave me be so I can go to sleep," she snapped.

"I'd be an even bigger fool to do that, don't you think?"

There was a rough edge to his voice that sent a fevered chill skating across her skin. The raw power and strength of him was undeniable, and for a fraction of a second, she hesitated. Perhaps he was right. Perhaps he was a fire she couldn't control. She mentally shrugged off the idea. Boldly, she stepped forward, and with a gentle tug, pulled his head down to hers. Her touch light, she brushed her lips against his.

"What I think is that I can pleasure you like no woman has ever pleasured you before."

A dark growl rumbled out of his throat as his hands slid up her waist to cup her breasts, his thumbs scraping across her nipples until they were hard, swelling with anticipation. Pressing deeper into his touch, she framed his face with her hands and kissed him. With a gentle nip to his bottom lip, she provoked another primitive sound from him as she sought the heat of his mouth. Her tongue twirled around his, plunging then retreating in an intimate dance of seduction.

Increasing the intensity of her kiss, her mouth teased, and yet demanded in bold strokes a passionate response from him. There was a leisurely bravura to her unhurried movements as she removed the cloth belt encircling his waist. Caught up in her spell, he didn't even consider resisting her as the material drifted to the floor and she slowly pulled his *gambaz* upward, enticing him to remove the oversized shirt.

Christ Jesus, but she was the most tantalizing creature he'd ever held in his arms. The image of Frances's face flickered briefly in his mind before his attention was quickly drawn back to the present. Having broken their kiss, Allegra's hot mouth had worked its way down the side of his throat and across his chest until her tongue licked at his nipple. An instant later, her teeth lightly bit down on him. Pain and intense pleasure mixed together to bring his cock to a full erection. In the space of less than a minute, she'd managed to bring him to the point of wanting to plunge into the heat of her, filling her until she cried out with the same need he was experiencing for her. Like an inexperienced young man intent on satisfying his first throes of lust, he half carried, half dragged her to the pile of pillows that served as his bed.

Tumbling downward, he tried to kiss her again, but she twisted away from him in an expert move to burn a path to his waist with her mouth. Unable to help himself, he groaned as her hand pressed firmly against his erection, stroking him through his *sherwals* in slow, mind-numbing strokes. The friction of the material against his skin intensified the pleasure of her touch, and he groaned a protest when her hand retreated.

Through the slits of his half-closed eyes, he watched her remove his boots before her hands slowly massaged their way back up to his waist. With agonizing leisurely strokes, she teased his body into a taut knot of need. God, he wanted her mouth on him, swallowing him with the same ease she had that damn banana. He reached for the waistband of his *sherwals*, but her hands stilled his.

"No," she said in a throaty whisper. "Let me."

Swallowing hard, he nodded his agreement. To his amazement, she grabbed the waist of his pants with her teeth. While one hand toyed with his nipple, the nails of her free hand raked across his buttocks as she pulled off the garment with her teeth and one hand. She stopped just past his erection to swirl her tongue around the tip of him.

Not once in all his years bedding a woman had he ever been driven to such an intense desire and lust with this kind of slow torment. He leaked a milky drop onto his stomach, and briefly closed his eyes in a fervent prayer that he wouldn't lose his seed before he buried himself inside her slick folds. And something told him she would be hot and creamy for him. It was there in the feverish glint of her green eyes as her gaze never left his the entire time she slowly removed the remainder of his clothing.

His cock jumped as she blew a cool breath across his skin before her teeth gently nipped at the inside of his thigh. He groaned with impatience, and yet she still didn't take him into her hot mouth. Tension gnawed at him with exquisite intensity.

"For the love of Christ, Allegra. Take me in your mouth." His hoarse demand brought her head up and she directed a seductive smile at him.

"Is that what you want, Shaheen?" She enunciated his name correctly, but there was a flavor all its own to the sound. It was the first time he'd ever heard an Englishwoman speak his Amazigh name, and on the tongue of this woman, it was seduction itself.

"Yes," he rasped.

Her eyes locked with his, she lowered her head toward the apex of his thighs. The heat of her tongue swirled across the head of his erection. Slowly, she licked and stroked her way down to the base of him. Seconds later she drew his bollocks into the liquid warmth of her mouth. With her tongue rolling his sacs around, she lifted her head pulling him slightly upward as her thumbs pressed firmly against the area of skin below. Surprised by the unexpected pressure, he uttered a guttural cry at the raw, primitive pleasure surging through his body. She rubbed at the sensitive spot, forcing his buttocks off the pillows in a sharp response.

Bollocks tight with the need to explode, he blindly reached for her, but she evaded him. Once again her tongue stroked his iron hard erection, all the while her thumbs continued to rub and apply pressure to the spot directly beneath his bollocks. When she took his cock into her mouth, he groaned deeply and shuddered at the sensations rippling over him. Christ, he wasn't capable of holding back. His hands grasped her head, urging her to move faster. Without hesitation, she obliged him.

Her name a hoarse cry on his lips, he exploded in the burning heat of her mouth. She swallowed his seed and continued to milk him as he throbbed wildly in her mouth. The intensity of the experience slowly eased, replaced with a sense of satisfaction and a trace of remorse. *Damm gahannam*, he'd been so caught up in his own pleasure, he'd failed to consider her needs. Completely spent, he didn't move as she sat up and stared down at him. A small smile on her face, she trailed her fingers across his thigh in a lazy move.

"I trust you were not disappointed." There was no hint of a question in her voice. She exuded the confidence of a woman certain of her skills when it came to satisfying a man.

"Your reputation doesn't do you justice, *ma belle*," he said quietly as he caught her hand and tugged her toward him. "But I regret not giving you satisfaction as well."

"My pleasure is unimportant," she murmured as she reclined back into the pillows.

He rolled onto his side to study her. Although she still wore her *sherwals*, the moonlight illuminated her full breasts and dark-colored nipples. Sliding his hand across her stomach, he brushed his fingers over one of the hard, peaked buds.

"On the contrary, *ma chérie*." He lowered his head to gently suck on a taut nipple for a brief instant. "I want to please you."

"Then send me back to Marrakech," she said in a throaty whisper that edged along his senses like a red-hot branding iron.

He came up on one elbow to look down at her. Her expression was soft and seductive as she stared up at him in wide-eyed expectation. Frances used to look at him the same way when she wanted something, exploiting every one of her feminine wiles to get what she wanted. This time he knew better than to allow himself to become tangled in the spider's web. In a casual gesture, he trailed his fingers from the base of her throat down to her waist.

"Do you really think I'm about to let you go now, *ma belle*?"

"I . . . I don't understand." Confusion darkened her eyes as she searched his face, a frown of bewilderment furrowing her brow.

"Don't you?" he said with a tight smile. "You just demonstrated to me why you're one of the world's most renowned courtesans. Can you blame me for wanting more?"

"M–more?" she stammered.

"Of course. I intend to avail myself of your charms as often as possible in the coming weeks."

Comprehension slowly dawned on her features, and she tried to sit upright. Arching an eyebrow at her, he quickly rolled over to trap her beneath him. Green eyes flashed with anger as she glared up at him. There was a fire in her that excited him, and he wasn't sure he liked the way it made him feel.

"If you think I'm going to give myself to you without hesitation, you're delusional," she choked out in a strained voice.

"I'm far from delusional, Allegra, nor am I easily swayed by your skills." Her eyes widened with alarm, and he smiled with satisfaction. "Did you really think you could seduce me into letting you go?"

10

She stared up at him, dumbfounded. She'd failed. Even at Madame Eugenie's she'd never failed to seduce and influence even the most difficult of customers. She'd never used her talent for personal gain, but it *had* protected her from the occasional ill-tempered lover or the unsolicited advances of an inebriated peer. She'd badly miscalculated his ability to remain unaffected by her.

The knowledge left her badly shaken. Her skill at seduction had sustained her all these years in her determination to shape her own destiny. Was it possible her ability to hold a man's attention, enthrall him, had been little more than an illusion, too?

Her failure to persuade him to let her go undermined her confidence in a way nothing else could. Now she had nothing left with which to bargain. All she'd done was whet his appetite for more. And hers, too, if she were being honest. She'd enjoyed pleasuring him, seeing him caught up in the heat of passion. The entire time she was caressing him with her mouth she'd been tempted to straddle him and take him inside her. The powerful image still lingered in her head, making her wonder what it would be like to give in to him.

She immediately shut herself off to such a choice. Surrendering was not an option. She refused to do it. The only thing remaining of her shattered independence was her ability to say no. If he meant to keep her here, he'd find her unwilling. She held her body rigid beneath his hard, muscular frame, and with a small shake of her head, she glared up at him.

"I have no intention of sharing your bed."

"Ah, but you're already here, *helwa jahannam meshsh.*"

Dear God, there was a dark arousal in his voice that threatened to destroy all her resistance to him. It was the tone of a teasing lover. And whatever name he called her in the language of the Bedouins, it sounded almost affectionate. His thumb brushed over the peak of her breast. The nipple tightened at the pleasurable sensation, and she cursed the way her body reacted to the hot touch. Deliberately, she closed her mind off in the same way she'd done when she'd been with the men she'd serviced at Madame Eugenie's.

"There is a difference between choice and necessity. Do not mistake a service performed for anything more than it was—a simple milking," she said coldly.

Every hard muscle brushing against her body grew taut at her words. His amusement disappeared and a grim expression swept across his face. "And is the price I paid for you any less than what Shaftsbury and others have paid for your *services*?"

The words sliced deep. It made everything in her life sound cheap and sordid. And she didn't believe that. She was simply a survivor. Her choices had been nonexistent at Madame Eugenie's, and when the opportunity had come to change all of that, she'd taken it. Her mother might have sold her into whoredom, but she'd never allowed it to own her. She wouldn't apologize to anyone for making the best of what life offered her.

Arthur had given her the world, and she refused to squander that gift. Her lovers might seek her out because of an illusion, but when she welcomed them into her bed, they received much more. She gave them her undivided attention. She soothed their frustrations, debated all manner of topics, eased their sorrows, satisfied their lust, and offered them her friendship.

In turn, they gave her independence. Something few women even dreamed of, let alone obtained. Being able to choose her lovers was the most precious thing she possessed. That was something this man didn't understand or refused to see.

"Just because you gave Nassar your horse for me, doesn't mean you own me." She shoved at his solid, muscular chest in a futile effort to free herself.

"Is the price I paid any different than the money and jewels your lovers give you?"

"How many times do I have to tell you that I *choose* my lovers," she said through clenched teeth. "They don't buy me."

"You didn't answer my question, *ma belle*. Is what I paid any less than what others have paid?"

She glared at him in frustration. It was as if he was accusing her of something, some fault of character. And she was certain it didn't matter how she answered him. His opinion of her would remain the same. His dark frown was a harsh reminder that she was still at his mercy.

"What you paid was the equivalent of perhaps two weeks of my undivided attention. No more," she said flatly. She had no idea whether it was an accurate statement. Until now, she'd never tried to put a price on her time.

"Two weeks?" he mused as if thinking out loud. "The question now is whether it was a fair price to pay."

She had no time to respond before his mouth captured hers. The unexpected shock of his lips heating hers stole her breath away. Pleasure danced across her skin, and she realized she wasn't even attempting to put up a struggle. Her mind dismissed the thought like one might deflect an insect buzzing around one's head. Instead, her mouth parted beneath his demanding kiss. Hot and tantalizing, his tongue mated with hers, circling, tempting, stroking the warm insides of her mouth with a skill none of her other lovers had possessed.

She couldn't remember ever wanting to melt mindlessly in a man's arms before, but she wanted to do exactly that right now. Every one of her senses was alive and crying out for more. From the earthy male scent teasing her nose to the warm spicy flavor of his mouth, her body craved more. Even the rough pad of his thumb scraping over her skin created a hunger for more of his touch.

A low growl rumbled in his chest, raw and primeval in nature. It tugged at her until her body arched up toward him like an instrument responding to a maestro's touch. She had no doubt the primitive note was meant to brand her. And it made her hover on the fine line dividing exhilaration and fear. Part of her rejoiced in the exquisite sensations he aroused in her, while another, smaller part of her cried out a warning.

She fought to hear the admonition, but lost the battle the moment his mouth slid gently, tenderly along her bruised jaw and down the side of her throat. Molten heat wound its way through her veins as his firm lips lingered on the frantic beat of her pulse while his thumb abraded her nipple. Each caress stirred a fire in her belly that streaked its way downward to her nether regions.

With a languid move, he slid his body down hers until his mouth was over one breast. His tongue flicked out to lave the stiff peak in a white-hot caress that sent pleasure rippling through her. God, she was out of her mind to allow this to continue, and yet she didn't want him to stop. Desire rocked through her at a blistering speed and she sucked in a quick breath of air.

The unique scent of him washed over her anew. Cedar with just a bite of licorice filled her senses. It was a tantalizing smell. All male and dangerously potent. His mouth burned a trail across her skin and she moaned softly. Sweet heaven, but the man was a master at manipulating her body until she wanted nothing more than to surrender to his fiery demands.

The moment the thought whirled through her head, she grew stiff with horror. Dear lord, how had she come to this moment—ready and willing to surrender her will to him? She couldn't relinquish her independence, no matter how hypnotically tantalizing the man's touch was. She'd given up too much already. The cold seeping into her made her shiver, and not even the warmth of his hands on her stomach penetrated the icy fear layering her skin.

He raised his head to look at her, and her mouth went dry at his expression. His features wore the look of a conqueror intent on showing mercy to a vanquished foe. It was evident he believed he'd won her surrender, and it deepened the fear winding its way through her. She didn't have the physical strength to fight him even if it were possible to crush the desire he aroused in her, but she did have her wits. And words were her most powerful weapon at the moment.

"I take it my performance is meeting your expectations, my lord," she said in a voice that expressed utter boredom. "I want to ensure you receive your money's worth."

Given how badly rattled she was by his caresses, it amazed her that she'd managed to make it sound as if her response to him had been nothing more than an exhibition of sexual skill. Almost instantly, the benign satisfaction on his face gave way to something dark and dangerous. The ferocity of his anger sent trepidation spiraling through her.

Refusing to let her apprehension control her reaction, she didn't avert her gaze from his furious glare. Instead, she arched an eyebrow at him in a mocking manner. It had been an enormous risk insulting him like this. And it *was* an insult to suggest she'd staged her response to his advances. Men didn't like being made fools of when it came to bedroom sport. The bitter twist of his lips wasn't nearly as harsh as the way his gaze slid over her with utter contempt.

"My money's worth? I think I paid too much." His voice was a blast of frigid air over her skin. "Your skills are exceptional, *chérie*, but like any other whoring slut, your duplicity in bed is more than transparent."

Unable to stop herself, she flinched beneath his dark rage. Once again, she'd made a mistake in her estimation of this man. Not even Charles in his anger had ever referred to her in such coarse terms. Whatever had made her think she could handle his wrath? He looked ready to kill her.

The thought sent fear skidding through her. This wasn't the reaction of a man who'd just had his prowess in the bedroom called into question. She should have known he was far too confident to ever believe he might be lacking expertise. The black fury on his features sharpened the contours of his face until he resembled an avenging angel. His expression made it clear she'd released something horrible and bleak from deep inside him.

With a powerful, lithe movement, he got to his feet and reached for his clothing. The strand of moonlight fluttering down into the tent lit up his entire body. Soft and translucent, the light was a sharp contrast to the hardness of his sinewy frame. It was the body of a lover she knew would please her in ways no other man had before. She turned her head away from him as he dressed. Hadn't she learned her lesson? She'd barely managed to avoid an entanglement with the man. Even if she appeased his anger, the last thing she needed to do was invite more trouble on herself.

Completely dressed, he strode toward the flap of the tent. One hand parting the wool door to one side, he stopped and stared out into the dark night. Even in the dim light, his fury was all too visible in his taut, tension-filled posture. She swallowed hard.

"Be forewarned, *ma chérie*," he said in a velvety tone that belied the inflexible steel beneath. "If you try to leave camp again, I'll not be as merciful with you as I have been tonight."

"Merciful?" she snapped in frustration. "Showing mercy would be to let me go. You don't have the right to keep me here." She sat upright and grabbed her *gambaz*, clutching it to her chest as he slowly turned his head to look at her.

"As Sheikh of this tribe, my word is law. You'll remain here as my guest until *I* say you're free to leave."

The icy words made the temperature in the tent drop even lower, and she shivered at the contempt glittering in his dark eyes. He didn't wait for her reply before he simply vanished in a flash of furious movement. The thick flap of wool serving as a door smacked angrily against the side of the tent as he left her alone. Closing her eyes, she sank back down into the pillows that covered the pallet.

The stillness of the night was almost absolute, and a tremor sped through her, followed by another and then another. The relief of having survived Shaheen's icy rage was second only to the fact that she'd earned a reprieve from his attempts to win her surrender. She inhaled a deep breath.

Remain here as his guest. More like a nightingale in a gold cage is what he meant, and all because he didn't want Charles finding him. Something had transpired in his past that had hardened his heart against his family. So much so, that he'd discarded his English name and lifestyle to live in obscurity as one of the Bedouins. Whatever had happened, it had to have involved a woman. His reaction to her insult had been that of a man scorned.

But not just any woman—a mistress, possibly even a courtesan like herself. He'd not tried to defend his abilities as a lover like she'd expected. Instead, he'd accused her of being a lying whore. She stared up at the moonlight filtering its way through the seam in the tent. Her words had stirred something in him much deeper than offended pride.

Whatever old memories her words had brought to the surface, they had only reinforced his decision to keep her here, at least until Charles was no longer in Marrakech. But even if his past had remained buried, she was certain he would have kept her here just the same. She was a challenge.

His stubborn nature would make it difficult to accept defeat where she was concerned. Her resistance only made him that much more determined to bend her to his will—to seduce her into choosing him. He'd almost succeeded. The thought terrified her. She'd never met a man who'd come so close to breaking through all of her defenses like this man could and *had*. She shivered again. If only she could go to sleep and wake up from this nightmare.

Exhausted, her eyes fluttered shut. The one thing she'd learned after Arthur had died was that things always looked better in the morning light. Tomorrow would be a better day. She was free of Nassar's vicious captivity, and while Shaheen's anger had alarmed her, she knew there had to be a valid reason for his fury. She forced her eyes open and she saw the moonlight dancing its way through the tent seam. Once more, her eyes drifted shut and when she opened them again, sunlight was streaming into the tent and outside the camp was bustling with activity.

A quiet sound drew her attention toward a young woman who entered with a small tray of food. Following close behind her, a child pushed past the wool flap carrying a pitcher, bowl, and cloths.

"*Manger, anasi.*" The woman gestured toward the food, and

Allegra found her friendly smile too engaging to resist. With a smile, she nodded her gratitude.

The boy eyed her with something that wavered between annoyance and dismissal. She remembered Cordelia had often worn a similar look as a child when ordered to do something she didn't like. The memory made her smile at him with amusement. When he tipped his nose up in the air, she experienced a wrenching wave of homesickness. Despite the yearning, it was impossible to keep from laughing when the boy rolled his eyes at her and scurried from the tent. The woman said something in the Bedouin language, a look of regret on her face. Waving her hand at what was clearly an apology for the boy's behavior, Allegra laughed.

"Les garçons seront des garçons." Relief swept across the Bedouin woman's face at the old adage that boys will be boys. With a slight bow of respect, she followed the child out of the tent.

The aroma of something hot and sweet pulled her over to the small tray sitting on a low pedestal. The smell wafted up from the bowl on the tray. She tested the gruel, savoring the honey sweet taste. Her stomach growled for more, and she quickly finished off the hot dish while enjoying the juicy pomegranate cut open on the tray. When she'd finished eating, she took a quick sponge bath, which left her feeling clean and refreshed. A short time later, she emerged from the tent with renewed hope that she would find a way to return to Marrakech.

Shaheen's tent, unlike Nassar's, didn't stand apart from the rest of the dark brown and beige-colored tents that surrounded his. She walked through the camp, waiting for someone to stop her, but no one did. Instead, she was greeted with friendly smiles and polite nods as she continued her explorations.

She rounded the corner of a tent and entered a large circle that seemed to be a hub of activity. She saw Shaheen in the midst of an intense discussion, towering over most of the men around him. Her heart skipped a beat at the sight of him. It wasn't a sensation she wanted to feel, particularly when she saw the cold disdain in his eyes when he caught sight of her. He was still furious, and his dismissing look sent regret pulsing through her at having put a barrier between them.

The alarming emotion made her swallow hard. God, she was a fool. That barrier was all that protected her from complete surrender. She needed to find a way out of this golden cage or she would be lost in more ways than she cared to imagine. Quickly turning away from Shaheen's stern profile, she retreated around another tent and walked around the outside of the encampment. She passed the horses, hobbled in the same spot as they had been last night. Sighing at her failure, she continued her walk.

As she rounded the last tent on the outer edges of the site, she drew in her breath at the sight of a large roan stallion grazing at what little he could find on the ground. The animal sensed her presence and threw his head up to turn and look at her. There was a wild, arrogant manner to the horse as if he knew he was king of his world. From where she stood, she saw him flick his ears back and forth.

When he seemed satisfied that she wasn't a threat, the animal lowered his head again with a haughty dismissal. She studied the stallion for a long moment, noting the power in his movements as he moved from one patch of grass to another. Here was an animal that could outrun even the horse Shaheen had ridden yesterday.

She ignored the small warning going off in her head. It didn't matter whether the horse had been broken or not. She was an experienced rider, and if she gave the animal its head in the right direction she'd let him run himself out to the point where he'd be more manageable. She just had to stay seated. Confident she could do so, she glanced around for a bridle.

Not seeing one, she hurried back to where the other horses were tethered and retrieved the tack she needed. When she returned, the giant roan hadn't wandered far in the limited space he'd been afforded. She experienced a sense of kinship with the animal.

Like her, he was hostage to the line that prevented him from running away. Slowly, she walked toward the animal, keeping her voice soft and steady like her grooms did with the high-strung horses in her stables. The horse snorted loudly as she closed in on him and she halted immediately. When he resumed eating, she moved forward again. As she reached him, he threw up his head with another loud breath of air puffing out of his nose.

Gently, she reached out to stroke his jowl. When he didn't move, she stepped closer. She continued to rub his cheek while speaking softly to him. He tossed his head, but didn't shy away from her as she ran the leather bridle across the side of his head and down his nose. With a shake of his head, he nipped at the bridle's leather. Quickly, Allegra slid the steel bit into his mouth and past his teeth. He gnawed at the metal bar, but didn't seem bothered by it.

Pleased with her success to this point, she hastily slipped the rest of the bridle over first one ear and then another. With the bridle secure on the stallion, she freed the animal from the lead line. The sound of a soft cry startled her, and she jerked her head around to meet the wide-eyed gaze of the boy she'd seen earlier.

Aware that her window of a head start had just narrowed, she led the stallion toward a nearby bucket. Kicking it over, she positioned the horse so she could use the pail as a step stool to mount the animal. The minute she was astride him, his entire demeanor changed. No longer docile and compliant, he tossed his head and reared up on his hind legs.

She buried her fingers and the reins in the stallion's wiry mane and clung to it in a death grip. At the same time, she clenched her thighs tightly against the horse's sides, determined not to let him prevent her from reaching Marrakech. She was through letting others control her and her destiny.

※

The moment the men dispersed to attend to their duties, Shaheen found himself searching the area for a glimpse of Allegra. When she'd appeared in the central gathering space of the encampment a short time ago, his gut had clenched with a mixture of emotions that ranged from anger to a stark hunger. He needed his anger to help him keep his distance from her, particularly when the woman had the power to twist him into knots.

Last night, when she'd tried to convince him that her response to his touch was nothing more than practiced skill, he'd been furious that she thought him a fool. Her mockery had hit too close to home. It had brought back vivid images of that night in Frances's town house in Mayfair.

His mistress had played a twisted game by fucking his brother at the same time she was sharing his own bed. Frances hadn't been just greedy, she'd been clever and deceitful as well. Neither he nor James had realized it until it was too late.

Frances's behavior toward the end had made him suspicious that the courtesan was seeing another man. The night of James's death, he'd called on her unexpectedly, but she'd been alone and denied involvement with anyone else. Like a fool, he'd believed her and allowed his lust to blind him to her treachery.

When James had discovered them in bed a few hours later, his brother's reaction to the sight of them had been one of uncanny silence. But the acrimony in his brother's gaze had sliced through him with the ugliness of a dull blade. The icy expression in James's eyes that night had hurtled him back to the pain of his childhood. A pain that his brother had made bearable by being his protector, champion, and consoler even into adulthood. But Frances had taken his brother from him.

He closed his eyes against the memory until the sound of someone clearing their throat made him turn his head and focus his gaze on Jamal's wry expression.

"I see you prevented the *anasi* from escaping last night," the Amazigh said with a chuckle. "I'm beginning to think that old witch Halah has the eye after all."

"What the devil is that supposed to mean?" he growled.

With a shake of his head, the Bedouin's grin widened. "Nothing at all, particularly if one ignores the *anasi's* fiery-colored hair and temperament."

"If that's your cryptic way of saying I've staked my claim on Allegra, you're wrong."

"Then you will have some explaining to do when Mahmoud arrives. It is the first time since the day Yasmia died that you have not had Hakim close at your side."

Shaheen scowled at his friend. "The boy is almost a man, and it's time for him to take on more responsibility. I didn't send him to Khalid's camp at Sidi Rahal alone. Should I have taken him with us to find Nassar?"

"No. It would have been a mistake to take him with us."

"I'm glad you agree," he snapped. "As it is, if Nassar is plotting something, we're ill prepared. Add to the night watch, and I want anything out of the ordinary—"

The sudden shouts echoing from the northern edge of the encampment took them by surprise, causing them both to jerk around. Not hesitating, Shaheen raced toward the sound. As he sprinted past other members of the tribe hurrying to answer the calls, he kept looking for Allegra's familiar figure among those he passed. Something in his gut clenched when he didn't see her anywhere.

Another cry went up again, and this time he was able to make out the words Ahmar Jinn. He grimaced. Some young fool was trying to ride Red Devil again. Rounding the corner of a tent, he slid to a halt, his skin growing cold as he saw Allegra astride the massive roan stallion.

The muscles of the animal's neck knotted with tension as he tossed his head angrily. Nostrils flaring, the horse rose up on its hind legs. He didn't know how, but somehow Allegra managed to remain on the animal's back. In a low, ominous voice, he ordered the gathering throng of spectators to be quiet.

With an angry cry, Ahmar Jinn arched his back and kicked his hind legs outward. The vicious whiplike movement sent his heart crashing violently into his chest as he saw Allegra slip slightly on the animal's back. Sweet Jesus, she wasn't using a saddle. She righted herself and reined the animal's head to one side until his nose almost touched her leg. The stallion squealed his protest as the move made it difficult for him to buck.

"Don't come any closer. You'll only agitate him that much more." Even though she never looked at him, Allegra's voice echoed harshly across the short distance between them.

"Get off the horse now, Allegra," he commanded in a low voice. Despite his anger and fear, he marveled at the skillful way she was handling the fractious animal. "He's dangerous. He's already injured two of my best riders."

She ignored his quiet order and leaned forward to talk softly to the horse. It was impossible to hear her words, but there was something about the set of her jaw that said she wasn't about to obey him. Ahmar Jinn danced restlessly in a tight circle, his powerful legs pounding the earth in angry repetition.

"Damn it, Allegra. Get off that animal now before you get yourself killed," he rasped.

Maintaining the grip on her reins, she ignored him to lean

forward again and murmur something in a soothing voice to the horse. With a gentle tug of the reins, she turned the animal around so he was facing the plains that stretched out in the direction of Marrakech.

"*Merde*," he exclaimed as he realized what she was planning.

He didn't wait to see her urge the stallion forward as he whirled around and raced around the perimeter of the camp to where the other horses were. As fast as he could, he bridled Tarek then launched himself up onto the animal's bare back. As he wheeled the Arabian away from the camp, he saw Jamal bridling his own horse as well.

With a sharp command, he urged Tarek into a flat-out gallop. Allegra had already put an incredible distance between them, and he could only hope he could catch her before something terrible happened to her. And when he caught up with her, he was going to flay her hide for daring to disobey him in front of his people, not to mention putting herself in harm's way.

He'd been riding at a hard gallop for almost half an hour before it became apparent he was gaining on her. She'd clearly not slowed her mount any, and he knew her desire to escape had made her push Ahmar Jinn too hard. The stallion was fast, but Tarek was exercised daily and better able to handle long distances at the pace Allegra was trying to maintain. The fact that she was still on the stallion amazed him. With her knowledge of horseflesh he'd automatically assumed she knew how to ride, but he'd never considered the possibility that she might excel at it. She was the only rider, aside from him and Malik's father, who'd managed to stay seated on Ahmar Jinn for any length of time. But she was the first to ride the stallion for this long.

More than a half hour ago, Marrakech had been a small strip on the horizon, but now it loomed large enough for him to easily identify the Koutoubia Mosque. He saw Allegra glance over her shoulder at him, her face filled with panic. Bending over Ahmar Jinn's neck, she slapped the reins against the stallion's hindquarters and urged him on to a breakneck speed that made Shaheen's mouth go dry with fear.

If the stallion stumbled, she'd never survive a fall. With a soft word to Tarek, he urged his mount to increase their speed. Lathered with sweat, the Arabian dug into the ground at a blistering pace, eating up the distance between him and the tiring red stallion. As he pulled even with Allegra, she tried to swerve away from him, but failed as his hands grasped Ahmar Jinn's reins.

As he gently pulled back on the reins of both animals, her nails raked across the back of his hand in her effort to break his grip on the leather. The sting of the scratch made him grimace, but he continued to tug on the reins so both horses slid to a halt at almost the exact same instant. When he looked at her, the desperation in her face was so powerful that he froze beneath the guilty weight of it.

In that split second, she leaped from Ahmar Jinn's back and ran in the direction of Marrakech. Unable to forget the look on her face, he watched her flee. Should he let her go—say to hell with his cousin discovering his identity? *No.* If the treaties collapsed, the tribes would return to warring among themselves, meaning more bloodshed. Once his cousin returned to England, he would send her back to Marrakech. He tried to suppress the taunting laughter in the back of his head, and the voice that called him a liar. Dropping Ahmar Jinn's reins to the ground, he rode after her. In a few short strides, he leaned over in the saddle and lifted her with one arm to set her in front of him. With an angry cry, she struggled hard and her fist caught him in the jaw. The blow sent pain ricocheting through his face and toward the back of his head.

"*Enough*, goddamn it," he rasped. "Enough."

"Let me go!" When she swung her fist at him one more time,

he ruthlessly pinned her arms against her sides as he tucked her tightly in his grasp.

"I'll let you go when I'm good and ready." Glaring down at her, he wavered between relief that she was safe and fury at her recklessness. "I ought to beat some sense into you. That little stunt of yours could have easily gotten you or someone else killed."

Her mouth drawn tight with mutiny, she met his gaze with defiance before turning her head away to stare out at Marrakech. The rebellious expression on her face disappeared as she studied the city she'd been trying so desperately to reach. Long, dark lashes brushed against rose-hued skin as she closed her eyes. Vanquished in her quest for freedom, she was the image of vulnerability and fragility. His forefinger caught a single tear that rolled down her cheek. Despite her despondence, she displayed her contempt for him by jerking her head away from his touch. Her sorrow and anger edged across his senses with the sharpness of a steel blade.

Damn it to hell, in the space of seconds, the woman had managed to erase his anger and leave him dangling in the wind. Once again, he considered letting her return to Marrakech. It was a fleeting thought. He turned Tarek around and headed toward camp. Jamal had caught up to them, and the Bedouin had Ahmar Jinn well in hand. As Shaheen rode past his friend, Allegra twisted violently in his arms.

"If you won't give me my freedom, the least you can do is let me ride with him."

She tossed her head in Jamal's direction, her anger a tangible force in the rigidity of her body. Ignoring her, he replied by prodding Tarek into a smooth canter. Her sharp inhalation of anger made him look down at her face. Gone was the defeated, vulnerable woman he'd seen seconds before. In her place was the stubborn, haughty courtesan who captivated and infuriated him in one breath.

His jaw clenched tight with anger, he glanced away from her. Hadn't his experience with Frances taught him anything? Last night Allegra had lied to him, out of self-preservation perhaps, but she'd lied nonetheless. And she'd used that incredible mouth of hers to try and persuade him to release her. It had been a deliberate attempt to manipulate him. She might not be as devious as Frances had been, but she hadn't hesitated to use her body to achieve her goal.

Still, he couldn't deny there was something special about her. Frances had been a shallow creature, but Allegra had hidden depths to her. And he admired her spirit. Few women would have stood up to Nassar the way she had. Then there was that amazing ride just now on Ahmar Jinn. No woman he'd ever met would have done either of those things, let alone defy him in the matter.

Beautiful, spirited, and brave. A hazardous combination in any woman, but in a courtesan—lethal. Grimacing, he barely suppressed his snort of irritation. He now had the unpleasant task of curbing that spirit of hers. She'd defied him in front of the tribe. It wasn't something he could let go unpunished or he'd be viewed as weak. Damnation, but the woman had made things that much worse. If she detested him now, she was going to loathe him when they got back to camp.

11

As they rode into camp, Shaheen's embrace tightened around her. She flinched as her body responded to the increased pressure of his arm about her waist. While her head protested, her body melted willingly into his as he pulled her closer. Oh God, why did her body have to betray her like this? This was the real reason she'd risked riding that brute of a horse.

She'd been running away. Marrakech meant she could return to England and the safety of a life she knew well. A life where she was always in control of her senses, her emotions. Not this unbridled desire Shaheen stirred in her. A hunger that threatened to spiral out of control at any moment, leaving her vulnerable in ways she didn't want to consider.

Uncontrolled passion had been something she avoided. While every man she'd welcomed into her bed had experienced both pleasure and desire, she had never shared herself completely or with abandon. Surrendering to passion meant she might lose her heart.

But with this man, it would be easy to surrender, and the thought terrified her. That fear had driven her to run as far away as she could. And she had almost escaped him. She'd almost reached the safe haven of Marrakech when he'd reached out and snatched freedom from her.

Dark brown hands pulled the horse to a halt, and in a lithe movement he dismounted. All too aware of his displeasure, she slid off the horse to land lightly at his side. He didn't look at her, but his anger was a tangible sensation across her skin. Retreat seemed the best option at the moment. Glancing toward his tent, she took one step in that direction. In that split second, his fingers bit painfully into her upper arm. Unable to suppress her cry, she wordlessly protested the bruising pain his grip caused.

"Not yet, *ma belle*, we have some unfinished business."

The grim resignation in his quiet words sent a chill sliding down her back. Without any other warning, he dragged her toward the center of the camp. As he did so, he called out in the Bedouin tongue that was that odd mix of French and Berber. She could only make out a word or two here and there, and while it was impossible to understand everything he was saying, she heard the words *disobedience* and *consequences*.

Whatever he was saying, everyone was listening and following them. The moment they reached the communal campfire, he sank down on a large log. With a sharp jerk, he pulled her across his knee. In the next instant, his hand cracked across her bottom through the thin *sherwals* she wore. The initial sting of the blow stunned her for a few seconds, her mind not fully comprehending what was happening. When he spanked her again, her disbelief evaporated and she fought wildly to twist away from him. He thwarted her efforts, and struck her once more.

"Let me go," she exclaimed with a hiss of fury.

"Do not struggle, *ma belle*. It will only go that much harder for you."

"Bastard!"

"Perhaps, but if I were any other man, I would be using a whip on you." His hand stung her backside with another sharp crack. "Everyone in the camp witnessed your disobedience when I ordered you off of Ahmar Jinn. I cannot let that go unpunished."

"Disobedience implies you have domain over me, and you do not," she bit out through clenched teeth as she fought back tears.

His paddling wasn't anywhere near as painful as the humiliation she was suffering. The public forum and method he'd chosen to rebuke her with was devastating. Again his hand made contact with her bottom. God, how she hated him. First he'd chosen to hold her hostage, now he was making an example of her. Mortified by the public manner in which he carried out his punishment, she closed her eyes, wishing the ground would open up and swallow them whole. She lapsed into silence, and when he finally released her, she slowly rose to her feet.

Fingernails digging into her palms, she fought to keep from leaping forward and scratching his eyes out. In a way, this incident was even more humiliating than the bartering he'd done with Nassar. Being sold had brought back horrible memories, but it had been accomplished in the privacy of Nassar's tent.

But this—he'd punished her in front of the tribe to solidify his authority. She shuddered. Facing Lady Bledsoe's condescension, spite, and hate in public would be far more bearable than this degrading experience. Calling upon every bit of composure she could dredge up from inside her, she squared her shoulders and held her head at a haughty angle.

"Are you quite finished, *my lord*?" she sneered. The insolence in her voice stressed that he was anything but a nobleman.

His head jerked sharply in her direction as he met her gaze with repressed outrage. Satisfaction clipped through her. Something had told her the use of his title would anger him. She'd struck him a blow and it elated her. Glaring up into his face with every bit of defiance she could muster, she silently announced how much she despised him.

His features could have been stone except for the single muscle that twitched in his cheek. He seemed to be struggling with an emotion she couldn't define, and for a brief second she wondered if he regretted inflicting his punishment on her. No, *remorse* wasn't in the man's vocabulary.

When he dismissed her with an abrupt nod, she whirled away from him. Forced to meet the eyes of those who'd watched her humiliation, she froze in her tracks. Then with as much dignity as she could command, she lifted her head higher and stalked back to Shaheen's tent. The silence was deafening as the crowd parted and made a path for her. Clinging to what little composure she had left, she forced herself to maintain a dignified pace. Only when she was hidden from view did she allow herself to run as fast as she could to the tent.

❦

Every one of Shaheen's muscles ached from the tension holding him stiff and immobile as he watched Allegra disappear from view. Christ Jesus, what the hell was happening to him? He'd never hit a woman before in his life, not even Frances. And her behavior had been far more deserving of a beating than Allegra's minor transgression. Why the devil hadn't he found some other type of punishment for her? Shoving a hand through his hair, he glared at one of the men who had lingered behind, causing the man to hurry away. With uncharacteristic fury, he slammed his fist into a nearby post that served as a support for a roasting spit.

"Take care with your hand, Shaheen. If the *anasi* misbehaves again, you will have need of it." Quiet condemnation filled Jamal's voice.

"What do you suggest I should have done?" he snarled. "Allegra openly defied me in front of the men. We both know a leader cannot lead if he has no respect."

"Agreed, I simply think her punishment could have been less humiliating. Nassar accomplished that task well enough with her. It disappoints me to see you do so as well."

"Do *not* compare me to that murderous bastard." Shaheen's hand slashed through the air in harsh rebuke. "Nassar would have beaten her with a whip for less, enjoying every minute of it."

"Perhaps I am too harsh in comparing your actions to Nassar, but you must look into your heart and consider whether it was the *anasi* you were punishing or another woman."

"Don't lecture me about my past, Jamal," he ground out between clenched teeth. "We both know it's not up for discussion."

"I think it is, given the current situation," Jamal said harshly. "The *anasi* is a courtesan. A woman much like the woman you loved a long time ago."

"Do not test our friendship in this way, Jamal." He directed a cold look of fury at the older man, but the Bedouin never flinched.

"The *anasi* is not the woman from your past. She did not pull the trigger the night your brother died."

With a roar of anger, he lunged toward Jamal with an explosive movement, but the Amazigh was quick and darted out of the way. Stumbling to a halt, Shaheen turned to face his tormentor and shook his head.

"You should have left me to rot that day in the desert."

"That would have made it easy for you, no? Die rather than face the truth about your brother's death." Jamal shook his head sadly and remained silent for a long moment.

"We're done here," Shaheen rasped as he turned and started to walk away.

"You must release the *anasi*, Shaheen. Whatever happens to the treaties will happen. It is in God's hands, not yours. Allegra Synnford bears no responsibility for your past or what happens among the Amazigh."

He came to an abrupt halt as Jamal's words pierced him with a keen sense of guilt. His friend was right, he should let Allegra go, but something inside him refused to part with her. He shook his head and glanced over his shoulder.

"Allegra stays."

"She will come to hate you," Jamal said with a sigh.

"We shall see."

With that grim reply, he strode away as if the devil was on his heels. Eager to find a quiet place to think, he left camp and walked the half a mile to the tribe's primary source of water. Small, yet vital to the countryside, the stream flowed well, thanks to the late winter rains. Rainfall over the past winter had helped to ensure the brook would meet his people's needs until the winter rains would fall again.

He squatted on the edge of the narrow channel to trail his fingers through the cool water. It was a precious commodity on the Moroccan plains, and he understood why the tribes had warred with each other for centuries. Water was the difference between life and death for the Amazigh and other Berber tribes. It had kept him alive that day Jamal had found him in the desert.

If not for his friend, he would have died. He'd not been grateful for the Bedouin's interference, but over time he'd found ways to keep the past from haunting him. But that had changed the moment he found himself craving Allegra's touch. There was guilt in that need. A culpability for desiring a woman who symbolized the very thing that destroyed his life and that of his brother.

A cold chill spread its way across his skin as he remembered Frances's unpleasant laughter when James had found him in bed with the courtesan. He'd dressed quickly, but his brother had disappeared by the time he'd managed to plunge his way out into the snow-covered street. For more than an hour he looked for James.

He'd searched everywhere before returning to the town house they shared to find the household in an uproar. James had tried to kill himself in the study, but the staff had thwarted his efforts. Bleeding from his botched attempt, his brother had staggered out of the house despite attempts to stop him. It hadn't been difficult to conclude where James was headed, and he'd raced back to Frances's house.

When he burst into Frances's bedroom, he'd found James standing over her, spattered with blood. The woman had fallen backward onto the mattress, her head turned toward the door so it seemed as though she were looking directly at him. But her wide-eyed gaze remained unmoving and vacant. Horror, fear, and panic held him in place as he looked at Frances and then his brother. James's voice filled his head again as if it were yesterday.

"She laughed about it, Robert. She found it amusing that she was fucking the two of us at the same time. She tried to tell me you betrayed me."

"James, listen to me. You need to put the gun down."

"You wouldn't betray me like that, would you?"

"No! You know me better than that. You're my brother, James, I wouldn't deceive you. I swear I didn't know she was seeing anyone else, and certainly not you. I would have finished with her if I had known." He took a step closer, his hands raised in a gesture of surrender. James nodded, his expression one of understanding.

"I told her I didn't believe her—that she was a liar. I knew you couldn't betray me. She lied to me, Robert. She said I was the only one she loved." His brother looked down at Frances with a bitter twist of his lips. *"That's why I had to do it. She lied. I loved her and she lied to me."*

"James, I want you to put the gun down." He moved deeper into the room, desperate to stop his brother. *"We can work this out together, but you need to put the gun down."*

"We both know I can't do that." James's voice held a flat note of resignation. The resolute acceptance on his brother's features sent panic streaking through him, and he took another step toward him.

"God damn it, James. Put the gun down."

"I'm sorry, Robert." Without another word, James swung the gun up to the side of his head and pulled the trigger.

Unable to help himself, Shaheen released a low cry of anguish as the pain of that moment washed over him once again. No matter how many times he replayed the scene in his head, the horror of it was still as vivid as the night it happened. He looked down at his hands, half expecting to see James's blood on his palms from where he'd held his brother until the servants had arrived with the police.

Springing to his feet, he swallowed the emotions closing his throat. It had been impossible not to blame himself for James's death. His father had been even less forgiving when he learned his eldest son was dead. He grimaced at the memory of his father's bitterness. It reminded him of the hostility and resentment in Allegra's eyes after her punishment.

He winced. She had good reason to hate him. He'd humiliated her in front of the entire tribe. It hadn't been his finest hour, and he should have made allowances for her. She wasn't familiar with the harsh life of the Bedouins or their culture. Could he have avoided all of this if he'd explained everything to her yesterday—the treaties, his cousin—all of it?

With a soft noise of disgust, he shook his head and headed back toward camp. She'd done nothing to prove to him she could be trusted. The memory of how she'd avoided Hakim at the Sultan's palace made him grunt. It was one instance—she'd done nothing else to inspire his confidence. She was a courtesan. A woman trained in the art of manipulation when it came to her best interests. She'd used those skills last night thinking she could persuade him to send her back to Marrakech. He was a fool to think her anything more than that. But he did.

She was strong, independent, courageous, and honorable. Even her attempt to manipulate him last night had been to regain control of her life. She was unlike any woman he'd ever met. Comparing her to Frances was impossible. No two women were ever so different. And there were few women in the peerage who could match her strength of spirit.

Then there was his physical need for her. It was a craving that came from deep within, and he didn't know how to control it. It threatened to get out of hand, and it cut too close to home. He didn't need Jamal to tell him the treaties were nothing but an excuse to keep her here. Yet it hadn't stopped him from using it as a justification for his actions.

He knew better, but there was something about her that set his blood on fire. Perhaps it was his belief that hidden behind the façade of a seductive, well-trained courtesan was a woman no man had ever reached. A woman who hid her vulnerability behind a mask of confidence and erotic sangfroid. He didn't just want Allegra the courtesan—he wanted the woman behind the mask.

Without even realizing where his footsteps were taking him, he found himself standing outside his tent. He strained to hear any noise emanating from inside, but heard nothing. He stood there debating his next course of action. Damnation, he wanted to see her, to explain. *Merde*, what was there to explain?

Everything and nothing.

Like a caged tiger, he prowled the area in front of the tent. Then with a growl, he pushed aside the flap and entered the interior. She sat curled up among the pillows on the pallet. The accusatory look in her eyes tore at him worse than anything Jamal could have said to him. When he stepped toward her, she scrambled to her feet, her expression cold with disdain.

"What do you want?" She enunciated each word in an icy tone.

It was a question he didn't know how to answer. He wasn't even sure why he'd entered the tent. No, he knew why, but it had been a futile hope he'd not even dared to let himself think. Her reaction was exactly what he'd expected. He clenched his teeth at how uncomfortable her contempt made him feel.

"I wanted to try to explain—"

"There isn't anything to explain. You made an example of me, by beating me in public."

"I regret the manner of punishment, but you left me little choice," he snapped as guilt flayed his conscience. "Other Sheikhs would have bared your back and drawn blood for less transgressions. Some, like Nassar, would have taken great pleasure in doing so."

"Are you implying I should be grateful it was *you* punishing me?" A bitter laugh parted her lips and he became even more defensive as he tried to make her understand his actions.

"Damn it, Allegra. My leadership hinges on my people obeying orders. It can mean the difference between life and death. You challenged that authority and jeopardized my ability to lead."

"I didn't challenge your authority, because you have none over me." She spat out the words at him. "Did you honestly believe I wouldn't try to escape—that I'd just do nothing?"

"No." He shook his head and watched her eyes widen in astonishment. "I knew you would do everything you could to find a way to leave."

"And yet you keep me here against my will." Her acerbic response scraped across his senses as her fury lashed at him. Turning away, he rubbed the back of his neck as her gaze burned his skin with scorn and accusation.

"I told you before, there's too much at stake to let you go back to Marrakech."

How in hell could he begin to explain why he refused to let her go? What could he say to make her understand his reasoning when he knew it wasn't just the treaties that made him keep her here? Desire wasn't an excuse for holding her here against her will. Even with his back to her, the heat of her anger whipped across his back.

"I have been a confidante to powerful men, including the Prince of Wales. My word is my bond, despite the fact that I am a mere courtesan." The bitterness in her words almost disguised the slight waver in her voice.

He wheeled around to face her. Did she really think herself ordinary? Narrowing his gaze, he stared into green eyes that briefly flashed with a fragile expression of pain until she looked away. Was this what drove the vulnerability he'd seen in her? Did she believe herself somehow less deserving than others simply because of her profession? Regret stabbed at him, her censure a searing reminder of his own complicity in everything that had happened to her over the past two days.

"You are far from insignificant, Allegra," he murmured as he closed the distance between them. Reaching out, he cupped her face and forced her to look at him. "And I have no doubt you would keep my confidence."

"Then why do you refuse to let me go?" She jerked her head away from him in anger.

"If I let you go back to Marrakech now . . . to Shaftsbury . . ." His gut twisted at the thought of her being with the Viscount or any man. "If you knew that returning to Marrakech might start a war, would you go?"

"A war?" Her anger abated some and she shook her head. "No, of course not. But how could something I do start a war?"

"When I came to Morocco, the Amazigh were dozens of tribes scattered across the country. Raiding parties known as *ghazu* were everyday occurrences—many of them quite bloody." His jaw tightened at the memory of Nassar killing Yasmia with such brutal fury. "With the Sultan's blessing, Sheikh Mahmoud and I formed alliances and treaties among the different tribes to stop the warring factions."

"I still don't understand what that has to do with me." She released a harsh sound of exasperation.

"A number of the treaties were parleyed in the presence of French, Spanish, and British officials, with me acting as one of Sheikh Mahmoud's council leaders."

"You didn't tell them you were British," she gasped as understanding swept across her lovely features.

"I'd negotiated a number of the smaller treaties under my Amazigh title, and it didn't even occur to us—me—that we should explain who I was," he said with a growl of disgust at his blundering. "When we realized the implications it might have on the treaties, it was too late."

"And if Charles finds out who you are and happens to speak to the wrong people . . ." Her voice trailed off as she met his gaze.

"Then you could be the catalyst for renewed violence among the Amazigh," he said with quiet conviction.

"But Nassar knows who you are," she said with a touch of suspicion. "Why aren't you worried about him?"

"Nassar is afraid of the Sultan. Mulay Hassan has the ear of the Consuls, and Nassar doesn't want his more questionable activities scrutinized by the French or the Spanish."

"Which means he'll not say anything until it suits his purpose," she mused with a frown. "But when he does, if he protests in the right forum, the treaties are likely to collapse and Nassar will take advantage of that to strengthen his base of power and influence."

"As usual, I've underestimated you," he said quietly. "Other than Major Hastings, there are few people outside the tribe who would understand the complexity of the situation."

It was impossible not to be impressed with her insight. His own prejudices had prevented him from seeing how intelligent and knowledgeable she was. The question now was would she stay of her own free will. Up until now, he'd not given her a choice, and she despised him for it. She exhaled a pent-up breath and looked at him with a resolute expression.

"It seems I have no choice but to remain here until Charles leaves Marrakech." She eyed him with mistrust. "But this changes nothing between us. I want your word you won't take advantage of the situation."

"Which I'll gladly give the minute you tell me you feel no desire for me at all." He raised his hand in silent warning at the look of objection on her face. "And I *will know* if you're telling the truth Allegra."

She glared at him for a long moment before turning her back on him. "What I feel changes nothing. I won't come to your bed."

"And I won't force you, but I do intend to be persuasive." With that, he turned and left her alone in the tent. She wanted him. She'd not openly admitted it, but her silence confirmed it. It was enough to give him hope that courting her favor would earn him a spot in her bed. And her decision would have to be her choice. But he would do everything in his power to convince her to choose him.

12

Vivid fingers of pink, red, and yellow streaked across the sky as another day melted into the heat of the Moroccan plains. The vibrant colors blended with a blue sky to create a beautiful painting that changed with each passing minute. The Atlas Mountains rose upward in a vain effort to touch the ribbons of color stretched so close and yet so far above their peaks. Below the craggy mountain range, the plains stretching out toward the setting sun were a mixture of stone rubble and small areas of verdant green. It was a harsh, but hauntingly beautiful landscape. Would Cordelia like Morocco? The thought of her ward sent a small wave of homesickness cresting over her.

Before she'd left England, she'd written Cordelia a letter explaining her trip to Morocco. She'd made no mention of having received a letter from her niece in hopes that Cordelia would assume Allegra hadn't received news of the engagement. It had been a way of buying time until she found a way to deal with the situation. She traveled frequently, so it was more than likely that Cordelia would not find her extended absence unusual. Perhaps her absence would prevent Lady Bledsoe from discovering her relationship to Cordelia.

Cordelia's happiness was all that mattered, and if it were destroyed because of her, she'd never forgive herself. Perhaps her agreement to remain here until Charles had left Marrakech was a blessing in disguise. She heaved a sigh. *Or perhaps not.* The past few weeks had been a severe test of willpower when it came to Shaheen. It had taken her some time to reconcile his actions in punishing her in front of the tribe. She understood the reasoning behind it, but the emotional aspect of his actions made it difficult to forgive him. Still, his explanation and obvious remorse had made it easier to come to terms with the event. Particularly when the word *persuasion* was a dangerous one in the man's vocabulary. He had been true to his word. His persuasive powers were far more potent than she'd expected.

She'd thought he'd do everything in his power to seduce her from the moment he declared war on her senses. But he hadn't. He'd done just the opposite. Oh, he'd flirted with her, teased her and been attentive as to her comfort, but he'd not even tried to kiss her. Something she didn't know whether to be grateful for or not. Particularly when she found herself longing for his touch. Without even touching her, he was wearing down her resistance to him.

He'd provided her with several of his books to read, and his friend Jamal had been teaching her the Berber language. And he'd made it his habit to take her riding with him in the mornings. They didn't talk much during that time, but she found his company pleasurable. He was intelligent and had an excellent sense of humor. In a number of ways, he reminded her of Charles. The family resemblance was even more pronounced when he was flirting with her, because he had the same devilish smile as his cousin.

The desire he felt for her, he kept hidden, but it was there. There were occasions when she would look up to find him watching her with a hunger that frightened and thrilled her in the same breath. He always disguised his expression quickly, but not before it ignited a response in her. Only in the past week had she come to realize his quiet pursuit of her was working. She found herself dreaming of him each night, waking up with an intense craving for his touch. It was a stark desire that threatened to drag her headlong into an attraction she knew would jeopardize her ability to easily walk away at the end of an affair with him.

But no matter how much she wanted to resist her attraction to him, she knew she was fast losing that battle. She was certain he knew it, too. It was there in the way his fingers would slide over hers when he handed her something or the way his hands held her just a little bit longer than necessary when he helped her off her horse.

With a sigh, she focused on the scenery in front of her. Over the past month, she'd fallen in love with the desert plain and its people. The Bedouins were happy despite the hardship of their existence. The simplicity of their lives gave them time to cherish family and friends. There was a peaceful serenity to everything here that soothed the soul. It reminded her of what she'd never had growing up. *A real family.*

In the evenings, she would sit with the Amazigh women on one side of the communal campfire for the evening meal, while the men sat on the other. Afterwards many of the adults spun magical stories for the children sprawled at their feet, clinging to every word. And somewhere in the dark, she knew Shaheen was there, watching her from the shadows, his strong, steady presence filling her with a myriad of emotions.

Sand crunched softly beneath a lightweight tread, and she turned her head to see Jamal coming to a halt beside her.

"*Anasi*," he said with a slight bow. Jamal had been teaching her his Berber tongue, and she now knew *anasi* meant *woman*. But the respectful manner in which Shaheen's people said the word made it sound like it was more of a title than a simple word.

"You enjoy watching our sunsets." The Amazigh smiled as he studied the horizon.

"I do. They're beautiful. We don't have sunsets like this in England."

She sent him a brief look then turned back to watch the colorful display before her. A comfortable silence fell between them as they stared out at the landscape. After several minutes, Jamal cleared his throat.

"*Anasi*, we've received news."

"News?" She frowned as she looked at him.

"Lord Shaftsbury is still in Marrakech," Jamal said quietly. "The man recently received a message from England and has strengthened his efforts to find Shaheen."

With Charles still in Marrakech, it meant she would have to stay in Shaheen's camp awhile longer. Her heart skipped a beat as she tried to quell her happiness at the thought. The emotion was a telling one, and she experienced trepidation at its meaning. She smiled at Jamal.

"Then it seems my stay with the Amazigh will last awhile longer."

"It would seem that way, *anasi*. I have tried to convince Shaheen to return you to Marrakech and let God determine our fate, but he is stubborn that one."

"I'm happy to remain until Charles returns to England. I know Nassar is not to be trusted." She fixed her attention on the dying sun and flinched as the image of her kidnapper fluttered through her head.

"He is a murderer." Jamal's face was dark with hate. She

understood the Bedouin's vehemence where Nassar was concerned. She despised the man, too.

"Tell me what happened," she said.

"Nassar led a *ghazu* on Sheikh Mahmoud's camp and murdered Khalid's wife. His men tried to kill Hakim, but Shaheen saved the boy. For that, Khalid made Shaheen the boy's bodyguard and a member of his tribal council."

The horror of Nassar's actions echoed in Jamal's voice. She remembered the pain in Laila's eyes that day in the *souq* when the young woman explained what a *ghazu* was. It must have been her mother's death she'd been thinking of that day. It made Allegra's heart ache to think of Hakim and Laila motherless at such a young age. She didn't question the man any further on the subject. He clearly found the topic painful, and she had no wish to add to his sorrow.

Returning her attention to the sun sinking lower on the horizon, she shivered as Nassar's face slipped so lifelike into her head. The man had much to answer for, and she wasn't the only one who wished to see him punished. They stood there in silence until the setting sun was little more than a strip of reddish orange on the horizon.

In the hush of the approaching night, she stared out at the Atlas Mountains. The rapidly fading light had changed them so they were sharply etched against the twilight that encroached upon their sturdy façade. They reminded her of Shaheen's strong and unyielding personality. Just as the mountains kept the Sahara desert from engulfing the Moroccan plains, Shaheen stood guard over his people, keeping them safe from men like Nassar. Almost as if he could read her mind, Jamal turned his head toward her.

"Shaheen is like a son to me. And I think him fortunate to have you as the *jahīm anasi*."

"The what?" she asked as she looked at the Bedouin's features darkened all the more by the twilight shadows. The Amazigh met her gaze then looked down at her hand.

"May I, *anasi*?" He reached for her hand that bore the hennaed bird of paradise. Gently, he touched several different marks that looked like small flames inside the design. "These marks show you are the *jahīm anasi*. The woman of fire."

"I don't understand."

"We Amazigh are a superstitious people," Jamal said with a smile. "More than a year ago, Shaheen was told that a woman of fire would come to him and leave her mark until his past united with his future. Everyone believes you are the *jahīm anasi*, except Shaheen of course."

"That's utter nonsense. These marks don't mean anything." She shook her head in vigorous denial as she jerked her hand out of Jamal's. The Bedouin arched his eyebrow at her.

"The Amazigh have a saying that it is the most improbable of things that shape our destiny, *anasi*."

"But that still doesn't mean it's me." She shook her head in denial as she recalled how the old woman in the market had said she was Shaheen's destiny.

"Perhaps," Jamal mused quietly. "But the woman of fire will force Shaheen to face his past. That's something he doesn't want to do."

"I doubt I could help him when I prefer to leave my own past in the dark." She turned her head away from the Bedouin.

"Shaheen is faced with his past every time he sees you." Silence fell between them once more. After several moments, Jamal inhaled and exhaled a deep breath as if suddenly reaching a decision. Frowning, he sent her a penetrating look. "If he knew what—"

"Knew *what*, my friend?"

Startled, the two of them whirled around to see Shaheen behind them, the dim light casting one side of his face into the shadows. His mouth was tight with disapproval. Before Jamal could speak, she met Shaheen's accusatory expression steadily.

"He thought you might be angry with him for telling me how you rescued Hakim from Nassar's butchery. That and the fact that Charles is still in Marrakech."

He sent Jamal a hard look. "There was no need to tell her anything."

"I saw no harm in telling her what I did." There was a challenge in Jamal's voice that made Shaheen narrow his gaze slightly.

With a sharp note in his voice, Shaheen said something in the Amazigh tongue, which caused Jamal's face to darken with anger. The Bedouin responded with the harshness of a parent chastising a child. Her knowledge of the language was still limited, and before she could even interpret the gist of their argument it was over. Throwing his hands up in a gesture of disgust, Jamal stalked away, leaving her alone with Shaheen in the near dark.

A hungry tension slid through her as she looked up at him. That familiar warm ache settled between her legs and she shivered. Every time she stood this close to him, her body craved his touch. She'd enjoyed the touch of other men many times, but this man was different. He made her body respond in a hedonistic way simply by standing next to her. No other man had ever done that to her before. She shivered again.

"You're cold." The warmth of his voice washed over her, flushing her body with heat.

"No." She shook her head. "I'm fine."

His knuckles brushed her chin as he forced her to look at him. "If you're worried about Nassar, don't. I won't let him come near you again."

"I'm not worried. I know I'm safe here."

She stepped back from the fire of his touch, her pulse racing with a dangerous excitement. The only thing she was worried about was how long she could resist him. Perhaps the real question was whether she wanted to. She looked up at the stars beginning to dot the night sky and breathed an inaudible sigh. It had been the truth when she said she felt safe here with him. She couldn't define it, but there was something comforting about his presence. He made her feel safe. Beside her, he cleared his throat.

"I've never told you how brave I think you are."

"Brave?" She turned her head and looked up at him with a frown.

"You must have been frightened and feeling all alone when Nassar was holding you prisoner, and yet you never gave in to him."

"I would have eventually given up if you'd not arrived when you did." The memory of the hopelessness she'd experienced in Nassar's camp made her close her eyes.

"But you didn't. Even when he hit you . . ." A fierce anger flashed across his face, followed by a stark remorse that startled her. "If I could have spared you the humiliation of that bartering I would have."

"I know," she whispered as she looked away from him.

Silence drifted between them for a long time before he reached out to touch her short curls. "Short hair becomes you, *ma belle.*"

"I confess it's much easier to take care of," she said with a wistful note in her voice as she touched the top of her head. The trauma following Rana's attack had eased, but she still felt a sense of violation. "Although, I'm certain it's not the most becoming of styles."

He caught her chin with his hand and forced her to look at him. "I think it makes you look adorable."

The soft words sent a tremor through her. Lord, but the man had a voice that could convince her to indulge in the most delicious of sins. He used it to coax her, tempt her. This was the man she feared, this charming seducer. With just a word and a smile, he'd adeptly eroded her self-control. It was a struggle, but she maintained her composure and arched her eyebrow at him.

"Why do I think you spent your childhood sweet-talking your nanny out of just about anything, including trouble?" she said with a light, teasing laugh.

"I won't deny being the apple of her eye. And yes she did forgive most of my sins." He sent her a wicked look of amusement.

"And your parents? Were they as forgiving as your nanny?" She smiled, curiosity lighting her lovely face.

It was a simple question, yet far more complicated than it seemed. He paused for a long moment, the bitterness of his childhood rising up to rake through him with a physical pain.

"I never knew my mother, and my father—" He grimaced. "My father and I didn't care for each other, so we avoided each other's company."

"I'm sorry," she said softly as she looked up at him. "It must have been difficult to grow up without a mother."

The sympathetic gleam in her eyes cracked something inside him that he didn't think could be touched. He'd bottled up every terrible childhood memory, and yet with a simple statement she'd reached down inside him and tugged those emotions to the surface. Emotions he didn't want to feel. *Damm gahannam*, she'd actually gotten him to speak about his childhood. Not even Jamal had ever been able to get more than two or three words out of him when it came to his days as a child at Pembroke Hall. It was time to change the subject.

"Do you have family?" he asked.

"Yes." She nodded. "A niece. She just finished her schooling."

It was just enough information to satisfy the curious, and yet it was vague and nondescript. Like him, she didn't give up her secrets easily. Still, it told him more than he'd known before.

"What's she like?"

"Cordelia?" Surprise flitted across her face as a smile curved her mouth. "She's beautiful, charming, thoughtful, sweet, and highly intelligent."

"Like her aunt," he said softly as he breathed in the scent of jasmine drifting off of her.

"Cordelia is *nothing* like me," she said in a tight voice. "She won't ever be touched by the darkness I've seen."

The change in her was instantaneous. She was a tigress determined to protect her cub. Suddenly, it was quite clear to him why she was so protective. She was giving her niece what she'd apparently never had in her own life. Someone who cared. He understood that all too well. The urge to pull her into his arms and just hold her welled up inside him. The unexpected need to comfort her—protect her—made his muscles stiff and wooden.

He didn't move. If he did, he'd have no choice but to wrap his arms around her. This was something completely different from lust and desire. It was an emotion that bored its way deep into his soul. And if he didn't take care, it would change him forever. Even if he'd allowed himself to give in to the impulse, she didn't give him the chance to do so.

"Excuse me, I think I'll retire for the evening," she said in a strained voice. As she headed back toward the tents, he quickly caught up to her. Gently, he pulled her to a halt.

"It wasn't my intent to stir up painful memories, Allegra." He cupped the side of her cheek in his hand. "I have my own demons, and I won't begrudge you yours."

She closed her eyes and stood frozen in front him, the pressure of her cheek heating his palm. Her mouth parted slightly, and a soft sigh whispered past her sweet lips. Unable to help himself, he lowered his head and brushed his mouth across hers in a gentle exploration. She didn't object. Instead, she leaned into him, and the white-hot taste of her fanned through him with lightning speed.

With a groan, he tugged her into his arms as the desire he'd suppressed for weeks exploded inside him. Soft, yet eager, her mouth parted beneath his allowing him to taste its inner sweetness. She tasted of pomegranate—tart and sweet in one stroke of his tongue. Christ Jesus, she tasted wonderful. Smelled wonderful. The jasmine soap he'd acquired for her bath scented her skin in a subtle way. It tantalized his senses, until every part of him ached for her, craved her.

Hard as iron, he longed to slide into her slick heat and have her sheathed tightly over his cock. The image pulled a low growl out of him as he deepened their kiss. In response, a mewl of pleasure escaped her and she melted into his embrace. It was a spontaneous display of emotion that told him this was the woman behind the mask. This was the Allegra he'd been looking for. Triumph surged through him as he dragged his mouth across her jaw to her soft earlobe. He nibbled on the small piece of flesh, delighting in the moan that parted her mouth.

"Say it, Allegra," he murmured into her ear. "Tell me what I want to hear."

She whimpered as his hand slid up over her waist to cup one breast while his thumb flicked over a stiff nipple. "I—"

"Shaheen, where are you?" Malik's voice had the same effect as a bucket of water dousing them.

The moment the boy's cry broke through the darkness, Allegra quickly jerked away from him. With a groan of frustration, he tried to keep her close, but she evaded him. As Malik called out again, she put several feet between them, her expression filled with the remnants of passion, confusion, and alarm. He stretched out his hand to her, but she swatted it away and raced back toward the camp.

Allegra hurried past the campfire, pretending she didn't hear the greetings called out to her by those sitting around the fire. She needed a quiet place to think—to understand what had just happened. For the first time in her life, she'd blindly responded to a man. No warning to take care. No voice in the back of her head controlling her reactions, guiding her as to what her lover needed from her. She'd simply kissed him back, her emotions completely in control of her body. If Malik hadn't interrupted them, she would still be in Shaheen's arms.

The realization tugged the air out of her lungs as she lurched into the tent's dark interior. What had she been thinking? *Nothing.* That was the problem. She'd allowed her guard to fall and instinct had taken over. Her emotions had been in control, not her head. Dear lord, she was out of her mind.

It was incredibly foolhardy to even *think* about becoming emotionally involved with the man. Particularly when she was on the verge of welcoming him into her bed. And she was on the edge of the abyss where Shaheen was concerned. She knew she would not be able to resist him for too much longer. The challenge was to keep her emotions in control and not forget that their liaison would eventually end. Emotional entanglements were unacceptable. She'd learned years ago that caring for people meant nothing but betrayal.

She sank down onto the pillows that made up her pallet. Not since the night Arthur had died had she felt so lost. The memory of that night washed over her as if it were simply a matter of days not years since the terrible event. The scandal had been horrifying, not because Arthur had died in her bed, but because of the lies the attending physician and coroner had spread. Lies that had guaranteed her ability to provide for Cordelia.

Dinner had been a quiet affair that evening, just the two of them. When Arthur had complained of being tired, she'd encouraged him to stay the night. Arthur's habit of sleeping in the nude had only sealed her fate the next morning. When the attending physician and the coroner arrived, they'd assumed Arthur had died while in the act of copulation. A heart attack—brought on by vigorous activity. The peaceful, happy expression on Arthur's features had only added to her mystique.

The next day, every London paper had blatantly or slyly commented how Arthur had died a happy man. In hours, gentlemen callers had inundated her home. For weeks, she'd hated Arthur for feeding her to the wolves, and her grief forced her to retreat from the world, seeing no one except a few old friends and the Prince of Wales.

Bertie had been a friend of Arthur's as well, and he seemed to understand the depth of her loss. He'd consoled her and sought to protect her when Lady Bledsoe's lawyers had tried to take her home and possessions. With Bertie's help, she'd found a skilled barrister who'd dealt with the court case, but the scandal had taken its toll on her.

In some ways, she understood Lady Bledsoe's malicious hatred. Made a laughingstock of the Marlborough Set, the woman had to live with the gossip about her husband suffering a fatal heart attack in the arms of his mistress. It could not have been an easy thing for Lady Bledsoe to bear. But it had been no more than her own sorrow.

She curled up into a ball, clutching a pillow to her chest. Arthur had been the first person since her mother and sister that she'd allowed herself to care about. In the almost two years they were together, he'd seen to it that she had lessons in every possible subject. She'd been his creation, molded to be the ultimate companion. And when he'd completed his task, he'd died.

The knowledge he'd given her hadn't eased the pain of his death, but it had enabled her to wear the illusionary mantle of courtesan extraordinaire. She'd not wanted the title, but when her dying sister had appeared on her doorstep with Cordelia, she'd had no choice. So she'd cloaked herself in the illusion and hidden her true self behind its façade.

Not once since Arthur's death had she allowed herself to care too deeply for any man. It had been her rule. A rule she'd invoked to insulate herself from further heartache. But it had also kept her from giving any of her lovers an uninhibited passion. She'd never opened herself up completely to any man. She'd never let them see the woman behind the courtesan. It kept her heart safe. Safe from the pain of loving someone only to lose them. It explained why she'd actually given Charles's proposal consideration. She didn't love Charles, but his proposal represented a stability and sanctuary she'd never known. The allure of it made her vulnerable. If she were to love, it would be the end of her. And that she couldn't allow.

Her destiny was to remain free and independent without emotional entanglements. She was a courtesan. A woman who catered to the needs of the men she was with. Courtesans didn't find love. They only found their next patron. With a quiet sigh of resignation, she tucked the pillow close to her body and lay still in the dark.

Could she risk choosing him? Did she have the determination to keep her emotions in check where he was concerned? It was a troubling question because it was one she didn't want to answer. She shuddered. Her indecisiveness where he was concerned revealed far more about herself than she wanted to admit.

13

The fresh morning air was still crisp and clean smelling without the heat of the day to dry it out. Allegra had awoken before dawn debating whether she should ride with Shaheen as she normally did. In the end, she'd decided that not riding with him this morning would only emphasize how much his kiss had affected her last night. And it *had* disconcerted her. So deeply that she refused to dwell on the subject.

Instead, she moved quietly through the camp toward the horses on the opposite side of camp. The soft whicker of a horse drifted through the air as she passed the last tent and saw the hobbled Arabians mingling together. Standing off to one side, Shaheen's stallion eyed her with suspicion and tossed his head with an arrogance that reminded her of his owner. The sudden frisson skimming over her skin made her stiffen. He was directly behind her. She could feel his warmth spreading across her back, and a small whiff of cedar drifted beneath her nostrils.

"I didn't expect to see you this morning," he said quietly.

She wasn't sure how to answer him as he walked past her and threw a blanket onto his horse. With his back to her, it was impossible to read his expression, but she could see the tension in him. It was there in his stiff and jerky movements as he saddled the chestnut stallion.

"Is that your way of saying I'm not welcome to ride with you today?"

He stopped adjusting the saddle girth and looked at her over his shoulder. Frustration glittered in his eyes as he sent her a hard look. "If you think to play games with me, Allegra, *don't*. You can only push a man so far before he breaks, and I'm already there."

"You accused me of playing games when we first met. I wasn't guilty of the charge then any more than I am now."

"And yet last night, you fled like a gazelle at the first hint of danger."

"Yes." She met his gaze steadily. "I ran because I won't be seduced into a decision that affects me so intimately. I choose my lovers in the light of day and not in the throes of passion."

"Then that means you *have* considered my proposition." There was a note of triumph in his voice as he studied her with that familiar arrogance of his.

"I didn't say that."

"You said it was a decision that affects you *intimately*. That tells me you're considering my request."

The gleam of satisfaction in his dark eyes made her swallow hard. He was right, she *was* contemplating a liaison with him, but she'd not meant to admit it. She flushed under his heated gaze and a tremor rippled through her as he moved to tower over her. His fingers trailed across her hot cheek, while a small smile tipped the corners of his mouth.

"Choose me, *ma belle*. You won't regret doing so."

The words caressed her, tempting her to say yes as he turned away from her to continue saddling his horse. Following his lead, she proceeded to saddle the dark brown mare she rode every morning. Before he had the chance to help her, Allegra jumped up into Adiva's saddle. She didn't think she could handle him touching her at the moment. Her body was more than ready to betray her if he came too close. He sent her an inquisitive look as he checked Adiva's saddle girth with a gentle tug.

"Did you eat breakfast?"

"No." She shook her head at his question. "Should I have?"

"I'd planned on visiting one of the tribe's herdsmen today." A frown furrowed his forehead under his kaffiyeh. "It's a long ride on an empty stomach."

In less than a minute, he'd retrieved a chunk of goat cheese from his saddlebag and handed the food to her before turning around to mount his horse. Hunger rumbled through her belly, and she bit into the cheese as she urged Adiva into a canter. Sprawled out in front of her, the rugged desert plains were as beautiful as they were untamed. She understood why Shaheen had chosen to stay in Morocco with the Amazigh. Here was a serenity London, with all its polite society, could never offer.

They'd ridden for over an hour when Shaheen motioned for her to halt, and she brought Adiva to a stop. Out of the corner of her eye, she saw him drink deeply from a water bag he'd removed from the side of his saddle. When finished, he offered the bag to her. The intimacy of sharing such a basic need wasn't lost on her as she drank the surprisingly cool water. Shaheen had dismounted to water the horses with another water bag as she quenched her thirst. When he'd finished, he turned to study the mountains with a puzzled frown.

"Do we have far to go?" She handed him their water bag, which he tied to his saddle in an absentminded fashion.

"No," he said as he remounted Tarek. "Actually, I'm surprised we haven't seen Omar yet. I didn't think he was quite this far from the camp."

"Why would he be so far away in the first place?"

"Omar likes his privacy," he said with a smile. "He'll only come so close to the encampment."

"Does he have a large number of sheep?"

"Enough," Shaheen said with a shrug as he surveyed the land stretched out in front of them. "It's why I'm surprised—"

She watched him stiffen in the saddle as he peered closely at something off to their left. Turning her head, she saw nothing except for a flock of birds in the sky.

"What is it?"

"I'm not sure." He glanced around as if looking for something else. Tension emanated from him, and Tarek shifted restlessly in place. "Let's go."

Together they rode in the direction of the birds. As they drew closer, she recognized them as vultures. The stench was the first thing they encountered. It was the sickening smell of rotting carcasses heated by the sun. The first slaughtered animal they saw was an ewe. Partially decapitated, it was bloated from the sun. Nearby, another ewe, its skull completely crushed, lay dead and swollen from the heat. Shaheen grabbed Adiva's bridle and brought the horses to a halt.

"*Stay here.*"

All she could do was nod obediently as she surveyed the grisly scene. Strewn out in front of them was carcass after carcass. Each one brutally hacked to death. Covering her nose with her hand, she watched Shaheen ride deeper into the carnage. Where was the Bedouin sheepherder? The answer was an insidious whisper in the back of her head. She swallowed hard as a vulture swooped down to steal another bird's carrion. It failed and flapped away in defeat.

The winner hopped to one side to peck at its prize from a different angle and as it did so, she screamed.

Shaheen wheeled Tarek around in a sharp turn. Nauseated and sick with fear, she could only point at the vulture's prize as the bird plucked at the eye socket of a decapitated head. Wrenching her gaze away from the horrendous sight, she twisted in the saddle to bend over and retch. When she'd finished, she rested her forehead against Adiva's mane.

Oh God, how could someone do such a thing? What kind of man— she immediately knew the answer. Despite the heat from the approaching noon hour, she shivered with cold. Strong fingers bit into her arm as Shaheen pulled her upright. Her stomach still churning, she moaned softly at his action.

"Look at me, Allegra."

The command was impossible to ignore, and she lifted her head. Fury had darkened his eyes to jet stones. She'd seen him angry, but not this type of cold wrath. It sent ice sluicing through her veins. Instinctively, she drew back from him, and his gaze softened. He offered her the water bag and she took a sip to rinse out her mouth.

"I need you to listen to me," he said with a crisp urgency. "We're in danger. There's only one person I know who would condone this type of behavior."

"Nassar," she said with conviction as she returned the water bag to him. Deep down inside, she'd known the Sheikh was responsible from the moment she'd seen the first dead ewe. He nodded his head in agreement.

"I need you to be strong, *ma chérie*, because we need to leave here *now*."

Despite her queasy stomach, she'd do anything to avoid Nassar. She nodded and they turned their horses around and left the carnage behind them at a hard gallop. The air grew fresher as they put distance between them and the butchery, but the memory of the heinous act didn't abate. It was difficult to blot out the memory of the sheepherder's severed head, but she fought valiantly to forget. The horrible sight was a reminder of how lucky she was to be out of Nassar's reach. She shuddered. They rode hard toward camp, continuously looking over their shoulders, but saw no one in pursuit. After almost a half hour, Shaheen motioned her to halt.

"We're not being followed, and the horses need rest and water," he said. Despite his calm tone, her fear didn't abate. He grasped her hand and raised it to his lips. "Just a few moments, *ma beauté courageuse.* I promise."

She trembled at the gentleness of his voice, and nodded as he offered her a smile of encouragement. While he watered the horses, she worriedly scanned the landscape for any sign of riders headed in their direction.

"Why would he do such a terrible thing? What purpose could it possibly serve?" She shook her head in disbelief.

"Fear," he said quietly. "It sends a message of fear. Nassar wants to expand his territory, and this is how he does it."

"Isn't this your territory?"

Confusion swept across her face, but it was the fear and horror glazing her green eyes that sliced viciously through him. Christ Jesus, he'd been a fool. He'd been so consumed with his need for her, he'd not bothered to assess the dangers of a ride so far from camp. He should never have brought her with him. He'd put her life in danger and if something had happened to her—he stopped himself. The thing to do now was calm her fears.

"In a manner of speaking," he said as he began to water Adiva. "This land and the people in my tribe have been entrusted to me by Sheikh Mahmoud, First Sheikh of the Amazigh."

"Sheikh Mahmoud . . . Jamal said something about him being the sovereign?"

"He's a descendant of the first Sheikh of the Amazigh. That birthright makes Khalid leader and sovereign of all the Amazigh tribes." With the horses watered, he quickly mounted Tarek and sent her an encouraging smile. "Come, we're less than an hour from camp."

She acknowledged his words with a nod, and urged Adiva forward. As they rode, he continued to watch the landscape for any sign of Nassar. He wouldn't feel at ease until he'd returned her safely to camp. He'd heard stories about Nassar's terror tactics in territories southwest of Marrakech, but nothing this far north. This meant the balance of power was shifting, and he didn't like what that meant for Khalid or the rest of the Amazigh.

Nassar seemed on the verge of a power play, which could mean war, something he knew Khalid didn't want any more than he did. More importantly, he didn't like how all of this affected Allegra's safety. She was in danger if Nassar knew where his camp was. He glanced over at her. She'd witnessed the horrifying work of a madman, and yet she'd not succumbed to hysterics. He was proud of her, and furious with himself for putting her in harm's way.

The moment the tents of his tribe appeared on the horizon, he found himself breathing easier. As they approached camp, two men rode out to meet them and he quickly issued several orders. His men raced away as he and Allegra came to a halt at the outer perimeter of the encampment. In a lithe movement, he leaped off Tarek to help her dismount. The warmth of her filled his arms, and she clung to him with what he recognized as relief. A tremor shook her body followed by another until she trembled violently against him.

He cradled her and murmured reassurance into her ear. Her reaction was understandable given the horror of her experience. The shudders wracking her body eased at the same time he saw Jamal hurrying toward them. Somehow, he didn't think the anger on his friend's face was entirely for Nassar. He grimaced and returned his attention to Allegra. He lifted her chin so he could look into her eyes. That haunting vulnerability of hers was back, and it tugged at him to keep her safe from whatever threatened her.

"Go rest. There are things I must do, but I'll come to see you shortly."

"We didn't even bury him," she whispered as she slipped out of his arms. Catching her by the shoulders, he forced her to look at him.

"If we had, and Nassar had returned, he would have known we'd been there. We have the advantage if he doesn't know. Omar would understand this."

"It wasn't right." Her stubbornness was offset by the softness of her voice.

"No, it wasn't. But here on the desert plains, we do what survival demands first, propriety second." He saw a glimmer of understanding flare in her eyes, and he brushed his fingers across her cheek. "Go now."

With a nod, she walked away like an obedient child. It wasn't her normal behavior, and he cursed himself for causing it. He'd give anything to have his fiery Allegra back in place of this docile creature. The possessive thought startled him, but he pushed it aside in order to deal with the current problem. Turning to Jamal, he faced his friend's anger.

"What possessed you to take the *anasi* into the desert without an escort? Taking her short distances is one thing, but this . . . this . . ." Jamal sputtered to a halt and glared at him with disgust.

"I know it was foolhardy," he bit out, not needing any reminders of his mistake.

"Foolish?" Jamal stared at him with a look of contempt. "It showed a total lack of concern for the *anasi's* safety. She's your responsibility."

Jamal's tongue-lashing was no more painful than the one he was subjecting himself to internally. He'd been a fool. He could have easily gotten her killed, or worse, if Nassar had found them— the thought of her in that bastard's arms chilled his blood.

"I realized my mistake the moment we found Omar," he said quietly.

"So the sheepherder took you to task as well." Angry satisfaction filled Jamal's face.

"No," he said harshly. "He was dead when we arrived. Hacked to pieces and left to rot."

Stunned, Jamal stared at him for a long moment then spat on the ground. "Nassar."

"Either him or Sheikh Cadi, but this kind of barbarism isn't Cadi's way. Nassar on the other hand . . ." He gritted his teeth. "Khalid needs to know Nassar might have formed an alliance with Cadi."

"Agreed. I'll send someone to Sidi Rahal immediately," Jamal said in a tight voice. The Bedouin turned away then stopped and bowed his head. "I am disappointed in you, Shaheen. You are not worthy of the *jahīm anasi*."

It was a slap in the face, and it stunned him. Never in their fifteen-year friendship had Jamal ever expressed anything but pride and satisfaction in him. It was as if he was a child again, and he was watching his father walk away in disgust. But this time, he truly deserved all the blame laid at his feet.

❦

Allegra pushed her way up out of the depths of sleep. When she'd returned to her tent, she'd raised the wool side panels before lying down. Now a soft breeze danced across her cheek, stirring her awake. Turning her head, she stared out at the Atlas Mountains. It was late afternoon, and the sun was illuminating the craggy rock face of the tall, mountainous range. The memory of what she'd seen earlier flashed through her mind, and she winced at the images fluttering through her head. The horrific scene seared into her memory.

Sitting up, she hugged her knees into her chest. She was certain Shaheen would never have taken her with him if he'd suspected something was wrong. In fact, she'd seen the self-recrimination in his face as they'd fled the dreadful scene. His tenderness had startled and warmed her at the same time. It was a side of him that she'd not seen before.

Over the past month, he'd flirted with her, teased her, but the regard he'd shown her today was unlike anything he'd exhibited toward her previously. His actions had revealed him to be a man capable of deep feeling. A man who made her feel safe.

Safe where her welfare was concerned, and yet he was danger-ous to every one of her senses. Last night, he'd nearly brought her to her knees with little more than a kiss. He'd not exerted any overt pressure on her in any way, but her body recognized him even when she couldn't see him. Raw and fiery, her senses pulled at her whenever he was near until she ached with need.

Just the thought of him made her skin tingle, particularly beneath her tattoo. And with each new thing she learned about him, it became all the more difficult to resist him. She was expe-rienced enough to know that Shaheen had suffered a terrible loss at the hands of a woman. A woman who had most likely been a courtesan. Whatever his suffering, he'd buried it deep inside, and then he'd built a wall around himself to keep everyone out. But there had been moments when he'd peeled back the layers to show her what type of a man he really was.

Another breeze blew through the opened tent, and it hinted at the night's chill. Rising to her feet, she quickly unrolled three sides, securing the woolen flaps in place as Jamal had shown her. When she'd finished, she moved toward the last open wall of the tent. One hand on the rope holding the wool material in place, she studied the unobstructed view of the Atlas Mountains. If someone had told her four weeks ago she could be happy living here, she would have deemed them a liar. And yet she had been happy. Despite the brutality of what she'd seen today, she realized she didn't want to leave this place. Leave him. She froze as a tingle skimmed across her back. She knew without turning around that he was behind her. She always knew when he was near. It was how her body responded to him, and she was tired of fighting the inevitable.

Slowly she turned around to meet his penetrating gaze. There was something powerful and magnetic about his dark brown eyes. They pulled her to him with the same force a mesmerist invoked on an audience. She didn't want to resist. As her gaze flickered over him, she drew in a soft breath. He still wore the familiar black *gambaz* he always wore, but this evening he seemed more potently dangerous to her senses. The garment emphasized his hard, broad shoulders, and accentuated the predatory aura that always emanated from him. He'd discarded the crisscrossed gun and cartridge belt he usually wore for a beige belt with a small curved blade tucked into the band of cloth. He was the proud Amazigh warrior and every bit the Bedouin Sheikh.

"You are well?" His concern revealed he'd been worried about her, and she nodded.

"I doubt I'll ever forget seeing that . . . that terrible sight, but I'm well. Thank you."

He studied her for a long moment, then moved to stand at her side to stare out at the mountain range. It was an easy silence, but she knew he was still troubled.

"I should never have taken you with me this morning."

He didn't look at her, but kept his gaze focused on the mountains. Regret echoed in his voice, but there was anguish mixed with his remorse. It made her want to comfort him.

"You had no way of knowing what would happen."

"No . . . but I should have been more cautious with your safety," he bit out with an anger she knew was directed at himself. "I knew Nassar was nearby. I underestimated his boldness."

"It doesn't matter. We're safe now, and that's what's important."

"But that's my point, Allegra. It does matter. What if we *had* met up with Nassar? I wouldn't have been able to protect you. And the thought of that bastard touching you has been eating away at me since we returned to camp." Something flared in his eyes as he looked her, and the heat of it stole her breath away.

"Why?" Her soft query made him go rigid. The tension in him was razor sharp, and his mouth was taut with an emotion she couldn't name. He spun away from her, and with repressed violence, he shoved his hand through the dark, silky waves of his hair.

"Because you're mine," he growled. "And because the thought of any man touching you is enough to drive me mad."

Her heart skipped a beat. There was something more than desire layered beneath that possessive note in his voice. She wasn't sure whether to rejoice or be terrified. Slowly, she moved to stand at his side and reached out to touch his arm. Uncertain of what to say to him, she remained silent as he turned his head to meet her gaze, his eyes dark with angry remorse.

"I should never have brought you here. I should have taken you back to Marrakech the moment I found you."

"I'm glad you didn't," she whispered as she stared up at him.

"Why are you glad, *ma belle*?" He cupped her chin in the palm of his hand. The moment he touched her, the heat of him melted into her skin, spreading its way downward until her breath was ragged.

"If you hadn't brought me here, I wouldn't have been able to . . . I wouldn't have been able to *choose* you."

The brown eyes gazing intently into hers suddenly sparked with a blaze that terrified and thrilled her in one breath. Slowly he lowered his head and lightly brushed his mouth over hers. Fire streaked through her, forcing her to draw in a sharp breath of need. It gripped her as easily as he did, and the power of it was impossible to ignore. As his mouth slanted over hers, the kiss deepened and pulled her down into a whirlpool of need and desire. The currents of the emotions tugged at her, insisting she not refuse his demanding lips. The heat of his tongue warmed the inside of her mouth as he teased and cajoled a response from her. Lost in the sensation of his touch, she struggled to keep breathing, and the fresh aroma of cedar caressed her senses as if it were a feather. She'd not realized until now how much she'd missed the scent of him.

Hungry for his touch, she moved closer, her hands resting on his hips as she pressed her body into his. The moment she did so, his arousal pressed into her thigh. Her heart skipped a beat before it started to pump wildly with excitement. Dear God, she wanted to feel him inside her, filling her with his hard, thick length. She wanted to experience the tip of him pressing into her as he teased her with his body until she cried out and he plunged deep inside of her. Erotic images of his naked body entwined with hers pulled a whimper from her throat. She wanted him. Craved him. Eagerly, she slid her hand across his hip until she reached his erection. Hard and thick, he jumped at her touch as she rubbed her hand over him through his clothing. The caress pulled a heavy groan past his lips and his mouth left hers to nibble on the edge of her jaw.

"You have no idea how hard it's been staying away from you, *ma belle*," he whispered.

From off in the distance she heard someone call his name, and as if they'd been indulging in nothing more than a quiet conversation, he quickly released her. On the edge of the abyss, Allegra stumbled slightly as he released her from his embrace. Disoriented, she pressed her fingertips into her forehead fighting to clear the fog enveloping her brain. Outside the tent, she heard Jamal's voice calling for him, and Shaheen quickly moved forward to sweep aside the wool flap guarding the shelter's door. As she turned around, Jamal entered the tent.

There was nothing in Shaheen's expression to denote he'd even been aroused mere seconds ago. The ease with which he shut down his desire stung her pride more than she cared to admit. She was a courtesan of the highest order, sought after by royalty, nobility, and powerful men. None of her lovers had ever exhibited the type of self-control this man did. The knowledge didn't just irritate her—it slashed at her confidence.

"He's arrived." Jamal said in a wooden tone of voice.

His manner surprised her because she knew the men were close friends. Watching them together she was suddenly reminded of tin soldiers. A frown furrowed Shaheen's head as he rubbed his chin.

"And Kasim?"

"He rode back with them."

A contemplative expression on his face, Shaheen nodded his understanding. "Then something else has happened. He wouldn't be here this early in the season otherwise."

"Khalid has always done as he pleased. Not unlike another man I know." The Bedouin shrugged, his voice filled with a veiled sarcasm.

Glaring at the Amazigh, Shaheen released a sound of irritation and turned his head to study her for a long moment. She met his gaze steadily and when she saw a sudden flash of emotion flare in his eyes, it startled her. *Indecision?* No, she had to be mistaken. Shaheen wasn't the type of man to doubt himself. He never questioned his actions.

"Have Malik saddle Tarek, I'll ride out to meet him."

With a nod, Jamal left the tent. Alone once more, tension charged the space around them. The tactile sensation edged its way across her skin in a way she'd never experienced with any lover. But then nothing about Shaheen or her relationship with him was even remotely like her past. The moment his piercing gaze met hers, she was mesmerized. The man's ability to hold her captive with just his eyes was a power no other had ever been able to exert over her before. Closing the gap between them, he stretched out his sun-darkened hand and gently slid his fingers through her short curls.

"You look like a girl barely out of the schoolroom." His quiet statement made her laugh.

"I think the sun has blinded you," she said with a smile.

"I'm far from blind, *ma belle*. I see a woman before me who's capable of great passion."

The soft words sent a shiver skimming down the back of her neck. They made her mouth go dry with a longing she didn't even think possible for her to feel. Everything about this man terrified her. He'd already stolen her independence and self-control, what would he steal next? Her heart? The thought of it made her freeze, incapable of responding to him. His eyes narrowed as if he could see the effect he was having on her.

Somewhere outside the tent, a loud chorus of voices erupted with shouts of excitement. He glanced over his shoulder, an expression of frustration tugging at his dark brow. With a sharp move, he turned back to her and jerked her forward to kiss her hard. It was a brief moment of passion that lit every nerve ending in her body. Lifting his head, he smiled down at her. It was a smile of confidence that unsettled her in more ways than one.

"Until tonight, *ma belle*," he murmured before he released her and left the tent.

As she watched him go, her heart skipped a beat. Tonight she would belong to a man who possessed the power to take her to the heights of heaven or the depths of hell.

14

Exhilaration roared through Shaheen as he raced out to meet the approaching caravan. She'd chosen him. In spite of all that had transpired between them, she was coming to him of her own free will. Tonight the woman behind the mask would be his.

A sudden cry tugged his attention away from Allegra. It took only a brief moment to recognize Hakim riding out to meet him on the plain. As the boy pulled his horse to a sliding halt, Shaheen narrowed his gaze at the haughty expression on his charge's face. Clearly the young man still resented being ordered to escort his sister and Allegra's maid back to Khalid's camp, rather than being allowed to help rescue Allegra. It also gave him a possible explanation for Khalid's sudden, yet timely, appearance here in Douar el Haj Brahim. As he studied Hakim in silence, he waited for the young man to speak. Defiance flashed across the young man's face as he arched his eyebrows imperiously at Shaheen. Amused by the boy's attitude, he smiled at Sheikh Mahmoud's royal heir.

"I have told my father everything," Hakim said coldly. A smug look rested on the young man's handsome face, and Shaheen studied him in silence for a long moment. Out of the corner of his eye, he saw Khalid riding toward them.

"I see," he responded quietly. "Does that include your desire to bed Allegra Synnford?"

"I am old enough to experience a woman," the boy blustered as color rose in his face.

"I think that is a matter of opinion. The one thing I'm convinced of is that you're too young for Allegra Synnford."

"And *that* is a matter of opinion." Hakim sneered. "I think you will find my father's thoughts are of a different perspective."

"But does he have the complete story or simply what you wanted him to hear?"

The color darkening Hakim's cheeks confirmed Shaheen's suspicions. His young charge had been selective in what he told his father. Biting back another smile, he turned his head as Khalid and his personal escort cantered up to them.

"*Ssalamū 'lekum*, Excellency." Shaheen bowed and touched his heart and then his forehead in the traditional Amazigh greeting.

A smile of pleasure curving his lips upward, Sheikh Mahmoud responded in kind. "*Ssalamū 'lekum*, Shaheen. You are looking well."

"As are you, my friend. I'm surprised to see you, but it's good you've arrived. I'm afraid the news I have to report is not good."

"I imagine it concerns my brother," Khalid ground out between clenched teeth. "It's why I came early. I have news of Nassar as well."

"What news?" He frowned at the underlying note of concern in Khalid's voice, expecting the worst.

"My brother is raising an army." Khalid's words were a fierce explosion of anger and Shaheen's jaw tightened. Given Omar's brutal slaying, Nassar didn't intend on taking any prisoners when he attacked.

"Did Kasim explain what happened to Omar?" Shaheen asked quietly.

"Yes. Omar was a good man." Khalid closed his eyes and murmured a brief prayer then met his gaze with a dark frown of concern. "You were right to insist we watch my brother all these years, Shaheen. Our worst fears have been realized, my friend."

"It doesn't please me to be right," he said with a sigh.

"But fortune favors us because you were." Khalid sent him a grateful look. "Because of you, we have allies, but we'll discuss all of this later. Right now, I wish to meet your guest."

"My guest?" His body grew taut with tension. He knew full well who Khalid was referring to, but a part of him wanted to keep her hidden away from everyone but him.

"Ah." Khalid shook his head as he met Shaheen's gaze with a mischievous glint in his eye. "So Hakim was right. Your mind has grown weak in your old age."

Irritated by the words, he straightened in the saddle as he met Khalid's amused look. With a quick glance at Hakim, he glowered at the younger man's gloating features. The boy needed to learn his place.

"Age brings with it the gift of wisdom, whereas the folly of youth is that one arrogantly assumes much and knows little."

Chuckling at the dark scowl on his son's face, Sheikh Mahmoud shook his head as he turned his attention back to Shaheen. "Then you do have a guest staying with you?"

"I do."

"Excellent. I will be most happy to return Miss Synnford's maid to her. A pleasant woman, but she's hounded me incessantly about bringing her to her mistress."

"I'm sure Allegra will be delighted to see her friend again."

"Allegra." The Sheikh rolled the name off his tongue in an experimental fashion. "It seems Hakim fancies the woman for himself."

The observation made him stiffen as he met the Sheikh's curious gaze. He noted Hakim's petulant expression and grimaced. Returning his gaze back to his friend, he shook his head.

"Allegra is a woman of principles. She refuses to rob a cradle."

"Cradle!" the boy sputtered with fury. "You only want her for yourself."

"Hakim." There was a sharp warning in Sheikh Mahmoud's voice as he sent his son a hard look. "See to the caravan. We'll set up camp west of Shaheen's position."

Anger darkened the young man's face as he scowled at his father and then Shaheen. It was clear he wanted to protest Khalid's orders, but with an explosive noise of outrage, he whirled his horse around and raced back toward the approaching caravan.

"He is obsessed with this Synnford woman." Khalid sighed.

"It's an infatuation. It will pass." He didn't look at the Sheikh as he kept his gaze on the boy he'd been a surrogate uncle to for the past fifteen years.

"I believe so, too," the Sheikh said as he gestured for them to continue forward. "Unfortunately, it has done little for his relationship with you."

"It's time he spread his wings." He grimaced and lifted his shoulders in a small shrug. "You always talk about how much he looks up to me. Best he learns now I have feet of clay."

"And the woman?"

Caught off guard, he stiffened in his saddle and shot his friend a quick glance. "Allegra? What about her?"

"Is Hakim correct in his belief that you've laid claim to her?"

He winced. While it was true in the beginning that he'd not had any plans to make her his, things had changed. Allegra had chosen him. Agreed to be his mistress. When Hakim learned that fact, there would be hell to pay. The question was—how to break the news to the boy without destroying their relationship completely. Beside him, Khalid cleared his throat.

"It would seem that Hakim's assertions are not without substance." The Sheikh's voice was neutral, but the thread of amusement running beneath his words as they drew close to the camp's outer perimeter was distinct. "You've claimed the woman as your own?"

Khalid's question forced a laugh out of him. He shook his head as he smiled with a sense of irony. "No man *ever* lays claim to Allegra, and God help the man who forgets it."

"You speak as though you have firsthand knowledge in these matters." This time a smile curved Khalid's mouth.

"I have," he admitted in a grudgingly exasperated manner. "But I know that if Allegra had been any other courtesan, she'd have eaten Hakim and spit him out four or five times over."

"And how many times has she done this to *you*?" Laughing, the Sheikh wagged his finger at Shaheen. "I'm eager to meet this woman who distracts you so easily."

The moment they reached the edge of the camp, their conversation ended as people surged forward to greet their leader. Grateful he was no longer the target of his friend's amusement, he found himself searching the crowd for Allegra. Not seeing her, tension tightened his body.

Seconds later, relief slammed into him as he caught sight of her auburn curls. From his position near Khalid, he could see her watching the caravan's arrival with curiosity. He took pleasure in studying her oval features. The woman was a conundrum. One minute she was filled with a fiery confidence, the next she displayed a vulnerability that aroused a protective instinct in him. Something he'd only experienced with those closest to him.

Damnation, he was reading more into his reaction than necessary. It was natural to protect what was his. When he'd had his fill of her, the urge would disappear. He ignored the laughter in the back of his head as he dismounted and waited on Khalid. With a glance in his friend's direction, he saw the Sheikh catch sight of Allegra. The Amazigh leader's head jerked in his direction as he strode over to him.

"Is that her?" Khalid asked. "Hakim described a woman with *long* auburn hair."

"One of Nassar's women cut it off." His gut twisted as he remembered when they'd brought her into Nassar's tent.

"My brother has a great deal to pay for," Khalid said with a dark scowl. "Come, introduce me to your guest."

The Sheikh clasped his hand on Shaheen's shoulder and they moved to where Allegra was standing. Despite her wariness, Khalid's gift of charm worked its usual miracle. Almost too well, he thought as he watched her flash a brilliant smile at his friend. It sent a jolt of jealousy surging through Shaheen. Gritting his teeth, he dismissed the sensation. Khalid had never forgotten his wife nor would he betray him by attempting to win her from him. Aware of his friend's amused gaze, he scowled. Khalid was going to be a nuisance when it came to his relationship with Allegra.

"Miss Allegra, oh my lord, is it really you?" Millie's strong English accent made Allegra's head jerk toward the sound. "I've been worried half out of my mind."

The sight of the older woman made Allegra sway on her feet as her face paled. Shaheen's hand steadied her, but she pulled free of the light grasp and ran to meet her friend. The two women hugged each other, with Millie chattering away. Allegra's happiness illuminated her features, and he found himself wishing he, and not Khalid, had been the one to reunite her with her friend. With a dark frown at the sentiment, he turned his head to see his friend studying him with a look of assessment.

"I noticed the henna markings on her hand," Khalid murmured. "Laila tells me the seer in Marrakech painted the markings of fire on Allegra's hand."

"Did she? I hadn't noticed," he muttered as he fought to bury his surprise beneath a mask of indifference. He'd been too preoccupied with other things to note the details of her tattoo.

"Apparently Fatima said Allegra was your destiny." Khalid chuckled. "And . . . how shall I put this . . . Halah has been quite eager to meet the *jahīm anasi*."

Jahīm anasi. The woman of fire. A deep groan rolled out of him. The seer would delight in reminding him that she'd foretold his meeting Allegra more than a year ago. At the time he'd laughed at the old woman, but now her words haunted him in a manner that was far from comfortable. *A woman of fire will leave her mark until your past unites with your future.*

He frowned. Halah's words could be interpreted many ways. It was all coincidence, nothing more. Allegra had already left her mark on him. As for his past uniting with his future, that was simply the inevitable meeting with Shaftsbury he'd be forced to endure when he returned Allegra to Marrakech.

"Come, there is much to do before the council meets this evening." Khalid laughed and slapped him on the back as they watched Allegra's joyful reunion with her friend.

With a sharp nod, he turned away from Allegra and walked with his friend to where the caravan was setting up camp next to his small tribe. Although they were all under Khalid's rule, his Amazigh were responsible for small reconnaissance missions as fewer numbers were able to travel more quickly.

Now as he watched his men and their families being reunited with other kinfolk, a sliver of envy wrenched through him. James had been the only real family he'd ever known. His mother had died giving birth to him, a fact his father took great pains to point out to him whenever the opportunity presented itself. Burying the past as deep as he could, he threw himself into the task of directing the gathering of the tribal council Khalid had called.

Hours later, when the council meeting adjourned, he strode out of Khalid's tent into a darkness filled with dying fires. Other council members emerged from the tent with concerned expressions as they retired for the night. He understood their fears. The First Sheikh of the Amazigh had informed his council that he intended to strike Nassar first. But to do that, he would have to negotiate an alliance with Sheikh Jabbar, a warlord who controlled the northwestern section of Morocco. The man had obtained his power by stealing cattle and horses. Oddly enough, the man had a sense of honor as he never took more than half from his victims.

Even the justice he administered was done fairly. Jabbar was a law unto himself, but if Khalid could convince the man to join the Amazigh, it might prevent war. Nassar wouldn't go up against Khalid with Jabbar as their ally. The only flaw in Khalid's plan was the possibility that Jabbar might refuse to form an alliance. Even Hakim, who had put his petulant nature aside, had thoughtfully expressed his doubts. It had filled him with a sense of pride to know he'd had a role in the young heir's education.

He rolled his head to one side and then the other in an effort to soothe the sore muscles in his neck. The moon was high in the sky, telling him it was at least midnight. He grimaced. Allegra would be asleep by now. He'd imagined many times what it would be like when she finally came to his bed, but none of his fantasies had included planning for war. It was a conflict that couldn't be avoided unless they found a way to stop Nassar, and all of it hinged on Khalid forming an alliance with a horse thief. Soon he'd have to send Allegra back to Marrakech for her safety, but until then he could enjoy the pleasure of being with her.

"You're troubled, my friend." Khalid emerged from the tent to stand at his side.

"Only for your safety. How many men shall I bring with us?" he asked quietly as he met his friend's resolute gaze.

"You're not going with me," Khalid said. Seeing Shaheen about to protest, he raised his hand in an authoritative manner. "I'm taking two of my own men and our fastest horses. I need you here in case my brother moves more quickly than I expect."

"And if Jabbar doesn't agree to this alliance of yours?"

"Then I'll go to the French."

The somber words made him jerk with amazement as he stared at his friend. Khalid had always resisted aligning himself with the French, Spanish, or British governments. He hated politics and knew the price the Amazigh would pay if they sought help from any foreign power.

"The French?" he asked as the Sheikh sent him an arched look.

"Nassar's men will not fight the Legionnaires."

Khalid was right. Nassar didn't have the stomach for taking on the French Foreign Legion. Deep sorrow marring his handsome features, Khalid stared up at the night sky.

"I never told you why Nassar hates me, or what drove him to kill Yasmia, did I?"

The question came as a surprise. Khalid rarely mentioned Yasmia's name, but his celibacy since her death indicated how much his wife had meant to him. He didn't speak, but simply shook his head at his friend. Returning his gaze to the stars, the Sheikh heaved a sigh.

"Yasmia was beautiful. When I look at Laila, I see my wife so clearly." Khalid clasped his hands behind his back and tilted his head as if he were studying a specific constellation.

"I fell madly in love with Yasmia the first time I saw her. I didn't know it at the time, but Nassar felt the same way and spoke for her first. Unable to bear seeing her marry my brother, I announced my intention to live in Marrakech. The night before my departure, Yasmia came to me, and the next thing I knew I was holding her in my arms."

The Sheikh released a quiet noise of grief and closed his eyes. Ice flowed through him as he absorbed Khalid's words. Jamal had once told him he could be of the same blood as Khalid. Was this what the Bedouin warrior really meant? That their stories were similar?

"When Nassar found us together, he didn't say a word. He simply turned and walked away. The next morning, he denounced Yasmia as a whore, naming me as her protector and demanding she be whipped."

The similarities between his past and Khalid's made him swallow hard. Like him, his friend had loved a woman and lost a brother. His friend's features took on a shadowy expression of fury as he turned his head toward Shaheen.

"I refused to let anyone beat her, and I took the whip in her place. Nassar left the next day, and Yasmia and I were married a short time later."

The Sheikh's voice faded into silence as he returned his gaze to the starry night above. Uncertain as to what to say to his friend, he remained silent and contemplated how they'd both wrestled similar demons from the past.

"You need to send the *anasi* back to Marrakech in the morning," Khalid said firmly.

"No, not yet," he growled. It was a gut response. Emotions he refused to name tumbled through him at the suggestion. With a shake of his head, he averted his gaze from his friend. "The moment Shaftsbury tells the British who I am, the treaties—"

"The French and British will not interfere in tribal matters. The treaties will hold. Fadi, Coman, and the others are men of honor, unlike my brother," Khalid said in a firm voice. "The reason you give for keeping the *anasi* here no longer exists."

The words were like a lion clawing his flesh open. He didn't want to let her go. He wanted more time with her. He stared out into the darkness and didn't respond.

"Shaheen, she's no longer safe here. I've received word that my brother's spies know she's still in your camp."

"If I take her back to Marrakech, what's to prevent Nassar from kidnapping her again?" he protested bitterly. "I can protect her better than Shaftsbury."

"She's your weakness," Khalid said quietly. "My brother knows that now, and he'll exploit it if he can."

"My weakness?" he growled. "Allegra isn't a weakness."

"If she's not your weakness, then why insist she remain here?"

"Because she's my responsibility until she's able to return safely to England."

He glared at the look of skepticism on his friend's face. Did Khalid actually think he had feelings for the woman? He scoffed at the idea, while crushing an answer to the question. An answer he didn't want to hear. Khalid's eyes narrowed with astute perception.

"Then send for Shaftsbury. He can escort her to Safi where she can sail for England."

The words hovered in the air between them, and he was certain he'd just been issued an indirect command. He didn't like it. Particularly when he knew Khalid was right. But he couldn't let her go just yet. Today he'd put her in harm's way, but he'd learned a hard lesson. Protecting her meant making the right choices, and sending her back to Marrakech wasn't the right choice. His gut told him that. Yes, he wanted her. *Wanted her in the worst way.* But he knew she was safer with him than Shaftsbury or anyone else, even Khalid. She was safe because she was his, and he wasn't about to let anyone hurt her. The possessive nature of his thoughts sent tension crashing through him until he was rigid. He gave the Sheikh a hard look.

"We've been friends a long time, Khalid. So do not misunderstand me when I say that *I'll* decide when and how to send Allegra back to England." The hard, ruthless edge to Shaheen's voice made Khalid look at him oddly.

"So be it, but God help you if you fail her the way I failed Yasmia."

The forbidding look on Khalid's face didn't trouble him as much as the sympathetic note he heard in his friend's voice. The silent look of warning in the Sheikh's gaze didn't comfort him either as Khalid turned and walked away. Shaheen uttered a noise of disgust. God, he was a fool. He'd been so obsessed with Allegra that he'd failed to use his head when it came to protecting her and his people. He should have realized Nassar would track his movements. Fear gripped his muscles, twisting them into painful knots. Adding to his discomfort, another emotion spiked through him. It was hunger. A hunger to see her, reassure himself that she was safe.

His stride swift, he walked quietly through the camp until he reached his tent. Lifting the wool flap, he slipped into the dark dwelling where he paused to allow his eyes to adjust to the darkness. It wasn't long before he could see Allegra's voluptuous curves stretched out on her pallet supported by pillows. The blanket she used barely covered her lush curves. Desire barreled through him at the sensual picture she made. A long leg bent at the knee was exposed to the night air, while the thin wool covering had slipped downward to reveal the tops of her full breasts.

The thin stream of moonlight washing in from above accentuated the roundness of her hip beneath the blanket, while highlighting her exposed skin like pale silk on a dark canvas. He wanted to see her painted this way. But not asleep. He wanted an artist to capture that expression of raw sensuality her green eyes always had when she was awake. With as much stealth as possible, he crossed the carpet to sit at her side. Her breathing was soft and steady as she slept.

She looked so peaceful. He could only hope that this afternoon would not haunt her dreams. He frowned. Khalid was right. He needed to get her to safety, but not Marrakech. Nassar would be looking for her there, and he wasn't about to let that bastard take her a second time. No, Safi was safer. English ships put into port there frequently. The idea sparked a rebellion in his head.

The internal protests didn't surprise him as much as their intensity. Whenever he considered setting her free, a raw, primal possessiveness surged through him. It wasn't a comfortable sensation. A small sigh passed her lips, and he watched as she shifted beneath the blanket. The wool covering slipped down to reveal the tip of one dusky-colored nipple.

Instantly, he was as hard as a rock as he stared at the stiff peak. Christ Jesus, what kind of power did this woman have over him? Even in the innocence of sleep she could make him ache with desire. Stifling a groan, he dropped his head to rest upon his knees. He sat there with his eyes closed, drawing in her scent, listening to the soft sigh of her breath, the quiet rustle of her body against the pillows as she moved in her sleep. The sheer essence of her floated up to encircle him and snare him in her net.

Hard and taut inside his *sherwals*, his cock throbbed for release.

Every time he drew in a breath, his body cried out for her. It was a demand he knew would take a long time to assuage, but not tonight. Given the horrors of the day, he wasn't about to disturb her peaceful slumber.

Raising his head, he sucked in a sharp breath at the sight of her. She'd moved again in her sleep. One arm was tucked behind her neck, while her other arm crossed one breast until her fingers brushed over the opposite nipple. Her mouth was slightly parted as if even in sleep something had aroused her sensual nature. She was everything he'd ever dreamed temptation would be. Unable to help himself, he stripped his clothes off his back, amazed that he didn't wake her with his movements. Quietly, he stretched himself out beside her and encircled himself with his hand.

Watching her sleep, he pumped his erection with a firm hand. As he adjusted his grip to catch the sensitive ridge near the top of his hard cock, the action tugged a ragged breath from him. His gaze fell to her breast, and he imagined licking and sucking on the stiff nipple as he tightened his hand around his rod. She moved again in her sleep. This time her head turned toward him, her tongue darting out to moisten her lips as she pillowed her head into the curve of her shoulder.

The sight of her tongue damping her lips pulled a dark moan from him as his hand clenched himself a trifle too hard. He pumped faster as his eyes took in the soft smile curving her mouth. God almighty, she was awake. How long had she been awake? Caught up in the base needs of his flesh, he kept stroking himself as her eyes opened to stare into his. Lightly, she touched the nipple of one breast, her tongue lacing her upper lip as she twirled her fingers around the tip of her.

"Does it excite you when I touch myself like this?" Her voice was soft and mesmerizing as her fingers continued to play with her nipple.

"Christ Jesus, yes," he growled, as he pumped his hand over his flesh until he was burning from the heat of his fast strokes.

"And this," she murmured with a seductive smile as her hand slid down toward a dark triangle of curls. "Does this excite you?"

Still stroking himself with a quick and furious hand, he watched her fingers dip into her curls. His mouth went dry as he stared in fascination at the way she caressed herself. Erotic and sensual, her movements only intensified the need for release in his body. Unable to speak, he released a guttural sound as he closed his eyes and spilled his seed with one last hard stroke of his hand.

15

Allegra leaned over him and brushed her mouth against his in a gentle kiss. As she pulled away, his eyes opened. There was just a hint of indecision in them before they narrowed to study her with an assessing look.

"How long have you been awake, *ma chérie*?" The gruff question pulled a smile to her lips.

"Since you took off your clothes," she murmured as she cleaned his stomach with a soft bit of fabric she kept near her pallet.

Her answer clearly stunned him as he stared at her in disbelief. Finished attending to his immediate needs, she rolled over onto her stomach and rested her head on her folded arms as she met his gaze with an inquisitive look.

"Didn't you enjoy yourself?"

"Of course, I—"

"Then does it matter how long I was awake?"

"I would have enjoyed giving you pleasure in return," he said in a husky voice as he came up on one elbow and stroked her cheek with his hand.

"But you did please me. I found it quite pleasurable watching you, knowing that I was the reason you were so hard." She smiled with mischief. "It *was* me you were hard for wasn't it?"

"You know damn well it was."

He brushed a short curl off the edge of her brow. It was a tender touch, and it frightened her. Charles had been tender with her, but his touch had never clutched at her heart the way this man's caresses did. She studied his face with an experienced eye. There was something different about him tonight. He was on edge. She could see it in the faint lines of tension pulling at his sensual mouth. Instinctively she stroked his bare shoulder in a soothing manner to divert his attention from whatever was troubling him.

"I like your Sheikh Mahmoud. Have you been friends for a long time?" Her question hung in the air for a moment before he shrugged.

"A little more than fifteen years." The taciturn response made her sigh, and she lifted her head to study his closed-off expression more easily.

"Trusting one's lover is part of the contract we made today, Shaheen. Our mutual pleasure is based on trust, and that means trusting me not to betray your secrets as well."

"Exactly what is it you want to know about me, Allegra?" There was a mocking note in his voice as he studied her with an unreadable expression.

The cynical gleam in his dark eyes aroused frustration and understanding all at the same time. Somewhere in his past, whoever had hurt him, had hurt him deeply. Experience had taught her that in most instances a woman was often the cause of the pain. Whatever this particular woman had done, it was seared into him like a brand.

"I'm not her," she said quietly.

"What the—who have you been talking to? Jamal?" His voice was tight with fury.

"Jamal hasn't said anything to me, nor has anyone else." She met his gaze steadily. "It was an educated guess. An accurate one if I judge your reaction correctly."

"You expect me to believe that?" he exclaimed, his mouth a hard line of anger.

"Yes. It was nothing more than simple observation. It's a part of who I am, what I do. I offer a man more than sexual pleasure, Shaheen. I'm companion, confidante, and friend. I anticipate my lover's needs, both physical *and* emotional. The men I choose find I'm a sanctuary where they can freely be themselves. They've no need of masks when they're with me."

She waited for him to say something, but he remained silent, a guarded expression on his face. When he didn't speak, she frowned. This wasn't going quite the way she'd envisioned it when she'd awoken and watched him masturbating beside her. She pressed one cheek back into her arms, but kept her eyes focused on his unreadable features.

"*I'm not her*, Shaheen. And I won't pay for her sins, whatever they were."

"No. You're not her." His soft words startled her, and the determination that flashed in his eyes sent a shiver down her spine. "And I'm not like any of your other lovers. I want what you've never given any man before. I want *your* mask stripped away."

"I'm not sure what you're asking of me." It was a lie, and she knew it. The chill tickling her spine raced across her skin until she was ice-cold. "You asked me to choose you, and I've done so willingly."

"But you're still hiding behind that courtesan façade you've created for yourself. I want the woman you keep hidden away from every man you meet. The woman who's afraid to experience true passion for fear of losing control."

The dangerous glint in his penetrating gaze alarmed her. She'd known he wanted the passion she'd never offered to any of her past lovers, but this was something different. Swallowing the knot of trepidation in her throat, she trembled as his fingers trailed with a lazy finesse across her shoulder and down her back. He wanted her to open herself up to him completely and without inhibition. It meant giving up control. It meant complete and utter surrender. He asked the impossible. Desperate, she tried to turn the tables on him.

"Are you willing to do the same?"

His fingers grew still against her skin, coming to rest at the small of her back. The heat of his touch thawed the chilled spot at the base of her spine, but the tension in him radiated its way into the muscles beneath his fingers.

"I think you need to explain that request, *ma belle*."

Cold and distant, his voice blew an icy wind across her skin as his brown eyes marked her with a wintry stare. She'd touched a raw nerve. The past had a greater hold on him than she'd realized. It was there in his harsh and forbidding expression. They were at odds again, and she didn't want that. The thought chilled her even more, and she shivered as she answered him.

"Are you willing to show me the man who prefers to bury himself in the desert rather than return to England to face his past?" Her question turned him into a cold statue.

"Exactly what is it you think you know about my past, Allegra?"

"Only what I've deduced—nothing more. It's not too difficult to guess that you're at odds with your family. You yourself told me you never got along with your father."

Her words echoed softly between them, and his mouth thinned

even more as he watched her with a cold eye. She wasn't lying. He
was certain of that. If anything, she looked puzzled as to why he
was angry. And he *was* angry. Furious because he'd allowed her
revelation to affect him.

From the first moment he'd learned Shaftsbury was looking
for him, he'd assumed it was because his father was dead. But not
knowing anything for certain had made it easy to dismiss the possibility. Without confirmation, he could easily bury his emotions
deep beneath the layers of detachment he'd built over the past
fifteen years without feeling anything because he knew nothing.
Rolling onto his back, he stared up at the stream of moonlight
pushing its way through the tent's ceiling.

He'd always thought the news of his father's death or impending demise would have little, if any, impact on him. God knows
he'd wished the bastard in his grave on more than one occasion
over the years. But the reality of the situation was completely different from what he'd expected. Instead of the blasé disinterest of
someone unaffected by the news, it was as if someone had stabbed
him with a knife. And it infuriated him that he cared, that he still
longed for his father's love and approval. That he found himself
wishing his father might still be alive and that he could return to
England in hope of— He was a fool.

Allegra's hand pressed against his chest, as she rose up to hover
over him. The compassion on her face was mixed with another
emotion he couldn't name. The sight of it warmed him more than
he wanted to admit. Even now, as he struggled to come to grips
with the emotions barreling through him, he was moved by her.

"Perhaps if you just listened to what Charles has to say—"

The instant Shaftsbury's name rolled off her lips his pain ebbed
as a new emotion took hold. Primeval in nature, it raced through
his blood with a primitive rhythm he refused to name.

"No," he growled before she could finish her sentence. "No more talk."

His hands slid across silky shoulders as he grasped her arms and rolled her onto her back in one swift move. Fever slashed through him as he stared down at her. She was his now, and he refused to share her with any man. After tonight she would be marked in such a way that not even she would be able to dispute that fact. Lowering his head swiftly, he took her mouth in a hard, demanding kiss.

She didn't protest, but welcomed the harsh caress with an eagerness that heated his blood even more. Her excitement betrayed itself in the way her arms curled around his neck to pull him deeper into her body. Beneath him, her soft curves met his hard, angular ones, while every inch of him sought to connect with the soft silk of her skin. It wasn't enough to simply feel her against him. There was this overwhelming need to absorb her into his body, bind her to him for as long as he could. It was the most base sensation he'd ever felt. There was no comparison to the raw intensity of it. To the fire that consumed him.

He shuddered as her lips parted beneath his and her tongue flicked its way into his mouth. Christ Jesus, but the woman knew how to tantalize him with one hot stroke of her delicious tongue. The fire in his blood was out of control. Impossible to stop. That he didn't *want* to stop should have alarmed him, but it was a fleeting thought in the haze of this blinding desire. It possessed him to the point that he was lost in her arms. Lost in realizing that he might never be able to let her go. The thought should have extinguished the blaze inside him, but it didn't.

Tossing it aside, he welcomed the consuming fundamental need that allowed him to immerse himself in her. It pushed everything out of his head. Shaftsbury, his father, his failures, James,

Frances—everything receded as he took from her what she willingly gave. And she *was* willing. Needy. She clung to him just as a jasmine vine embraced a tree. The flower's scent and the sharp bite of mint cloaked her skin, but he also detected the faint hint of musk. Desire's scent.

God, she was already wet and slick for him. He didn't even have to touch her to know it. His mouth broke free of hers as he ravaged her throat, drinking in her sultry perfume as he lightly nipped at her skin with his teeth. Another soft moan escaped her mouth as she squirmed beneath him. Her fingernails bit into his back as she tried to press her hips against his. Tried to meld her soft heat to his rigid cock. Triumph rolled through every muscle of his body. Eagerly, he worked his way downward with his mouth as she arched her back in an attempt to keep her body joined with his. Cupping a full breast in the palm of his hand, he dragged his thumb across a stiff peak. The small hiss of air she inhaled called out to every predatory instinct in his body.

The rawness of the sound and the emotions gripping him stretched him until he was certain he would explode before he even buried himself inside her. This wasn't just a simple moment of lovemaking. This was desire at its most powerful, its most base. It fed his primitive need to wipe any trace of the past from his soul. His body hummed for her as he lowered his head again and swirled his tongue around her hard nipple. A whimper of craving poured out of her. It wasn't enough. He wanted more.

Deep and dark the emotions rose up in him until he wanted to devour her. Tonight she would help him drive out his demons. His hand slid down her stomach, straight for the white-hot center of her. She tensed at the stroke. His mouth released her nipple, and he raised his head to stare down at her. There was no deception or hesitancy in the depths of her green eyes. Only a naked hunger for him. He was certain no other man had ever seen this look on her face before.

He waited for the ultimate victory.

Her eyes darkened to a deep green, and her expression was filled with a silent plea. Still he waited. Only when she surrendered completely to the passion gripping her would he be able to satisfy this insatiable desire burning its way through his body. Her eyes closed for a brief moment, her mouth forming a small moue as she tried to shift her hips beneath him. When she failed, she whimpered with need.

"For the love of God, Shaheen. Please. I want you. I need to feel you inside me."

Triumph surged through him. It tightened every muscle in his body with fiery need. He'd drawn from her the one thing he'd wanted most. Her passion. Her open soul willing to mate with his. A decadent madness stormed its way into every limb of his body as he raised himself higher so he could study her. Memorize every inch of her. The moment he pressed himself against her curls, she thrust her hips upward in a silent demand for him. He needed no other invitation.

With a growl that rumbled deep in his chest, he plunged into her. Barely suppressing his cry of pleasure at the way her hot cunny gripped him, he withdrew from her slightly. Ripples convulsed over his hardness as her body clung to his, trying to hold him prisoner inside her. Sensation after heated sensation pounded against his cock as he plunged into her over and over again with increasing speed. God almighty, he'd never experienced anything like this before.

Every part of his body was on fire for her. Staring down into her face he released a groan of pleasure as she arched up into him. The open passion in her expression made her exquisite. Eyes closed, her mouth was parted in small pants of pleasure as a pink tongue flicked out to wet her lips. She was an alluring siren, bowing to his demands, his will—his need. She was his.

"Look at me, *ma belle*," he rasped. Her eyes flew open, her gaze blazing with unrestrained pleasure. "You're mine. You belong to no one else. *Say it*."

"I'm . . . Shaheen's woman." She panted as he ground his hips against hers. "I belong . . . to no other . . . man."

The soft words pushed him over the edge as his hips slammed into hers at a blistering pace until a dark cry rolled out of him and he purged his soul inside her.

❦

The heat of the day was in full force as Allegra stood beneath the roof of her tent. Even with all the wall panels raised, there was little fresh air drifting through the dwelling. Staring out at the desert plain, she remembered the ecstasy of last night. Never in her wildest dreams had she ever imagined that lovemaking could be so exhilarating or passionate.

From the moment she'd surrendered and declared she was his, Shaheen had spent the rest of the night pleasuring her almost to the point of madness. His hands and mouth had teased and tormented her until she could do nothing but beg for him to take her again and again. The sheer bliss of it all still sent shivers of delight across her skin. Her nipples grew hard and the soft wool of her *gambaz* rubbed across them much in the same manner Shaheen's thumb had done last night.

She ached for him in a way she'd never ached for any man, and her body was hungry for more. It was a hunger she'd never expected to feel for a lover, and it was unsettling. She was in way over her head where he was concerned, but she didn't care. That in itself was alarming.

Heaving a sigh, she turned her head as she heard children laughing and shouting near her tent. The sight of Millie walking toward her as the children dashed past the older woman tugged a smile to her lips. Even despite living in the desert for a month, her friend still dressed as if she were going to the market for the evening's meal. The woman traversed her way around the children and low-burning campfires as she headed toward her. Behind her Jamal carried a large trunk on his shoulders. As they reached her tent, Millie directed the Bedouin to set the trunk down under the peaked roof of the dwelling.

The trunk safely settled in its new home, Millie nodded her gratitude to the Bedouin as she brushed past him to open the luggage. An odd look crossed Jamal's face as he remained where he was and watched Millie. For a moment, she was almost certain the Amazigh's features were filled with lust as he studied the maid. Suddenly aware that he was being observed, he jerked his head toward Allegra. Even beneath his dark skin, she could see a flush of color rising up in his face. Muttering something under his breath, he gave her a swift bow and hurried out from underneath the tent and quickly disappeared. Amused by the man's behavior, she wondered if Millie might find the Bedouin attractive. The two of them were about the same age, and the Amazigh was quite handsome. The maid pulled out a dress and turned to face her.

"Here we are, Miss Allegra. I'm certain you've missed wearing your own clothes," Millie said as she held up a day gown. "I think you'll find this much more to your liking than those native clothes you're wearing."

Laughing, she shook her head. "I don't think so, Millie."

"But miss, you can't possibly want to continue wearing those pants and that shirt," Millie exclaimed in horror.

"I do indeed." She smiled at her friend. "They're comfortable, and I'm not so eager to give them up. You should try them."

"That Jamal suggested the same thing." Millie sniffed with disdain.

"He likes you," Allegra said with a smile.

"Who? Jamal?" The woman jerked with surprise and her cheeks flared with color.

"Yes. I saw the way he looked at you a few minutes ago."

"Harrumph. I think your imagination is running amok." Millie waved a hand in dismissal. She turned quickly back to the trunk, rummaging through it. When she didn't find what she was looking for, she lifted her head. "I must have left your brushes in my trunk. I'll go get them."

Cheeks still tinged with heightened color, Millie darted out of the tent just as Laila was arriving. Delighted to see her friend, she crossed the shelter's carpeted floor and greeted the younger woman with a warm hug.

"Laila, how wonderful to see you again."

"I am delighted to see you are safe," the young Bedouin woman said as she hugged Allegra tightly. As Laila stepped back, her gaze flew to Allegra's short, curly hair. The dismay in the young woman's expression made Allegra reach out to squeeze her hand.

"It looks much better than it did. Actually, I've grown accustomed to it, and it has its advantages. It's much cooler, and Shaheen has nothing to grab hold of when he gets angry with me." She grinned mischievously at the younger woman.

"I imagine that's quite frustrating for him." Laila laughed then grew sober. "Still, if I'd just been more observant—"

"Stop," Allegra said sternly. "What happened was beyond our control."

"Perhaps, but it still doesn't make me feel any better," Laila said with a sigh. "And now there's the threat of war again."

"War?" she exclaimed.

"My uncle has negotiated an alliance with Sheikh Cadi to

challenge my father. It's why he's so far north of his territory."
Laila's voice was filled with bitterness. "Not content with killing
my mother, he must now try to take my father from me as well."

"Surely it won't come to that," she said in a soothing voice as
her heart skipped a beat.

What would happen to Shaheen if there was fighting? Would
he fight alongside the Sheikh? She already knew the answer, and
it terrified her. Laila spread her hands in a gesture of troubled
concern.

"I wish I could believe that. Unless Father can negotiate a treaty
with Abd al Jabbar, then there will be fighting."

"This man your father went to see; do you think he'll sign a
treaty?"

"I'm not sure. I think Jabbar will agree only if it's in his best
interest, but Father can be quite persuasive. Almost as much as
Shaheen." Laila sent her a sly look and Allegra's cheeks grew hot
under the other woman's scrutiny.

"You forgot autocratic and demanding," she responded in a wry
tone.

"And what is this to the *jahīm anasi*?" Laila scoffed as she
reached out to touch Allegra's tattoo. "You are fire, and fire molds
steel. I should have known that when Fatima painted these marks
on your hand. You are the woman of fire. Even our own seer foretold your coming."

A dark shadow fell across the carpet, and she looked up to see
Shaheen standing behind Laila with a scowl on his face. "You listen to Halah's old wives' tales too much."

It was impossible not to smile her pleasure at seeing him. It had
been hours since he'd kissed her good-bye this morning, and her
body was alive with sensation just being near him. Laila looked up
at him and laughed.

"And you *don't* listen, which is why Halah is gloating like a child pulling a prank." The good-natured teasing pulled a smile to his lips, and Laila scrambled to her feet. "I have chores to do, so I'll come visit later, Allegra."

With a wave of her hand, the young Bedouin woman left the tent. The moment Laila left them alone, the air crackled with heat. Shaheen leaned into her until there was a mere thread of space between them, and she trembled at the way her skin tingled as his gaze slid over her.

"Wearing my mark suits you, *ma belle*," he murmured.

A strong hand cupped her cheek, while his thumb slid sensuously across her lower lip. It was a teasing caress, and she could see the wicked amusement in his gaze as she inhaled a sharp breath. Determined to prove that two could play at this game, she parted her lips and drew his thumb into her mouth. Sucking on him, she delighted in the warm, salty taste of his skin. Her gaze never left his face as she swirled her tongue around his thumb. Desire flared in his eyes as he drew in a swift breath of pleasure at her hot caress. Slowly, she eased his thumb out of her mouth and offered him her most sultry smile.

"Did that please you?" She smiled as he gave her a sharp nod. "Then perhaps I could please you in a similar fashion elsewhere."

The suggestive statement drew a ragged breath from him and he jerked her against him. Staring down into her eyes, he shook his head as if trying to clear it.

"In a few hours, *ma belle*, I'm going to make you pay for that."

"Why wait, when I'm willing to pay now," she teased as she caught his hand and returned it to her mouth, her tongue flicking out to swirl around his forefinger.

"Sweet Jesus," he groaned as he tugged his hand free and pressed her hips into his hard, thick erection. "Do you have any idea how badly I want your mouth on me right now?"

"Yes." She laughed softly. "I think I do."

Another groan rumbled in his throat as he rested his forehead against hers. "I promise you, *ma chérie*, tonight I intend to extract full payment for this blatant attempt at manipulation."

"I'll look forward to it," she said in a husky voice and pulled his head down so she could brush her lips over his. "But until then, remember that I've marked *you* as well."

The low growl of desire rumbling in his chest made her smile with satisfaction. A movement out of the corner of her eye forced her to shift her gaze, and she saw Hakim standing just outside the tent, his face red with anger. Realizing someone was behind him, Shaheen turned around and waited for the younger man to speak.

"Coman has returned, and he has a prisoner," Hakim said in an icy tone.

"Very well, I'll be there in a moment."

"I'll wait for you." The young man's voice was a whip cracking between the two of them.

Narrowing his gaze, he studied Hakim for a long moment before he gave him a sharp nod and turned back to Allegra. One hand stroking her cheek, he bent his head toward her.

"Until tonight, *ma chérie*," he whispered as his mouth brushed against her earlobe.

Not waiting for her reply, he left the tent, Hakim keeping pace beside him. The silence between them bordered on the brink of freezing, but he knew nothing he said would make him look any less guilty in Hakim's eyes. Working their way through the camp, they headed in the direction of Khalid's tent, which was serving as the tribe's command post.

"You lied." Hakim's snarl broke the tense silence. "You wanted the *anasi* for yourself."

Coming to a halt, he faced the young man he'd guarded since childhood and shook his head, keeping a strong grip on his temper. "I did *not* lie to you. That is your pride talking."

The young man turned away with a grunt of anger. "I saw her first. She should be mine."

"*Damm gahannam*, you sound like your uncle," he exploded with fury. "Is this what I've taught you? That a human being is nothing more than a piece of property one owns? If so, then I've failed miserably in my duty to you *and* your father."

Wheeling away from Hakim, his furious stride carried him toward the command post. God, he was a hypocrite. He was every bit as guilty as the boy for treating Allegra as property. He'd wanted her from the moment he set eyes on her. Even if he'd fought that need every step of the way, he was no less guilty of claiming her when she wanted nothing to do with him. A strong hand grabbed his arm and dragged him to a halt.

"I am *not* like my uncle." Hakim shook his head in umbrage before his expression changed to one of respect. "You are more my uncle than Nassar ever was or could be."

Studying the young man before him, he heaved a sigh. "Then start acting like the man I know you can be because your father needs you now, more than ever."

"It sounds simple when *you* say it." Hakim scowled with frustration. "I will never be the man my father or you are."

"Perhaps not, but you *will be* the man we've taught you to be. That is all either of us have ever asked of you."

"And what of the *anasi*?" Hakim's voice clarified that there was still bad blood between them where Allegra was concerned.

"I never lied to you about Allegra. She rejected you simply because you *are* too young for her. She is a rare woman in that she has principles, Hakim. Most women in her profession would have broken your heart and made you bitter."

Although there was still a trace of anger in the young man's face, there was also discernment reflected there, too. The boy would heal, and their relationship would continue, but in a different form. As the Amazigh heir tipped his head in a nod of understanding, Shaheen offered him a small smile.

"Come, we need to see what news Coman has brought us."

Together they continued toward the command post. Relieved to have things settled between the two of them, he recognized that their relationship had changed. He was no longer the boy's guardian, but a friend and mentor. It was a small payment on the debt he still owed for James's death. The boy would do well by Khalid, especially if Nassar forced them into a war.

An hour later, Shaheen realized there was only one way to avoid an armed conflict with Nassar. The man had to die. As Coman and the other men escorted their prisoner away, a vicious fury slashed at him. The bastard had gone too far this time. He relaxed his fist and opened up the crumpled piece of paper he held.

My dear Newcastle,

As you can see, I've decided to let you live. Your whore on the other hand . . . well, did you really think I would let you keep her? If I cannot have her, then neither shall you.

Sheikh Nassar

He crumpled the paper in his fist again with suppressed violence. The man his men had captured had been sent to murder Allegra. The note was simply the message Nassar had intended for him when he found Allegra dead. She was in danger. God, he'd done nothing but make mistake after mistake since he first met Allegra. He should have sent her back to Shaftsbury weeks ago. No, he should have placed her on a boat to England himself. Khalid's words echoed through his head. *God help you if you fail her the way I failed Yasmia.* And he *had* almost failed her. It wouldn't happen again. She was going back to England with Shaftsbury.

"He'll do to her what he did to my mother if we don't stop him," Hakim said with a haunted expression on his young features. "What are you going to do?"

The boy's grim words sliced through him and he nodded. A fear he'd never known before closed his throat, and not even when he'd searched for James that terrible night had he experienced this kind of dread.

"I'm going to send for Shaftsbury. He can take her to Othmane, and from there they can travel by train to Safi. It will be a safer route than taking the train from Marrakech. Nassar will be looking for them there."

"Let me fetch Shaftsbury."

"No," Shaheen exclaimed with a sharp hand gesture. "It's not safe."

"Is it safe for any of us?" Hakim asked quietly. "If it makes you feel better, I'll take Jamal with me. We can travel in the dark to avoid any of Nassar's scouts."

He hesitated as he considered the boy's suggestion. It was a sound plan despite the danger involved. But Hakim's status as Khalid's heir was a problem. If something happened—

"I'll be in good hands, and as you've said, I need to take on greater responsibility." The younger man sent him a sober look.

"I didn't mean putting your life in danger," he snapped, glaring at Hakim. "If your father were here, it would be me going after Shaftsbury."

"But he's not."

Still he hesitated to agree to the suggestion. It would be just as easy to send Jamal by himself. Stepping toward him, Hakim touched his shoulder.

"Let me do this. Let me make my amends to you *and* the *jahīm anasi*."

The request wiped away his reservations as he realized how

much the young man had matured almost overnight. Or was it simply that he'd not given the boy a chance to prove himself? Narrowing his gaze, he studied Hakim's eager expression.

"Send for Jamal so we can hammer out this plan of yours. I want both of you to return safely with Shaftsbury in tow."

Satisfaction turned Hakim's mouth upward as he nodded and bolted out of the command tent. Left alone, he opened his fist and looked at the note he still held. The sudden image of Frances sprawled lifeless across her bed flashed through his head, only this time it was Allegra's green eyes staring up at the ceiling. A shudder blasted its way through him as he threw the image back into the dark pit it had emerged from. Allegra wasn't going to die.

With Shaftsbury's help, he'd see to that. But something told him she wouldn't go willingly. The idea that she might want to stay with him in spite of the danger filled him with mixed emotions. Whatever happened, he wouldn't let her stay here. He'd do whatever was necessary to make her leave. All that mattered was her safety. Not even the pain he was going to feel when he gave her into Shaftsbury's care mattered. A primal surge of emotion raced through him. After tonight, she'd no longer be his. But until then he was going to memorize every breath she took, every turn of her head, everything about her that he could commit to memory.

16

Reclined among the jeweled-toned pillows on the carpeted floor of her tent, she didn't hear Shaheen enter, but her body vibrated from his presence. She looked up from the book she'd been reading to see him standing just inside the doorway watching her. With a smile of welcome, she stood up and walked toward him.

He met her halfway, and she melted into his embrace with a sigh of pleasure. His arms were hard and solid around her, but she could feel his taut sinews were rigid with tension. Something was wrong. *Terribly wrong.* There was a sense of desperation about him that frightened her. As he turned away, she shivered. Whatever news he'd received earlier had disturbed him greatly.

The sudden sound of childish laughter echoed outside the tent, and she turned her head to see Malik and a young girl scurry into the dwelling with two baskets. As the children set down the handwoven containers, Shaheen dropped the sidewalls of the tent with the exception of the opening that looked out onto the Atlas

Mountains. When the children were gone, Shaheen extended his hand to her. Slipping her hand into his was like entering a home she'd lived in forever. The sensation warmed every part of her heart and body. As if he felt the same way, he smiled down at her and gently squeezed her fingers. They sat down at the pommel rests situated in front of the low table with his shoulder pressing into hers as he leaned toward one of the baskets.

"Close your eyes," he ordered with a wicked grin curling his lips.

With a wary smile of amusement, she eyed him carefully. "What are you up to?"

"Close your eyes, Allegra." This time the command dared her to disobey him as his brown eyes glinted with determination.

"As you wish." She laughed and closed her eyes.

There was the sudden aroma of a pungent fruit, and she tilted her head to one side as she breathed in the scent. *Bananas.* Without permission, she opened her eyes to see him watching her with a sinful spark of mischief in his dark eyes. In his hands, he held a banana with its skin peeled back.

"Would you care to demonstrate the proper way to eat this fruit, *ma belle*?" he asked. Laughing, she stretched out her hand, but he pulled the banana out of her reach. "On second thought, I don't think I care to endure the torment you put me through the last time you ate this particular type of fruit."

"I won't deny that I enjoyed winning our wager," she said with another laugh as she gestured for him to let her have a bite of the fruit.

"I didn't know whether to throttle you or keep you with me until we were both satisfied," he said gruffly as he offered her the banana.

Her hand resting over his, she leaned forward and swirled her tongue around the tip of the fleshy fruit before she bit off a small piece. His low growl teased her senses as she met his brown-eyed gaze. This was what she'd never experienced with her other lovers. *This intimate knowing.* There was an invisible thread binding her to him. It was so strong she didn't think she could break it even if she wanted to.

His fingers gently touched her cheek before he opened up another basket and handed her a flat loaf of bread. Minutes later, she was looking at a buffet of fruits, cheese, and bread. As they ate, the rapport between them was natural and comfortable, and she laughed as she playfully fought him for the last piece of cheese. Relinquishing the tasty morsel to him, she reached for a date instead. As she bit into the sugary sweet fruit, Shaheen poured them a cup of tea. He watched as she took a sip. Eyes widening, she uttered a soft gasp. "Earl Grey!"

"I asked your maid for the last of her supply." He smiled with satisfaction.

"Thank you," she said with a happy sigh. "I love mint tea, but this is like being at home."

The moment she spoke, he turned his head away from her and his profile was sharply defined in the fading light as he stared out at the mountains vivid with color from the setting sun. She couldn't see it, but she sensed the sorrow in him. It prompted her to reach out and touch his cheek. There was just the hint of an evening shadow bristling beneath the pads of her fingers. He stiffened slightly at the touch before he captured her hand in his and pressed his mouth to the inside of her wrist.

It was a simple caress, but the tenderness of it tugged at her heart in a way she never could have envisioned. The intensity of the emotion held her in place as he stood up and crossed the carpet to stand where the wall of the tent was drawn back. Arms folded across his chest, he studied the desert plain that stretched out to the foot of the mountains. His air of impending disaster had returned, and he looked like a sentinel guarding against an unseen enemy. Had something happened between him and Hakim? The boy had not been pleased to see her with Shaheen earlier, and it was more than possible they'd had a falling-out.

"I haven't thought about home for a very long time."

His words were so soft, she almost didn't hear them. In fact, she was certain he'd not meant to speak them out loud. Quickly rising to her feet, she moved to his side and entwined her arm in his.

"Do you miss it?"

Silence hung between them for a moment before he shook his head. "No. I've found the home here that I never had in England."

"I understand why you feel that way. I love the simplicity of it all. There are no complications for the Amazigh. They live in the present believing their destiny is already foretold."

"And you? What of your destiny, *ma chérie*?" He looked down at her with an unreadable expression.

"I always thought I fashioned my own destiny." She lifted her hand to examine the somewhat faded mark on her hand. "But I don't believe that anymore."

As she spoke the words, she suddenly realized how little control she had over her life. The choices she'd made were the only control she'd ever had. Her every decision had layered the outcome of subsequent choices. But the real truth was that from the moment her mother had sold her to Madame Eugenie, she'd had only one choice.

Survival.

That wasn't shaping one's destiny. Her gaze returned to the mark that proclaimed her the *jahīm anasi*. No, she didn't shape her destiny, it shaped her, and she was Shaheen's woman. His destiny. This was exactly where she was supposed to be. It was a heady revelation, and it stole her breath away. His touch was gentle as he ran his forefinger over her henna tattoo.

"Then let us live for the moment, *ma belle*, and let destiny take care of itself." His warm breath teased her cheek as he whispered the words in her ear.

Capturing her face with both his hands, he kissed her gently. It was a caress that made her want to weep from the sweetness of it. Dear lord, she had no defense for this type of tender regard. With one warm touch, he'd sent her heart spiraling out of control. His fingers trailed across her cheek as he released her and moved to drop the tent's last open wall. When he turned to face her again, she saw something akin to hopelessness flash in his dark eyes. With a slight shake of her head, she went to him and pressed her hand to his heart.

"You're troubled, *mon coeur*."

The endearment slipped past her lips before she could stop herself, and beneath her palm, the muscles in his chest grew hard and taut. Sweet heaven, what had possessed her to use such an intimate endearment? She swallowed hard and took a step back from him in shock. An odd expression swept over his face, and with a swift jerk he pulled her back into his arms.

"Say that again," he growled.

Startled, she met his penetrating gaze and paled. She flinched with dismay as she averted her gaze from his. She'd revealed too much with her words. A strong hand caught her chin in a firm grip, and he forced her to look at him.

"Now, Allegra." The demanding arrogance was back in his voice, and she shuddered with the realization that she had surrendered every last piece of her soul to him.

"My heart," she whispered as another tremor rippled through her.

With a soft groan, he captured her mouth in a kiss that set her entire body on fire. His mouth singed her, marked her, demanded her response. She gave it willingly. With each fiery brush of her lips against his, she offered him her heart. She'd thought yielding to him had meant giving up complete control—giving up her sense of self, but it didn't. Surrender only meant she would finally be complete. With him, she was the *jahīm anasi*. She was his, and nothing would ever change that. Loving him was what made her whole.

His mouth took everything she offered him, and she spiked her fingers through his hair as she pressed into him. A low growl rumbled in his chest as his erection brushed against the apex of her thighs. Sweet and fragrant, the scent of her tickled his nose and the faint taste of sugared dates swept across his tongue. How was it possible the woman could be as intoxicating now as she had been the first time he'd kissed her? With a skilled move, she teased the inside of his mouth with a languorous stroke of her tongue.

Christ Jesus but he wanted her—needed her. He deepened their kiss, his tongue mating with hers in heated strokes until a mewl of need echoed out of her. The sound sent a rush of excitement through him. She wanted him. But the triumph he'd expected to feel was missing. Instead, it was gratitude he was feeling. Appreciation for this moment—this last night with her. He lifted his head to stare down at her. He'd always thought her a sensual creature, but tonight she was exquisite.

It astonished him that his hand shook as his fingers traced the smooth softness of her cheek downward to the small hollow of her throat. He wanted to draw out this moment as long as he could. He'd told her they would live in the present tonight, and that was exactly what he intended to do. Morning would come soon enough. With an eagerness that pleased him, she tugged his head down and kissed him. It was a caress designed to entice, and he groaned his willingness to be seduced by her. With a skillful move, she nestled her hips snug against his stiff cock. Sweet Jesus, but the woman knew exactly how to touch him so he had little choice but to simply show her what he couldn't say.

Roughly, he tugged her *gambaz* up over her head. She didn't protest, but reached for his shirt and pushed it up to his shoulders so she could press her mouth to his skin. He discarded the *gambaz* while her hot tongue darted out to swirl around his nipple. A second later, she gently bit down on the tip. He drew in a sharp breath at the pleasure surging through him. *Merde*, the woman was going to make him spill his seed before he even finished undressing. It was time to bring her to her knees. Tossing his shirt aside, he knelt in front her and tore her *sherwals* downward. Dark auburn curls dusted the apex of her thighs, and the light fragrance of musk filled his nostrils. Fingers biting into her soft, plump thighs, he forced her legs apart then leaned forward to slide his tongue through her thick folds, licking his way to her sensitive spot. Above his head, he heard her release a deep moan, and with his thumb he applied pressure to the rim of her sex. Her fingernails bit into his shoulders as he swirled his tongue around the small fleshy nub. A drop of cream flavored his mouth, the bite of her fresh and hot. Eager for more, he licked the rim of her before he delved deeper into her hot core. God, she tasted good. Hot and silky smooth. Her knees buckled and her hands pressed deeply into his shoulders. With one last stroke of his tongue, he pulled away from her and allowed her to sink to her knees.

An iron vise tightened its grip around his heart at the emotion darkening her green eyes. It was the unrestrained passion he'd asked her to give him. But there was something else flashing in that beautiful gaze of hers. An emotion he knew he wasn't worthy of. Christ Jesus, he was a condemned man. Tonight he was living in paradise with the knowledge that he'd be in hell come morning. It didn't matter. All that mattered was her. Desire made her skin glow as she wrapped her arms around his neck, her breaths soft pants of excitement. He'd pleased her. Of that, he was certain and it increased his ardor as they tumbled backward into the pillows on her pallet. Their movements feverish, they tugged the remainder of their clothing off. She was free first, and in a quick move, she straddled him. Slowly, her hands glided across his shoulders and down over his chest. Hard and strong, his well-sculpted body was like the desert, hot and beautiful. Leaning forward, her tongue trailed a path from his breastbone up to the base of his throat. He was salty and all male. As she tasted him, a deep sound rumbled in his chest.

Her lips pressed against his hard muscles, she breathed in his spicy scent. Sitting up, she gently scraped her fingernail along the hard length of him. The rumble in his chest became a deep growl.

"You're playing with fire, *helwa jahannam meshsh*."

"As the *jahīm anasi*, isn't that what I'm supposed to do?" she teased. "Perhaps I'll just keep playing with fire until you tell me what *helwa jahannam meshsh* means."

She'd barely finished speaking before she was on her back and the weight of him was pressing her into the pillows. Pinning her hands up over her head, he bent over her and flicked his tongue across one nipple, his touch as light as air, but agonizingly delicious. As the tip of him brushed against her sex, she whimpered and arched her back in a silent plea for more. He obliged her with a sharp thrust as he sheathed himself inside her. She uttered a small cry at his possession. Dear lord, she'd never dreamed it could be like this—so intense—so exquisite. She was on fire from the inside out.

The pleasure of it carried her into a white-hot abyss as a shudder gripped her. Her body tightened around his hard length, and she bucked her hips against his as he uttered a sharp cry and throbbed with his own release. Buried deep inside her, he gingerly lowered his weight down on top of her. She welcomed the warmth of him, and clung to him as the sound of his harsh breathing echoed in her ear. It mimicked her own frantic breaths. She kissed his shoulder, enjoying the hot, spicy taste of him that flooded her senses.

After several moments, he rolled off of her to stretch out on his back. His eyes closed, and she saw an expression of contentment settle on his features as he pulled her into his side. Slightly drowsy, she was happy to simply burrow into him and cherish the quiet aftermath of their lovemaking. The strong beat of his heart sounded in her ear, and the steady rhythm made her feel safe. He'd not yet spoken the words she wanted to hear, but she knew he would. Stubborn and proud, it would take time for him to admit his feelings for her, but she was certain he cared for her. What they'd shared just now had been a passion born of deep emotion, and she rejoiced in it. Content and happy, she pressed a kiss into his side and snuggled deeper into his warm flesh.

❦

The soft streaks of dawn pushed their way through the folds of the tent as Shaheen stirred beneath the light blanket that covered him and Allegra. The warmth of her penetrated his skin, stroking his senses. Nestled into his side, her voluptuous curves were a perfect fit against his body. Her breathing was soft and warm against his skin, and he didn't move for fear of waking her. No, that wasn't why he remained still. He simply didn't want to let her go. Pain forced his eyes closed as the full impact of the knowledge hit him. Despair sliced through him, and he did what he'd done since he was a boy. He buried the pain.

He reminded himself that the only thing that mattered was her safety. By the end of the day, she'd be in Safi and on a ship setting sail for home. She'd be safe. She'd be with Shaftsbury. The thought of his cousin sent a wild stroke of hostility through him. His gaze dropped down to study the way Allegra was holding him in her sleep. Had she ever slept in his cousin's arms like this?

The uninvited image slipped through his head, followed by a wave of fierce jealousy. Had she been like this with all her lovers? Had she slept this quietly, this easily with them as well? Even if she had, it wouldn't matter, because he was the one she'd willingly stripped her mask away for. She'd dropped her courtesan façade and given him the passion he knew no other man had seen. She'd surrendered her heart to him.

And yet she would come to hate him before the day was through. He swallowed hard. Did he really have the fortitude to execute the plan he'd formulated while Allegra had slept quietly beside him? He had no choice. He'd failed James, but he refused to fail Allegra. Life would not be worth living if he allowed anything to happen to her.

The guilt alone would be unbearable, knowing he'd selfishly kept her with him instead of sending her to safety. He'd made a critical error in underestimating Khalid's brother. He'd not do it a second time. That Nassar had come so close this time to hurting Allegra chilled him to the bone. The bastard would try again, he was certain of it.

No, the only thing he could do was send her away. He'd have to if he wanted to keep her safe. He sure as hell didn't have the courage to tell her the truth. Particularly when he didn't even want to admit it to himself. He studied the softness of her face with a need to memorize the way she looked when sleeping.

After last night, he knew without a doubt that Allegra wouldn't return to England willingly. She'd fight him tooth and nail to stay here. The only way she'd leave was if he could convince her there was nothing here for her. That she meant nothing to him. He closed his eyes against the painful thought. *Merde.* He'd have to humiliate her again and the thought of doing so sickened him. Did he have the strength to be that cruel to her?

As she shifted against him in sleep, her hennaed hand covered his heart and she burrowed deeper into his side. He stared down at the fading tattoo the seer in the *souq* had applied to her hand. The *jahīm anasi* was meant to unite his past with his future. And his past was about to take his future from him. The irony of it was almost laughable.

If he'd not been so stubborn, he could have avoided this entire scenario. He could have returned her to Marrakech when Jamal had advised him to. He could have trusted Allegra to keep his identity a secret. It would have been easy to disappear into the wilds of the Moroccan landscape where Shaftsbury couldn't find him, even if the reasons for doing so no longer existed. He could have done all of that, but he'd chosen not to. Now he was to pay a price that was as high as the one he'd paid the night of James's death.

Taking care not to disturb her, he extracted himself from her arms and dressed quickly. Without looking at her, he moved to the entrance of the tent. His hand fisted around a portion of the wool flap, and he paused to look back over his shoulder. God help him. She was the most beautiful woman he'd ever seen, and he was a bastard for doing what he was about to do to her. He drew in a sharp hiss of air and left the tent.

The Amazigh were preparing for the worst, and the path to the command post was busy despite the early hour. Ahead of him, he saw Hakim standing in front of the command tent. Standing beside him was an Englishman. He steeled himself for what was to come as he came to a halt in front of the two men.

"Newcastle." His cousin extended his hand in greeting. "It's been a long time."

"Shaftsbury."

Not caring that his response was abrupt he ushered the man into the command post with a sharp hand gesture. He didn't bother to extend any of the usual civilities. There wasn't time, and the last thing he wanted to do was befriend the man taking Allegra away from him.

"I believe Hakim has explained why I sent for you?" He arched his eyebrows at the Viscount and waited for a response.

"He indicated Allegra has been here with you for the past month and not in England as I was told. He said she was in danger, and I needed to take her to England today. What I don't understand is why you didn't bring her back to Marrakech when you first rescued her."

He ignored Shaftsbury's unspoken question and retorted with one of his own. "How familiar are you with Moroccan politics, cousin?"

"I know that the French and Spanish share jurisdiction, while the British Foreign Office watches." Shaftsbury shrugged at his limited knowledge.

"True, but the Amazigh control the land, and for the past five years I've been working under my Amazigh name to form treaties meant to unite the Amazigh as a nation. If the French discovered my nationality, they would take great offense to an Englishman negotiating alliances. They might even suggest Her Majesty's government was behind my efforts, which would cause problems as well."

Understanding lit Shaftsbury's dark gaze. "And my arrival in Marrakech compromised you."

"It did." He jerked his head in an abrupt nod.

"But that still doesn't account for why you held Allegra here."

"If I'd returned Allegra to Marrakech, you might have started asking questions in the wrong places," he snapped with suppressed irritation. He didn't remember his cousin being quite this annoying the last time they'd met. "And I wasn't about to let anything endanger the treaties."

"So now you are." There was just a hint of sarcasm in Shaftsbury's voice, and he sent the man a hard look.

"The treaties are in jeopardy because Nassar is preparing for a war, and he's prepared to kill anyone who gets in his way." He folded his arms across his chest. "One of my men will guide you to Othmane where you'll be able to catch a train to Safi. I'm also sending Sheikh Mahmoud's daughter and Allegra's maid with you as well."

"How far is Othmane from the camp?"

"A little more than two hours. You stop for nothing. If a horse goes lame, then leave it. No matter what happens, you don't stop. Is that clear?"

"You make this sound as if it's a matter of life and death."

"It is," he ground out between clenched teeth. "If Nassar's men find you, your chances of survival are slim."

"What about you?" Puzzlement furrowed the Viscount's brow as he shook his head.

"Me?" He shrugged. "I'm staying here."

"You can't be serious." Shaftsbury stared at him in stunned outrage. "These people aren't your family."

"Family isn't limited to blood," he bit out fiercely. "The Amazigh took me in when my own father rejected me. They've shown me more love and kindness than my own father did. They're my family now."

"That may be, but it doesn't change the fact that you have responsibilities in England. Your father is gravely ill, and he's been asking for you."

Turning away he strode to the open doorway of Khalid's tent. "The last time I saw my father, he made it perfectly clear he never wanted to see me again. I'm more than happy to grant him that wish."

"Good God, man, he's dying. I don't even know if he's still alive, but he wouldn't have asked for you if he didn't really want to see the only son he has left."

Furious at the way his cousin was pushing him, he whirled around and stalked his way across the carpet to put himself within inches of Shaftsbury's face. "I'll say this one time, and one time only. My father is already dead to me."

"And so is your brother." His cousin's face was a forbidding mask as he glared back at him. "But if he was alive—if he asked you to at least listen to what your father had to say, would you refuse him? Are you willing to abandon the responsibilities that your brother can't accept?"

The question knocked the breath out of him as if Shaftsbury had hit him with a left jab. Frozen where he stood, he simply stared at his relative, only the man he saw in front of him was his brother. James faced him, berating him for being so stubborn and unwilling to grant a dying man his last wish.

"What do you know of my brother?" he rasped deep and low as he turned away from his cousin's probing gaze.

"I know that you idolized James," Shaftsbury said quietly. "I used to envy you having James for a brother. He looked out for you."

"And my brother is dead because of me," he choked out. "*I* was the catalyst that drove my brother to pull the trigger."

"I don't believe that." Shaftsbury shook his head. "James had a choice, and he made the wrong one. Blaming yourself accomplishes nothing."

"Think what you like." He rolled his shoulders in a dismissive shrug. "But the only thing you need to concern yourself with is getting Allegra to Othmane before the midday train."

"Allegra!"

He didn't need to hear his cousin's exclamation to know she was behind him. There was something about her that always told him she was nearby, even when he couldn't see her. When he turned around, he saw Shaftsbury embrace Allegra in a close hug. The sight of her in another man's arms made his muscles grow taut. Instinct demanded he take back what was his, but he couldn't. Her life was in jeopardy and he'd forfeit his happiness, even his life to save her.

"What the hell happened to your hair?" Shaftsbury pushed her back slightly, one hand going to her head. Clearly confused by his presence, Allegra remained mute as she looked at him then back at his cousin's angry expression.

"Did you cut her hair?" Shaftsbury didn't let Allegra go as he turned his head to glare at him.

"No, Nassar is responsible for that." Regaining her voice along with her composure, she shook her head as she defended him. She pushed herself out of Shaftsbury's arms as her lovely gaze flew to meet his. The questions darkening her green eyes made him look away from her. The confusion and fear in her expression were too much for him to bear. Just as he'd destroyed his brother, he was about to destroy her, and he despised himself for it.

"I don't understand." She pressed her fingertips into her forehead as if she were struggling to concentrate. "How did you find me? How did you get here?"

"My cousin sent for me." Shaftsbury nodded in his direction. "He explained everything. Now that I've delivered my message, I can go home. And Robert says I'm to take you with me."

"Robert?" Confused she looked at Shaftsbury with a blank expression.

"Shaheen is my cousin Robert. The man I came to Morocco to find," his cousin said. "He's asked me to take you home."

"Home?" her confusion slowly ebbed away as comprehension dawned on her face.

"But of course, my dear." Shaftsbury squeezed her hand and smiled at her. "I'm taking you back to England."

The fiery determination in her eyes ripped through his heart. He had no choice now. She was about to force his hand, and the thought of what was to come made him close off his expression. He couldn't let her find one crack in his resolve, and that meant destroying her.

17

The words sucked the air out of her lungs as she stared at Charles in dazed bewilderment. He was taking her back to England. But she didn't want to go, and certainly not with Charles. Her gaze flew to Shaheen's impassive features.

He was sending her away.

Frozen in place, her mouth went dry with fear. Dear God, he couldn't do this. Not after last night. Her stomach roiled with nausea as she breathed in the thick, exotic musk incense that layered the air in the tent. It was a scent that spoke of secrets, mystery, and danger. There were still secrets between them, but the only danger now was facing a life without him. Last night had convinced her there was more between them than sex. She was bound to him now, and she refused to simply walk away. She studied Shaheen for a long moment, but his gaze told her nothing. While she couldn't tell what he was thinking, it was easy to see the tension in his stiff posture. Still looking at Shaheen, she touched Charles on the arm.

"Charles, I'd like a moment alone with Shaheen."

"But, Allegra—"

"Now, Charles." She turned her head toward him. "Please."

As if remembering other times when she'd been equally set on having her way, he nodded sharply. Charles left the tent without another word, followed by Hakim. Relief jolted through her as the two men left her alone with Shaheen. Closing her eyes for a brief moment, she tried to center her thoughts in hopes of making sense of everything. She sensed his gaze on her, and her eyes flew open. He watched her in silence, his expression little more than that of a disinterested bystander. Uncertainty swelled her throat shut as she tried in vain to swallow the knot lodged there.

The man facing her bore no resemblance to the man who'd held her in his arms last night and taken her to heights she'd never dreamed possible. This was a stranger staring back at her. A cold reflection of the man she thought she was coming to know. Gathering her courage, she licked her dry lips and tried not to tremble in the face of his bleak presence.

"Why are you sending me away?" she asked in a hoarse voice.

"Because I have no further use of you."

The harsh cruelty in his voice made her head snap backward as if he'd hit her. Suddenly it was difficult to breathe, and the indifference on his features made her grow cold. He couldn't mean that. Not after last night. Heat slowly returned to her limbs, and she straightened to her full height.

"I don't believe you."

"Believe what you will, *ma belle*. But it *is* the truth."

With a shrug, he turned away from her and moved to a waist-high table that contained several maps. His beautiful hands brushed across the surface of a diagram as if he was studying it intently, but she knew better. Although his expression hadn't changed, his profile revealed a twitch of tension in his cheek. Something was wrong. He was hiding something from her. Beneath his cruelty she was certain there had been something else. *Regret? Pain?* Her heart skipped a beat. *Nassar.* He'd been preparing for a confrontation with Nassar, and as Sheikh, it was his duty to protect his tribe. Protect what was his. She breathed in a sharp breath of hope.

Protect her.

Was that why he'd sent for Charles? Was that the real reason for this cold, callous manner of his? Was he trying to make her believe he didn't care so she'd simply leave and return to England with Charles? It was the only possible explanation. He was worried Nassar's men might take her again if the camp was attacked. Well, she wouldn't have it. She refused to be shipped off like some coveted prize jewel. She was the *jahīm anasi,* and she would stay with him. It was her destiny.

"I won't go," she said stubbornly.

Despite the calm way he straightened upright, she could see the lethal power in him. Anger hardened his dark eyes, and his expression was one of contempt.

"Perhaps I wasn't clear enough, Allegra," he growled. "There's nothing for you here."

"*You're* here. That's all that matters to me."

With more confidence than she really felt, she stepped forward and tugged his head down to kiss him. His body gave way slightly, welcoming hers into his. It was a sign he might concede and her heart soared with hope. A second later, strong hands bit into her upper arms as he shoved her away from him.

"You seem to be under the mistaken impression that I *want* you to remain."

"You wanted me last night," she said angrily.

Last night he'd cried out her name in the midst of their love-making. A passion he'd demanded. The same passion she'd withheld from other men, but had yielded to him willingly. He was the only man she'd ever given herself to openly and honestly, asking nothing in return. And the idea that he no longer wanted her was unthinkable. She would never have revealed her heart to him if she'd not been certain it was safe to do so.

"I don't deny your attractions, *ma chérie*." He stretched out his hand to brush his fingers over her breast in a contemptuous gesture. "But don't mistake desire for affection."

"Don't you dare stand there and try to tell me last night meant nothing to you," she snapped.

"But it *didn't* mean anything, *ma belle*."

He turned away from her and returned to reviewing the map on the table. She flinched. It wasn't true. Last night had meant something to them both. She believed that with all her heart. With determination, she pushed his rejection aside. He was lying. Fingernails digging into her palm, she shook her head. She didn't know how she knew that, but she was certain of it. Maybe it was the tension holding him rigid. Or the way his body had almost betrayed him when she kissed him. He could deny it all he wanted, but last night had meant something to him. She released a noise of disgusted anger and tugged on his arm to make him face her.

"Please credit me with some intelligence, Shaheen. I've been with too many men not to know when a man harbors feelings for me."

"The only harbor I found with you, *ma chérie*, was a resting place for my cock." The crude remark made her suck in a painfully sharp breath.

"You bastard."

"Perhaps you would prefer a lie?" he asked blandly.

"So—just like that—you decide to send me back to Marrakech."

"Actually you're going to Othmane to catch the train for Safi." His calm, detached response infuriated her. "But yes, I'm sending you away, as I said I would."

"With Charles?"

His response was a sharp nod and his mouth thinned. She eyed him carefully. There had been a flash of anger in his eyes when she'd mentioned Charles's name. If he did care for her, it stood to reason he might be jealous.

"How kind of you to ensure my escort is not only capable, smart, and handsome, but a good lover as well," she said in a honeyed tone.

The mask he wore slipped the moment she mentioned Charles in the context of a lover. Fire blazed in his dark eyes as he stared down at her with an expression that would have made most of his men shudder, but she wasn't afraid of him. The only thing that frightened her was the thought of him tossing her aside. Something deep in the depths of his penetrating gaze made her catch her breath. Was that need she saw flickering there? Oh God, if he would just kiss her. Take her into his arms and tell her that he'd only been trying to protect her. Kiss her and say it was all a mistake. Tension threaded its way between them. It was a palpable sensation that edged its way across the top of the skin. He shook his head in disgust.

"Forgive me, *ma chérie*, but we both know there isn't much difference between a brothel whore and one dressed up like a lady." The callousness of his words slammed into her with the force of a physical blow. "My cousin is being well paid for his trouble. As are you."

"What does that mean?" she choked out as her stomach churned.

"I believe my offer was my stallion for one night in your bed," he said in a low, even voice. "Unfortunately, Abyad is gone, but you'll be well compensated, particularly since you provided me with two nights of entertainment. Shaftsbury will instruct my solicitor in London to pay into your bank account the sum of ten thousand pounds for services rendered."

Stunned, she simply stood there not making a sound. There was no pain, just numbness. Not since the night her mother sold her into Madame Eugenie's brothel had she felt so betrayed. She was being traded, but this time the price was her heart. For the first time, she considered the timing of Charles's arrival. To reach the camp so early, it would have meant leaving the city before dawn. That meant Hakim would have left last night.

Dear God. Shaheen had sent for Charles yesterday—*before* making love to her. Last night had truly meant nothing to him. *Nothing at all.* She swayed slightly as pain etched its way through every pore in her skin. Raw and biting, it ate away at her with the slow precision of a pendulum slicing through her skin.

She wanted to die.

No. She refused to give him the satisfaction of knowing how devastating his rejection was. Inhaling a deep breath, she drew herself upright and held her head proudly erect. Drowning in a dark lake would have been preferable to meeting his gaze, but she forced herself to look at him. Just as she did that first night at Madame Eugenie's, she shut off every emotion she possessed.

Except one.

Anger unfurled its dark nature inside her with methodical slowness. She allowed it to steady her. It would sustain her until she was someplace secluded where she could lick her wounds. She wouldn't make a fool of herself over the man any more than she already had. Bitterness mixed with her anger as she turned away from him and walked toward the open doorway of the tent. At the entrance, she paused and looked at him over her shoulder.

"I might be a whore, Lord Newcastle, but I'm not ashamed of who I am nor do I hide what I am. You, on the other hand, hide here among the Amazigh, pretending to be something you're not." Bitterly, she sent him a hard look. "I pity you, my lord. Even Nassar for all his barbarity is more honest about who he is and what he desires."

Not waiting for his response, she turned around and stalked out of the tent. Anger made her back rigid and straight, only emphasizing the stiffness of her step. With her head held high, she stalked away. Shaheen watched her disappear around one of the tents in silence. Then with a low cry he whirled around and with a vicious swipe of his hand, he cleared the table of the maps. Hands gripping the sides of the table, he bent over the table and closed his eyes.

The desire to go after her spiraled through him with the pull of a raging river. He resisted, but it took every bit of self-control he possessed to do so. When he'd said she'd be well compensated it was as if he'd struck her. Ashen and devastated, she'd been mute with horror. God, he was a bastard. How could he have done this to her, even if it was for her own protection? He should have found some other way of convincing her to leave.

Pain lashed at him, and with another tormented snarl, he lifted the table up off the floor and flung it to one side. Mocking laughter echoed loudly in his head as the table crashed noisily to the carpeted floor of the command tent. There had been another option, but he'd been too much of a coward to even consider it. He could have told her the truth. Explained that everything he was doing was because he loved her and wanted her safe. And he did love her despite every barrier he'd raised to keep her at a distance. She'd stolen his heart. Last night had merely sealed his fate in that regard. But it changed nothing. Her life was in danger, and sending her away was the best way to protect her. Hands clutching at the back of his neck, he bowed his head, eyes closed as the anguish rolled over him in wave after wave. While he'd made her hate him, it was better than losing her now or in the future. And he would lose her, just as he had his brother and the love of his father.

❦

The sun was nearly directly overhead as Allegra and the rest of her friends rode north across the desert plain. Ahead of her, Jamal led the way with Laila and Millie riding close abreast of her and Charles drawing up the rear. Over the past two hours, the intensity of her pain had slowly become a draining numbness that weighed down her entire body.

She'd done the unthinkable. She'd broken the one rule she'd vowed never to break. Falling in love with one's patron was the cardinal sin. And God help her if Shaheen were ever to realize how deeply he'd wounded her. It would only amuse him, and she'd suffered enough humiliation at his hands. The man had been so eager to be done with her he'd asked the one person he cared for the least to come fetch her.

When they were preparing to leave camp, Laila had joined the rest of them at the horses. Hope had burned anew in her breast at the sight of the young woman. If Shaheen was sending Khalid's only daughter with them it might mean he'd been lying to her simply to convince her to leave. Laila had destroyed that hope almost as quickly as it had flared into life. Her friend had relatives in Othmane she'd promised her father she would visit, and Laila's words had made anguish slice deep into her heart.

A sudden shout from behind her jerked her out of her thoughts, and she looked over her shoulder at Charles, who'd increased his pace to move around them. He reached Jamal's side in a matter of seconds and shouted something to the Amazigh as he pointed to the left. Following the direction of his sharp gesture, her mouth went dry. In the distance, she saw a large party of riders heading toward them. Her gaze flying back to Jamal and Charles, she saw them exchange only a few more words before they both dropped back to her and the other women.

"We're only a few miles from Othmane," Charles called out. "Jamal says Sheikh Mahmoud has men there who'll protect us."

"I can't go any faster than this." Millie, her eyes wide with fear, shook her head.

The woman's loud cry of panic drew Jamal's attention as he finished calling out an order to Laila, who had already nudged her horse into a flat-out gallop. As the Amazigh woman began to draw away from them, Jamal pulled even with her.

"Millie, I protect you. Ride." The Amazigh's accent made the English words that much harsher, but he caught the maid's attention. *"Ride!"*

She only had time to see Jamal slap the hindquarters of Millie's horse as Charles did the same to her own mount. In seconds, the five of them were riding hard toward a midsized town she could now see low on the horizon. The small Arabian she rode didn't seem the least bit strained by the increased pace, and she was certain the moderate pace they'd maintained since leaving the Amazigh camp had saved the animals from being exhausted at this point.

Once more, she glanced at the approaching riders, and her heart thudded wildly in her breast. They were gaining on them. The minutes dragged on as Othmane grew in size, but the distance between the riders chasing them and their small party decreased. It was now possible to see the riders clearly and their rifles waving in the air. A loud scream from Millie jerked her attention to the right and she could see another party of riders riding up from behind them on the opposite side. The men shot their rifles into the air as they quickly encircled their small party and forced them to a halt. It was a scare tactic, and it worked. Glancing at her companions, she could tell the shrill sounds had set their nerves on edge just like her. Charles was arguing with Jamal when the Amazigh's expression grew dark and forbidding. He said something to her old lover, and Charles's face became equally grim as the two men watched a lone rider approaching. She turned her head and her stomach lurched. *Nassar.*

As the noise died down, he uttered a harsh command, and several of his men dismounted and dragged all of them off their horses. Millie was the only one to protest, and Jamal charged quickly to the terrified woman's side. He squeezed her hand and said something to her beneath his breath. His efforts earned him a crashing blow to the back of his head, which made him stagger into the maid.

Holding him upright against her, Millie helped Jamal reach the rest of their small group. When Nassar's men had disarmed Charles and the Bedouin, they forced them to stand in a straight line. From where he sat on his horse, Nassar studied them in silence, his thick, black eyebrows arched with derision. It only emphasized the cruelty in his expression. He quickly dismounted, and with his fists planted into his sides, he slowly walked past Millie and Jamal then halted in front of Laila, whose face was a mixture of anger and fear. An odd look crossed Nassar's face as he tilted her chin upward.

"Newcastle was right. You do look like your mother." His words drew a hiss from Laila, and she jerked away from his touch and spat on the ground.

"Do not dare to touch me, you filthy murderer."

Nassar's response was to strike the young woman's face with the back of his hand. The force of the blow drove Laila to her knees, her hand cupping her face. Charles immediately stepped forward with a cry of anger, but one of Nassar's men restrained him. Jamal held himself rigid, but Allegra could see the murderous rage on the Amazigh's face. She looked back at Nassar and saw him studying her with a mocking smile. She knew how the man thought, and she deliberately kept her expression neutral.

"What is it you want?" Steel threaded through Charles's quiet words. With a sudden look of interest, Nassar moved to stare into the other man's eyes. It was a look of assessment, and Charles didn't flinch beneath Nassar's harsh contemplation.

"Why your women of course." A low laugh accompanied his words, and a shiver slid through her. With a dismissing wave of his hand, he turned his back on Charles. "Kill the men, and take the women to camp."

Horrified, Allegra strained against the tight hands that held her in place. "*No!*"

Her cry made Nassar stop. Slowly turning around, he stared at her coldly. The flat, reptilian look in his black eyes made her body grow icy with fear. God, how she hated him. Hated him for what he was forcing her to do. His thin lips tight with anger, he walked toward her.

"You dare to say *no* to me, Allegra?"

"Let them go," she said quietly. "In exchange for their lives and freedom, I will let you do with me as you like."

"Allegra, no!" Charles's harsh cry was joined almost immediately by Jamal's protest.

"*Anasi*, do not do this."

"Oh dear lord," Millie gasped.

"No, Allegra, no," Laila sobbed through her tears.

Ignoring them, she held her head erect and met Nassar's assessing look with a quiet assurance she didn't feel. She gave another tug against the hands that held her, and the Sheikh nodded at his man to release her. Arms folded across his chest, he offered her a feral smile.

"As usual, you do not understand your situation, *ma chérie*. It is no different than the last time we met. As I recall, you offered a similar bargain then as well. I have no time for games."

"No," she said quietly with a shake of her head. "I told you the last time we met that I *choose* the men I take into my bed. If you release them, I will choose you and refuse you nothing. Your pleasure will be my sole concern."

"A pretty speech, Allegra. But again, I can take what I want from you."

"But will you take or receive? What I'm offering you is absolute obedience."

Suppressing the bile rising in her throat, she stepped forward and slowly sank to her knees. Her movements deliberately subservient, she bent over in a prostrate manner at his feet. The protests of her friends filled the air, but she blocked the sound out of her head. As she waited for his answer, she fought to suppress a shiver of revulsion. She couldn't let him see how repulsed she was at the thought of being with him. It would take all of her skill and willpower to do what she intended, but the lives of her friends were at stake. She had little choice in the matter if they were to go free. Nassar's silence pressed down on her as she prayed fervently for his agreement. Squatting in front of her, the Sheikh grabbed her chin and forced him to look at him.

"I have your word on this bargain?" he asked.

There was a distinct warning in the question. If she broke their agreement, he would most likely beat her until she was dead. Shaheen's face flashed before her, and her heart released a painful spasm in her chest. Without Shaheen, death was infinitely more preferable. The moment the thought churned through her head, the fighter in her slapped the notion aside. She would survive as she'd always done. Her destiny would not end on the Moroccan desert plain under the feet of a sadistic monster like Nassar.

"You have my word." She met his cold gaze steadily, sealing their bargain with a nod.

"Release them." Nassar's sharp words snapped over her head like a whip.

She shivered as she remembered how he had threatened to take a lash to her back the last time they'd met. Again, protests filled the air, but she remained where she was at Nassar's feet, head bowed.

"I approve of your behavior, *sabhā emîra*," he murmured with a lascivious twist of his thin mouth. He lifted her chin once more. "You'll find me most generous if you please me. And to show you how generous I can be, you may watch your friends reach the gates of Othmane."

"And I have your word as an Amazigh that your men will not follow them into the city?"

A fierce scowl of anger drew his jet-black eyebrows together, making the sinister expression on his face all the more pronounced. His hand released her chin so roughly her head snapped to the side. "You have my word as an Amazigh," he snarled.

Relief expanded her lungs as she realized she'd been holding her breath until he'd agreed. A moment later, he grabbed her by the arm and yanked her to her feet. Stumbling, she was forced to steady herself against him, and she fought to keep from recoiling from him. She watched as Charles took a step toward her, a fierce fury blazing in his eyes. A split second later, a knife was resting against his throat as Nassar snapped an order. Frightened that he might lose his life in a fruitless effort to save her, she glared at him.

"Stop, Charles. I've made my decision."

"Don't do this—" The knife against his throat pressed deeper into his skin, and a drop of blood rolled across the top of the blade.

"For the love of God, Charles. Just go. Take care of Millie for me."

Anguish replaced the anger in his eyes as he slowly accepted the hopelessness of their situation. They were outnumbered, and any rescue effort on his part would only result in his death and that of the others as well. As she watched him grapple with the reality of their situation, her heart ached for him at the torment carving its way into his face. She recognized the great effort it took for him to turn away from her, and she swayed slightly as she watched him convince the others to walk to their horses. Millie protested vigorously until Jamal silenced her with a stern word in her ear. Laila refused to budge from where she stood when Charles approached her. Roughly, he grabbed her arm and pulled her toward the horses. Tears streaming down her face, the young woman kept her eyes on Allegra until Charles forced her to mount her horse. In a matter of minutes, they were riding off toward the city gate and safety. Impatient, Nassar grasped her arm and tried to pull her in the opposite direction. She turned her head to look at him.

"You said I could watch until they reached the city."

He frowned with anger, but relented with a sharp nod. Turning back toward Othmane, she watched her friends disappear into the city less than five minutes later. As they vanished, she shuddered. It was time to make good on her bargain. Numb with the reality of her situation and what she'd agreed to, she turned to Nassar and bowed her head in a submissive manner.

"I am yours to command, Excellency."

Faint from the thought of what was to come, she swayed slightly but managed to remain upright. Nassar issued several harsh commands, and strong hands dragged her back to her horse. Moments later, she was riding back into the desert.

18

Allegra swallowed hard as she realized the sun had dipped below the horizon some time ago. If there was anything to be grateful for, it was the fact that Rana had not come into the tent. She didn't care why the woman stayed away, just that she did. After a bath she'd put on the clothing provided her. They were more suited to the harem than the harsh life in the desert, but then she knew why Nassar had sent them.

The thought of him touching her was revolting. And she *would* have to endure his touch. If she wasn't accommodating, Nassar would see to it that she changed her mind. Charles would return to rescue her, but it would take time to find help. She inhaled a deep breath in an attempt to quiet the churning in her stomach. The first place he would go would be back to the Amazigh camp. Would Shaheen even care that she was Nassar's prisoner again? She flinched at the memory of his brutal behavior this morning.

She squeezed her eyes shut against the pain rising back to the surface. God but she'd been a fool.

She jerked as she heard Nassar issuing commands outside the tent. Steeling herself for the night to come, she deliberately sank to her knees and waited for him to stride into the tent. When he did so, she immediately bowed forward until her forehead touched the luxurious carpet on the tent floor. She waited until his black boots came into view before she looked up at him.

"How may I serve you this evening, Excellency?" She worked hard to keep her voice soft and soothing. A thin smile crossed his face as he towered over her.

"You are an enchanting creature when you want to be, *ma chérie*."

He slowly circled her, his hand lightly touching her hair. It sent a rush of revulsion through her, but she managed to suppress the shiver threatening to ripple through her. She'd made a deal with the devil, and now her survival hinged on pleasing him. If he thought she was trying to break their bargain she knew he'd think nothing of having her throat slit or torments far worse. Deliberately, she forced herself to reach for his hand. Beneath her touch she could feel him stiffen, but she didn't hesitate. He stroked her cheek with his finger.

"Come, I wish to eat. Serve me."

He gestured toward the food a woman had brought into the tent upon his arrival. Quickly rising to her feet, she forced herself to walk slowly toward the center of the tent where the food tray sat among several pommel rests. As Nassar sank down against one, she reached for a branch of grapes and turned to face him. The expression on his face was one she'd seen on the men at Madame Eugenie's. She tried to remember what she'd done to make those men happy and couldn't. The knowledge made her throat close in horror. Oh God, she couldn't do this. She couldn't just give in to him without a fight. She'd saved her friends. They were safe.

But you aren't, Allegra.

The cold, detached voice in the back of her head was one she recognized. It had seen her through three years at the brothel. It was what would keep her alive now. She shut down every emotion inside her and got down on her knees. With the grape stem between her teeth, she crawled toward him. When she reached him, she carefully picked a plump fruit off the stem. With a slow stroke of her tongue, she swirled it around the tip of the grape before sucking it into her mouth.

Hypnotized, Nassar didn't move as she plucked another grape from the stem. Without pricking the skin of the fruit, she placed one end of it between her teeth then leaned forward to offer him the grape. The man didn't hesitate and lunged forward to take the fruit from her with his mouth. His scent was heavy and thick with a mix of jasmine and frankincense. It overpowered her in its intensity, and her control slipped as she almost gagged. The grape squirted a small amount of juice when he bit into it, and his tongue darted out to lick her mouth where it landed. It reminded her of the way a serpent flicked its forked tongue out. A hard hand snaked around her neck as he pulled her down on top of him and kissed her wetly.

God, if only Nassar were Shaheen. If only it were last night.

Her heartbeat accelerated at the memory. In that split second, she realized how she might survive the degradation of Nassar's touch. She would imagine it was Shaheen touching her. Shaheen's skin her mouth was caressing. The fantasy wouldn't block out everything about the night to come, but his image would enable her to do what was necessary to satisfy Nassar. It would help her endure this horrible night.

Nassar pulled her to him. A glint of dark lust lighting his eyes, he ran his hand down the front of her bodice before sliding over to stroke one breast. Unprepared for the caress, she pulled in a sharp breath of disgust. She forced herself to smile as his gaze flitted up to her face.

"I like being touched like that." Her lie was nothing more than a whisper, and she fought to school her features into a beckoning smile. He grinned.

"Excellent, because I intend to touch you a great deal tonight, *ya atruğulla*."

The cold voice of survival instructed her to slowly remove the top that barely covered her breasts. The obscene hunger crossing his face made her stomach roil, and once again, the stench of his heavily perfumed body assaulted her nostrils as he leaned into her. Closing her eyes, she pictured Shaheen in her head. It was his hand that pushed hers aside so his fingers could stroke first one nipple and then the other.

Her eyes flew open, hoping it was all a nightmare and that Shaheen was the one touching her. Instead, it was Nassar who hovered over her. His gaze followed his hands as they moved downward and burrowed inside her *sherwals*. His fingers stroked her, but the only sensation his touch produced was bile rising in her throat. Dear God, she was a courtesan. A woman skilled in pleasure, yet her body couldn't summon up the merest hint of desire. She wasn't even wet between her thighs, and the moment he realized it, she was doomed. Desperate to distract him, she forced herself to caress his cheek.

"Excellency, we've not yet finished our meal."

Relief sailed through her as he pulled his hand out of her *sherwals* with a grunt. "You're right, Allegra. In fact, you've not had anything to drink. We can remedy that right now because you're going to milk my prick dry."

The crudity of his words left her feeling as though she'd been tossed into a cesspool. With the speed of a cobra, he undid his *sherwals* to release his fat erection. Deep red, almost purple, his staff bobbed with his excitement, and a drop of clear semen dripped onto her breast as he shifted his body so the tip of his erection was touching her lips. Revolted she shuddered and closed her eyes again, knowing he would see the disgust in her eyes. God, what if she refused? The detached voice in her head ordered her to do whatever necessary to survive.

"Open your mouth, Allegra."

Tears lodged in the back of her throat as she did as he ordered, and she visualized Shaheen in her head. She remembered his groans of pleasure as she'd stroked him with her tongue, teasing him with her mouth. His body had shuddered with delight at her mouth on him, his voice calling out her name with each thrust of his cock into her mouth.

Clinging to the memory of Shaheen's body against hers, she heard a dark cry above her as Nassar released his seed. In that instant, Shaheen's face vanished from her head. Caught unprepared for her captor's quick orgasm, she choked and her teeth sank into his softening member as she struggled to breathe. The sound of his pain echoed loudly in the tent and he jerked away from her. Fury slashed across his swarthy features as he ruthlessly struck her in the face. The vicious blow sent her whole body rolling to one side.

"You vicious little cunt," he snarled as he scrambled to his feet to examine himself.

Stunned from his blow, she moaned in pain as she tried to flex her jaw. Already her face was beginning to swell, and she struggled into a sitting position as Nassar glared at her with deadly intent. She realized then that it was doubtful she'd survive the night.

❦

Shaheen stood in the darkness on the edge of camp staring out into the desert. He'd thought losing James had been painful. He was wrong. Nothing could equate to the pain he felt now. Allegra's departure had left a hole in him. A hole that no one could ever fill except her.

Behind him, he heard a shout of laughter. He didn't bother to look over his shoulder. Khalid and Jabbar had ridden into camp with an escort just as the sun was sinking below the horizon. The two men had signed a treaty of alliance and the tribe was celebrating. The light tread of someone behind him made him spin around. Khalid stood before him with an expression of sympathy on his face. With a glare, he waved his friend away.

"Save your pity, Khalid. I don't need it." He turned his back on his friend.

"I am not offering you any." The Sheikh released a sigh as he moved to stand at Shaheen's side. "Hakim tells me that you destroyed the interior of the command post."

"It was set to right," he growled.

"If you—"

Shouts suddenly exploded in the night air, followed by a rifle shot. Neither one of them hesitated as they raced through the darkness toward the sound. He stumbled over a stone, but recovered his balance as he ran toward the outcry with the Amazigh leader close on his heels. More shouts filled the air, followed by another shot.

A woman's shrill scream broke through the air at the volley of gunfire, and his gut clenched instantly as a vision of Allegra flashed through his head. In front of him, a large crowd gathered on the opposite side of the camp. Pushing his way through the masses, he entered the inner sanctum of chaos to see several riders hunched over in the saddles of their horses. Although there were several men holding torches aloft, it was still difficult to see clearly in the dark. But there was something far too familiar about the man dismounting from his horse. Striding forward, he came to a halt as he met his cousin's desolate gaze. A swift count of the horses told him that all but one person had returned. Icy dread gripped him, and he lunged forward to grab Shaftsbury by his clothes.

"Where is she?" he snarled. "Where the hell is she?"

"Nassar—" He didn't allow his cousin to say another word as he dropped the man with a hard swing to his jaw.

"Get up you son of a bitch," he roared as he dragged his cousin to his feet.

He was going to kill the bastard. His hand drew back a second time, but Khalid's strong hands pulled him away as Jamal stepped between him and his cousin. Guilt washed over him. He should never have trusted her safety to anyone but himself. It was his fault Allegra was in Nassar's hands again. Just as he'd failed James, he'd failed her.

"It is not the Viscount's fault," Jamal snapped. "It is no one's fault. Nassar and his men had faster horses and they surrounded us."

"And he just let all of you go while he kept Allegra." He jerked himself free of the hands restraining him and glared at his old friend.

"The *jahīm anasi* went with Nassar willingly." There was a note of deep pain in Jamal's voice as he turned his head away. "We could not save her."

Sand from a brutal desert storm could not have bit more deeply into his skin as he took in the Amazigh's words. The guilt he'd experienced only seconds ago returned with a vengeance, flaying him with a pain that was raw and physical. She'd gone with Nassar willingly. Why would she do such a thing? God, she was in that bastard's bed, allowing him to touch her. The thought of it sickened him. In a daze, he saw Jamal step forward to lay a solid hand on his shoulder. He shook his head at the older man's pained expression.

"Why?" he ground out between his teeth. "Why would she go willingly with that bastard?"

"Why?" Laila shoved her way past Charles and Jamal. The accusation in her glare was as sharp as a knife. "Because he was going to kill Jamal and Lord Shaftsbury then take Millie and me to his camp. I told you it was a mistake to go, but you wouldn't listen. She gave herself to Nassar in exchange for *our lives.*"

The bitterness in Laila's voice threw him back to those terrible minutes in his father's study when he'd tried to explain James's death. The only difference was, Allegra was alive and she was giving herself to a man she despised. Another image of Nassar caressing her flashed before him, and raw fury flooded his veins until he was almost blind with rage. He wheeled about sharply, his gaze searching the crowd until he saw Malik standing in front of his father. With a sharp gesture of his hand, he motioned the boy to come to him.

"Saddle Tarek for me now," he snapped. With a nod of his head, the boy disappeared into the crowd as Khalid grabbed his arm.

"Are you mad? You have no hope of saving Allegra if you charge into Nassar's camp by yourself."

"I don't intend to charge in." Shrugging off Khalid's grasp, he sent his friend an icy look. "I plan on being very quiet."

"Perhaps this matter calls for something a bit more strategic . . . a broader scope."

Jabbar's manner was quiet, but held a note of deadly purpose as he stepped forward into a beam of light. Despite his compulsion to go after Allegra immediately, he recognized the need to keep a cool head. If Jabbar had an idea, he was willing to listen, because he didn't have a plan.

"Explain."

"First, you don't even know where Nassar's camp is, do you?"

The brutal observation sliced through him as he realized how hotheaded he was being. For the past fifteen years, he'd taught himself to think before acting, but ever since the day he'd met Allegra he'd lost all of his reasoning ability. God, he was behaving just like James. His anger and pain were controlling his actions. His jaw flexed with tension as he shook his head.

"I know where it is," Jamal injected quietly. "When we reached Othmane, I turned around to follow the *jahīm anasi*. It's why we are so late in returning."

Humble gratitude swept over him as he acknowledged the danger his friend had risked in following Allegra to Nassar's camp. Swallowing hard, he met the man's gaze with a look of thanks. Jamal's nod in his direction was almost imperceptible, but he could see the understanding in his friend's eyes.

"Then what you need is a distraction, my friend." Jabbar's tone was lighthearted.

"A distraction?" He narrowed his gaze at Jabbar. There was an air of amused arrogance on the man's features, but his gray eyes were devoid of emotion.

"If there's one thing my men and I are experienced in, it's nighttime *ghazus*. Perhaps this is the opportunity you've been waiting for, Sheikh Mahmoud. After all, there's nothing quite like the element of surprise."

"Didn't you say that your main forces won't be here until sometime tomorrow?" Khalid's voice indicated he was far from convinced that the brigand's suggestion was a good one.

"True," Jabbar nodded. "But I've raided Nassar's camps before, and I never did it with more than thirty men. If Sheikh Shaheen is determined to go after this woman, he can hardly do it alone. We've already agreed that striking Nassar first is to our advantage. Wouldn't it make just as much sense to use the night to our benefit as well?"

Shaheen turned his head toward Khalid. The Amazigh leader

folded his arms and stroked the small beard on his chin with a contemplative frown furrowing his brow. After several moments of silence, he slowly nodded.

"There is sound logic in your suggestion, Jabbar. While it is not quite what we had planned, perhaps it is better to surprise the serpent in its nest than wait for it to strike." With each word he spoke, Sheikh Mahmoud seemed to grow more confident in his demeanor. "How many men do you have with you?"

"Fifteen of my best," Jabbar said quietly. "Most of them were with me the last time I raided Nassar's camp."

"How far is it to Nassar's camp, Jamal?" Shaheen asked his old friend.

"Almost three hours from here," the Amazigh said quietly. "I would judge their numbers to be at least two hundred, maybe more."

A soft murmur rustled through the crowd of men and women. Shaheen glanced around, not surprised to see the worry on the faces of the Amazigh. Even when his tribe was combined with Khalid's, they were barely one hundred fifty strong. It was why they'd sought Jabbar's help. But the other man was correct. The night could be a strong ally, and even if Allegra had gone willingly with Nassar, the bastard might still kill her before the sun rose simply for the pure pleasure of doing so.

"We should attack in two waves. The first group should be our best fighters," Shaheen mused out loud. "Nassar and most of his men will be sleeping. It will only take a few men to silence his guards, and with Nassar our prisoner, his men will surrender easily."

"I agree." Jabbar nodded his head "My men and I will volunteer to enter the camp first. I assume you will ride with me, Sheikh Shaheen?"

"Yes." He sent the man an abrupt nod as Shaftsbury stepped forward.

"I'm going with you."

He sent his cousin a sharp look, but the man's face grew more stubborn. Shaftsbury's decision didn't surprise him, and he had mixed emotions about the man joining them. If anything, Shaftsbury would be useful to have along if Allegra refused to let him near her. And he'd be a fool to think she would be glad to see him after the way he'd treated her this morning. She'd suffered so much already at the hands of Nassar, but if there was one thing he knew about her, she was a survivor. Still, even someone as courageous as Allegra had limits to what they could endure. Tonight might well be her breaking point. He clenched his teeth at the thought of what the bastard was doing to her at this moment.

Beside him Khalid shouted out several commands, and the crowd erupted like bees from a hive, intent on preparing for the battle to come. Hakim pushed his way past several men to join them, and the young Amazigh heir bowed formally in front of his father.

"I wish to ride at Shaheen's side, Father."

Sheikh Mahmoud's expression reflected an immediate rejection of his son's request. Then as if realizing it would be a mistake to refuse the boy, he grasped the young man by the shoulders and pulled him into a tight hug. When he released him, he nodded.

"Only because it is Shaheen you ride with will I grant this request. Be brave and wise when you enter the battle, my son."

With a fatherly smile, he ordered Hakim to take charge of seeing that the horses were properly saddled and ready to leave as quickly as possible. Khalid's expression was a mixture of pride, sorrow, and fear as he watched Hakim hurry off to accomplish the mission he'd been given. With a sigh, the Amazigh leader turned to Shaheen.

"He has become a man almost overnight. If something happens to me, he will lead the tribe well."

There was a hint of despondency in Khalid's voice, and Shaheen laid a hand on his friend's shoulder. "I'll take care of him."

With a small smile, the Sheikh nodded. "I would never have agreed otherwise."

Close by, Jabbar finished consulting with two of his men then turned back to Shaheen and the Sheikh. "The last time I visited Nassar's camp, my men and I covered the hooves of our horses with strips of material to deaden the sound of their movement. It worked amazingly well."

"An interesting approach," Khalid murmured as he arched his eyebrows. "I confess to being delighted that you are not Nassar's ally, otherwise I fear we would be in dire straits."

"Even if we'd not come to an agreement on our alliance, I would never join forces with a man like Nassar." Jabbar's gray eyes became icy and cold. "The man is a menace, and we'll be well rid of him."

Shaheen frowned at the man's steely tone. Something unpleasant had transpired between the two men, and Jabbar was out to extract vengeance for whatever sins Nassar had committed. He studied the man's expression for a moment, wondering if Jabbar was any more calm and collected about what they faced than he was. As if suddenly aware of being watched, the other man met his gaze and a cold smile curved his mouth.

"Don't look so surprised, Sheikh Shaheen. We all have our dark monsters haunting us. Nassar is one of mine, and I've simply been biding my time."

Sheikh Mahmoud frowned at Jabbar's words. Looking first at Jabbar and then Shaheen, his face hardened into an angry mask. "My brother is mine to deal with, is that clear? It is my right to avenge Yasmia, and I'll not let anyone steal that from me."

Jabbar looked ready to protest, but the hard look Sheikh Mahmoud sent him tugged a sharp nod of acquiescence from him.

When his friend turned to study him as well, Shaheen grimaced. He wanted nothing more than to cut Nassar's heart out for what he'd done to Allegra. For what he was no doubt doing right now. Tension threaded his muscles into hard knots, and he clenched his jaw as he nodded his agreement. He might have just given up the right to slit Nassar's throat, but Khalid hadn't forbidden him to give the man a sound beating.

19

Fire. Raw and fierce, it layered her back. It held her rigid beside Nassar as he slept, his loud snores filling the candlelit tent. Earlier, he'd used a whip on her as punishment for injuring him and his subsequent impotency. She'd stubbornly taken each lash in silence, gritting her teeth while her fingernails dug into her palms. Her silence had only enraged him further and he'd whipped her until she'd finally given in to the pain and screamed out.

The mineral odor of dried blood on her back mixed with Nassar's thick, heavy scent to permeate her skin. The smell sickened her. She desperately wanted a bath to rid herself of the man's stench, despite knowing how bad it would hurt. And she was certain that no matter how much she scrubbed her skin, she would always smell him, feel his touch. She suppressed a whimper of anguish. She was fortunate he'd only beaten her.

Many of the women she'd left behind at Madame Eugenie's all those years ago were not so lucky. There were women who'd suffered far greater pain and horrors than she'd endured tonight. And their efforts had all been in vain, whereas she'd made her sacrifice to save her friends. No matter how much she hurt, she'd made the right choice. She had no regrets. With great effort, she climbed to her feet as quietly as she could. Now was her chance to escape. The snoring stopped and she froze, unable to move. Terrified he'd awakened, she glanced over her shoulder only to see him shift positions in his sleep and resume his loud snores. Relief choked her throat with tears, but she swallowed them to keep any sound from escaping her lips.

She needed to move quickly, but it was difficult. Every movement made her body throb with pain. In the far corner of the tent, she saw the clothes she'd been wearing when she'd entered Nassar's camp. With as much stealth as her battered body allowed, she crept toward them. She'd expected pain, but when she crouched down to retrieve her clothes, her back screamed its protest. It grew worse when she slid her *gambaz* over her head and her stomach roiled, making her dizzy. How she managed to dress without making a sound she didn't know, but after what seemed a lifetime she shuffled barefoot toward the tent doorway. She'd just reached the tent entrance when Nassar's snoring came to an abrupt halt.

Her heart in her mouth, she turned and saw him sitting up, a groggy expression on his face. The moment he saw her standing at the doorway his sleepy look disappeared. Malice flashed in his dark eyes as he watched her. She'd yielded to his beating, but she wouldn't give him the satisfaction of knowing how badly she hurt at this moment. Heart pounding, she bowed her head in his direction. Anything more than a nod would have drawn a cry of pain from her.

"Excellency, forgive me if I disturbed your rest. I needed to relieve myself and didn't mean to awaken you." She lifted her gaze so she could look him directly in the eye, and waited for him to accuse her of trying to escape.

"Well hurry up then," he snapped with a disgruntled snort as he waved his hand at her.

With another bob of her head, she turned away from him and stepped out into the crisp night air. The moment she was out of view, her legs wobbled beneath her and she fought to remain standing. Oh God, it was impossible to escape now. He'd come looking for her if she was gone for too long. She dragged in a deep breath of cool air, clearing her lungs of the man's repugnant smell.

Overhead, a large bank of clouds drifted across the moon until there was little light to see by. Keeping her hand on the side of the tent to guide her in the darkness, she shuffled forward. Perhaps if the moon remained hidden behind the clouds she could find the horses. She released a half laugh, half sob beneath her breath. What in heavens name made her think she could possibly ride a horse if she managed to steal one. She could barely walk, let alone mount a horse.

A tear rolled down her cheek. The thought of going back into that monster's tent sent bile rushing up into her mouth and she stumbled around the side of the tent to vomit. Wiping her mouth on the sleeve of her *gambaz*, she closed her eyes. She couldn't go back inside that tent. She wouldn't. This was no longer about survival. It was about exchanging a slow death for a quick one. The bastard could come find her. When he did, he'd be so furious, he'd put an end to her misery. Every step a painful one, she moved forward. She didn't care where she was going as long as it took her away from Nassar.

She'd not gone far when she heard a soft thud in the dark. Fear slithered through her and she froze, waiting for someone to drag her back to Nassar's tent. When she didn't hear anything else unusual, she shuffled forward, only to hear the noise again. It was the muffled sound of fighting and a tremor swept through her. *Shaheen.* He'd come for her. The clouds overhead parted to light up the darkness around her, and she tried to draw back into the shadows.

"Bloody hell. *Allegra.*"

Charles's harsh whisper proved her undoing as she turned her head toward him. Slowly, she sank to her knees, giving way to the tears she'd blocked since arriving in Nassar's camp. The last bit of hope burning in her breast was extinguished once and for all. He hadn't come for her. God, even to the end she'd been a fool.

Why would Shaheen come looking for her when he'd said in no uncertain terms that they were through? Why had she even dared to dream he would rescue her from Nassar a second time? Her silent sobs shook her body hard, and Charles uttered a soft expletive as he knelt beside her to cradle her in his arms. He held her for only a minute before he forced her to look at him.

"You're safe, Allegra. It's all right." He gently brushed his fingers across her damp cheeks and smiled. "Tears? Are you still bewailing your refusal of that emerald necklace I offered you?"

The absurdity of his whispered comment brought her crying to a halt, and she choked out a low laugh. Arching his eyebrows at her, she saw the relief flash across his features as her tears disappeared. He immediately pressed his finger to his lips in a gesture for her to be quiet. The faint noise of fighting echoed nearby, followed by shouts and then gunfire. In the next instant, the entire camp erupted with the sound of several bloodcurdling cries and the thunderous sound of horses racing into the camp.

Nassar's voice echoed close by and she turned her head to see that she'd only passed four tents since leaving his dwelling. They had to move. If he found them here, he'd kill them both. Her hand squeezed tightly into Charles's arm to get him to move, but it was too late.

"My dear, Allegra. Surely, you're not about to leave me for another lover." Nassar's voice was lethal venom.

She turned her head to see the man facing them with a curved saber that glinted in the moonlight. The memory of Omar's beheading pushed its way into her mind, and a shudder ripped through her. Charles quickly helped her to her feet before pushing her behind him.

"We have a score to settle, Nassar." His words quiet, but forceful, Charles leveled his gun at the Sheikh. "I don't like being threatened, and I sure as hell don't like my friends being hurt."

"Then you'll not like this either." Nassar nodded swiftly to someone behind them.

Caught off guard, Charles didn't have time to react, and he crashed to the ground from a terrible blow by one of Nassar's bodyguards. The scream welling up in her throat broke past her lips, and Nassar's smile vanished as he strode forward. His fingers wrapped around her wrist as he jerked her toward him with a hiss of anger.

"Shut up, you bitch, or I'll kill you right where you stand."

She glanced down at Charles's still form, half expecting to see the bodyguard killing her former lover. Relief sped through her when she realized the bodyguard had gone to join in the fighting. Her gaze flew from Charles's still form back to Nassar's malevolent expression. An explosive rage, violent and powerful, crashed through her, stirring another emotion to life. *Hate.*

She'd never hated anyone in her life before. But she hated Nassar. The emotion swirled in her belly like the rustling of a nest of snakes. Dark and powerful, her hate and anger mated until the emotions danced and slithered their way through her, seductively hissing a cry for revenge. She wanted Nassar to feel pain. But most importantly, she wanted to see him writhing in agony from some torture she devised. She wanted to see that flat gaze of his filled with terror.

The dark, intense emotions flowed hot through her veins. They screamed in silent fury at the memory of a whip cracking through the air. The sting of it biting into her shoulders as Nassar beat her, each blow harder than the last. Lashes she wanted him to feel. She wanted to hear him plead for mercy as she flayed the skin off his back, the rough leather handle of his own whip scratching the palm of her hand. She wanted to smell the fresh scent of his blood dripping onto the sandy earth as he tried to crawl away from her. Her expression must have revealed her emotional state to him because he tugged her close, his body and weaponry brushing against her.

"There's nothing to fear, Allegra. No one will take you from me," he sneered.

His confidence flamed her hatred to a blinding, fevered pitch until the fire scourging her back diminished to a mere twinge as she pushed hard to free herself. In doing so, her fingers brushed over the dagger tucked in his sash. Without a second thought, she ripped the blade from his cloth belt and stabbed him in the shoulder. In a split second, he shoved her away with a loud cry of fury and pain. She couldn't tell whether it was a deep wound, but it was serious enough that blood stained his white robes.

Satisfaction empowered her to step forward and jab at him with the knife a second time. He dodged her attempt, and with bitter fury darkening his face, he knocked her to the ground. The blow blinded her with pain as it sucked the air from her lungs. Fighting to remain conscious, she lifted her head to see Nassar raise his saber, his eyes glittering with fury as he stared down at her. Fear didn't exist in her mind when she looked at him.

Hate took over and sent her staggering to her feet. She swayed slightly, her hand shaking as she held her small weapon in front of her. His laughter added fuel to the fire inside her, and she lunged forward with the blade. In the next instant, a powerful force slammed into her and dragged her away from Nassar. Furious, she released a primal wail of rage. Where was her knife? She'd dropped it. She needed it to kill Nassar. Her fury numbed the pain in her back as she went down on her knees. Her fingers dug viciously through the dirt to find the blade. A large hand found the weapon first and tossed it out of reach.

For the first time, she recognized Shaheen's unmistakable spicy scent as his harsh breaths echoed in her ear. He'd stopped her. He'd prevented her from attaining the vengeance she so desperately wanted. Rage sharpened the edge of her hate and her blood pumped fiercely through her veins as he pulled her to her feet. The dark strength flowing through her pushed her beyond reason and she clawed at Shaheen's face. He'd rejected her, and now he thought to protect her. She didn't want him anywhere near her.

"Let me go, you bastard," she screamed with pained fury. "Let me go."

She swung her arm and the force of her blow sounded loudly against the side of his face. When he pinned her hands against his chest, she resorted to using her feet and knees.

"For the love of God, Allegra. Stop fighting me," Shaheen rasped.

Behind them, the sound of steel against steel caught their attention and they both turned their heads. The moment she saw Khalid facing off with his brother, she sagged against him like a rag doll. Concerned she might faint, he wrapped his arm around her to provide support. The moment he did so, her soft cry of agony filled him with remorse. He'd hurt her.

"Where are you hurt?"

"Get away from me." Her voice was a savage hiss of fury and hate.

The sound of it sliced through his heart with vicious precision. She shoved free of his touch and put several feet between them. The moment her gaze met his, he wanted to cry out from the excruciating pain of her contemptuous look. The scorn in her eyes burned him. Condemned him. Christ Jesus, what had he done by sending her away this morning? At that moment, Shaftsbury stirred on the ground, and he went to help his cousin to his feet. Allegra staggered toward the man and collapsed into his embrace. A wild cry of anguish rose up inside him as he watched her go willingly to Shaftsbury. She'd suffered tonight, and Shaftsbury was a friend she trusted. *Friend and lover.* He shoved the thought aside. No, he needed to give her time. Behind him, he heard Nassar taunting Khalid.

"Well, now, *brother.*" A nasty smile curled Nassar's lips as he sneered his greeting. "Somehow I knew you'd be responsible for this unwarranted attack and massacre of my people."

"Massacre?" Khalid's voice was icy as he faced Nassar. "This is justice."

"For what? Killing a slut who betrayed me for you?"

The slur drew a loud cry from Khalid as he lunged forward, his sword whipping up into the air. It descended downward toward Nassar, but the sharp clang of steel against steel echoed through the small area as Nassar blocked the attack. With a dazzling display of speed, Khalid twirled his sword in his hands as he attacked his brother again.

Steel crashed in the air as the two men swung their weapons with a swift and deadly strength. The intense look on Khalid's face was troubling. It was the first time he'd ever seen his friend allow emotion to enter into his fighting. The usual methodical expression on his face was gone. In its place was a sinister emotion he didn't care to name.

"Come, brother. Surely you can do better than this," Nassar said with a cold smile. "Your whore is better off dead than living with a man who can't fight."

The Sheikh's only response to his brother's taunt was a flash of steel as his sword bit through cloth and into Nassar's sword arm. The stroke drew a bright spurt of blood, and for the first time Khalid smiled. Seeing his brother's satisfied expression, Nassar moved with the speed of a cobra. Quickly switching sword hands, he struck out at Khalid. Blood flowed as his sword left a long nasty cut across Khalid's face.

A red river streamed down his friend's face onto his shoulder, and Shaheen grimaced at the sight. It was only a flesh wound, but Khalid's emotions were getting the best of him with every taunt his brother threw out at him. He could tell by Nassar's smile that the other man knew it, too.

"*Enough*," Khalid snarled. "We finish this, *now!*"

Moonlight flashed off the weapons as metal struck metal with sparks flying off the swords. With a skillful twist of his body, Khalid moved through an opening in Nassar's defense. The moment he did so, his expression said he recognized the trap. Nassar danced to one side and dragged his sword across Khalid's stomach. There were no words, only a look of calm resignation on Khalid's face as he slowly sank to his knees.

Shaheen didn't wait for his friend to collapse onto the sandy desert floor before he charged forward. He ignored Nassar's smile of contempt and focused on the fact that the man was nursing a wound on his shoulder. Khalid had struck his brother in the arm not the shoulder. Had Allegra stabbed the bastard before he and Khalid had arrived? Blood soaked the Sheikh's robe, but he moved as if it were a minor wound. Despite that, it was clear he was favoring his sword arm. He was protecting it with every move.

Blocking out everything except the battle to come, he focused on the man opposite him and finding his weakness. With each move the man made, he listened and watched his response to every thrust and parry. The smell of blood filled the air, its soft coppery scent a reminder that Khalid was hurt. As he fought Nassar, he heard the subtle change in his opponent's breathing. It was an indicator that the man was tiring.

Elated, a surge of energy swelled through him, and he swung his sword up and to the side. Nassar simply arched his body like a bow as he leaped back from the bold swing. Pressing his attack, he swung his sword again and again. Each time his sword met Nassar's the other man's blows were lighter than before. It was then he saw it.

Nassar was favoring his left foot. Leaping forward he feinted an upward swing of his sword, and as the other man parried upward, Shaheen dropped and sliced across Nassar's right thigh with his weapon. Rolling to one side, he lightly sprang to his feet, then whirled around to face the man, who'd sunk to his knees, one hand pressed against a dark, bloody wound.

Not hesitating, he lunged forward again, and with a vicious thrust, he sent his sword into Nassar's chest. The man's face became a mask of stunned amazement. Staring down into the face of his enemy, he thrust the sword deeper. As the life light flickered and died in Nassar's eyes, he braced his foot on the man's shoulder and withdrew his weapon. Somehow, he'd thought killing Nassar would free him, but it didn't. He wasn't sure anything would ever alleviate the guilt he felt at letting Allegra out of his sight.

He turned back to where Jabbar was tending to his friend. Allegra sat with his head in her lap. Pale and drawn, she looked ready to collapse. Guilt and pain crashed through him at having been the catalyst for her suffering. His gaze didn't leave her face as he moved forward. Silently, he willed her to look at him, but she didn't spare him a glance. A wave of hopelessness sailed through him and he knelt down at Khalid's side. The warlord had opened the Amazigh Sheikh's *gambaz* to examine the wound, and as Shaheen studied the extent of his friend's injury, he knew the man didn't have much time. Raising his head, he shouted for Jamal. Khalid's hand gripped his arm.

"Hakim . . . where is . . . Hakim?" The Sheikh's voice was already weak.

Biting the inside of his cheek, the salty taste of his own blood slid across his tongue. *Merde*, what was he going to tell his friend? How could he tell Khalid that he'd left Hakim in Jamal's care when the boy had taken a blow meant for him? The boy would live, but Khalid— Again he threw his head back and roared for Jamal. A hand gripped his shoulder and he looked up into Charles's sympathetic face.

"Tell me where the boy is. I'll fetch him."

"I left him with Jamal about six tents back." The irony of the situation was not lost on Shaheen as he tossed his head toward the direction of where he'd left the young Amazigh heir. The man who'd come to take him back to see his dying father was now going to find the son of another dying man.

"Right, I'll be back in a moment."

"Charles . . ." Allegra's voice was little more than a whisper as she looked at Shaftsbury. "Hurry."

His cousin circled past her as he hurried away, but he saw the possessive way Shaftsbury touched the side of her cheek as he'd left. Jealousy twisted inside him, followed by a sharp edge of guilt for not protecting Hakim well enough that he would have been here when Khalid had fallen. He'd failed again.

"Nassar . . . dead?"

"Yes," he bit out as Khalid offered him his hand.

"You . . . are . . . good friend." A sigh rumbled in his friend's chest, and he recognized it as a death rattle.

"Save your strength." He squeezed Khalid's hand gently.

Where the hell was Hakim? The boy's father wasn't long for

this world. At the sound of running feet, he saw the Amazigh heir charge into the open area. The young heir's shoulder had been bandaged, but the strips binding his wound were already dark with blood from his racing to his father's side.

Eyes dark with fear, Hakim hurried to Khalid's side. Making way for the boy, he rose to his feet and stepped aside as the young man knelt next to his father. In painful silence he watched Khalid weakly raise his hand to touch the side of his son's face. With equal measure of love and grief, Hakim covered his father's hand with his own. The sight of their affection for each other cut deep. His father had never loved him. The earl had always hated him for taking his wife from him, and when James had died, his sins had multiplied as far as his father was concerned.

He couldn't hear what Khalid was saying, but he saw Hakim nod his head. Another rattle sounded from Khalid's chest, and his hand slowly fell from his son's face. Grief swallowed his heart as he heard Hakim offer up a shrill howl of sorrow. Over and over again, the boy cried out his pain. Across from him, Allegra sat with her eyes closed, the mask she wore devoid of any emotion. It was as if she were a marble statue, oblivious to the pain and sorrow surrounding her.

Then he saw it. A single tear slid out of the corner of her eye to trail slowly down her cheek. God, what had he done to her? To them? Khalid and Jabbar had arrived only hours after he'd sent her away. It was because of Allegra that they'd attacked Nassar's camp tonight. If they'd waited, would things have turned out differently?

It was like reliving the night James had died all over again. The questioning, the agony of second-guessing himself. It was excruciating in its intensity. He'd done all of this when James had died, and now he was doing it again. The steady hand on his shoulder made him jerk. He turned his head to see the sorrow in Jamal's eyes.

"He would not want us to grieve. He's with her now, and he's happy." There was a heartrending truth to Jamal's words that tore at his gut.

"Yes." He nodded his belief that the Bedouin was right. There was work to do, and their grieving had to wait. "We need to take him home. There are arrangements to make."

"I'll see to a litter," Jamal said quietly and walked away.

Not moving from where he stood, his attention returned to Hakim sobbing over his father. Allegra gently stroked his head as he cried, although she didn't say a word to him. Gently, she shifted Khalid's head out of her lap and onto the ground. Before he could move forward, Charles was already beside her to offer her his hand. As she rose to her feet, she uttered a low cry of pain. Alarmed by the sound, he strode forward until he was standing in front of her.

"You're hurt."

"It's nothing," she said in a cold, unemotional voice.

He almost believed her until he saw the dull, listless cloud darkening her gaze. For the first time, he realized she was in a state of shock. When he'd stopped her from attacking Nassar her reaction had been one of fury and outrage. But he didn't recognize this lifeless creature standing before him, and fear clutched at his gut. Out of the corner of his eye, he saw his cousin look down at Allegra's back. A look of horror crossed the man's face.

"*Good God*, you're bleeding, Allegra." At Shaftsbury's words, she swayed slightly, her hand going to her forehead.

"Am I?" Again that lifeless note in her voice. It scared the hell out of him.

"Let me see," he said with a gentle ferocity as he turned her around to examine her back. Stripes of blood had soaked through her *gambaz*, and he frowned. He couldn't tell where she was injured. Fear rising in his throat, he quickly yanked her shirt up to her neck.

The moment he did so, she screamed a sound of agony that chilled his blood. To his horror, he realized the cloth had adhered itself to her injuries in the form of a scab. His action had literally torn open her wounds. Remorse sliced through him with a sickening lurch as he stared down at the thin stripes of blood crisscrossing her back. For a moment, he didn't understand what he was seeing. It took several seconds for the full impact of her injuries to sink into his head. When it did, rage flooded his body. Christ Jesus, the bastard had whipped her. He'd beaten her with a whip. His hands shook as he gently turned her to one side so he could see the wounds better in the moonlight. God, he wanted the bastard alive again just for the sheer pleasure of torturing the man. A shudder rocked through him as his hand touched her shoulder.

"Shaftsbury, we need to get her to a doctor." He motioned to her back with his head as his cousin shifted his position to see what had been hidden by Allegra's shirt.

"Sweet Jesus," his cousin hissed.

"Charles?" Her voice was weak and weary, and his cousin quickly moved around to face her. Her hand stretched out to touch his chest as she swayed on her feet. "I want to go home. I want to go home to England now."

Her words were physical blows to his body, and his hand released her as if he'd been burned. She wanted to go back to England with Shaftsbury. The anger and hate he'd seen in her eyes earlier had been real, not a figment of his imagination. Despair tightened around his chest like a vise until his breathing was labored.

"Allegra, we need to get you back to the camp. We need—" Shaftsbury protested with a shake of his head.

"*No.*" Her voice was strong and sharp. "Tonight. *Now.* I want to go home, *now.*"

"But you can't—"

"Fine, I'll get there . . . on . . . my own."

With a vicious sound of disgust, she jerked away from the two of them, her *gambaz* falling down to cover the marks on her back. She had only taken two steps when she swayed on her feet. Leaping forward he caught her as her legs gave way and she fainted. A grimace twisted his lips as he cradled her close to his chest, all too aware of her blood seeping through the material that covered his arm. He stared down at her pale features. He'd denied her so many times in the past he didn't have the strength to deny her this time. If she wanted to go home, then he'd make it happen. His eyes met Shaftsbury's worried gaze.

"Where the devil are you going to take her?" Charles growled angrily.

"We'll ride to Othmane. I believe there's a noon train to Safi, which will give us time to find a doctor to tend to her back."

"For God's sake man, she's in no condition to travel."

"What do you propose, cousin?" he snarled as he glared at the man opposite him. "Whether we take her to Othmane or back to the camp, the distance is the same. In Othmane, there's a doctor and a train that will take her home. I've refused her too many times before. I'll not do it again. If she wants to return to England, I intend to see to it that she does."

20

Shaheen watched in grim silence as the doctor examined Allegra's back with a number of clucking noises passing his lips. When he and Shaftsbury had arrived at the small hospital in Othmane just as dawn broke over the horizon, he'd not expected to find a Frenchman running the facility. That the man had once been a surgeon with the Legionnaires had been such a stroke of good fortune that it made him believe a higher power was watching over Allegra. The man had immediately recognized she was in great pain, and he'd given her a dose of laudanum, which had taken effect almost instantly. The man sent him a quick scowl as he cleaned the wounds on Allegra's back.

"What manner of man would do this to a woman?" the doctor asked in a fierce manner.

"A dead one." Arms folded across his chest, his rage still simmered below the surface as he now wished he'd taken his time killing Nassar.

"*Bon, mon ami, bon.*" The Frenchman nodded his approval. "No man who commits a sin such as this deserves to live."

"How bad is it?" His jaw clenched as he prepared himself for the worst. If she required sutures—the thought of her hurting was bad enough, but that he might have been able to prevent it only strengthened his feelings of self-reproach.

"Actually, her wounds look worse than they really are. The man who did this knew how to inflict great pain with the least amount of damage. There are only one or two places where the whip sliced deep enough to cause any real concern of infection. I believe she'll heal better if I refrain from suturing them, but there will be scars."

The doctor's words eased some of his tension as he bowed his head and released a sigh of relief. At least she'd be spared the ordeal of sutures. The Frenchman finished applying several poultices to her wounds, his movements fast and efficient. Through it all, Allegra didn't make a sound, and he was grateful for the laudanum keeping her oblivious to the world.

Fingers biting into his biceps, he remembered her reaction yesterday morning when he'd rejected her. She'd been devastated by his cruelty. The pain of that moment washed over him again. It didn't matter that he'd been trying to protect her. He should have declared his feelings, told her how much he loved her. He could have persuaded her to return to England with the promise that he'd join her there. His gaze settled on Allegra's pale features.

He loved her more than he'd ever thought it possible to love someone. If only he'd revealed his heart to her. The contempt and hate in her eyes last night had soaked its way into him to fester in his gut like a poisonous wound. His body constricted with a sharp, torturous pain. He'd earned every bit of her scorn with his actions, and he didn't think anything he did could ever make things right with her. With them.

The Frenchman straightened then turned to meet his gaze with an air of grave concern.

"Although her physical condition is good, her mental state concerns me."

"Allegra is a survivor. She's faced worse things than this," he said harshly.

"Even survivors have their breaking points." The doctor washed his hands in a basin on a nearby table. "She is apt to suffer sudden bouts of unprovoked behavior that could range from fits of anger to deep depression. She may even attempt to take her own life."

"Not Allegra," he ground out as he studied her lacerated back. The whip marks the doctor deemed less severe remained uncovered and crisscrossed her back in bright red streaks against the pale silk of her skin. No, not his beautiful, stubborn *helwa jahannam meshsh*. She was a survivor. The doctor arched his eyebrows with skepticism as he continued to scrub his hands.

"I still believe it wise to monitor her mental state as well as her physical one. I've made her comfortable, and the laudanum will help her sleep for at least the remainder of the afternoon." With a grunt he nodded his understanding beneath the Frenchman's forbidding gaze.

"When can she travel?"

"Travel?" The Frenchman stared at him in amazement. "Monsieur, the woman has suffered a terrible beating. While her wounds aren't life-threatening, you see what her back looks like, and her jaw is swollen from where she's been hit several times. She needs rest."

"She'll recuperate better in familiar surroundings. She wishes to return home to England immediately, and I intend to grant her that wish."

He owed her that much. He'd see to it that she got home safely and quickly. She would heal faster if she knew she was out of Morocco. Away from all the horror she'd experienced here. Away from him. Again his pain gnawed at him for what he'd lost. At least Shaftsbury would be with her. The man cared for her and would see to her every comfort. But the thought didn't offer him any solace. It tortured him to know that his cousin would be the one to soothe her when she was frightened. It was Shaftsbury who would be there to protect her, not him. The doctor sent him a dark glare.

"If you insist on doing this, monsieur, then you must see to it that she is transported in a bed. She's not capable of walking." The doctor gestured angrily toward Allegra's back. "And with these poultices on her back you cannot carry her."

"Then I'll arrange for a litter." Brushing past the man, he knelt at her side. "Leave us."

With a snort of disgust, the doctor threw his towel onto the table and stalked out of the room. The door banged loudly behind the man, and he grimaced at the sound, certain it would penetrate Allegra's sleep. Gazing at her face, he watched for some sign the noise had disturbed her, but her breathing remained slow and steady.

His fingers lightly traced the dark bruise along her jaw, and he closed his eyes as remorse tore him apart. God, if only he could relive the past two days. Perhaps Khalid would still be alive and Allegra wouldn't have suffered so terribly at Nassar's hands. In the back of his head, a small voice told him going back wouldn't change things. He'd done what he thought was right, and reliving the past wouldn't change his decisions.

Destiny had shaped the events of the past two days, and the outcome, as painful as it was, couldn't be altered. From the first moment he'd spent in her presence he'd done nothing but make mistake after mistake where she was concerned. His actions had been selfish and tyrannical. Then the one time when he sincerely believed he was acting in her best interest, he'd only managed to cause her more pain and anguish. Instinct had told him she'd object to being sent away with his cousin. When she'd challenged him and refused to leave yesterday, it had nearly killed him to reject her the way he had. He'd wanted nothing more than to pull her into his arms and agree to whatever she asked of him. But reason had held him back from doing so.

In hindsight, he should have listened to his heart. The muscles in his body twisted into hard, painful knots as he remembered the tortured look on her face the moment he'd informed her of the money he was paying into her bank account. With that one callous action, he'd reminded her of some terrible event in her past. He'd seen it in the way her eyes had darkened with horror. He shuddered. God, if he could simply take it all back. Opening his eyes, he stared at her pale features marred by purple and blue splotches where Nassar had hit her.

"*Je t'aime, mon coeur*," he whispered. "You have my heart, now and forever."

Leaning forward he brushed his lips across her brow. His soul roaring with the agony of leaving her, he rose to his feet and strode out of the sick room. The door to Allegra's room closing softly behind him, he saw Shaftsbury spring to his feet. When they'd arrived at the hospital, he'd not given the man the opportunity to do anything but sit outside Allegra's room and wait.

"The doctor said she's going to be all right," his cousin said quietly.

"Yes." He had no desire to discuss Allegra with the man, and he headed toward the door. "I'll be back shortly. I need to make arrangements for a litter."

"For what?" Shaftsbury stared at him in puzzlement.

"Allegra wants to go home to England, and I'm going to see to it that she does."

"*Good God.*" The Viscount shoved a hand through his hair. "You can't seriously think to move her. She was in shock last night."

"There's no other option." His jaw flexed as he narrowed his gaze at the other man. "Othmane has no hotels, and I'm not letting her stay here. She made it quite clear last night that she wanted to go home. She'll heal faster in familiar surroundings, and it's time I honor at least *one* of her requests."

"So just like that you're going to send her away." His cousin's gaze narrowed as a sudden gleam of understanding sparked in his eyes. He looked away from the man's perceptive gaze.

"I'm doing what's best for Allegra." He grimaced as he moved toward the door. "While I'm out, I'll see to your train tickets as well."

"You love her."

The quiet words resonated through the antechamber with the strength of a loud, tolling church bell. He inhaled a sharp breath then just as quickly released it. Did it matter that the man had guessed his secret? It changed nothing. Allegra despised him. That was an emotion he was well acquainted with since childhood. He ignored his cousin's observation and tightened his grip on the doorknob.

"Once you arrive in Safi, you should find it easy to secure passage on a ship to Southampton."

"Damn it, Robert," his cousin exclaimed. "Don't act as if this were some social engagement you were planning. If you're in love with the woman, why not tell her?"

He jerked around at the sound of his English name. It was the name of the man he'd once been. But had he really changed all that much? He was still failing those he loved. His mouth tightening with anger, he sent Shaftsbury a hard stare.

"My feelings for Allegra aren't your concern," he snarled.

With a fierce tug of the metal knob beneath his fingers, he yanked the door open. Already the heat of the day was making itself felt, but he was too cold inside to feel the warmth. But his cousin wasn't willing to let him go so easily as he stepped forward and tugged on Shaheen's arm.

"I'm finally beginning to understand why you buried yourself out here in the desert," Shaftsbury snapped. "Out here, you can play the martyr and hide from the truth."

"What the hell are you talking about?" He turned around to glare at his cousin.

"I'm talking about why you feel so guilty about your brother's death. It has nothing to do with your failure to stop that gun from going off. You feel guilty because you lived and he didn't. Your father always blamed you for your mother's death, and when James died, you simply gave the man one more reason to hate you."

Shock ripped through him as he stared at Shaftsbury's harsh, unforgiving features. Unable to move or speak, he fought a desperate battle inside him to reject the truth in his cousin's words. The knot in his throat making it difficult to breathe, he shook his head in denial.

"You're wrong," he choked out in a hoarse rasp.

"I'm right and you know it. I can see it in your face." Shaftsbury's face suddenly lit up with comprehension. "It's why you're just going to let her go. Loving her is a risk you're not willing to take."

The brutal reality of his cousin's words propelled him through the door and onto the unpaved street. Reeling from the fiery revelations his relative had shared with him, he strode through the heart of Othmane. He passed through the busy market, oblivious to anything except his cousin's words playing over and over again in his head. He didn't want to acknowledge the truth in those words, but he was hard-pressed not to.

All this time he'd wracked himself with guilt because he'd not stopped James from murdering Frances and killing himself. Now, for the first time, someone had forced him to realize it wasn't his failure to save his brother that tortured him. His guilt had been nurtured in the knowledge that he'd survived while someone else his father loved was dead. The death of his mother had always been placed squarely on his shoulders, and it hadn't been a surprise when the earl laid the blame for James's death at his feet as well.

What would life have been like if his father had been a more forgiving man? He grimaced. Dealing in what-ifs was pointless. It was impossible to change the past. The earl had hated him because he'd lived and his mother hadn't. James's death had only made his presence unbearable for his father. But while he couldn't change the past, he could at least face it. To do that he had to return to England to see his father.

It was unlikely the earl had suddenly had a change of heart, but the time had come for him to put an end to the guilt he'd lived with for all these years. It was time to let go of all the sorrow. Even if his father wanted only one more chance to rail at him, then so be it. He needed to rid himself of this guilt and accept that he bore no more responsibility for James's death than he did for his mother's. Guilt had been the weapon he'd used to keep himself from getting too close to Allegra.

He'd wielded it over and over again to keep her from getting past his defenses. But she'd broken through every one of his barriers until she'd touched something deep inside him. Shaftsbury had been right. He'd not been willing to risk telling her the truth. It had been easier to drive her from him than to tell her how much he loved her. And he'd done his work well. Allegra despised him. Even though she'd been in shock last night, it had been Shaftsbury she'd gone to—not him.

The pain of that moment had been worse than witnessing his brother's suicide. Now, there was little he could do except honor her wishes and see to it she went home to England. She'd suffered enough because of his mistakes. He wouldn't make her stay here a moment longer than necessary. Ahead of him was the train station, and gritting his teeth, he steeled himself for what he needed to do.

❧

Shaheen stood at the library window staring out at the rain-drenched gardens of Pembroke Hall. It had been raining just as hard weeks ago when he'd entered the manor only to learn his father had died just hours before his arrival. He turned away from the dreary view and crossed the library's hardwood floor to the table he'd been using as a desk.

As a boy, he'd spent many hours in the massive library, reading everything he could get his hands on. It was the one place the earl rarely visited, which had made it a sanctuary from his father's cold temperament. His fingers pushed aside several papers on the desk until he found the handwritten note. He studied it for a few minutes before he clutched his wrists behind his back and stared up at the portrait over the enormous fireplace.

Commissioned when he was just a boy, the painting of his father revealed things he'd never noticed before. The harsh twist of his father's mouth had thinned even more as he'd grown into an older man. Even more enlightening was the depth of misery and sorrow in his father's eyes. Emotions he fully appreciated. His father must have been miserable without his mother.

It didn't excuse what the earl had done, but for the first time he finally understood the man. He knew what it was like to lose someone you loved. The portrait was a reminder of what life might hold for him if he wasn't able to persuade Allegra to forgive him. Once again, his eyes were drawn to the note on his desk.

She would have loved you, but I never could. I simply could not forgive you for taking her from me. For that, I ask your forgiveness. You deserved better.

James Camden, Earl of Pembroke

After years of discord, his father had apologized. Sorrow gripped him with an unexpected strength. But it wasn't for his father. It was for what his father had never given him. The love of a parent for a child. It was a worse sin than burdening him with the idea he'd been responsible for his mother's death. He shook his head. All that time wasted. A lifetime of struggling to make his father proud in hopes of earning a smile, a fatherly pat on the shoulder. He would not make the same mistake as the earl. No child of his would ever be denied his love. But first, he had to win Allegra back.

Something he was attempting to do with the help of an unlikely ally—Shaftsbury. His cousin had been a frequent visitor to Pembroke Hall since his father's funeral. At first he'd found it difficult to be in the same room with the man given Allegra had gone so willingly to him in Morocco. He'd tried not to like him, but his cousin had made it damned difficult. Particularly when Shaftsbury seemed determined to help him win back Allegra. Fingers tugging at the snug collar around his neck, he looked at the clock. Shaftsbury was late. It had been more than a week since Charles's last visit and he was eager for news of Allegra.

The library door burst open, and his cousin walked in with

an apologetic smile on his face. The two of them met each other halfway and shook hands.

"My apologies, Robert. One of the horses threw a shoe and we were forced to stop and find a blacksmith."

His body grew taut at the sound of his given name. He didn't think he would ever grow accustomed to it again. He much preferred Shaheen. There was a solid rhythm to it, but he knew better than to expect anyone in England to call him by his Amazigh name.

"How is she?" he asked in a pointed tone.

Charles sent him a sympathetic look before concern filled his features. It was enough to make his gut lurch. Something was wrong. Fearing the worst, he walked to the sideboard and poured two brandies. His cousin joined him and accepted the snifter he offered.

"She's doing well physically, but according to her niece, she's suffering from horrible nightmares."

"Cordelia's with her then?"

"Yes. You know her?" A look of surprise creased Charles's forehead.

"We've not met, but Allegra mentioned her." He stared into the softly rounded glass he held. It seemed like just yesterday he'd found himself listening to Allegra talk about her niece.

"Well, the girl is taking excellent care of her." Charles took a drink from his glass. "Did you know Jamal was at Fairfield Oaks?"

"Yes." With a nod, he set his snifter down on the liquor cabinet. "He managed to convince Allegra's maid to marry him."

"Well, I think Allegra is grateful he's there." With a frown, Charles finished off his brandy and set his glass aside. "She won't admit it, but these nightmares of hers have left her badly shaken."

"I need to see her, Charles." His fingers dug into his biceps as he glared at his cousin. "It's been almost three months. I should have gone to her the moment I finished burying my father."

"And you know damn well what the doctor said—no excitement." Charles glared at him. "I know you're worried about her—so am I. She's stubborn, and if you showed up on her doorstep, I don't know how she'd react."

"Because she blames me," he ground out with dark remorse.

"You don't know that." Charles winced as he met his gaze with commiseration. "No one knows, because she absolutely refuses to talk about Morocco with *anyone*."

Shaheen turned back toward the sideboard and poured himself another drink. Yes, she was stubborn, but she was strong, too. Nonetheless, it worried him that she refused to discuss Morocco at all. The doctor in Othmane had warned him she might be prone to depression and other things as a result of Nassar's treatment. Christ Jesus, what if the bastard had raped her? The air in his lungs dried up and tightened his chest. He needed to see her—to beg her forgiveness. And what if she wouldn't even let him cross the threshold of her home? The possibility struck at the deepest part of him. If she refused to see him, everything would be lost. But he also knew that it didn't matter whether he tried to see her tomorrow or a year from now. Her answer wouldn't change. Either she'd forgive him or she wouldn't. Not even touching the drink he'd poured, he turned to face his cousin.

"I want to see her."

"I don't think that's—"

"I don't care what you think." He snapped his hand in a dismissive gesture. "If she blames me, then she can take her anger out on me. But if she's hurting because she believes I don't love her, then that's something I *can* fix."

Charles arched his eyebrows with a frown of disagreement.

"Are you so damned sure of yourself that you're willing to risk losing her?"

"I'm not sure of anything anymore." He closed his eyes briefly, then met his cousin's troubled gaze. "I just know she'll either listen to what I have to say or she won't. Time won't change that."

He was living in a fool's paradise if he thought she would have anything to do with him at all. But he needed to hear her answer. And God help him if she turned him away because he could easily become the man his father was without her in his life.

21

Malevolence twisted Nassar's lips into a cruel smile, and she fought the urge to flee. Heart pounding with fear, she tried to scream but when she opened her mouth nothing came out. The whip dangling at his side danced against his leg like a poisonous snake eager to inflict its venom. Shuddering, she flinched as she saw his expression change. He'd seen her fear.

Dark and malicious, his smile made her want to weep with terror. Oh God, she wanted Shaheen. She needed him to come for her. The whip bit into her skin, its fangs drawing blood with each bite. Unable to help herself, she shrieked beneath each crippling lash. Where was Shaheen, why didn't he come for her? Frantic sobs poured out of her throat as she tried to crawl away, but there was nowhere to run. Nowhere to hide.

Gentle hands squeezed hers, as a soft voice spoke her name. With a shrill scream, she jerked awake. Tears streaming down her face, she pulled in deep gasps of air in an effort to breathe. The

nightmare still vividly real, she shrank back from the figure leaning over her.

"It's all right, Aunt Allegra. You're safe now." A soft rustle of
silk accompanied Cordelia's voice as her niece's fingers stroked her
forehead to brush a stray curl aside. "The man's dead, dearest. He
can't hurt you now."

Trembling with the remnants of her fear, she wiped away the
tears from her cheeks. She was no longer in Morocco. She was
at Fairfield Oaks. Far away from the desert, but not the horror.
Despite Cordelia's presence, the terror of her dream didn't fade as
she slowly took in the papered walls of the salon. She knew Nassar
was dead and couldn't hurt her anymore, but it didn't ease her fear.
It hovered beneath the surface like an insidious creature slithering
along every nerve ending until she wanted to claw at her skin to
destroy the fear any way she could.

The terror of that night would never leave her. She knew it
with a horrible certainty that chilled her. There would never be an
escape from it. It was a terrible part of her that would remain with
her until she took her last breath. All she could do was pray that
the nightmares might fade with time. Cordelia touched her cheek
then sat down in the chair opposite Allegra's to study her with an
air of deep concern. Guilt pushed through her fear as she met her
niece's gaze.

"You should be in London."

"Nonsense." Cordelia snorted in an unladylike manner. "You
need me. We've only delayed the wedding a few months. Edward
understands."

"Does he?" She shook her head in disbelief. "I wonder."

"He doesn't care a fig about the gossip." Cordelia's brisk words
made her flinch, and her niece was immediately contrite. "Oh
dearest, I'm so sorry. I didn't mean it like that."

"I know. I'm simply sorry that there *is* gossip." Allegra averted her gaze and picked at the upholstery of her chair.

Millie had been the one to summon Cordelia to Fairfield Oaks shortly after they'd returned from Morocco. Although she'd angrily questioned her friend's judgment, she couldn't deny being happy to see her niece. What she hadn't expected was for Cordelia to inform her that her secret was not really a secret at all. Since that first awkward moment when her niece had confessed she knew everything about Allegra's notoriety, she'd skillfully danced around the topic to avoid answering any questions. Cordelia released an exasperated sigh.

"We need to talk about it."

"No we don't," Allegra snapped.

"I've known for several years now." The quiet statement made her jerk her gaze upward. *That long?* She swallowed the knot in her throat at the steady and forthright gaze meeting hers. Cordelia shrugged. "One of the girls at school thought to have a bit of sport with me by telling me all about you and her uncle, Lord Stretton."

"Oh my dear, I'm so sorry." She closed her eyes for a brief moment as she realized how devastating such an event must have been for her niece.

"I confess it was a bit of a shock when Patricia told me, but I managed to make her think I'd known all along." Cordelia shrugged. "But I understand why you did it, and I adore you for it."

"Why . . . I did it?" She stared at her niece in bewilderment.

"When I asked Millie about the matter, she explained about Grandmother . . . my mother and you." Cordelia bit her lip as her eyes welled with tears. "When someone loves you, they protect you. You did what you had to do to keep me safe. I've had the home and love you and my mother never had as children, and I shall love you for it always."

The love and acceptance in her niece's voice created a knot in her throat as she saw the tears in Cordelia's brown eyes. She was the image of Elizabeth, and she knew her sister would have been so proud. As if embarrassed by her emotional state, Cordelia pulled a handkerchief out of the cuff of her sleeve and dried her eyes. With a sniff, her niece returned the linen to its resting place and shook her head.

"I need to go see why Jamal is taking so long with that pot of tea I asked him to bring us."

"Perhaps he's trying to sweet-talk Millie out of one of those scones he loves so much." Allegra smiled as she visualized the Bedouin teasing his new wife into giving him one of the delicious treats.

"Blast! I forgot the man loves those scones as much as I do." Cordelia leapt to her feet. "I'd better make sure he left some for us."

"It doesn't matter. I'm not really in the mood for tea, and I have some correspondence to answer. As I recall, you have some mail to respond to as well." She laughed at the flush of color that rose in Cordelia's cheeks. Edward's missives were always the highlight of her niece's daily activities.

"I do need to write him back." The color in Cordelia's cheeks heightened before her frown returned. "Are you sure you won't let me send Jamal in with some tea for you?"

"Perhaps later. I really do need to answer some of my letters. If I don't, some of my friends are apt to come drag me back to London before I'm ready," she said as she rose from her chair. She sent Cordelia a reassuring smile, but her niece's frown darkened.

"But—"

"It was only a dream, Cordelia." She kept her voice firm and devoid of emotion.

"Yes, but I'm sure if you talked about it . . ."

"I just want to forget, Cordelia," she said quietly as she crossed the drawing room floor to her secretary. "Discussing the matter will only bring it all back, and I simply want to forget what happened."

"If you're sure. . . ."

"I'm quite sure, dearest. Now hurry before all of those scones are gone."

With a grimace, Cordelia nodded and left the salon, leaving her alone with her thoughts. Nassar's face was still vivid in her head, and she forced herself to focus on her mail, determined to put the man's visage out of her mind. It would take a few minutes to crush the bad memories and destroy the images of Nassar. It always did after a bad dream. She drew in a deep breath to quell the queasy sensation in her stomach. Her nightmares always left her feeling weak and helpless. She hated it. Hated it because when she felt that way, Nassar won.

Restlessly, she sifted through the letters strewn about her desk. Several of her friends had written to say they would come fetch her back to London if she didn't return soon. They all meant well, but she had no intention of returning to town anytime in the near future. Not with things the way they were now. She sighed as she picked up the letter from Charles. Briefly skimming its contents, she smiled. His amusing anecdotes about life in town provided an excellent view into his thoughts, and it pleased her that he was taking an interest in women again.

He'd mentioned several ladies in a conversational tone, but it was the anonymous lady he'd referred to several times that piqued her interest. Especially when he referenced the woman as needing someone to tame her shrewish tongue. She tapped the missive against her fingertips. What woman in their circle of friends had enough of a silver tongue as to set Charles on edge? Lenora

Haywood. That had to be who Charles was describing. But Lenora was much older than him. She wouldn't bother to give him the time of day, let alone a sharp riposte. No, it had to be someone else.

A quiet knock on the drawing room door interrupted her train of thought, and she looked up to see Jamal enter with tea.

"Miss Cordelia said you didn't want tea, but Millie refused to listen."

His gaze that of an indulgent father, he crossed the floor and set the food-laden tray on the oval table in front of the couch. Almost three months ago, Jamal had arrived at Fairfield Oaks unannounced and to the distinct consternation of Millie.

That the Amazigh had been willing to give up his home to follow her longtime friend to England spoke volumes as to his feelings for the maid. As she watched Jamal pouring her a cup of tea, she marveled at the way Millie had the man wrapped around her finger. Completely enamored of his new wife, Jamal did almost anything she told him to do. That is until he'd had enough, and then it was Millie who was jumping to the man's orders.

"She insists that you eat again, *anasi,*" he said as he handed her a cup of tea.

"Good heavens, Jamal, can't you control the woman?" She heaved a sigh. "I couldn't eat another thing after that immense lunch she had Mrs. Barfield put in front of me."

"Perhaps I should feed some of this to the dogs?" he asked with a mischievous wink.

"That's an excellent idea," she exclaimed. "I know Millie means well, but I'll soon be able to float down the Thames if she keeps this up."

"Is there anything else I can get for you, *anasi?*"

There was an unspoken question layered beneath his words that made her heart skip a beat. Was he offering to share news of

Shaheen if she were to ask him? She shook her head and took a sip of her tea.

"No, thank you, Jamal."

He hesitated for a moment, and out of the corner of her eye, she saw him grimace as he tried to make a decision about something. When she didn't look at him, he removed a plate of food from the tea tray and went through the French doors into the garden. When he'd moved outdoors, she turned her head to stare after him.

What if she'd asked him about Shaheen? Would he have news? It had been Millie who'd accidentally revealed Shaheen had returned to England to see his father. Her friend had been mortified when she'd blurted out the news. Although she'd managed to reassure Millie that she was fine with knowing Shaheen was so close, inside she'd been anything but. When he didn't come to her, the knowledge only served as a painful reminder that she meant nothing to him. But still she'd held out hope, torturing herself with dreams of Shaheen suddenly appearing on her doorstep. But as each day passed without any sign of him, her dreams had died one by one. Everything inside her was gone.

She took another sip of her tea, just as she heard the sound of a carriage pulling up in front of the house. Leaning back slightly, she peered out of the window and saw Charles climbing the front steps. Delighted her friend had come to pay her a surprise visit, she rose from the desk and returned her cup to the tea tray. Behind her, the salon door opened and she turned toward the door with a smile.

"Charles, how lovely to see you," she exclaimed with a smile as she extended both her hands to him.

"I'm not staying, I was in the area to inspect a piece of property I'm thinking about buying, but I wanted to look in on you." He kissed each of her cheeks then stepped back and smiled at her.

"Perhaps you can come back for supper?" she asked.

"No, I think you'll be otherwise occupied, or at the very least not speaking to me."

"What a peculiar thing to say. Why on earth would I stop speaking to you?" She tipped her head to one side in a quizzical look.

"Because I convinced Charles, under duress, to bring me with him." Shaheen's words echoed quietly from the salon doorway, and she jerked her head toward the sound of his voice. Their gazes met as he stepped deeper into the room. Trembling, her hand flew to her throat, and he immediately knew his appearance had thrown her off balance. She was far too pale, and his gut wrenched as that vulnerable expression of hers flickered across her face.

God, she was beautiful. More so than the last time he'd seen her. There was a glow to her skin that made her radiant. Soft and feminine, her curves simply enhanced the picture of sensuality she made. Her surprise ebbing, he could almost see the tension streaking through her until a mask of polite indifference settled on her features. Her body was stiff and rigid as she turned back to Charles.

"You won't stay?" The desperation in her soft plea cut deeply into him as he watched his cousin shake his head. God, did she despise him so much that she needed Charles to serve as a buffer between them?

"I really do have some property to inspect, my dear." Charles kissed her check. "So I'll say my good-byes, but I know that Robert has several things he'd like to discuss with you."

Not even waiting for her response, his cousin stepped away from her and barreled his way to the door. He understood the man's desire to flee. If he were any less desperate, he'd be fleeing as well. She turned to look at him, her green eyes fiery. There it was, the anger he'd expected. But there was something else mixed in with it. *Fear?*

"Why are you here, *my lord*?" Her stilted formality made him wince. She knew exactly how to hit him when it came to using the title he'd been born to. He'd never expected it to be easy convincing her of his sincerity, but she wasn't going to make it any less difficult for him either.

"I needed to see you."

"I can't imagine why," she said sharply as she turned away from him. "There's nothing more for either of us to say to each other."

The collar of his shirt tightened around his neck like a noose. Resisting the urge to tug at his clothing, he studied her in silence for a long moment. Framed in the light of the window, her soft curves were even more pronounced, and he ached to simply hold her again. Ached for her to love him as much as he did her.

"Whatever you might think, things aren't finished between us," he said quietly.

"We were finished with each other the day you sent me away."

Her anger had dissolved into cold antipathy, and his heart contracted in his chest with a spasm of pain that was quickly becoming far too familiar where she was concerned. Christ Jesus, did she blame him for allowing her to fall into Nassar's hands? He'd made a mistake sending her away, and he was in hell because of it.

"For the love of God, Allegra, do you have any idea what it cost me to do what I did that day? All I wanted was to keep you safe."

He could hear the desperation in his voice. The fear that she wouldn't forgive him, the need for her to believe what he said. But did she hear it? Would she allow herself to hear it? She sent him a cold stare. If she'd heard his desperation, she ignored it.

"Please spare me your regrets, my lord. We have nothing left to say to each other. If you'll excuse me, I need to change for a social engagement. I'll have Jamal show you out."

She headed toward the door, but he reached it before she did. Quickly closing the exit, he stood with his back against the wood carved panels, effectively blocking her departure.

"Forget your damn social appointment. I'm trying to tell you I'm sorry."

"I don't want your apologies, my lord. Now get out of my way," she snapped as she ordered him to step aside with a sharp wave of her hand. "We're no longer in the desert, and this is *my* house not yours."

The lace on her wrist fell back at her arm's movement to reveal dark red pigment. The sight tugged a sharp breath out of him. *Merde*, she was wearing a henna tattoo. He quickly grabbed her hand and pushed her sleeve up as far as it would go. Staring down at the bird of paradise marking, he restrained her easily despite her efforts to pull free of his hold. The markings were recent, and they carefully layered an older design. A spark of hope streaked through his veins as his eyes met hers.

Although her expression was closed and unreadable, her eyes were stormy with anger. This was the Allegra he loved, fiery, passionate, and alive. With a gentle tug, he pulled her into his arms. Immediately, the heat of her sank into him, warming him as if he'd come home. God how he'd missed her. Missed just holding her. His nose caught the tantalizing scent of jasmine wafting up off her skin, and his mouth watered for a taste of her. He rubbed over the fire markings on the back of her hand with his thumb, and his heart leapt at the tremor that rippled through her.

"These are the markings of the *jahīm anasi*," he said softly. "My markings."

Trying once more to free herself from his grip, she glared up at him with her mouth in a tight, recalcitrant line.

"They mean nothing."

"No? Then why not let them fade away to nothing? Tell me, Allegra. Why did you have someone redraw the tattoo?"

"Let me go," she gasped as she arched away from him, her hands pushing against him.

"Tell me why you kept the markings of the *jahīm anasi*."

"Because I wanted a constant reminder of what it means to love someone and be destroyed by them," she cried out hoarsely.

The declaration made him sag as if from a physical blow. Her anger was a tangible force between them, but it was the pain in her green eyes that crippled him like nothing else could. Her gaze revealed not only the suffering he'd caused her, but a darker anguish burned there as well. Something he knew he'd not caused, but was ultimately responsible for.

Dazed, the reality of what he'd done slowly sank into his consciousness. He'd crushed the only thing on earth that he wanted—her love. Unable to move, he simply stood there staring at her. When he'd arrived, he'd expected her to be angry and resist him, but he'd never really doubted she wouldn't take him back. Now, for the first time, he realized he'd been wrong. If he didn't find a way to convince her of his sincerity, he would lose her forever.

As his hold on her relaxed, Allegra jerked free of his arms to put several feet between them. The tension in the room was a tangible force, and she trembled beneath his dark gaze. It was difficult to believe he was here, in her salon, apologizing to her.

Dressed in the height of English fashion, he was almost a stranger she didn't recognize. His dark hair was swept back off his forehead, while the tight cut of his jacket emphasized a new leanness about his frame. Had he not been eating? She immediately jeered at herself for even thinking the question. Why should she care about him? Anger burned hot and deep inside her. He'd nearly destroyed her in Morocco and now he thought to waltz into her home and resume where they'd left off. She was no longer in the business of pleasing a man, least of all this one. It was bad enough she'd revealed her reasons for keeping the tattoo, but if he even thought she still loved him . . .

"I want you to leave." She flinched as she heard the anguish layered beneath her cold, angry demand.

"Not until you listen to what I have to say."

"Why? Because the great Sheikh Shaheen of the Amazigh says so?" She glared at him. *"Go to hell."*

"I've been there since I let you leave with Shaftsbury, and I'm ready to come home," he rasped. Ignoring his declaration, she shook her head.

"There's nothing you can say that will change what happened in Morocco."

"Don't you think I know that?" he growled. "Don't you think I'd change it all if I thought it would spare you the pain? I love you. I've loved you almost from the first moment I saw you."

The words filled the space between them, and she dragged in a deep breath of horror. *The bastard.* He had no right to say something like that to her. After sending her away in the manner he had, he had no right at all.

"It took you three months to tell me this?" she spat out with a vicious hiss. "You're a *liar.*"

"I'm not lying, *mon coeur.* I love you," he said as he closed the distance between them. "I would have come the moment I finished burying my father, but Charles insisted you weren't ready to hear what I had to say."

Her arms extended, she kept him from getting too close. A shudder rippled through her. Had he reached his father in time to resolve the differences between them? She dismissed the thought. The man didn't deserve her sympathy. If he really loved her, he wouldn't have let anyone stop him from coming to her before now. No one dictated to Sheikh Shaheen of the Amazigh. God, how could he lie so easily? To just blithely stroll in here and declare his love for her after the way he'd rejected her. He'd thrown her aside in the worst possible way. She'd given herself freely, but he'd tried to buy her. A vise squeezed her heart, and she almost cried out from the pain. She didn't believe it. She couldn't afford to.

He'd destroyed her once before—she couldn't survive losing him a second time.

"I don't believe you," she said in a flat voice.

"Then I'm going to prove it to you."

Harsh determination darkened his features as he grabbed her tattooed wrist and pulled her none too gently out of the salon and into the main hall. Her initial surprise quickly subsided and her fury returned with renewed fervor. This was England, and she wasn't his to command anymore. She belonged to no man, and she would never again allow any man to do to her what Nassar had done. Resisting his strength, she tried to yank free of his hold.

"What are you going to prove? That you're just like Nassar? Forcing me to do something I don't want to do?" Her words brought him to an abrupt halt as he whirled around to face her, his hand releasing her wrist as if he'd been burned.

"Is that what you think?" The stark torment on his face suffocated the anger in her body as he shook his head. "Do you honestly believe I would hurt you?"

Uncertainty slashed through her as she watched the emotions of regret and pain filling his expression. Turning away from him, she shuddered at the deep longing that was taking root inside her. She wanted to believe him. Wanted to believe him because she loved him. And God how she loved him. She wanted nothing more than to turn around and throw herself into his arms and forgive him everything.

"Why did you really come here today?" she asked without facing him. "What was it you hoped to gain by all of this?"

"You. I came for you. I came because wherever you are, that's where I belong. Wherever you are is home for me." The sincerity in his voice wrenched at her, and she closed her eyes.

"I can't do this," she said softly as she shook her head. "I just can't. Please, leave."

Strong hands gripped her shoulders as he pressed himself into her back. The heat of him spread its way through her until an answering warmth flowed through her. Nothing had changed. He could still affect her with a simple touch. And she could feel herself weakening.

"Allegra, look at me." He turned her around to face him, his hand cupping her chin in a commanding, yet gentle, touch. "If you want me to go, then you're going to have to tell me to my face that you feel nothing for me."

Drinking in a deep breath, she shook her head. What he asked of her was impossible. She couldn't lie about her feelings. As she looked up into his face, an emotion she didn't want to name warmed his sun-darkened features. Closing her eyes to block out the tenderness she saw on his face, a tear forced its way out from beneath her eyelid. Oh God, she didn't want him to see how vulnerable he could make her. She didn't want him to know the power he had over her.

The world shifted abruptly as he swept her up into his arms and carried her up the stairs. Startled, she looked up at his dark profile. His declaration had shaken her to the core. Could he be telling her the truth? Did he really love her? It didn't make sense. He'd been in England for almost three months and yet this was the first time he'd tried to contact her. Had he really stayed away because Charles had told him to?

Desperately she stirred her anger, knowing it was one of the few emotions she possessed that would give her the strength not to surrender to him. And she knew surrender was only a heartbeat away. It was there in the warm, spicy maleness of him, the heat of his hand on her skin, and the dangerous edge to his voice. It was so close she found herself relaxing in his arms. Worse still, it was impossible not to feel the strength of him as he cradled her so masterfully, yet gently. Frightened, she renewed her protests.

"What are you doing?" she whispered hoarsely. "We're not on the desert plains of Morocco anymore."

"Perhaps not, but you're the *jahīm anasi*, and I want to show you what that means."

"How? By using force to make me admit it?"

"I told you," he said in a strong, quiet voice. "I will never hurt you, and I won't force you to do anything you don't want to do."

At the top of the stairs he set her down, and with his hand clasped gently, yet firmly, around her wrist, he led her down the hall. It was the tenderness in his touch that silenced her protests as she followed him like a meek lamb. He opened first one door and then another as if searching for something. When he opened the door to her bedroom, he stood frozen in the doorway for a moment as if assessing the room. Gently pulling her in after him, he turned and locked the door. In a quick move, he bent over and slid the key under the door and out into the hallway. Appalled, she could only stare at him in mute dismay.

His eyes didn't leave hers as she watched him shrug out of his jacket then undo the tie encircling his throat. There was a raw, animalistic power flowing through him that made her mouth go dry as she watched his long fingers methodically remove the layers of society off his body. The way he undid the buttons at the cuffs of his shirtsleeves stirred something deep inside her as he swiftly removed his shirt. The sight of his sun-darkened flesh produced a familiar tug of emotion deep inside her.

Some small part of her marveled that she wasn't frightened. After what Nassar had done to her, she'd been certain she would find a man's touch difficult to bear. She'd been wrong. Perhaps any other man, but not Shaheen. Her body was screaming for his touch. She averted her gaze from him for fear he would see hunger in her eyes. Hunger for him, for his touch.

"Do you despise me so much that you can't bear to look at me?"

His quiet question caught her by surprise, and her gaze jerked back to drink in the beauty of him.

She shook her head, unable to speak as she stared at a hard, muscular chest. The strength of him was still there, but she'd been right earlier, he'd lost weight. She bit her lip as she pondered the reason why. He continued to undress, his hands peeling off the English layers until Sheikh Shaheen of the Amazigh stood before her in all his naked glory.

God, she wanted him to fold her into his arms and love her as he had the night before he sent her away. She wanted that quiet, desperate tenderness that she'd thought was his way of declaring his love. Had she been right then? Had he turned her away because he knew she wouldn't leave him if he'd declared his love? She swallowed hard as he walked past her to sit down on the bed.

She looked over her shoulder at him. He sat quietly, his gaze filled with what she could only define as warmth and tenderness. The expression rattled her badly. What if it was simply another lie? A dream she'd wake up from? Closing her eyes, she knew now what he'd already surmised. She would surrender to him the moment he demanded it. Her blood rushed through her veins, dragging heat to every part of her body. He was only slightly aroused, and she frowned at the fiercely intent expression on the sharp, angular lines of his face.

"Show me your back."

The soft command astonished her as she met his steady gaze. Why did he want to see her back? It was nothing but a scarred mass of tissue, something she was grateful she couldn't see. But every day she felt the ridges rubbing against the silk of her dresses. They were a constant reminder of what Nassar had done to her.

"Please, Allegra. I want to see your back."

The sorrow and regret echoing deep in his voice compelled her to reach for the pearl buttons that lined their way down her back.

As her fingers slipped and fumbled on the buttons, he called her to him. She didn't even think of refusing as she joined him at the bed. His hands were gentle as he turned her away from him and proceeded to undo her gown.

The bodice of her dress quickly fell to her waist, leaving only her chemise covering her scars as a corset was still too painful to wear. Warm fingers gently slid her chemise up and over her head. His sharp intake of air made her glance over her shoulder the moment he was able to see the full extent of Nassar's handiwork. Anguish swept over his dark features, and he closed his eyes. Arms crossed over her breasts, she stepped back as she faced him once more.

Shame suddenly flooded its way through her. She didn't know why, it just did. She had nothing to be ashamed of, and yet she felt as though she'd done something to cause his pain. His dark gaze locking with hers, he stood up. Leaning forward until there was next to nothing between them, he simply bent his head and kissed her. It was a gentle touch. Tender, sweet, and devoid of passion, but the emotion flowing through it shook her to the core of her being. She swallowed hard at the caress. Always he'd been so masterful, so demanding, but this . . . this was a touch that sang to her soul. He drew back from her, and she saw his jaw flex with tension.

"I love you, Allegra. I know I'm not worthy of you, but I love you."

Her mouth went dry as she closed her eyes to keep her tears at bay. His sincerity seemed so real. She felt him move to stand behind her. He lightly touched her shoulder, and she shuddered as the rough calluses of his fingertips traced over the scars on her back. Seconds later, his lips gently kissed first one scar and then another. A light dampness lingered where his face had brushed across her skin. With each scar his mouth caressed, the ridged tissue became wet beneath his tender touch. Slowly he continued to make his way down the scars lining her back. A drop of moisture slid across her skin, and she stiffened with surprise. As she started to turn around, his trembling fingers sank into her waist to hold her in place.

"No," he choked out in a hoarse voice.

Stunned, she realized the dampness on her back were tears. *His* tears. His shudders vibrated through her as he continued to kiss the scars on her back. He was giving penance for what she'd suffered at Nassar's hands. Oh God, he was telling her the truth. Only a man who loved her deeply could offer up such a tender tribute of remorse. With a low cry, she jerked free of his hands. Whirling around to face him, she bent over him, her hands turning his face upward so she could press frantic kisses against his skin.

"I love you, Shaheen," she murmured as she feathered his face with kisses. "I love you so much."

A deep groan poured out of his throat as he stood up to tower over her and crushed her mouth beneath his in a kiss that made her shudder from the depth of emotion it conveyed. The caress was without passion, yet it was filled with a heated tenderness that only love could render. When he released her, she murmured a protest. Brushing his fingers across her mouth, he returned to the bed, his eyes locked with hers. Tension held his upper body taut, and she saw him swallow hard.

"I don't know what that bastard did to you, *mon coeur*, and I'm not sure I can handle knowing." He winced and stretched out his hand to her. "But today and for the rest of our lives, *mon amour*, you'll be the one in control in our bedroom."

"I don't understand." She met his troubled gaze with bewilderment as she slid her palm over his.

"I want you to be the one to say what pleases you or not. I don't ever want to see you look at me in fear when I make love to you."

"I could never be afraid of you, Shaheen. When I'm with you,

I feel safe." He closed his eyes, and the pain lashing across his face pulled a soft cry from her. "Oh don't, my darling. Please don't."

Her skirts rustled quietly as she sank down on the bed next to him, and buried her face in the side of his neck as she held him close. He wrapped her in a tight embrace, his mouth pressed into her hair. They remained that way for a long time until Shaheen forced her to look up at him. The love she saw in his dark brown eyes made her heart skip a beat, and she stroked the side of his cheek. A look of incredulity swept across his face, and he shook his head.

"I don't deserve you, *mon amour.*"

"Ah, but *I* deserve *you*," she teased with a small smile.

Determined to banish the darkness from their lives, she stood up and swiftly removed the remainder of her clothing. She didn't take her eyes off him as she did so, and her heart jumped at the love and need glowing in his expression. With her hand, she gently pressed him backward onto the bed. Although a troubled look crossed his face, he said nothing, simply giving her complete control over the moment. The doubt and concern in his eyes warmed her as nothing else could. He was questioning his worthiness, and she didn't want him to. She wanted him to understand that with him there was no darkness, only the light of their love warming her, protecting her.

Keeping her touch light, she ran her fingertips across his chest and downward toward the narrow line of hair that pointed toward his swiftly growing erection. Her fingers circled the tip of him, and his entire body flexed beneath her touch. She loved staring at him, at his beautiful body and the way he responded to her. Her palm skated over the hard, thick length of him, and she watched as he grew larger just from her touch.

A deep groan rumbled in his throat, and she looked up at his face. His beautiful eyes were closed, but the pleasure on his dark features told her how much her touch delighted him. Sliding her body up over his, she braced her palms on either side of his head then brushed her hips against his. The tip of him rubbed across her sex, and she pulled in a sharp breath at the rush of liquid heat that suddenly drenched her curls. His eyes flew open at the sound, and she smiled down at him.

"The *jahīm anasi* has a request of Sheikh Shaheen of the Amazigh."

"You have only to ask, *mon amour.*" A dark hand caressed her cheek, and his gaze blazed with a desire she knew he was desperately fighting to keep in check.

"The *jahīm anasi* prefers that Sheikh Shaheen takes charge of her pleasure as only he can."

For a long moment, his gaze seared hers. Then with a guttural sound, he rolled her onto her back. His mouth sought hers in a hot kiss as his hands lovingly slid along her curves. One hand cupped a breast, and he flicked his thumb across the stiff peak. The touch drew a soft cry from her as she arched her back, offering him access to her throat. His mouth slid downward across her skin, and a nipple brushed invitingly across his lips.

Unable to help himself, he suckled her. God, but she tasted wonderful. Hot and sweet in his mouth. He rolled the hard tip of her nipple back and forth across his tongue. A soft moan slipped past her lips, and her fingers spiked their way through his hair. The joy that squeezed at him nearly stole his breath away. To love someone like this and to be loved in return was something he'd never believed possible. But for her to love him after all that had happened—it was beyond anything he could ever hope for. Slowly, his hand glided across the curve of her hip before brushing inward over her thigh. As his fingers dipped into the creamy, white-hot seat of her, she bucked beneath his touch.

"I want you," she whimpered as he gently stroked the tiny nub between her folds. "Please, my love."

The soft plea tugged at his heart, and he knew he'd never be able to deny her anything. Rising up over her, he poised himself at the center of her heat then slid into her hot silken sheath. A spasm ripped through her, tightening her grip on him. Hot cream flowed over his cock as he slid in and out of her with increasing speed until she shattered around him and tugged his own release from him. A shout of fulfillment roared out of him to mingle with her cry of joy.

As the heat of their lovemaking died into a soothing warmth, Shaheen pulled her into his side. It would always be like this with her. This insatiable need to keep her close at his side. There would never be a time when he wouldn't feel this overwhelming love for her. She lightly trailed her fingertips over his jaw as she stared up at him.

"I love you," she whispered.

"I'm not letting you out of my sight until you're legally bound to me. You know that don't you," he said in that arrogantly masterful way he had.

She didn't answer him. Instead, she nestled deeper into him, her face pressed against his hard chest. He wanted to marry her. Instinctively she knew he would accept nothing less than marriage. She was more than willing to give up her independence to be with him, even though she knew he would never take her free will from her.

He'd shown how much he loved her by offering her the ability to control how they made love. He would do the same in other aspects of their lives. But would he love the child? His relationship with his father had been such that he might very well not want children. Then there were the rumors and innuendos that would no doubt arise once word spread that she was with child. A strong hand caught her chin and forced her to look at him.

"I realize it was a less than romantic proposal of marriage, but somehow I expected a response from you." Tension had drawn his mouth taut as his gaze swept over her face.

"Are you certain that's what you want?" She quickly slipped away from him and off the bed.

"What the hell is that supposed to mean?" he growled as he tried to prevent her from escaping him.

Not looking at him, she crossed the room and retrieved a peignoir from her wardrobe. As she shrugged into the lightweight garment, she glanced over her shoulder at him. "It means nothing. I'm simply thinking about your new responsibilities."

"Why do I think you're trying to avoid answering my question," he snapped as he got out of bed to face her.

"I'm not trying to avoid anything. I'm simply pointing out that you have new responsibilities and with them come certain . . . expectations." A frown creased her forehead as he stepped toward her.

"Expectations?" He frowned. "If you're referring to what people will think when I make you the Countess of Pembroke, I don't give a damn what they think."

"I confess I have no inclination to be the focal point of another scandal, but there will be one."

There was a catch in her voice that made his heart ache for her. She was no doubt remembering the last scandal she'd been embroiled in. Charles had told him everything Allegra had suffered then, but this time *he'd* be there to shield her from the gossip. They didn't even have to remain in England.

"Then we'll return to Morocco. I'll arrange for an estate manager to see to my properties, and I'll offer Charles a nice stipend to keep them honest."

"An Earl's responsibilities lie in England, not elsewhere," she said quietly. "You know that as well as I do."

"Then we live here," he said with a growing frustration. "Damn it to hell, Allegra. I want you for my wife. I don't care where we live, because home is wherever you are."

"It's not that simple," she protested with a sharp shake of her head.

"It is that simple. Once we're married, we'll go back to Morocco until the gossips find new fodder for the gristmill," he said with a confidence he didn't really feel. The truth was, her hesitation was scaring the hell out of him. "In fact, we'll spend half of every year in England and the other half with the Amazigh for the rest of our lives."

He took several steps forward, anxious to hold her and convince her of his sincerity. When she shied away from his approach, he immediately retreated, despite the urge to pull her into his arms. She was still so vulnerable, and even though she'd given control to him moments ago, she would never willingly give up *all* control. Warm sunshine framed her silhouette as she stood staring out the window, and his gaze hungrily glided over her body. God, how he'd missed her. Just being close to her was enough to lighten the darkness he'd existed in for the past three months.

She'd gained a little of the weight she'd lost in the desert. It gave her a softer, rounder look, and her face glowed. His gaze drifted downward, and he frowned in puzzlement. He knew every inch of her by memory, and yet he didn't recall her breasts being quite so round. And had her lush hips suddenly become fuller? He went rigid with shock as his gaze jerked back up to her face. She was with child.

The realization clutched at his insides with such a vicious twist he wanted to double over from the pain. Christ Jesus, the bastard had gotten her pregnant. How was he going to accept Nassar's bastard living in his home? He swallowed the knot constricting his throat. God, not only did he have to live with the fact that he'd surrendered her to Nassar's touch, but that the man had seeded her as well.

No wonder she was putting him off about marriage. Shoving a hand through his hair, he cupped the nape of his neck as he stared down at the round rug that covered the wood floor. The muscles in his stomach contracted with a brutal twist once more. What the hell was he going to do? He couldn't give her up. He didn't have the strength to do that. But did he have the courage to raise a child that wasn't his? He didn't have a choice. He loved her. He loved her enough to accept a child that wasn't even his. For her sake, he'd be the best father possible to the child. And he'd work hard to do the one thing his father had never been capable of doing. He'd find a way to love a child that had had no control over the circumstances of its birth. This time she didn't shy away from him as he drew close and cupped her face in his hands.

"I love you," he said softly. "I want you for my wife."

Her fingers curled around his as a look of fear filled her eyes. "I need to tell you . . . I just don't know how . . ."

"There's no need, *mon amour.* I love you, and the child need never know I'm not the father." She stiffened as he wrapped her in his arms and pulled her close. "I'll love the babe as if it were my own."

His words flowed over her with a warmth she'd never experienced in her entire life. The magnanimity of his gesture left her speechless. If she had even thought to doubt his love before, she would not be able to do so now. To offer complete acceptance to a child he believed was created in an act of violence was a testament to the depth of his love for her. It was the most selfless demonstration of love he could have offered, and as she stared up at him in dazed confusion she tried to comprehend how destiny had given her such a man to love and be loved by. In all her efforts to shape her own destiny, she had never even dared to fashion the image of someone so wonderful as a part of her life. Tears flowed down her cheeks as she shuddered in his arms, and a low growl rolled out of him as he held her tight against him.

"It's all right, *mon coeur*," he murmured. "I promise you, it will be all right."

"No, you don't understand," she choked out as a shaky smile curved her lips. "The child is yours, my love. I'm carrying your child. Nassar didn't touch me in that way."

Her tears soaked his skin as she pressed her face into him, clinging to him as though he were a lifeline. For the longest moment, he wasn't certain he'd heard her correctly. As she shuddered against him, her words kept echoing over and over again in his head. The child was his, not Nassar's. She was carrying *his* child. The emotions crashing through him did so with blinding speed. This had to be what joy felt like. This incredible rush of happiness mixed with excitement. Picking her up in his arms, he carried her to the bed and sank down into the mattress to cradle her in his lap. His fingers brushed away her tears before he pressed his mouth to her forehead.

"My *helwa jahannam meshsh*," he whispered. The moment he did so, she pulled away from him with a gleam of determination in her eyes.

"I think it's high time you translated that phrase." The demand in her voice made him chuckle.

"It means 'my sweet hellcat.'"

"All this time you've been calling me a hellcat?" Green eyes widening with annoyance, she glared up at him.

"No." He laughed softly. "I've been calling you my *sweet* hellcat. There is a difference. More importantly, you are *my helwa jahannam meshsh*."

She released a small harrumph as she eyed him with just a touch of suspicion. "Why am I so uncertain it's a compliment?"

"It is very much a compliment, *mon amour*. Only my *helwa jah-annam meshsh* could have survived all that you have over the past few months."

Lowering his head, he kissed her gently, almost reverently. Her love for him welled up inside her, spreading its way through her body until the heat of it unfurled in her belly to become a rush of desire. He pulled back from her, and in his eyes a small flame of need flared.

"I'm still waiting for an acceptance of my proposal."

Sliding out of his arms, she stood in front of him. With all the skill she'd learned over the years, she slipped her peignoir off one shoulder and then the other, until it fluttered to the floor in a silent invitation of desire. Slowly, she trailed her fingers down over one breast to circle a stiff nipple. Love and passion burned in his warm brown gaze as he watched the movement of her hand with a needy expression that thrilled her. As her hand slid slowly over her belly, she flicked her tongue out to lick her upper lip, which tugged a deep growl from him.

"Yes, I'll marry you," she murmured. "But right now, the *jahīm anasi* has a pressing need to show Shaheen of the Amazigh exactly how much she loves him."

She stretched out her hand toward him, and as he tugged on her wrist she fell into his arms, causing them to tumble backward onto the bed. Hands on his shoulders, she pressed her body into his. The spicy scent of him filled her nostrils as she sought the heat of his mouth with a love she had never thought to feel for any man. Once she would have found the thought of marriage confining. A sacrifice of her independence. But with Shaheen she had no need of independence. She was whole and free when she was with him.

He'd given her the one thing she'd been searching for all her life. This connection to someone she loved and who loved her. His fingers glided gently across her back, lightly stroking the scars there in a gesture of love that made her heart weep. There would always be a part of her haunted by Nassar, but with Shaheen's love that piece of her would have little say in the joys to come. Whenever she felt frightened, worried, or sad, she would have Shaheen to run to. She'd never be alone again, and for a courtesan that was an offer of a lifetime.